SLEEPING DOGS

SLEEPING DOGS

WENDY TURBIN

This edition published in Great Britain in 2021

by Hobeck Books Limited, Unit 14, Sugnall Business Centre, Sugnall, Stafford, Staffordshire, ST21 6NF

www.hobeck.net

ISBN 978-1-913-793-08-1 (pbk)

ISBN 978-1-913-793-09-8 (ebook)

Cover design by Jayne Mapp Design

Printed and bound in Great Britain

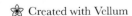 Created with Vellum

Are you a thriller seeker?

For my mum and dad, with love
'The novel wot I wrote'

Prologue

✦

The girl screams, flailing against the weight of water, crying out for help.

There must be someone who can hear.

A strand of hair floats over the surface, above her open eyes. It's drifting slowly. She doesn't understand — and then she does. The noise she's making, the movement, it's all happening inside her head.

She needs to cough the water out, to gag and spit, to give herself a chance of drawing breath.

One breath.

Please, one more breath.

Please.

Her throat's closed tight. The water can't get in — nor can the air.

Nerves are firing. Neurons flare into the dark that's closing in.

A shape. A shadow. The sound of someone laughing.

Her chest heaves once, and once again.

Then stops.

Chapter One

I woke screaming from the nightmare, tangled in the twisted sheets, hitting the switch before conscious thought caught up. The room flooded with light. My heartbeat slowed as I confirmed the droplets on my skin were sweat, not brine. The sea wasn't going to get me. Not today, not ever, not if I had any say in it.

My mouth was sticky, as if some marine creature had slimed a trail across my tongue. There was blood on the pillow and a sore spot on the inside of my cheek, but the panic began to lessen as the nightmare slipped away.

I checked the clock, relieved to find only ten more minutes to getting up time. I'd no desire to fall back into the dream that haunted me whenever I was stressed – which was pretty much all the time these days. Especially since I'd had to repay the debt my father had run up before he died. The strong chance of an "accident" – the sort that ends in life-changing injury if you're lucky and a headstone if you're not – made payment the only choice, but it left me broke. Now I was running Dad's detective agency on a shoestring – and even that was stretched.

The alarm beeped. Time to face the day. Clients to see, cases to solve. No point in dwelling on what's done.

THE WIND COMING OFF THE NORTH SEA HAD BITE, A GOOD excuse to drive the short distance to the other side of Haston. As I approached Emily Dunker's comfortable semi, I wondered why she needed a private detective. Whatever she wanted, I hoped it would pay well.

Mrs Dunker directed me into a cluttered room overlooking the street. She was a scarecrow of a woman, straw-haired, thin-lipped, in her mid-thirties. She could have been younger. Her careworn, worried air did little to enhance her looks.

Pot and kettle, Penny-lope? my father would have said. Fair enough. No one would describe my look as polished and my current woes were carving lines round my mouth.

'Tea?' she said, seeming anxious to put off the moment when she had to give away her secrets. Her voice barely rose from whisper to mumble as I shook my head.

'Are you sure? There's cake too. It should be home-made but ...' Her explanation died under the world's weight on her shoulders.

Dad claimed rapport meant higher fees. I wasn't in his league when it came to charming clients, but I cranked out a smile. By the time I'd got the details of the case the Tetley's would have cooled anyway.

Left alone in the front room, I snooped around the items on display. Baby pics took most of the shelf space, but one image of an older child caught my attention. Round-faced with a blunt fringe, she was slightly blurred as if she couldn't hold still for long enough to be captured by the camera. A framed swimming certificate for Jasmina Dunker, aged eleven, gave me a clue to her identity. I straightened another photo, this of her hugging a floppy-eared hound, and beaming into the lens. I lined it up with the others, then blew on my fingers. The silver frame felt icy.

On the far side of the chimney breast, the source of low-level noise turned out to be a baby monitor. The tinny nursery rhyme seemed half familiar but the RNLI calendar distracted me. Volunteers like these had saved my life once. February's page showed a photogenic crew leaning against the lifeboat, bare-chested, sun-tanned and faintly embarrassed. The sight was warming but my fingers were losing circulation.

It had seemed toasty when I came in, a contrast with the chill outside, but the radiators which had clunked and gurgled were now silent. The temperature was dropping. The fake log fire was dark and lifeless.

A radiator ticked twice, like a fingernail tapping inside the metal. I shivered.

Emily Dunker broke the sudden silence, returning in a flurry of plates, cups and coasters.

'I'm sorry,' she said, bending to switch on the electric bars. 'Heating's on the blink – again. I've put in another call to the landlord, but they can't seem to find the fault and it's a draughty house.'

As if to prove her point a door slammed somewhere at the back and she flinched, then half-laughed. 'Makes me jump. Don't know why because it's always doing that. Let's sit here, by the fire, shall we?'

We settled, a small table between us set with tea and cake, and I was glad to warm my hands on the cup.

Emily's gaze strayed to her wedding photograph on the wall, all smiles and confetti behind the heart-shaped glass, then came to rest on me. She opened her mouth, closed it again. Twisted the tissue in her hands.

The silence between us stretched.

I cleared my throat. 'So, Mrs Dunker, what can Wiseman Associates do for you?'

Emily sipped from her cup, rattled it down, then licked her thin, cracked lips. Finally, she got started, peeping through lowered lashes like a poor man's Lady Di.

'My Brian's a good man.'

Of course, chipped in my mean internal voice, that's why you're talking to me.

'He travels for his job sometimes, and I'm not naive, I know things can happen to attractive men – and since the baby came along it's been so hard for him.'

And it's a breeze for you, I thought, motherhood's a picnic in the park.

'He's been through it all before, you see, the nappies and sleepless nights. And Jasmina – my step-daughter – she's a credit to him.' Her gaze rested briefly on the girl's picture which had somehow crept back out of line, and her expression softened. 'She's a joy, and I never thought I could get pregnant so when I did it seemed like fate, you know? To have a child together, sort of complete the family.'

I nodded, though I wondered if her husband had been keen – and whether young Jasmina was quite so pleased to have a sibling vying for her father's attention. My own sister had sometimes seemed a cuckoo in my nest, and there were only five years between us.

'Okay,' I said, wary but hopeful. Infidelity can be a grubby gig, but it plays to our strengths – observe, photograph, report – and brings in a decent fee.

Emily's nerves retreated as she made her case. Out it

tumbled – the distance between them, his distraction when he was home, going out with unnamed 'friends' more often.

'Then Brian told me he was rehearsing last Friday night.' She hesitated, blinking fast. 'Only I bumped into their director and he was hopping mad because the hall was double-booked. He'd had to cancel.'

I shifted in my seat. 'Rehearsing?'

'Amateur theatrical stuff, Brian's done it for years and other men go to football, I suppose.' She waved that away. 'The point is, he lied! And he's been acting strange – not sleeping properly and going for walks early in the morning when he's always loved his lie-in.' She took a jerky breath. 'Then there was the letter. He said it was nothing, something sent by mistake and he'd send it back – but he looked furious. Then he went to his office,' she pointed through the wall to the back of the house. 'And I heard him open his desk.'

I raised an eyebrow.

'The drawer sticks. He banged it and he swore – and that's not like him – then he stormed out.'

Her cup was gripped between her hands. I hoped it was more robust than it looked.

'He must have taken the envelope with him only ...' Her fingers whitened against the china, but her head came up. 'Right down the back, behind where he keeps his passport, I found this.' She put down her cup and half stood to take a glossy picture from her pocket. 'I think he's being blackmailed.'

The photo showed her husband sprawled sleeping on a rumpled bed, eyes closed, mouth open. A twisted sheet failed to disguise a lightly furred potbelly but was placed, by luck or design, over the parts other beers can't reach.

I was grateful.

The smeared stain across his mouth said the lipstick of

7

this 'blackmailer' was the same colour as her underwear – the slut-red bra that lay beside him. She was a well-built girl if this item was to be believed.

His five o'clock shadow was way past midnight and the whole scene seemed staged to show the aftermath of illicit sex after a heavy night.

I turned the photo over. Written on the back in a loopy hand it said, "Great night! Let's do it again soon, Honey." Someone had planted a kiss underneath, and the pale pink smile seemed to mock.

It felt like a set-up, or a practical joke, and why would Brian Dunker leave this photo in his desk but take the envelope away?

But if it was a joke, his wife wasn't laughing. She was on the edge of tears.

'It doesn't prove anything, Emily,' I said. 'Could it be a stag-night gag?'

Hope flickered in her eyes, then died. 'He's been drawing out his savings – and he's ever so stressed. He's not even eating properly.' She blinked at the rich fruit loaf she'd brought in with the tea.

Her anguish was so real I could hardly point out that losing a few pounds might do his arteries a favour. Then I sucked in my own stomach and pushed my plate away.

Tears spilled over, dripping off Emily's chin. 'He says it's all inside my head and I should go back to the doctor or ...' She gulped and the tissue tore. 'He *says* he loves me, but he might just ...'

She couldn't bring herself to finish, but he wouldn't be the first to leave an exhausted wife alone with the nappies and the broken nights while he flitted off to greener pastures.

She lowered her voice, as if the spoken word might linger

in the air for her husband to find later. 'He mustn't know I've hired you, he'd be so mad, but I need the truth!'

'Everything's confidential,' I assured her, but something didn't feel right – and not just the case. I had a growing feeling of discomfort – as if I was being watched. The hair on my neck began to stir.

'He's meeting someone on the pier. Friday. Nine in the morning. He said he'd bring the money.' Her eyes skimmed past the baby monitor, giving me a fair idea of how she'd overheard her husband's conversation. It crossed my mind that someone else could be upstairs, listening in. 'You've got to tell this "Honey" to leave him alone. Leave *us* alone.'

Her eyes were puffy with dark shadows underneath, her nose red-raw where she dabbed with the sodden tissue. Her nails were bitten down, scabbed around the edges. A tide of misery rolled from her in waves.

I'd sympathise but it was an unlikely yarn and it would involve the pier – a place I preferred to avoid. Still, the rent was due again next week, and work was scarce. I couldn't afford to be fussy – and I'd had enough of being in that house.

Emily signed the standard contract, and I agreed to do my best.

ONCE OUTSIDE I PAUSED TO BRING MY E-CIG TO MY LIPS AND suck steam into my lungs. I glanced in at the Dunkers' window. Emily had turned on a lamp. It lit the room like a stage set as she headed towards the window. She glanced out, half waved at me, then pulled the curtains shut.

In the sudden gloom a figure appeared, shimmering on the Dunker's driveway and, for a micro-second, I thought it was their daughter. This girl was twelve or thereabouts, but she was nothing like the vibrant Jasmina. Hollow-cheeked and skinny-legged in jodhpur jeans with shadowed bruises on her arms. Below her t-shirt sleeves big thumb prints stood out clearly. They were the most solid thing about her.

Because this girl was dead.

The ghost girl pointed to my feet where a small tabby, the kerbstone visible through its body, was trying to wind itself around my ankles. She giggled soundlessly as it passed right through. A momentary chill cut into my bones, but the cat was fatalistic, grooming its stripes with a busy tongue a time or two before it strolled across the road.

In the bungalow opposite a curtain twitched and when I looked back the girl had drifted closer. She floated just above the pavement, head on one side and stared at me with black, unblinking eyes.

Then she reached out and touched my face.

There was a deep aching chill, as if the bone beneath my cheek had turned to ice. I tried not to cry out, but it hurt – it hurt a lot. It always did.

Now I'd have to find out what she wanted because the dead don't speak – and though she faded into nothing, she'd left me some of her pain.

Chapter Two

In the distance, the reflection of Haston's pleasure pier shimmered on the North Sea tide. Gulls huddled on shingle to the east of the town where, a few streets inland, a glow from an attic window diffused into the night sky.

Underneath the lights, in her workroom, Alice leaned over her sewing machine. It whirred against the backdrop of soft TV voices. Guided beneath the foot, the fabric emerged neatly joined on the far side, a cascade of satin and tulle.

The dress rehearsal was fast approaching, and she must get Titania's dress finished tonight. Unlike some of her clients, these actors were amateur, but the dramatics would be worthy of Hollywood if the costumes weren't ready on time.

Some of the players took themselves so very seriously, and none more so than director Terence – "not Terry, *if* you please" – who had begged Alice to help them out. Their usual wardrobe mistress had deserted, and Alice couldn't blame her. The East Coast of England was no match for sunny Tenerife.

The doorbell, emphasised by Monty's warning woof,

disturbed her musing. Like a devil summoned by her thoughts, Terence materialised on her front step.

'Just popped in while passing,' he announced breezily. 'See how you're getting on.' Alice had little doubt he was also hoping to run into the professional performers whose rent helped pay her bills. If any of her lodgers found fame, Terence would be in heaven, proclaiming bosom friendship to anyone who'd listen.

This evening he was out of luck. The only residents at home were Monty and herself. The Basset, naturally, greeted his arrival with great enthusiasm. Visitors meant treats although the fussy hound decided week by week which brands were fit for purpose and turned his nose up at the rest. Terence's offering did not pass the test, dropping untouched to the carpet while Monty gazed at him reproachfully.

'Sorry, Terence. He won't change his mind.'

'He's such a darling when he begs,' Terence said. 'Don't you have any others I could give him?'

'Only a few then,' she said, handing him a bag of Monty's current favourites. 'He'll get problems with his back if he gets too heavy.'

'Won't we all, dear heart,' said Terence, 'But sometimes it's worth it for a little of what we fancy.'

Alice sighed, then offered tea.

When they were seated in her lounge and Monty had gobbled his reward for raising first one paw then the other, Terence said, 'I just wish doggie chocs could make us all so happy. Honestly, I'm at my wits' end. Not only was the hall double-booked – I had to postpone the run-through! – but our "Helena" is still disrupting our evenings.' He raised one eyebrow. 'I thought it was called *morning* sickness, darling, and who knows whose it is? I'm sure she doesn't. I thought the young were better prepared than in my day.'

He waited, taking a sip from his cup, but Alice kept silent. She would not add fuel to the old gossip's fire. His "Helena" in Haston's version of *A Midsummer Night's Dream* had quite enough to contend with already, and whoever the father was, it wasn't anyone else's business.

Terence pursed his lips, then shrugged.

'And what's going on with Brian? He's usually one of my best, but his Demetrius is all over the place, missing cues, messing up his lines.' He sipped his tea again, regarding her over the rim. 'He seems to have developed a bit of a thing for you, darling, hardly took his eyes off you in rehearsal yesterday, and you were having quite the cosy chat in the car park before we left. Care to share?'

No, thought Alice. Absolutely not, or it would be all around the town in a nanosecond and if rumours got back to Brian's wife there would be fireworks worthy of Guy Fawkes. The solid Basset provided inspiration.

'Actually, he wants to be discreet, but I know you won't tell.' She leaned towards him, lowering her voice and silently apologising to Brian. 'He asked me to cut his costume to hide his paunch a bit.'

Terence snickered. 'Oh, my. Well, we all have our little vanities – that goatee he's been nurturing, for example. Suits him beautifully.' Terence stroked his own clean-shaven chin. 'He had become a touch over-padded for a leading man, only ...' His sharp eyes pinned her own. 'I rather thought he'd been reversing that of late. Trying to impress a lady love, perhaps?'

Drat the man. He notices everything. Alice tried not to react.

Terence went on, after a pause. 'Of course, he's wasting his time with you, darling, isn't he, unless you're thinking of switching sides?'

He smirked, making Alice wonder who on earth he'd been talking to now. She made no secret of being gay, but she didn't broadcast her private life on an open channel either.

Ignoring Monty, who nosed his arm hoping for attention, Terence continued. 'Well, it's obvious Brian's carrying a torch, my dear, and him a married man. Tut, tut.'

Terence prattled on while Alice could only imagine what he'd say if he discovered the truth and, more importantly, who he might tell. Brian had sworn her to silence, practically on pain of death, and though Alice disliked subterfuge, the customer was always right. Once she'd agreed to help, she'd kept his secret and enjoyed the extra income.

She tuned back in as Terence returned to the company's upcoming production.

'Thank the lord the costumes are under control.' He paused briefly to peer over his specs. 'They are under control, Alice, aren't they?'

'They'll be fine, Terence, but only if I can get on, so if you don't mind …' She continued to reassure as she ushered him to the door, but he wasn't quite finished.

'You will just alter "Helena's" dress – let it out a bit, won't you? I could drop it round,' he offered.

'No, Terence. Sorry. I've too much to do already. Someone else will have to do it.' She bit back the reminder that she had a living to earn with real paying clients, with deadlines, whose dresses wouldn't make themselves.

He drew his mouth down at the corners and steepled his hands in a theatrical plea. She remained unmoved. With her father's imminent arrival in town, she'd have one drama queen to indulge soon enough. She wasn't encouraging another.

'Oh well, if Helena splits her seams on stage the *Gazette*'s critic might give us a better review – old lech that he is.'

Takes one to know one, thought Alice, shutting the door firmly.

SHE WAS SMOOTHING TITANIA'S FINISHED COSTUME WITH satisfaction as *News at Ten* came on. As if cued by the music, Monty rose to his feet. She followed him to the kitchen where she tried without much hope to interest him in the rest of his dinner. He ignored it, making a beeline for the door into the garden. There he stopped and huffed reproachfully.

Why hadn't she opened it already, he seemed to ask. Surely, she understood his night patrol was more important than mere food? Alice rolled her eyes at his smug expression, as she watched him trot away to snuffle in the shadows.

It seemed darker than usual and she realised the outdoor light had failed. Mentally she added buying new bulbs to her list of things to do. She heard the hound plough his way to the top end of her wilderness and give one gruff bark. Perhaps the ginger tom was lurking in the undergrowth. If so, Monty might rush back whimpering from a scratched nose any minute. She waited but all was quiet so, keen to clear her workspace ready for the morning, she hurried back upstairs.

Monty would bay loudly when he wanted to come in. If he wasn't promptly attended to, this would be followed by an unearthly howl. The neighbours, already touchy about her lodgers' late-night lifestyle and the occasional flamboyant gathering, were only too happy to complain.

Hopefully she'd have five minutes before Monty sounded out his summons.

ALICE RETURNED THE LAST REEL OF THREAD TO ITS PLACE AND turned off the TV. The clock chimed the quarter.

Silence from below.

She frowned. Once, in the early days, Monty had escaped: Alice checked the new fence regularly. Even so, a stirring of concern was making her fingertips itch.

She started down the stairs. He wouldn't come in before he was ready even if she called – Monty could give mules a masterclass in stubborn – but she could shine a light on whatever he was up to. Digging up old bones beneath the overgrown shrubs probably. Still, he never stayed out this long at night. Could he have dug his way out if he smelled something interesting enough? She hurried across the kitchen.

Naturally, the torch batteries were dead and, beyond the patch of light spilling from the back door, all was black. Alice peered out. It was useless.

She could either rattle the treats bag, but that was unlikely to work as he'd already had more than his usual quota, or dash upstairs for the light on her phone. She was dithering when the doorbell rang. This was swiftly followed by a loud rapping on the front door. Alice's heart quickened. No one knocked like that without good reason.

A woman was turning away as Alice answered, facing towards the road as she spoke. 'There's a dog lying in the gutter, do you know …' but Alice flew past her. The woman's words followed, something about a thud, a car speeding away. Alice absorbed almost nothing.

Monty!

Three words did reach Alice as she fled down the path. They pulsed in her mind in red neon letters. 'Unconscious or dead.'

Unconscious, she begged throwing herself on her knees beside him. Please, please, let him just be unconscious.

. . .

As her Good Samaritan accelerated Alice's car through the empty streets, Alice prayed for Monty to wake. His head lolled; his heavy body swayed with the car's movement, soft and unresisting. She stroked his face with feather touches, fearful of what damage lurked beneath the muddy patches that streaked his smooth, warm fur. She greeted each rise of his chest, with relief, whispering, 'Hold on, Monty. Hold on,' then held her own breath till he took his next.

An eternity later the car swung into the parking place on the far side of the surgery. Dan Kitson and Val, his nurse, were waiting. The vet was the best, Alice reminded herself, highly trained in the US, where wealthy owners demanded the same healthcare for their pets as for their children. But would it be enough?

She could only hope and pray as Monty was transferred from the car onto a gurney and wheeled away. Alice kept pace until her path was barred with an apologetic gesture. Val pointed to the waiting room.

'Sorry,' she said. 'I'll update you as soon as I can.'

The pink-haired girl had always seemed both kind and competent, but her manner was distracted now, her focus on her patient as they disappeared through double doors, leaving Alice on her own.

It was only then she realised the stranger who had helped so much had disappeared into the night. She didn't even know her Good Samaritan's name.

She resolved to find the woman later and thank her properly. For now, all her thoughts centred on the surgery.

Monty's life was in Dan Kitson's expert hands. All Alice could do was wait.

Chapter Three

Having climbed the two flights of stairs from street level, I paused for a moment to catch my breath. The frosted glass door said "Wiseman Associates". My father's agency. Now it was mine – for now.

My trainee-cum-receptionist was on the phone, but touched a key to blank the screen as I went in. The habit is a good one – letting someone read over your shoulder is bad practice. Of course, he may have been checking the current job ads. Business was not brisk. He looked faintly embarrassed and jerked his chin in greeting.

My father's assistant had been competent and experienced, an asset to any firm. Sadly, when I inherited the agency, she had chosen to retire. I discovered replacing her expertise cost more than I could afford – which was almost nothing. I made do with her nephew, Nathan.

Nate did his best. He even pushed the chewing gum to one side of his cheek as he agreed an appointment with the caller. New business, hopefully.

I'd completed an ongoing case, so once in my office I updated the job log and set a reminder for Nate to invoice the client tomorrow. A drop in the bucket of my overdraft but it all helped.

A glance at my naked wrist, where my father's Omega Seamaster used to be, did not improve my spirits. I was trying to break the habit of checking it twenty times a day, along with the occasional cigarette – one more thing I could no longer afford.

A moment later, Nate was leaning against my doorway. I waved him in.

'I've put a Mr Haddock in for Friday at two,' he said. 'About his wife's yoga instructor, something fishy apparently.'

'He never said that!'

'He did.' Nate grinned. 'Dunno how I kept it together. I put it in the book.'

'That's fine, Nate, thanks.' He still hovered. 'And?'

'You're showing as unavailable for part of tomorrow, but no details? What do I say if anyone asks?'

'Just that I'm out.' I declined to enlighten him about my scheduled meeting with the bank.

'Coffee?' he asked.

'No, don't bother. You get off home. I'll hold the fort for the last hour.'

I heard him whistling down the stairs a few minutes later. Oh, to be young and carefree.

Pushing the hair out of my eyes, I set to work on the Dunker case.

Time sped by as I researched and made file notes. I reviewed the basics, rubbing absently at the ghost touch on my cheek from time to time.

The Dunkers seemed solid: credit rating reasonable; no

criminal convictions; social media presence limited. They were both registered to vote, could drive and had no outstanding speeding tickets or fines. They didn't own the semi in Carlton Drive, but had moved there from another rental, a two-bed flat, a few months ago. They'd lived at their previous address for several years, so not the type to flit. Most likely they'd just needed more space with the baby on the way.

Such solid citizens were good news for me. They paid their bills.

The land registry showed the property belonged to a Mr Salford-Peters who also owned a six-bedroomed property close by Stansted airport. From the electoral register I gathered he chose to reside in the larger house which was worth a little over ten times the one in our little seaside town. Sensible choice.

More trawling brought up random details on the Dunkers. The *Gazette* billed Brian as a leading light of the Haston Amateur Dramatic Society, and he was on a quiz team in the local league. Emily had been a teaching assistant at Haston High. She was pictured smiling prettily with a bouquet and a baby bump – presumably now on maternity leave – and had helped run the hospice fete. Other Dunker news mentioned the daughter. In addition to her swimming prowess, Jasmina had taken a minor role in a school musical. A picture showed her taking a bow. An Oscar winner could not have looked happier.

The ghost girl's touch flared like a tooth signposting a root canal in the not-too-distant future. No other child was mentioned in my searches. No red flags as far as dead teens were concerned. No deaths in the family, no accidents or illnesses, no mysteries at all. The only abnormality was the normality of their existence.

My dead girl didn't seem to be a Dunker.

If she'd lived at their address in the past, I'd have to dig deeper to find her. I set an action for Nate to do some research into previous occupants. Specifically, I wanted details of any dead children who might have reason to come back to haunt, though I didn't phrase it quite that way. Sudden deaths, suspicious circumstances, disappearances perhaps. I asked for anything connected to a teenaged girl, but ghosts were not something I shared lightly – or at all if I could help it. A reputation for anything smoke-and-mirrors would put paid to my business faster than the bank pulling the rug.

The icy touch on my face faded to a background ache. I chose to interpret this as having done enough for now. She wouldn't help me pay the bills, so I turned back to Emily Dunker's case.

She'd said her husband worked at Kendall's Textiles – but she'd proved him a liar once already, so it was worth a double-check. Kendall's website listed him as an employee. He'd been runner-up for "Salesperson of the Year" two years ago. The photo showed the man with the lightly furred potbelly, clean shaven and in a rather trimmer incarnation, being presented with his award. Perhaps success had gone to his stomach. Or failure to win had sent him comfort eating.

Thinking of eating, I had an appointment with a microwave curry and two episodes of the compulsive but implausible *Silent Witness*. They'd probably both give me indigestion, but we all have our vices. My stomach rumbled. Time to go home.

Fortunately for my hunger pangs the office was where I now lived. Above it, to be precise, in a tiny bedsit.

I was just locking the office door when my sister arrived, not even slightly out of breath after running up the stairs. I hadn't told her of my change of abode, so she followed me up the next flight in silent puzzlement. The silence was short-lived.

An estate agent might have said "bijou".

'Not big enough to swing a cat,' was Sarah's verdict. She twirled a pillow from my bed to demonstrate.

'I don't plan to take up cat swinging,' I said, catching the alarm clock and replacing it on the windowsill, 'and the housework is super-fast. I can even make tea without leaving my bed.'

She ignored me. 'What happened to that lovely seafront apartment? You loved it there.'

'They put a wind farm on the sandbank, spoiled the view,' I said, straightening the pillow.

It didn't take her long to pull at a new thread when she noticed, a moment later, my left wrist was bare.

'Oh, Pen. Dad's Seamaster, you haven't lost it?' Her voice was tight with distress.

'Of course not.'

I treasured that watch. Dad was given it by one very grateful client back in the day. It was the sort of timepiece designed to last, to hand down to your children and your children's children. Not much prospect of that at present.

'You sold it,' she said, narrowing her eyes.

'I haven't lost it and I didn't sell it.'

Her silence was more effective than burning bamboo beneath my fingernails. I couldn't meet her gaze. My fists clenched, then uncurled as I bowed to the inevitable.

'I hocked it.'

She started quiet, but I could see her working up a lather. 'You pawned Dad's watch?'

She got louder, huffing through her long Wiseman nose. 'You pawned it, Pen?'

I sighed, too overwhelmed with failure to explain.

She tilted her head, examining my face. Frown lines appeared between her brows. Then, before my eyes, my bossy little sister turned into our mother.

'Penelope Wiseman, tell me exactly what's going on.'

Chapter Four

In the streets outside the vet's surgery, revellers laughed and slurred farewells, then their voices faded. Occasional headlights swept shadows across the notices on the waiting room walls. Inside, a lamp glowed softly over the empty reception counter.

Alice paced, veering from hope to despair with every circuit. Her mind filled with imagining: the slow beep of the monitors; the voices murmuring vital signs; the clink of surgical steel as scalpels dropped into bowls. Hushed and unhurried expertise under stark theatre lights.

Now and then she stopped at the window, staring through her own reflection out into the dark. Insubstantial as a ghost, her hollow eyes stared back. Please, she silently begged the universe, let him live.

Imagining her life without Monty started her tears again.

At the start she had tried to resist his charms. A messy and demanding pet was not on her shopping list when she'd moved to the coast and started her own business. She needed absolute focus, to concentrate on making *Dress to Impress* successful. No distractions.

Then disruption had arrived in the shape of a warm and wriggling bundle – and Alice held her father entirely responsible.

'YOU NEED A GUARD DOG, LIVING HERE ALL ALONE,' POPS declared, nudging through the door with an armful of tri-colour fur. 'Ta-da!' With a flourish he tipped the squirming heap into her lap. 'Housewarming present.'

'Don't be absurd!' She tried to remove the doggy-fragranced gift from her silk crepe-de-chine skirt. Alas, all too late as a claw caught and heart-wrenching yelps commenced. 'Oh, for heaven's sake! Hold still, pup, and I'll get you free … honestly, Pops, what on earth made you imagine I'd want a dog.'

'Told you. Guard dog. And he'll get you out and about – nothing like a dog to help a girl make friends.'

'I don't need friends. I need work or I'll be going broke fast. And I can't take a dog with me when I'm meeting clients.'

There was a scuffling during which the pup managed a taste of her make-up and snuffled in her ear when she turned her face away. Alice got to her feet, holding him firmly to prevent further personal indignities or his escape. She didn't need damage on her new furnishings either. He nuzzled at her, whimpering excitedly. She tried to focus on the cold, wet nose but couldn't quite ignore the cheeky face and the feel of velvet fur.

'Take him,' she said, thrusting the pup forward. 'I can't keep him.'

Pops stepped away, holding up his palms. 'Tosh and fiddle,

Alice. You work from home and your clients mostly come to you. And I'll take care of the vet's bills so don't worry about that.'

The pup stared adoringly up at her and Alice found herself beginning to be charmed. Her father's expression, eye-to-eye with her at his own six-foot height, turned as soulful as the pup's.

'He needs a home, sweetie, and you need something without a thread at one end and a sharp point at the other. Anyway,' he went on, forestalling further protest with a flap of his hand, 'if you really don't want him, it's no problem. I can take him back. It's entirely up to you.' He arched an eyebrow. 'Of course, he's just the runt, unwanted and unloved.' He sighed. 'I expect they'll have him put to sleep.'

Alice glared, but he knew her too well.

Starting to grin, he pushed on. 'He'll be good company and make you laugh, and you can set him on any unwanted visitors when he grows a bit. And, er … he might need to visit the garden.' The pup's wriggling had become more focused.

His dumpy legs and compact body swiftly developed into a solid mass of unconditional love. It proved impossible to resist. Walking him along the seafront, the white tip of his tail waving like a flag, gave her a daily shot of happiness. And Pops was right about the friends. Everyone stopped to say hello to the amiable hound with the comically mournful face.

As for the idea of the valiant guard dog, everyone was treated like a long-lost friend after a token growl or two, and the first time he discovered his *Hound of the Baskervilles* voice he nearly fainted in fear of himself.

Alice had dined out on that story for a month.

. . .

In the vet's waiting room, minutes stretched into hours. Alice huddled by the radiator, staring blankly at walls adorned with posters and certificates. An appeal for canine blood made her eyes flood again. Monty loved all the attention and the extra titbits that came with each donation, searching Val's pockets for treats with gleeful snuffles even before he'd done his bit. Val always pandered to his fussiness, checking the brand with Alice on the day to make sure he wasn't disappointed. Perhaps, behind the surgery door, they were transfusing some other generous dog's blood into his veins.

Two hours went by before Val put her head around the door.

'Hey, Alice. Sorry it's taking so long. He gave us a fright, but we've got the bleeding under control and it's looking more hopeful. No promises, I'm afraid, but he's holding his own.'

Alice murmured her thanks and tried to stay positive, knowing Val would be doing everything possible to help him through. Maybe it was just the lateness of the hour, or the shock, but Alice couldn't stop the chill spreading despite the warmth of the waiting room as another hour crawled by.

Minutes stretched into eternity, but eventually Dan Kitson emerged. Alice rose to face him. Her breath stopped as she waited for the verdict.

She searched his face for clues. His skin was almost grey, smudges beneath his eyes. Exhaustion seemed to weigh his shoulders down, obliterating the air of quiet competence he usually carried. He pushed his fingers through the blonde waves flattened by the surgical cap dangling from his other hand. His jaw was locked, expression grim. A tiny muscle quivered at the corner of his mouth. Alice thought it might be anger as well as distress. Anger at his failure.

'I'm so sorry, Alice. I'm afraid the damage was just too

much to get on top of. We tried everything we could but …'
He shook his head.

Alice felt she should apologise somehow, as if it were her
fault they'd been put in this position. She wanted to touch his
arm, acknowledge all he had tried to do, but grief rose in her
throat, stifling speech.

She barely heard the professional phrases designed to
comfort. The peacefulness of Monty's passing was no
consolation.

A Basset-shaped hole had been punched through her life
and nothing would ever be quite the same.

.

Chapter Five

A sleepless night followed Sarah's visit. I'd explained about the debts, but that wasn't the only problem.

She'd listened, perched on the one chair in my bedsit, then cut to the heart of it.

'You've run the agency into the ground in less than a year? Come off it, Pen. Dad must have made a profit, and even you can't be that incompetent.'

'Thanks for your understanding!' I'd slumped on the bed. 'A lot of the firms Dad dealt with don't want to hire me.' And some I didn't want to do business with.

'Dad's contacts are old school,' she said, waving a hand as though it didn't matter. 'You just have to show them you're as tough as he was, and not some soft-hearted pushover. They probably think a woman's not up to putting the thumbscrews on when needed.'

'It's not a gangster movie, Sarah! And it's not that easy.' She'd no idea what debt collection looked like, up close and personal, and though "soft-hearted pushover" was harsh it contained a kernel of truth.

When I first started as a P.I., I was skip tracing for a find-er's fee. Dad arranged it with a firm in London. 'A training scheme,' he'd said, 'See if you can cut it before you're let loose on home turf.'

Tracking down those who'd chosen not to pay was satisfy-ing, but these were few. Most targets scraped by on minimum wage, paid an extortionate rent for substandard housing, and relied on pay-day loans to feed their kids. The interest spun it out of control – and then they ran. When found, the people who'd paid us to find them offered a way to work off what was owed – prostitution or drug running was rumoured to be the choice.

Dad told me I should toughen up.

Instead, I quit.

It took a long time and a lucky break before I got a second chance. A small outfit where I wasn't working for the bad guys, and legs weren't broken when I turned in my report.

Dad beamed. Said he always knew I'd turn into a real P.I. one day. Chip off the old block.

The block was tougher than I wanted to be.

Then he went and left his agency to me.

'ANYWAY,' I CONFESSED MISERABLY TO MY SISTER. 'I THOUGHT I could do it my way, but regular money's mostly corporate and that goes to the big outfits on a retainer. I'm small fry – no way to get my foot inside that door.'

Sarah seemed inclined to argue, but a glance at my expression changed her mind. We stared at each other in the sudden silence, then she shrugged. 'Well, Pen, it's clear you need a different business model – and some time to get it established.'

'I'm all out of time,' I told her. 'Whatever I do now will be too little and too late.'

She sipped the tea I'd made, thought for a little while then, wearing her most annoying enigmatic smile, she said, 'I've got an idea that you'll like, and some useful contacts of my own.'

While my blood did not quite run cold, it did chill by a degree as she told me how she could come to my rescue – and what she wanted in exchange.

I WENT DOWN TO THE OFFICE THE NEXT MORNING, contemplating Sarah's lifeline, and trying not to think about my impending meeting at the bank. The residual ache from the ghost girl's touch had settled behind my left eye this morning where it lay along my optic nerve like frost on a powerline.

'Morning, boss.' All keen and eager, Nate looked up from his desk. 'I've emailed you some stuff. Background on the Dunker house, but there's nothing on the public register about it being rented out before. Nothing about murders or manslaughter, or missing kids. Do you want me to keep digging?'

'Yes, but let's try something else as well.' I thought for a minute. 'Run a search on death notices for all girls aged between say, nine and sixteen, in the local area. Get photos if you can, especially where it was sudden or suspicious. Let's see if we can narrow it down and then check for connections to the house.'

If he found her picture, I'd know her straight away.

Leaving him whistling over the keyboard, I went into my office, glanced at my bare wrist and sighed, then checked my phone. I had just enough time before the bank appointment to see what Nate had found so far.

The current owner of the Dunker's rented semi was a surgeon, high level apparently, a string of letters after his name. A series of articles outlined his prizes and achievements in the world of medicine but little on a personal note. He was married with one daughter. An announcement in *The Times* a year ago was interesting.

Barbara and John Nash. Mr. and Mrs. R. J. Salford-Peters are pleased to announce the marriage of their daughter Barbara Victoria to John Mark Nash of Haston-on-Sea. The marriage took place on Saturday the 14th April 2018 at Leez Priory; a wonderful day was had by all.

No pictures of the wedding had been published but Nate had found a grainy image courtesy of Google. Chubby-faced, shapeless in cap and gown, Barbara Salford-Peters had received her BSc some years before. She was shown on the arm of her stern-faced white-haired patriarch. The brief article covered her acceptance into medical school but mainly concentrated on the brilliance of her father. His stellar career was with a Cambridge biotech company, making strides in immunology to much acclaim. The use of "mouse models" to "investigate allograft rejection and the induction of tolerance in mixed chimerism" sounded hard both on the rodents and on his daughter. Dad sounded a tough act to follow in the medical world.

Time was passing, and I didn't want to be late for my last-ditch attempt to stave off financial ruin.

Nate looked up as I passed through, his ginger freckles highlighting his normal pallor. Too many hours spent in the office or playing *SpyHunter* on Xbox. Maybe I should let him out more.

He spoke as I reached the door. 'I've found a girl who went missing.'

I turned back.

'She was eleven years old. Assumed dead when a Luftwaffe Heinkel bomber crashed into a house in Vista Road. She was playing there with a friend according to a news report.'

The annual Haston air show crossed my mind, but there'd been no recent crashes – and I'd hardly have forgotten an aircraft landing on the town.

I sighed. 'When was this, Nate?'

'About 1940.'

I'd take a bet they were still wearing those baggy-thighed riding breeches back then, not jodhpur jeans. I couldn't share that thought with Nate without explaining its relevance.

'Just kidding!' he grinned. 'I'm going back ten years initially – I've sent you the results so far.'

'Nice one, thanks,' I said. 'Try looking for anything in the name of Nash. The owner's daughter married a Haston man – maybe the house was for them.'

'Roger, wilco.'

As I left him trawling through the internet and set off towards the bank, I found myself thinking of Barbara Nash and her medical ambitions. The GMC listed no licence to practise in her name so maybe she didn't follow her father into the profession after all.

I could empathise. My own father's shoes were proving hard to fill.

MEETINGS AT THE BANK HAD SET ME ON EDGE SINCE I WAS summoned to discuss my overdraft and a plan for its reduction some months ago. For me the barred windows were a grim reminder I might not emerge unscathed from the "restructuring" of my debt. Every month I had to earn more money to pay off fees and interest; the capital sum seemed set in the same stone as the building.

Inside its hallowed portals were Business Managers who talked about investments in "stakeholders". It made me think of vampires. "Debt to earnings ratio" broke me out in a sweat.

Then a new man had taken over my account. I recognised his name but, in the flesh, he'd been a shock. In my head, he'd remained a nerdy schoolkid, but at that first meeting I found him all grown up – square-jawed and broad-shouldered. Colin Palmer, son of the lifeboat captain who'd once saved me from drowning under the pier.

Colin and I had history. Not the good kind.

Schoolboy Colin had traded on my rescue for a favour. He called in the "debt", though I hadn't exactly owed him – his dad had been my saviour – but Colin was also my first crush.

He'd told me what he wanted. I'd done my best.

I was caught with the stolen goods – shoplifted Cadbury's Flakes which were meant to be our ticket into the school "crime gang". After such abject failure, a gap had opened between us.

When the adult Colin took over dealing with my overdraft, it yawned wider than ever.

My nerves at our first meeting had made me solemn. The memory of doodling "Mrs Penelope Palmer" in my school notebook a thousand times added to my self-consciousness and his fanciable status did the rest. Colin had the handsome, rugged features of his father and some fine muscles beneath his sharp suit.

He shook hands firmly, in keeping with the seriousness of the moment, then indicated a couple of armchairs by a low table where we could talk. Perhaps realising my discomfort, he didn't pause to chat about old times but went straight to the business of the day – my impending financial doom.

'There's too much money going out, Penny,' he said. 'Fixed costs are high – and with so little business coming in – and clients who owe you seem slow to pay. I'm afraid you're in danger of trading insolvent.'

'Not a good idea?'

'Knowingly doing that is a criminal offence.' He said it with a smile that looked a little grim, then came at me with questions. 'Can you cut your overheads? Personally, too, so you take less salary out of the business. Can you do more to chase up the slow payers? And,' he paused, 'does your assistant really earn his keep?'

I'd taken his advice about cutting my overheads, my lovely seafront flat was an early casualty, saving the rent helped slow the slide, but I couldn't take much less in salary. Running up debts I couldn't pay could land me in a lot of trouble according to the banking world. Pots, kettles and financial crashes came to mind, but nothing would be gained by pointing that out.

OUR NEXT MEETING HADN'T BEEN MUCH BETTER. AFTER A brief chat about my prospective business, he laid it on the line.

'Here's where we are, Penny. We've had a look at the historic accounts you provided as well as the up-to-date picture, and it's clear that – as things stand – the business isn't viable.' He raised a hand to stifle the objection I hadn't made. 'I know you've plans to turn it round, but frankly it's difficult to see how anyone could take a reasonable salary, pay a permanent staff member, and cover the bills on the revenues you're showing here. From your dad's books, I can't see how he did it either.'

'Can't you increase my overdraft?' I resented the plea that crept into my voice but was grateful he hadn't mentioned Dad's accounts. They'd more likely win the Costa Fiction Prize than a gold star from the treasury.

'I'm afraid not.' He sighed. 'Look, maybe there's another way.'

I sat up straighter. 'I'm listening.'

'You say you have some regular business coming up soon – so it's a temporary fix you need?'

'Exactly.' I sounded a lot more certain than I felt but that pitch I'd made to some major companies in the area might work. Someone must handle their employee vetting.

'You list some assets. A painting? An Omega Seamaster watch?'

I nodded.

'The bank can't use them as collateral but – and this is unofficial – have you thought of asking one of your dad's contacts to help you out? Pledge them against a temporary loan?'

'Well, I could sell the painting.' Grandmother might be spinning in her grave, but I'd never liked it much and Sarah wouldn't even give it house room.

The low point had been pawning Dad's watch.

It hadn't helped for long, but now, with Sarah's plan, there was a chance the agency might make it – but it would have drawbacks. I'd rather give the banking world, in the shape of Colin Palmer, one last chance.

This meeting was no different from the last. He was patient while I gave it my best shot. I tried not to notice the fullness of his lower lip and the laughter-lines that seemed to emphasise his baby-blues. Just an echo of that first crush.

Concentrate, I told myself sternly. 'I have a new client, and another coming in tomorrow. Word's getting around.'

He flushed a little beneath his tan, perhaps embarrassed by my desperation. 'I don't think it will be enough to save the business unless ... what about the employee-vetting contracts you were hoping for?'

I swallowed. Now I was the one embarrassed. 'No go,' I muttered. I'd been undercut by a bigger firm. They'd offered all the same checks and had the staff to turn the work around much faster than I could manage.

'I'm so sorry, Penny,' he said and sounded so convincing I was tempted to believe it. 'I don't think there's much choice but to contact your creditors and try to negotiate.'

'I may have another option,' I said, then added, trying not to beg. 'Give me a week?'

'I can do close of business Friday.' he said. 'After that, I can't hold back the tide any longer.'

He wasn't anything like King Canute, I told myself as I left – too dark-haired, too cleanshaven, smelled better than any ancient Dane thanks to *Eau Sauvage* – but did he have the same mad gleam in his eyes, or was I just imagining that?

Chapter Six

Alice's lodgers rallied round, taking turns to pop home and check on her between rehearsing a new cabaret – "We've got a tour! Too exciting!" – and performing in their current show.

'We must give Monty a proper send off – funeral procession, eulogy – the works! He'd have loved it, darling.'

'I don't know,' said Alice. 'It's too much to cope with.'

'We'll sort it all. You won't have to do a thing – except show up. You'll feel so much better when you have closure.'

Closure. The word echoed inside her head. The only way she'd get that was to find out who was responsible for mowing him down. It was so hard to accept it was just some random act of cruelty.

The boys made sure she had all the company she needed. And she did. Except for Monty. She missed him through every minute of the day.

Work was her refuge; the costumes for the Dream still needed work, and Brian would be here soon, but in the meantime, Alice walked around her garden checking everything again.

The gate seemed to shut properly – she rattled the metal, pushed and pulled at the bars, but nothing made it open except her hand lifting the tight-fitting latch.

The fence had no gaps, nowhere Monty could have wriggled through a broken slat, or dug his way into her neighbours' gardens. The top fence was secure; he couldn't get into the junk-filled alley at the back even if he'd heard a cat or rat and wanted a game – and he certainly hadn't jumped the six-foot barrier.

Then Alice discovered another strange thing – the bulb in the outside light was loose. When she realised, she screwed it tight. It worked perfectly again. How odd.

That seemed more than coincidence.

It couldn't hurt to ask, Alice told herself, as she stood on the doorstep of number thirty-four.

'Yes?'

'Hi, Mrs Priestly.' Her neighbour had never offered a first name. 'I'm sorry to bother you, but I wonder if you saw anyone in the gardens at the back on Monday evening, or hanging about in the driveway ...' Alice's voice faded. How unnaturally bright she sounded.

Her neighbour raised her hand to her pearls, her expression horrified. 'Not a burglary? Not here?'

'No, nothing like that, it's ...'

'Good! We've Neighbourhood Watch after all, and the insurance is quite high enough, thank you very much indeed.' Her nostrils flared. 'Multiple occupation puts the premiums up for the whole street as I'm sure you're aware. It's not only you, of course, but ...'

'I'm wondering if someone might have opened my gate.' Alice cut in. 'Monty got out, you see … and he was …' Alice's throat began to close and she hoped she was not going to cry.

'Oh, the dog.' Her neighbour peered past Alice on the doorstep to the immaculate flower beds beyond. 'I hope he didn't do any damage – you ought to keep him under control … and the noise he makes some nights …'

Alice caught her breath. She could not explain Monty had been silenced forever – not to this woman.

'… and that goes for your *gentlemen* too. Laughing and singing till *all hours* and being very silly when I ask them to be quiet.' She sniffed. 'I know it's not always tobacco they're smoking. In that state, perhaps they left the gate open!'

Alice tried to focus on her task. Her nails dug into her palms. 'Everyone was out except for me, and it was only ten o'clock. Did you see anyone, hear anything?'

'Monday? No,' she shrugged, 'Ladies Circle dinner. And my taxi was late – I didn't get back till after eleven.'

The door was firmly closed but hope glimmered. Neighbourhood Watch.

When Alice had moved in, the man from number forty had been her first caller. He was bald and short, over-muscled and almost every inch of visible skin was inked. Anchors, crucifixes and ruby-eyed skulls all jostled for position with large-breasted mermaids and ornate script. His eyes had crawled up, then down her torso, then up again lingering in places. Eventually they reached her face. His chest had puffed as he offered her a leaflet, snake coils writhing around his fingers.

Neighbourhood Watch.

She had taken the literature politely and invited him in, but just then her furniture delivery arrived. Jerry, the boss man, blew her a kiss as he supervised her sewing table's emergence from the van. One of her father's showbiz connections, Jerry had recently swapped stunt driving for opening his own training school instead – with a side-line in removals. He'd given her a great deal – a thank you for making his uniform – and, more excitingly, he'd taught her a few driving tricks. Handbrake turns and rollovers had been thrilling. Another tick on her bucket list, just like starting her own business.

He was a good advert for her dress-making skill – the stylish jumpsuit fitted his six-foot four frame perfectly – but adding *Get-a-move-on, Darling* in a rhinestone rainbow on the back was all his idea – and perhaps the purple fascinator he'd teamed it with was a step too far.

Her neighbour seemed to think so. Alice had hardly seen the short man since. A glimpse now and then when walking his own dog had been the sum of their interaction. She always nodded. He stared back. Still, he was Neighbourhood Watch – it was worth a try to get justice for Monty.

The lion-head knocker triggered a storm of barking. It was silenced at a sharp command.

He held the bulldog with one hand and wore a t-shirt that proclaimed, 'Straight Pride'. The dog looked the friendlier of the two.

'I wonder if I could ask your help …'

'Piss off,' he said and slammed the door.

She returned home, disheartened, and even if she discovered how Monty got out into the road, she'd still be left trying to trace the car. The driver must have known they'd hit something. They should have stopped!

That night, she lay awake as thoughts turned in her head – was she to blame somehow? Could her neighbour hate her so much he would have done this? Could someone else?

She should have noticed more at the time. She'd been so shocked she hadn't even asked her Good Samaritan's name.

Maybe the woman could identify the car but so far there'd been no response to Alice's social media appeal to find her. The ad in the *Gazette* would be out today. Perhaps that would bring a result. She'd offered a reward.

Brian and his attitude whirled in her mind too. It was not her fault his ID documents had been returned to his home address instead of hers. That was down to the competition organisers. But he'd been on the phone complaining about it, and about the fitness plan she'd suggested.

'You didn't have to make me walk to the end of the pier yesterday, Alice. It's a damn long way – and then the passport. If Emily had seen it in the envelope ...'

Alice was tired of it all. Helping him had gone from a fun project to a constant worry and then Monty ...

'For heaven's sake, Brian.' She knew she'd spoken sharply. 'There's nothing I can do about that!'

'I'm sorry, Alice, I'm sorry. You're right, of course – I shouldn't unload it all on you.'

She'd accepted his apology, but then he had to spoil it.

'The last thing I want to do is upset you when you must be in bits. You're bound to be a bit sensitive.'

She'd fumed at his using Monty as an excuse for her very reasonable exasperation. He was the one with a secret, not her. She'd only agreed to keep quiet because he'd begged but if it was going to cause all this bother perhaps it wasn't worth it.

'Oh, Brian. Why don't you just tell her. She's bound to find out at some point.'

'Look, if Emily finds out about the competition now, she won't understand. She'll think it's just a waste of time and money and I don't want to upset her. She's having a hard enough time already. Even the house is getting her down. Says she keeps seeing things moving out of the corner of her eye –

and maybe its haunted! Honestly. Going to get her eyes tested, but if ...' Alice could hear the yearning, the "dream come true desperation" in his voice. 'If I win – or even just do well – it could make such a difference. She'd realise it's worth taking the risk.'

'I don't know, Brian. Show business is a tough life – especially for a family man.'

'I know but I have to give it my best shot – I can't be a salesman all my life! And with your help ...'

Alice sighed. He had talent, and he'd learned a lot – worked harder than she ever thought he would – and playing midwife to a new creation was undeniably great fun.

'So, we can just keep it between ourselves?' Begging again. 'And if I get nowhere, then no one ever has to know.'

'Ashamed?' she said, suddenly annoyed to think he might be.

'No! I'll be shouting it from the rooftops if I make it through the heats – you know I will. But there's no point in upsetting Emily if I fall flat on my face in the first round.'

He was good too. Even before they'd started to work together, she'd seen his potential, and been flattered he wanted her expertise. And he was paying for her coaching. A perfect arrangement.

Unless her father threw an eyelash-curler in the works.

Chapter Seven

L eaving the bank, I headed for my favourite thinking place on a raw day – the library café. A snug space between the rows of ordered books which wouldn't be too crowded with schoolkids till later in the day. There, over a large hazelnut latte and a Cadbury's Creme Egg, I pondered Sarah's proposal.

I loved my sister, of course I did, but her solution meant handing over control of part of my life to her, at least until I figured out a way to pay her back ... and I wasn't at all sure I was ready for that.

Her idea of background checks on potential partners – aimed at professionals with a sensible approach to on-line dating apps – had merit. Disposable incomes were high and with enough demand it could be a nice earner. According to Sarah, it was a "growth area with potential". We just needed to do some targeted marketing.

'Doesn't that kill the romance?' I'd asked, surprised to find her quite so practical.

'Too many of my friends have had bad experiences. I'm not so starry-eyed myself these days.'

I remained unconvinced – she was hopelessly romantic – but perhaps she didn't go on dating sites. Certainly, she'd always had a surfeit of admirers. I'd even had to lend a hand when she'd turned down a second date with her Chief Executive a while back. The woman turned vindictive.

I'd discovered this was not the first time that particular boss had lashed out when refused. I took some statements from sources who preferred to remain anonymous – though wrongful dismissal might have won large damages.

Sarah just wanted what she was owed. She had plenty of money anyway thanks to canny investments from her IT work. She left that company with her head held high, the proper compensation as stated under her contract and, more importantly, her business reputation still intact.

'I thought she was quite fanciable,' Sarah had said over a celebratory drink afterwards, 'until she ordered dinner for us both without asking what I wanted.'

In my sister's opinion we could turn Dad's agency around, and without stepping into shady corners. She'd outlined her proposal with enthusiastic idealism, and I found myself beginning to sway.

'You'd be helping lots of women – lots of people – make the right decisions about their future,' she had urged. 'And I could help out a bit. With money, of course, but I've got some time and I'm good at drilling down into data, spotting anomalies and figuring out where they came from. You know I never give up.'

That was true. She had the bulldog gene. There were times past when I could have cheerfully locked her in a cupboard and walked away for a week or two just to stop her worrying at a loose thread in my life.

She found out why my boyfriend in junior school had dumped me (Tina Pike had more pocket money), why I was taken back to the 7–11 in tears one day (Mum made me apologise for shoplifting two Cadbury's Flakes), and what my GCSE results were before I did. I'd have gone to the school for them but had a fair idea of how bad they were going to be. I feigned a stomach-ache and hoped a meteor would wipe us all out before the postman arrived the next day. My lovely sister intercepted him on the path and opened them for me. She always had to *know* everything.

For the mail tampering crime, Dad was supposed to make her see the error of her ways, but he was too busy laughing at *the apple not falling far from the tree*. I was the child with the Junior Master Detective Toolkit including fingerprint powder and magnifying glass. She got the looks and the brains and could do anything she liked. Infuriating.

Where I was tenacious, she was just plain stubborn – and smug with it.

So, my baby sister bailing me out … how could I accept that?

But without it, Dad's agency would go down – and Nate's livelihood was at stake, and mine. I was out of options, but still protesting.

'I can't take your money, Sarah. It wouldn't be right.'

'Not giving it. I'm investing – as a partner. I'll own an equal share.'

'A share that might not be worth much unless I pull a rabbit out of a hat over the next few months.' And as things stood, I couldn't even afford the hat.

'You don't get it, Penny-lope,' and she giggled like we were still kids. 'I *am* the rabbit!'

. . .

My chocolate egg finished, I crumpled the silver paper into a little ball and, when no one was looking, flicked it at the small child opposite who'd been making faces at me for no reason. I resisted the urge to stick my tongue out and sipped the latte instead.

I felt slightly sick, but sugar overload wasn't to blame. With the bank's attitude and that preliminary creditors' meeting about to be scheduled, I didn't have a choice.

I sent my answer by text so she wouldn't hear the defeat in my voice.

Welcome to the firm, partner.

Chapter Eight

P ops bustled into Alice's house, a whirlwind of warmth sweeping her into his arms.

'I've checked into the Grand and come straight over to give my best girl a hug,' he announced, suiting words to action. He kissed Alice's cheek then held her at arm's length to see her face, before drawing her back in close.

'I know,' he said after a while. 'But you can't hide in your workroom mourning for the rest of your life, sweetie, no matter how much it hurts.' He stepped back, handing her a clean tissue from his pocket, then wiping his own eyes with another. 'Come on, let's go for a stroll along the prom. You're way too pale and besides,' he patted her arm, 'I need some fresh air in my lungs. There's precious little in Vegas and I have to replenish my ozone when I can.'

Reluctantly Alice took her coat from the rack and tried not to dwell on the sight of Monty's harness. He'd have been bouncing around her feet, always eager for a walk.

No! She blinked furiously. Enough crying for now.

'Got gloves, scarf, a hat?'

'I'm not five years old, Pops.'

'It's cold out there and you'll always be my little girl.' He pulled her into his arms again and kissed her nose, and Alice wondered if he'd chosen those words deliberately. Her journey from Alan to Alice had been tough and he'd lived it with her, supportive from the moment she'd tracked him down. He'd coped with the surprises she'd sprung on him – first news of his parenthood and later, her plan to transition. He'd been her rock.

Now his face was full of concern, but her sorrow was reflected too. Hers was not the only heart Monty had left his pawprint on.

'I miss him so much, Pops. I don't know what I'm going to do without him.'

'I know, sweetie, I know.' His own eyes were brimming again as he rocked her gently until the storm abated. 'Come on, mop up and paint your face afresh, my darling girl. We'll put our best foot forward and face the world. He'd expect nothing less.'

'He'd just want the walk,' she corrected, sniffing, 'and to meet lots of friends to fuss him.'

'True – and that would have made him happy – as he did us. So, let's honour his memory by being happy we had him, even if it was just for a little while.'

Arm in arm, they headed for the seafront in the bracing chill, and Alice asked the question that had been burning in her mind since he'd first mentioned the possibility.

'Are you definitely stepping in to host the talent show at the Pavilion, Pops?'

'I am! The screen test went well, and they've made an offer I'd be mad to refuse. It'll be a bit manic rushing back and forth but it's doable, just.' He smiled at a child in duffle-coat and wellies chasing wavelets under the close eye of a teenage girl. A scampering spaniel circled them both. 'And it means I get to see you a bit more, my darling, so that's a bonus. We rehearse this weekend with technical and dress. Then I'll pop back to town for the spot at the Palladium on Sunday, and high tail it back next week with the TV crew. Bit of a mad dash but so lucky I was available when JoJo Lovington dropped out!'

'And you'll be judging?'

'Oh yes,' he beamed. 'Mine is the casting vote! Bring on those bribes, my lovelies!' He laughed. 'Seriously though, I only get to have my say if the celebrity panel are tied so hope-fully, I won't have to do it.'

'Don't you want to make someone famous?'

'That would be great – but think of those who lose. I don't want them sticking pins in my voodoo doll!' He grinned. 'No, let the panel take the heat. I'm happy hosting. We'll do all the regionals on a whistle-stop tour – highlights to be televised, of course – then I get to do the live London final *if* the powers-that-be are pleased with me.'

'You'll be the best, Pops, and never mind the panel – you'll be the best celebrity,' Alice said lightly while her mind was absorbing the news. Would a judge's daughter coaching a participant be grounds for disqualification? She hoped not, but there'd been a lot of small print. She'd have to check again. Best keep Brian under wraps for now.

Pops was still preening from her endorsement but playing modest.

'One Channel 5 documentary, a Queen Bee award and a few teatime quizzes don't quite make me a superstar, sweetie.'

'And a lifetime on the circuit – London, Benidorm and now Vegas, Pops!'

'Love your loyalty to your dear old dad, but I'm getting long in the tooth for this business.' His voice turned serious, started to lift. 'But this is what I've been hoping for, Alice. A real chance to break through, and they are gearing up for an international franchise if this goes well. Guest appearances world-wide on the cards – my pension plan assured – so fingers crossed!'

'That's great.' Alice hoped she sounded more enthusiastic than she felt, while wishing desperately it was another show in another town her father's future depended on. What if she had to tell Brian he'd wasted all that time and effort – and all because of her.

'They tell me the acts have been carefully selected so even the first round shouldn't be *too* dire, but there are the big numbers to rehearse – lots of dancers and backing singers. The producer wants the "professional talent" to dazzle in case the audience gets restive with the amateurs – can't think who he means.'

'What happened to JoJo? Is he ill or something?' She wasn't proud of the tiny hope he might recover from whatever it was and claim back the role.

'That would be me, sweetie – the "professional talent". What's the point in fishing for compliments if you never catch any?'

'Sorry, sorry.' She squeezed his arm. 'Not that you need to fish – you're fabulous and the audience will be mesmerised.'

'Now you're getting the idea.' He laughed then stopped. 'Actually, rumour has it my predecessor's back in rehab. Showbiz can take a toll.'

'It can.' Alice tried to concentrate but her head was whirling. She'd need to check on the competition rules – that bit would be easy – but what exclusions were in her father's contract, and how was she going to check without Pops wondering what her interest was? She'd never lied to him. He knew her too well.

He was glancing sideways at her now.

'Try not to worry, Alice,' he said. 'I know you miss your darling boy, and it hurts so much – but you will get through this. And I promise I'll get to Monty's funeral, even if I have to sneak out of rehearsals.'

Chapter Nine

꧁❀꧂

Against a leaden sky herring gulls wheeled. From the pier I watched the rubbish truck crawl along the prom. Huge birds fought over last night's chips. They needed to be quick or their breakfast would be ground to slime inside the roaring machine.

Choppy waves spat and slapped the pier's concrete supports; whirlpools churned in lazy circles, slurping like toothless crones with thick brown soup. I tried not to look.

I twisted my hair into a band – me and glamorous never did belong together and the ponytail was functional even if it did the Wiseman nose no favours.

A dark waterproof, navy scarf knotted at my throat, kept out some of the cold and I blended into the scenery. It helps that I'm of average height and weight for a female of my age. Five foot six and size fourteen.

I eyed the narrow hoarding I was trying to use for shelter. Okay, size sixteen, on a bad week.

So, there I was, freezing on the pier, waiting for Dunker and his alleged blackmailer and trying to be invisible. I had a fine view down the shingle beaches, so I fumbled with my phone, pretending to take a snap or two. Then nearly dropped it when it buzzed.

I slipped off my glove and swiped to cancel yet another withheld number – "An accident that wasn't your fault" or "Not too late to claim for PPI", it was an even bet.

The noticeboard bore a graffitied flier for the Haston Players, to which someone had pinned a business card advertising a lady with a whip. Below that a ripped poster featured showgirls with sky-high feathers and glittering leotards. I shivered.

A long minute passed.

The gulls, robbed of their breakfast, were gliding on the North Sea wind. It's what the locals term a "fresh breeze", and what visitors might call a "howling gale".

Or should that be a Howling Gail? I watched the ghost of Gail Monterey rise through the planks of the pier, her dripping hair making shadowy splotches on the planks. She looked at me. I looked back. I knew she'd be here. She always was.

Ten feet below, the tide surged around the pylons keeping me safe. She shook her head gently as if to say, *Your turn soon, my girl*, before she vanished into nothing against the stained cinder blocks of the public convenience.

Not me, I thought. I'd kept out of saltwater since the day I'd nearly drowned, but every time I found myself here, she'd pop up to wave hello.

Gail had been my babysitter a long time ago and I'd pestered to get my way as only a small child can. Gail loved everyone, especially children, especially me. I'd sulked when she said no, been obnoxious till she changed her mind, and finally she'd given in. We took an inflatable out onto the waves. Beneath the waves were currents. They swept us beneath this pier.

Without me, she might have had a brood of her own, and

grandkids by now too. All her generations lost. The sea did its part, but she wouldn't have been in the water if not for me.

She was my first ghost. I make what amends I can when the dead come to me, but when Gail looks me in the eye, I know it's not enough.

A gust tugged at my hair and dashed salt across my face. Brooding about the past wasn't going to make it better, any more than this wind was going to improve my complexion, despite the fancy skin cream my sister gave me pointedly every Christmas.

I swept my gaze around the pier head but there were few daft enough to loiter. One young couple, in thick coats, did their best to preserve body heat by wrapping themselves around each other, and giving mouth to mouth. I looked away.

A woman, stout in her sheepskin, waited for her equally stout dog. The Westie sniffed the plank Gail had risen through, then squatted, wheezing slightly. It had a zipper pattern on its side. I hoped the effort of marking Gail's favourite spot wouldn't burst a stitch.

The woman shot me a sharp look as I meandered past, then called. 'Come along, Betsy.' The dog sniffed the wall where Gail had disappeared before trotting off after its owner, giving me a wide berth.

If Gail had the chance, she might try to convince me her death was not my fault. She'd always had a generous soul. She might even tell me what my ghost teen wanted at the Dunker house. But the dead don't have a voice. I think that's why they come to me.

My mind was wandering.

I tried to look interested in the container ship on the horizon, then casually glanced around again.

A locked gate to my seaward side led to the fishing jetty,

which pointed across the Channel like an index finger from the pier's fist. Over the rail from this side, I watched a small motorboat bump against the pontoon dock below. A caged metal ladder gave access to where it rose and fell in the chop, but I'd need a key to get through the gate. That didn't matter. I had no desire to get closer to the water.

Still no sight of my quarry.

Hours passed, though the pier clock said it was less than twenty minutes. I caught myself seeking confirmation on Dad's watch and cursed. A good run of cases and I might be able to get it out of hock. The thought was cheering, but my face was raw, and my lips were cracking. I stifled a sneeze and then a yawn and gazed out to the horizon.

I'd wanted to be in place before Dunker arrived. Less suspicious, just part of the furniture, but I was having second thoughts. The blackmailer had chosen well. Nowhere to hide and nothing much to do there at this time of day. It was bitter, and any watcher would think masochist, not tourist.

I'd find out what Dunker was up to, but where did my ghost girl fit in? My cheekbone ached where she'd touched me, like an icicle was being driven through my sinuses.

I blew on my fingers, numb despite my gloves, and lifted my phone as if pointing the camera shoreward.

Then, finally, the wait was over.

Mr Brian Dunker was not quite as tall standing up as he'd appeared in the "Honey" photo. His legs were short on a lengthy torso. He was muffled in a zipped-up anorak but even so, less bulky than I had expected. He strode towards the shut-tered Jolly Roger Theatre to my landward side and took shelter against its bulk. His hair, now flat and plastered down with sea-spray, was thick and dark. He sported a neat goatee. It suited him rather well, and his eyebrows had been trimmed from bushy to well-groomed.

He sniffed the air, rolled his shoulders once then planted his feet "at ease". He stuck his hands in his pockets, like a man taking a breather from his stroll. But the flush on his face spoke of exertion and his eyes were never still. They darted here and there, alert for any threat.

They passed over me as I leaned casually on the rail. Well, why wouldn't they? I was facing away, phone in hand, just an out-of-season tourist determined to get the perfect postcard shot. The reverse camera is so useful, eyes in the back of your head.

He stood twitching slightly now, glancing at his watch. Then someone shipped up to meet him.

I'm not sure I ever really understood what "sashay" meant before I saw the woman who came to greet him. In her tightly belted raincoat and high black boots, she stepped out like she owned the universe and everything in it. She trod the rough planks like a catwalk. She'd always be noticed. And she wasn't the owner of that slut-red underwear arranged on the bed next to Dunker in the photograph. She was long and lean and nowhere near that cup size.

I watched him offer an envelope. She leaned forward as if to whisper in his ear. She took it and he seemed frozen to the spot while her lips grazed his cheek. She smiled for all the world like they'd just met at a cocktail party. Then she carefully wiped lipstick, or some imaginary trace of it, from his face with her thumb before stepping back.

This lady had some nerve.

I snapped a couple of shots of them together, managing to get myself out of frame with a bit of not too awkward manoeuvring, and then set off at an idle stroll back towards the prom. She overtook me as I dawdled past the kiddie carousel. The little painted teacups were being unveiled to face the day, their owner bending to check the guard rail. No sign of Brian. I picked up speed and followed at a discreet distance, but she never looked back.

We walked at her pace, which seemed leisurely but made me uncomfortably warm with the effort of keeping up. She slowed a bit when she took a call on her mobile and I was grateful for the breather. I stopped half-hidden by a shelter. She glanced in my direction, then I could see her head move as she spoke. Her free hand waved in the air punctuating the conversation, but I was too far away to hear.

I followed her along the seafront towards the radio mast, but long before we reached it, after just a mile or so, she crossed the coastal road and made her way inland through the maze of elegant Victorian avenues that made up this part of town.

She walked on. I followed. She turned left and right at intervals but kept heading away from the town. I was sweating inside my coat, wishing she'd just get where she was going so I could have a break.

Finally, she did just that. But it wasn't a house she went into, or even a block of flats. It was the vet surgery on the corner of Blackstock Road.

Okay. I squared my shoulders. Time for an imaginary Tiddles to get some premium lunch. I walked confidently up to the entrance that had swallowed my prey and nearly broke my wrist on the locked door.

Maybe someone had seen her through the glass panel and let her in. I peered through. My view was blocked by a second set of doors. On the doormat of the small lobby sat the faint ghost of a short-legged, long-eared hound. His front feet were turned outwards neatly like a ballet dancer and his legs were wrinkled. He regarded me mournfully. I suppose it's difficult for a dog with a face like that to regard in any other way.

I stepped back from the door. The surgery was a sprawling

low building covering the corner lot and had car parking on three sides. I could hear dogs barking at the back. Pet hospital at the rear, I guessed, and client entrance at the front where the pointy bit would be if it weren't chopped off by a wide porch and double doors. There were probably several exits and, no matter how hard I tried, I couldn't watch them all at once.

Right on cue I heard a motor start. I hurdled the low hedge and the path, ignoring the angry protest from my muscles. Blinking against the pain, I was just in time to see a small red hatchback speed off in the opposite direction. I got EJ62 then it was gone. Hyundai i10? Every third vehicle in Tesco car park was one of those, and most of them were red. Oh, joy.

I folded from the waist, leaning my hands on my knees till things stopped hurting quite so much, then somewhat despondent, I limped to the front door and checked their surgery hours. They should be open, but the door was still unyielding. The barking took on a note of mockery.

Chapter Ten

❦

Alice was walking along the seafront and congratulating herself on how much fitter Brian looked as she picked up the call. She failed to take in what Carol said at the beginning, her thoughts still on what her exercise programme was doing for Brian's posture as well as his waistline. Then she stopped walking and listened to her friend's tale with growing scepticism.

'Why would some random woman be following me?' she asked, but Carol was insistent.

'It's a good question, pet, and I can't answer it – but I'm sure she is. There are some funny folk in these parts.'

Alice could hardly argue with that. She rented rooms to some of them. The Pavilion's cabaret chorus capering along the road in new satin gowns and six-inch heels came to mind. They needed to "see how it all moved with the dance routines" or so they said. They just wanted to show themselves off, Alice thought fondly. It was a fair example of why some of her neighbours raised an eyebrow.

But Carol was still explaining. 'She was hanging around the end of the pier acting a bit strange – and my little Betsy didn't like the look of her. She sort of dithered about for a bit, and then she started to take pictures on her phone, but she still had her gloves on, so *I* knew she was only pretending.' Carol sniffed.

'They do have touch-screen gloves now,' Alice pointed out.

'I know – my grandkids have them for their iPad thingies – but if she'd been wearing that sort why would she take them off to answer a call!'

The current series of *Midsomer Murders* had just finished, and Carol was desperate for mystery. She wouldn't make something up exactly but let her imagination get a bit over-excited? Perhaps.

Sweet of her to care.

'Well spotted, Miss Marple,' said Alice. 'Amazing eye for detail.'

'Thirty years married to a cheating man, pet. You learn to notice things.' Carol chuckled. 'Anyway, I popped into the Coffee Bean for one of their lovely breakfast rolls when I saw you go by. A couple of minutes later there she was, the same woman, skulking along behind you. I walked up to the top prom, to keep an eye on her like, and she was almost jogging in pursuit – your long legs, pet. I felt quite sorry for her, not built for speed if you get my drift.'

Carol was not exactly slim herself and those rolls were high calorie – though she always shared with the little Westie. That thought brought a pang. Betsy would need a new *Petslim* buddy now Monty wasn't there. Maybe she'd suggest Colin's Basset. Unlike her fussy boy, Brooke had a greedy nature.

'I thought I'd best give you the nod, pet, in view of Monty – well, you know. In case it was connected to his accident in some way.' She left a respectful little pause. 'Anyway, I'll see you at the chapel, to pay my respects. Keep your chin up, pet.'

Tucking the phone into her raincoat pocket, Alice glanced behind at the figure in the distance, suddenly taking the idea more seriously.

Could she be the driver of the car trying to track Alice down? She could stop and ask – only the officer she'd spoken to yesterday had given her food for thought.

'IT'S LIKELY SOME RAT-RUN RACER HIT HIM BUT,' THE DESK officer said, 'there'd be no compensation unless you could prove fault.'

'I don't care about that! I just want to know how it happened – and make sure they know there are consequences. It could be a child next time! Surely, it's an offence not to stop?'

'It is,' he agreed gravely, 'but the thing is, and I know it seems unfair, but this is your responsibility – not having the dog under control, you see – and there could be a counter claim – vehicular damage, whiplash, emotional distress ...' He shrugged. 'So, *if* we found the driver, we *might* get them on leaving the scene, but it'd be just a small fine unless there's another offence – speeding, drink/driving, even mobile phone use maybe – but the chances of proving that are practically zero. And in law, well, it's just a dog. Sorry.'

So much for a pet-loving society!

'What if I said I did want compensation? He was a pedigree, after all. Would you trace the driver then?'

He sighed and took the details, generating a crime number "for her insurance", but it was clear investigating was on a par with cycling on the pavement. The station notice board included a missing fourteen-year-old and an appeal about a stabbing near the pier.

Perhaps she was being unreasonable.

ALICE INCREASED HER PACE ALONG THE SEAFRONT STILL contemplating Carol's call. She wanted to look Monty's killer in the eye and tell them what they'd stolen from her world. But it was absurd to think this woman was some maniac driver following her.

Her thoughts turned to the car. Would damage to it indicate its speed? And the driver might have spent the night in the pub. She might never be able to prove anything. Still, no one could stop her trying, and if they wanted to sue her, she'd fight it all the way and make sure their friends and family knew they were a cold-hearted killer!

Alice checked over her shoulder. The woman was still there, keeping pace. Carol's idea was ridiculous. A figment of an overactive mind.

Still, she increased her speed again, leaving the seafront and weaving through the labyrinthine roads towards her destination. The woman was never far behind.

ALICE DROPPED THE LATCH AS SHE HURRIED THROUGH THE main doors of the vet surgery. If this woman was some unlikely kind of stalker, it would slow her down. If it was all coincidence, it couldn't do any harm.

Kathleen, guardian of the reception desk, looked rather startled at the speed of Alice's entrance but summoned her usual smile. Then she turned solemn. 'Oh, Alice, I'm so sorry for your loss. Monty was such a lovely boy, and in his prime. What a tragedy!'

'Yes. Thanks.' The tone of her own voice was clipped. Sympathy just made her tears begin to rise.

'Poor Val was so upset – had a fit of the vapours the next day then had to go home. Of course, they'd worked so late and she was so fond of Monty – well, we all were but,' she sniffed. 'Some of us have to stay at our posts.'

'Of course,' Alice said, not caring right that minute about anyone else's feelings. She was holding on by a thread.

'I've come to ...' then her throat closed over the words. Her breath hitched and she blinked, tried again. 'I've ...'

'Of course.' Kathleen reached below the counter and placed a plain brown paper carrier carefully on the desk. 'He's right here, all ready and waiting for you.' She patted the bag gently then pushed it towards Alice. 'I'll see you tomorrow if I can get away. Two o'clock?'

Alice nodded as she fumbled for her purse, but Kathleen waved her away.

'No need just now. We'll send the bill. Deal with it when you can. Please, Alice, don't worry about a thing.'

Alice took a shaky breath and held the bag tight, closing her eyes for a moment. Grief punched her chest like a fist, it felt like her heart stopped. It took all her concentration not to break down completely.

The lock rattled as someone tried the front door.

Alice opened her eyes.

'Thanks,' she managed as she fled out through the side entrance.

Once safely in the car, she paused only briefly to peer into the bag. The gold-topped urn she had ordered gleamed back at her. She breathed deeply and started the engine. She'd let tears come when she was home, away from prying eyes like those of the woman who had just flown around the corner like she'd been shot out of a gun.

She was being followed! But Alice couldn't face a confrontation. Not right now.

She placed one hand gently onto the urn on the passenger seat in silent apology as she drove away.

'I promise you, Monty,' she said. 'I will find out what's going on.'

Chapter Eleven

❧

When the surgery door remained stubbornly shut despite my best efforts, I finally rang the bell. I was admitted by a matronly woman with a greying perm wearing a blue tabard-type overall with "Kathleen" embroidered on the pocket. She apologised profusely on seeing me locked out.

'The catch must have slipped. We'll have to get someone to look at it. Mustn't keep out the paying clients now, must we?' She fiddled with the door while observing a pink-haired young woman who was rounding the corner of the building. Kathleen's lips grew thin as the newcomer approached.

Kathleen's voice was saccharin. 'Oh dear, Val. Not car trouble again, I hope?'

'Nope. Hairdresser was running late.' Val's hair swung neatly as she turned. 'Pinkissimo – it's still my favourite!' The colour did nothing for her complexion, but she seemed happy with it. Then Kathleen's expression registered.

Squaring her shoulders, Val raised her chin and mirrored

her colleague's arched eyebrow to perfection. 'The boss okayed it so do feel free to mention it to him.'

Their mini-spat was interrupted by a young man wrestling a reluctant German Shepherd in from the street. Val nodded to him, then strolled unhurriedly through a door marked "staff" while Kathleen scurried to her post behind the desk.

I waved the man to go in front, not wanting the unhappy mutt between me and the door. Its desperate snarl displayed impressive fangs. I knew that look – I felt it on my own face when my dentist started the drill. Biting was not allowed there either, but I understood the temptation.

My six-month check was due, but that hadn't caused the sudden pain in my own canines. The dead girl's touch flared, like liquid nitrogen flowing along my facial nerves. The mournful hound's ghost from the lobby reappeared. It sat in the corner, watching.

Perhaps ghost called to ghost. One walked over my grave.

The German Shepherd's owner had it on a short, and tightly held leash so I felt safe, at least, while Kathleen looked up its notes. Poor thing had its tail tucked under its hind quarters and was whimpering. Ghost or vet, I wondered. Something was spooking the poor thing.

I stood back, turning to the notices pinned up around the walls: pet slimming club; health insurance; fleas lead to disease. In a framed photo, a handsome captain whose smile missed smug by a millimetre, stood at the helm of the *Liberty Belle*. The brass was shiny; the paintwork gleamed white, perfect as his teeth.

The same man also topped the "Your Caring Team" array pinned on a corkboard. They all posed with an animal of some kind. Daniel Kitson had a firm grip on a squash-faced cat, and a Robert Redford smile for the camera. Val was there too, her companion a bug-eyed lapdog. Kathleen held a plump bunny. It might have made a tasty pie.

I turned to watch the ghost hound sniff around while I considered my next move. P.I. work would never earn me a thirty-foot cruiser. Half-hour on the boating lake might be too rich for my pocket, but it was a job I loved.

So, had my quarry locked the door on purpose, then slipped out of the side door? Her car must have been parked here for a reason. Perhaps she was meeting someone. Though there had only been the driver in the car.

Unless someone had ducked out of sight before I turned the corner. My head began to ache more generally.

The big dog was wrestled to the far side of the waiting room with Kathleen's assurance someone would be right along, then she switched her focus onto me.

'So, dog, is it? Or cat? Or rabbit, hamster, gerbil, guinea pig?' She'd rattled them off almost without pause and I probably looked as blank as I felt. Her smile faltered. 'Oh, reptile ...' Rather disapproving, but by then I'd caught up. I'd prefer to claim a ruby corn snake or Komodo dragon, but that might not win Kathleen over, so I chose small and fluffy.

'Cat,' I interrupted rapidly to make up for my slowness off the block. 'I need food for my cat.'

'Science Diet, Royal Canin, Hill's ...' The woman was stuck on reciting lists. Unfortunately, none of these names were familiar. What happened to the common brands? Perhaps the margin on generic kibble wouldn't cover mooring fees on that boat.

I took a punt and opted for the Hill's. Sympathy made her chatty.

'Thyroid, is it? Poor thing. They do suffer when they get older, don't they?'

My imaginary kitten aged in a blink.

'Wet or dry?' she inquired.

A vision of a half-drowned Tiddles prompted my reply and a large bag of what sounded like Rice Krispies was placed on the counter. It could be mine for an outrageous sum.

'Oh, no,' I patted my pockets, not too theatrically, I hoped. 'I've left my purse at home. How silly of me. I'll have to come back later. Unless ...' Her jaw began to tighten as she prepared to refuse credit. 'I thought I saw someone I know come in just before me ... maybe she's still here. Tall, elegant, tan raincoat ...'

'Oh, Alice,' she said, perhaps relieved I wasn't looking for supplies on tick. 'I'm afraid you've missed her. She just picked up Monty and ran out the door, poor thing.'

'Ah, never mind.' I waved away my lack of cash and donned a look of friendly concern. 'And how is Monty?'

In the weird little pause, the dog ghost ambled over. He sat at my feet looking up and waved one large forepaw in the air. I was sorry to disappoint, but there's no way to give the dead a titbit. Not that I know of.

Then Kathleen said, 'Why, hadn't you heard? Monty died.' The ghost rolled over and put all four feet in the air, keeping that hopeful look fixed on his face. The receptionist looked at me rather closely.

'What a shame, he was such a beautiful creature.' I injected as much buttery warmth into my voice as I could without feeling queasy. 'Such a clever dog with all those tricks, and those fabulous ears.' The spirit got to his feet and shook his head, preening a little.

Reassured by my obvious acquaintance with the animal, she went on. 'Bassets are so adorable, aren't they? Poor Alice, she's devastated.'

'Oh, dear. I knew Monty was ill of course, but I had no idea it was so serious.'

'He wasn't ill. He'd not been here since his routine check three months ago.'

'Ah, just a bit of tummy trouble a while back – maybe she didn't need to bother you with it.'

A hint of furrow appeared between her eyes, but suspicion was too slight to still her gossip. 'He was run over. Such a lovely boy, he was. One of my favourites. Alice was picking up his ashes ready for the service tomorrow.'

'How tragic,' I murmured. 'And the service …?'

'The Assisi Chapel. Two o'clock tomorrow afternoon. Family flowers only though.'

I was grateful for the information. She killed any thought of mourners saving money on the wreath with news of donations to pet charities in lieu while I was wondering how to find out Alice's surname.

The Basset, who had been sitting at my feet apparently fascinated by our conversation now performed another of his tricks, a "sit up and beg" manoeuvre. His paws were huge, his legs short and balancing on such well-padded haunches did not look easy. His forehead fell into worry lines, but he held the pose.

Do people put death notices in the papers for the pets, I wondered, or chapels advertise their running order somewhere? Worth a try.

'Are you going to the service?' Kathleen asked.

'I'm not sure,' I said. I might end up there to track my suspect.

The dog jumped up, turned a tight circle, wagging his tail. He looked towards the door and back at me. *Let's go*, he signalled, as clear as if he'd spoken. The freeze-burn in my cheek throbbed again.

The sound of barking from the back had gone up a notch.

Then it got louder as the door beyond the reception desk opened.

The strong-jawed "captain" of this ship – sailing gear swapped for green scrubs – appeared in a doorway marked consulting room and laid a hand on the German Shepherd's head.

'Take her through, Kevin, and we'll run some tests. I'll be there in just a moment.' The dog shied, despite the vet's soft tone, but was dragged away. Kitson hung back.

'Have you heard from Val this morning?' he asked Kathleen. His voice was mild, but his fingers tapped against his thigh.

'She's just arrived.'

'Great. Thanks.' His smile grew warmer, and he included me in it. I felt a slow heat rise in response. The cleft in his chin was rock-star cute. He had a merest hint of Jon Bon Jovi's laid-back accent too. I wondered if he'd learned it to go with the look, or if it was natural. He was welcome to read me the shipping forecast anytime.

The staff door opened, and "Pinkissimo" emerged. The white tunic and trousers pulled against a generous figure and the fabric rustled as she moved.

'Morning,' said Kitson mildly. 'Could you stay on later, make up the time?'

'Sorry,' she said not sounding it. 'Not tonight.' She stomped away past the desk and into the corridor leading towards the rear. He hesitated a fraction before taking the paperwork Kathleen offered and disappearing into the consulting room.

'Trouble?' I asked.

'Second time she's been late this week.' Kathleen said, leaning forward on the desk. 'Honestly, she's great with the animals and the clients love her but just lately ... well, if I were boss, I'd have a word.'

'Plenty of couples meet at their workplace,' I suggested.

'No! He's got a new lady friend. He likes to keep her private but she's very chic – I've met her, just the once, and his taste is more refined than ...' Either words failed her, or she reconsidered what she was going to say.

She glanced reverently back at the consulting room. 'We're so lucky. America's loss is our gain, honestly – and he trained at one of the best vet hospitals there and keeps up with all the latest treatments. Your little pussycat couldn't be in better hands than his, so if you want to book an assessment ...'

I wondered if she really cared about his medical skills or whether she had just been trained to win his approval. Pavlov had a lot to answer for – she was practically salivating. I was barely resisting the urge to wipe my own mouth on my sleeve.

I took a deep breath and returned to reality. 'Well, I'll think about that. Thanks very much.'

The ghost Basset was back begging at my feet, his expression woeful. My facial nerve flared with graveyard frost.

'I'll maybe pay my respects at Monty's memorial.' The frost began to melt, and the dog trotted to the door. He looked back at me expectantly, tail waving.

'Thank you for your help, Kathleen,' I said. 'I'll pop back for the ...' I pointed at the waiting bag of cat crunchies and left.

Better dig out my funeral black, ready for tomorrow.

Chapter Twelve

❧

The Basset's ghost trotted around the vet's outer wall, his backside swinging from side to side. He kept his nose to the ground as he circled towards the back of the building. I followed, stopping at the pole which kept unauthorised cars out of the employee parking area.

I hung around watching him, idly wondering what the solid brick-built outhouse was used for. Not a garage – the doorway was too narrow. Bars over the windows and a keypad said it was kept secure.

A shadow at an upstairs window reminded me I might appear suspicious, staring into the staff car park – especially if that outhouse stored anything worth stealing.

I pulled out my phone and dialled the office, trying to look natural.

Waiting for Nate to answer, I watched the Basset doing what dogs do. He ignored the high-end BMW and a black Toyota Yaris, and finally chose the rear wheel of a custard-yellow Beetle.

'Hi Nate, it's me,' I said as the Basset cocked his leg. He left no trace against the shiny hub cap. 'How's things?'

'Quiet as the grave, boss.'

The dog wandered back inside through the closed door: his silent bark had been ignored.

'Same here,' I said. 'I'm heading back. I'll pick up my car and be there before your lunchbreak.'

'Okay. Oh, I've got that list together, girls to check against the Dunker house. I'm working through it.'

'Photos?'

'Yes, for most of them.'

'Good stuff, but I've got something else for you – high priority.' No point wasting his time if I could identify my girl at a glance.

'Great!'

'More research.'

His sigh was almost silent.

I explained the pet funeral service. 'Track the Assisi down. The dog's called Monty, for an Alice somebody. See if you can get her surname – phone them up and say you want to send a card or something. Be creative. I'll be back in a bit.'

'On it!' he said, cheered.

NATE HAD BEEN NAGGING, BUT EACH TIME HE MENTIONED aspirations towards field work I'd dodged the issue. His expectation was my own fault.

The day he came for interview he'd been early. His frameless specs, gelled ginger hair, and guileless grin had made a reasonable impression, as had his earnest attention when I outlined the office duties. When I invited questions, he'd leaned forward with fervent hope.

'I'd be a trainee, though, right? Learn to do the P.I. thing?'

'The P.I. thing?'

'You know, unmasking the bad guys and all that. Planting bugs, spying on people. Catching murderers. Aunt Maggie kind of said it's what you do.'

I suspected Maggie was "kind of" desperate to see him gainfully employed.

Disappointment loomed large in his future and obliged me to be clear. 'It's answering the phone, updating records, invoicing – that's the job on offer. It's more boredom than Bond.'

His expression said kicked puppy; his reference praised his enthusiasm; he was cheap.

I said I'd think about some basic training – after he'd proved himself reliable at the desk work – and we'd see how it went.

He'd proved surprisingly good at all the admin, but gangly, ginger and uncoordinated were not great assets for an investigator – and every case speedily solved was a precious drip into the dry well of my bank account.

So, I'd put it off, but he was getting restless. Now Sarah and her investment had come on board, if something not too complicated came along, I might just risk it.

THE DOG DID NOT COME BACK, BUT THE CURTAINS MOVED IN the apartment above the surgery. It was time to go. If they did keep drugs in that store, someone might call the boys in blue to check on me and that could be embarrassing. I'd gone to school with some of them.

Besides, if I walked back the direct route along the seafront, I'd have time to stop off at the bank. I was keen to look Colin Palmer in the eye and tell him of my change of circumstance.

As I walked back to my car, I had the feeling things were finally looking up, and not only financially. For whatever reason, I was on the road my ghost girl wanted me to travel. The feeling in my face was almost back to normal, and if Alice was the "Honey" who had left that message, and that lipstick kiss, on Brian Dunker's photo, I might be close to solving a case.

Given her catwalk model poise, it crossed my mind she might be a "therapist", the kind with a whip whose business card I'd seen pinned on the pier. She seemed too upmarket to advertise there, but agencies operated at the higher end. Keeping what he was buying quiet could be a nice little earner on the side – and she might not work alone.

It could be useful to see who else turned up for the mutt's send-off. The phone call she'd taken as I followed her to the vet could just have been to say the ashes were ready for collection, or from a look-out warning her about me. She could have had a minder keeping an eye out. Or be part of some larger blackmail gang.

Maybe I'd been infected by Nate's view of my business, but I thought back to the pier head and the possibilities of an accomplice. The young couple had seemed oblivious, and the woman with the Westie had left before me. Of course, I'd left before Alice, so anything was possible. No one had stood out.

As I reached my car and found it had not been ticketed, my optimism surged. Things were definitely looking up.

I risked leaving the car a little longer to cut into the pedestrianised High Street. I saw the bank ahead, and a small glow warmed my soul. I'd have to add my sister to the account, and it would be clear my dazzling business skills had not saved the agency. Still it would feel good to look my account manager in the eye and not feel at a disadvantage. It had been a long time since I was in that position.

Naturally, as I had such great news to impart, Colin Palmer was at a meeting elsewhere. I left a note about the partnership and a request he'd reassure my creditors till the funds had been transferred.

Despite all my exercise this morning, my jeans were pinching round my middle. Perhaps, it might pay to take up some activity. Join a gym? Take up a sport? According to a poster in the bank, the RNLI had a sponsored 10k run coming up.

Colin Palmer's sculpted physique and the scent of *Eau Sauvage* wandered through my mind.

A 10k run? I'd be hard pushed to manage it at a walk.

I diverted into the Subway take-out queue and said yes to extra coleslaw on the side. When I got back to my car the traffic warden had been round – a penalty notice was stuck fast to my windscreen.

Chapter Thirteen

✦

Alice arrived at the Haston Grand next morning at precisely nine forty-five. The hotel had seen better days, but Pops maintained he'd rather have "the fading elegance of a Grande Dame than some upstart motel with no soul at all" and it did have the best view of the Victorian Gardens with the sea beyond.

Pressing the desk buzzer, Alice tried to look casual despite the thumping of her heart.

The duty receptionist emerged from the backroom tugging down his uniform jacket and brushing crumbs from round his mouth. She relaxed a little. Most of the staff knew her, but friendly young Jamie was just perfect for her purposes.

'Good morning, Ms Mayford. How are you today?'

'Morning, Jamie. Fine, thanks. He's expecting a package. Thought I'd take it up if it's arrived?'

'Came a few minutes ago.' He put the large envelope on the desk. 'Are you sure you want to beard the lion quite so early?' Pops had a standing *do not disturb* instruction on non-rehearsal mornings. He would not emerge before the "civilised hour" of ten o'clock barring fire, flood or earthquake.

'I think I can risk it,' she said, tucking the envelope under her arm. 'But perhaps best not to phone up – if he wants to bite someone's head off, better mine than yours.' She smiled. 'How about you let me have a key so I can sneak in and make his coffee for when he wakes?'

'Of course.' He beamed and handed it to her. 'Not that Mr Mayford is ever anything other than charming.'

'I know – but he's not a morning person, bless him. Could you send up the full English for two in about twenty minutes?'

'My pleasure.'

Alice let out a silent breath as she headed for the stairs.

She'd phoned the production company yesterday.

'Send a hard copy – is that possible? – only the internet is rubbish in the sticks,' she'd said, 'and Mr Mayford's having problems accessing his emails – he's horribly afraid he's being hacked – fans stop at nothing these days.'

The HR assistant had been sympathetic. 'Comms are such a nightmare outside the cities,' he said, 'and stalkers … such horror stories! Poor Mr Mayford. It hardly bears thinking about. Not a problem.'

Alice could almost see his shudder. 'Courier delivery to the Haston Grand, then? Before ten o'clock would be just perfect! Thank you so much.'

Now the contract copy was in her hand. She dropped it into her shoulder bag and went in to wake Pops. With luck, he'd never need to know anything about it.

LATER THAT DAY, BACK AT HOME, ALICE ANSWERED THE DOOR.

'Did they come?' Brian said immediately, and at her nod went on without a breath. 'Are they the right colour? Have you checked the size? What if they give me blisters – or I can't walk in them at all? Where are they?'

She pointed up the stairs. She'd never known so much fuss over shoes, but these would make a difference. Tall worked well for this game – more dramatic for the stage – and he needed the advantage. His legs needed lengthening and these heels should do the trick. He was good but not unbeatable – not yet.

He'd need luck too, but she hoped "break a leg" was not about to be too literal. That would end the dream that burned in Brian like a fever – and he'd spent an arm and leg on it. He wouldn't want to give up now.

Her steps were heavy as she trailed in his wake to the top of the house.

'I'll have to practise in them,' he said as he fought to keep his balance. 'But they're just the job. The dog's danglies!' Then he remembered Monty was no more. 'Oh, God. Sorry, Alice. Didn't mean to remind you …'

Alice didn't need reminding – Monty was always in her thoughts – but missing the Basset wasn't the sole cause of her distress. 'It's fine.' She bit her lip. 'It's Pops – he will be judging.'

Brian turned away, kicked off the shoes, and the back of his neck went red.

'So what? It's only if you're an employee, or a close relative of someone who works at the production company that you can't enter –'

'That's true …'

'– and I'm not!'

'It's my father's contract that's the problem.'

Brian turned, his face now the same beetroot as his neck. 'Not *my* problem.'

Alice felt sick. 'No,' she agreed, 'but it is mine.'

He stared, shook his head. 'I've spent a fortune on this, Alice. Worked like a Trojan on all the stuff you said I should learn – even risked my wife divorcing me, for Chrissakes!'

The last seemed like exaggeration though he'd always said Emily's reaction would be extreme if she found out what he'd been spending so much money on. Once he'd proved himself, he hoped she'd see it differently.

Now he might not get the chance. Muscles were working in his jaw; his fists were clenched but it was misery not violence she saw emerge.

'There must be something we can do,' he said. 'Some way …' He shook his head again. 'I'm not accepting this, Alice. I can't.' He took a breath and looked up at her. 'How do you know exactly what this contract says? Perhaps it isn't what you think.'

Alice opened a drawer in her workroom cabinet and took out the envelope with the production company logo. She handed it over. 'Page seven.'

He held it loosely, looking at her. 'Your dad's?'

'A copy.'

He scanned the page. 'The *appearance of impropriety* bit?'

'That's it. It means if you win, Brian, if there's even a suspicion of undue influence, and if the production company found out the connection then Pops could be fired from the show – his reputation would be ruined!'

'That's a lot of "ifs", Alice …'

Her voice rose. 'He might never work again. And the runner-up could even sue – it's already happening in America!'

He threw the contract onto the sofa. 'Now you're being hysterical!'

'I'm not being …' Alice took a breath. Perhaps she was, just a little. She held up her hands. 'Okay, so he probably wouldn't end up in court – but it would damage his career and you have no idea how important that is to him right now. This is his last chance to really make it.'

'I get that, Alice, I really do – but don't you see, this is my only chance ... the one time I have to find out if my dream is worth anything – or if I'm going to be nothing but a second-rate salesman all my life.'

Alice laid a hand on his arm, then picked up the contract and sat down. Brian slumped beside her, head in hands.

'You're a great salesman,' she said. 'Or I wouldn't be ordering all those very expensive fabrics from you.'

He sniffed and, after a moment, conceded. 'Yeah, that's what Emily says ... but is that all I am?'

'A husband,' she said, 'a father ...'

He sniffed again, then chuckled, ruefully. 'My Jasmina wants to be a singer,' he said.

'Is she good?'

'Awful – but she's a great little actress ...,' he waved a hand. 'Whatever the future holds, I want my kids to know it's okay to reach for the stars ... seize the chance and give everything their best shot – even if it fails.' He sighed. 'I know I might not get anywhere – but one day I want to tell my kids that I tried!'

'So why keep it a secret?'

'Look, it's not her fault, but my acting's always been a bit of a joke to her side of the family, Brian's little hobby, and then there's all the money I'm forking out. There's bound to be a row.

'Besides, if I mess up, I don't want Emily to be there. She'd want to support me because she's always loyal, but then her sister would stick her nose in. Then suppose I get so nervous I can't perform or I'm just not good enough? No, I couldn't bear it, not Emily's disappointment, or her sister being all "Well, don't give up the day job," and whispering *I told you so* in her ear.'

'It's best for everyone to keep it quiet till it's over.' He raked his fingers through his hair. 'I'll come clean when I've come to terms with it and I can tell Jasmina she's got to reach for her dream if she wants.

'And if I do get to the finals – well, it won't be a secret anymore.' He sat up a little straighter. 'So, what are we going to do about my dream, Alice?'

Chapter Fourteen

✹

All seemed well at the office. Nate was working industriously at the reception desk, but then he'd have seen me on the security screen, puffing my way up the stairs. Before my arrival he could have been playing *Covert Action* or sexting a girlfriend for all I knew.

'Hi, Boss!' His greeting was cheery.

Perhaps hunger was making me snippy. Nate was a good lad and had worked hard computerising our data base. Dad's rolodex worked well enough for me, but Sarah wanted to delve into our old case files and go through our contacts for potential marketing so Nate's update would prove useful. The diversion would give my new partner something to sink her teeth into. I hoped it would keep her out of the way of my active investigations.

Poor Nate. He prepared the bills for me to pay, and he'd surely seen the final demands come in. It wasn't much of a leap from there to bankruptcy court – and his acting skills were not the best. He looked horrified when I told him there would be some changes.

'Good news,' I added hurriedly. 'My sister's coming on board and she's going to look into our' – I did the bunny ears with my fingers – '*business model* and see how we can be more profitable.'

He ran both hands through his hair, raising pale carrot-coloured tufts, and blinked at me.

'Don't worry, Nate. Sarah will be a lot of help. You'll see,' I said, as much to reassure myself as him, then I diverted him onto the results of his morning.

'I've found your Alice,' he said, cheering up a bit. 'Alice Mayford, designer and dress maker. Advertises a company called *Dress to Impress*. Very upmarket – dresses for posh do's and stage costumes. There's a mobile number and an email, plus social media accounts. Nothing seems strange – except the things some people want to wear.'

'Great.' I averted my eyes from his fashionably ripped jeans. They revealed skin so white it would make milk look tanned. His t-shirt was the red of recently dried blood and had "Dyslexia Rules, KO" emblazoned across it in dayglow orange. It lit up his acne from below.

Not for the first time I wondered whether he was colour blind or just dressed in the dark.

'I've sent everything I can find on Alice Mayford to your inbox, and don't forget Mr Haddock's due in half-an-hour.'

TELLING NATE TO GIVE ME A BUZZ WHEN OUR NEW CLIENT made his appearance, I settled at my desk, mozzarella sub in one hand, mouse in the other as I scanned the information Nate had pulled together. Teenage deaths in Haston in the last ten years made depressing reading.

He'd categorised by cause of death and from the numbers, it was carnage out there for young drivers. Suicide, drugs and alcohol accounted for many others, then stabbings and summer drownings from beach and boat. Bright faces full of promise smiled out from news reports. None of those pictures matched my girl.

I put my lunch aside, sipped at the coffee Nate brought in, and ploughed onwards.

Leukaemia, epilepsy, asthma, other cancers ... the list seemed endless. None of the photos matched either, but something tickled in my brain. Epilepsy — or not exactly that but something like it ... and there she was.

Hair neatly pulled back in a band, narrow-faced with high cheekbones, light shadows in the faint hollows beneath. Wide-eyed, laughing at the camera through long dark lashes. Healthy, happy, vibrant Lizzie Nash.

My skinny, little ghost girl.

I turned to the basics Nate had pulled together, then googled her for more. There were a lot of hits. Lizzie's death had made the national press.

Schoolgirl, 13, drowns in bath during mystery seizure shouted the *Daily Mail* headline from last October.

Elizabeth Nash, 13, who was described as fit and healthy, is believed to have suffered an unexplained seizure and fallen unconscious under the water in her bath.
Elizabeth's father, John Nash, 42, battered down the bathroom door at their home in Haston on Sea, Essex, and attempted resuscitation as Barbara Nash, her stepmother, called 999. Paramedics arrived within minutes, but the schoolgirl was pronounced dead at Colchester General Hospital.
Elizabeth Nash, known as Lizzie, died just ten weeks after being given the all-clear by doctors. She had suffered several seizures previously. She had been taken to hospital unconscious in May last year but had not had a seizure since.

In a statement to the press an anguished Mrs Nash said: 'Words cannot begin to express our desolation at losing our beautiful Lizzie.'

Asked if she believed the medical profession might have questions to answer, Mrs Nash commented, 'It's hard to understand how they could have said she was fine when this was clearly not the case. Her father and I will not be satisfied unless there is a full investigation.'

The Head of Neurology at the hospital where Elizabeth was treated declined to make a statement.

Tributes have flooded in for the tragic teen. Her father was too distraught to comment, but fellow pupil, Jodie Channing said: 'Lizzie was my best friend and nothing will be the same without her. I'll miss her every day.'

Jane Ryland, Proprietor of the Sunshine Animal Rescue Shelter, where Lizzie was a volunteer, said: 'We will miss Lizzie's beautiful face and sensitive demeanour, her loving care for all the animals here. Our hearts go out to the whole family and her many friends.'

Susan Harper, Headteacher at Haston High, described the schoolgirl as 'a valued and loved member of our school community, a lively and academi-cally gifted student who had recently shared her ambition of becoming a vet and working for the RSPCA. She was thoughtful and generous and will be missed by everyone in school.'

An inquest into her death will be held at Chelmsford Coroner's Court.

The inquest had been opened and adjourned pending reports, but all the indications were that scandal, if there were any to be had, lay with the neurologist. Poor man looked harried and wan in the photos – but colleagues were staunch in their support, saying this was a tragedy which could not have been predicted. The story had spluttered like a damp squib. Depending on the inquest result, no doubt it would ignite again.

My fingers went to my cheek. Lizzie's icy touch was buried beneath my skin, but it ached again below the surface like a wisdom tooth gone rogue. Knowing the "who" took me one step forward – but the "why" still felt a marathon away.

Nate's face appeared round the office door. 'Hey, boss. Client's on his way up.'

'Give me a minute and bring him through – then look up everything you can on Elizabeth Nash – see if the inquest findings are available yet.'

'Will do. I figure Haddock might need to get his breath back for a mo' before he comes in, anyway. He's a big bloke.'

I tidied the remains of my lunch into the bin under my desk and wiped my mouth with the napkin. My teeth should be alright given my forethought in removing the lettuce before biting into my sub, but I ran my tongue round just in case. Then I put my hair up into its usual ponytail and walked round the desk as the door opened.

He was a "big bloke" but he wasn't out of breath. The slabs of muscle looked steroid-fuelled and overdone. I suggested we sit at the lounge end of the office.

The sofa might just take the weight.

Chapter Fifteen

Vincent Haddock was not my favourite client but despite Sarah's investment I couldn't turn work down – not if it was legal, and this was. Like Emily Dunker, he had suspicions of his spouse.

'She's always been *my* woman, my Jenny-wren,' he said. 'Only one for me and I love her to bits. Do anything to make her happy. Give her the best – car, clothes, holidays – anything she sets her heart on. She don't have to work or nothing. Her job's just keeping herself nice and looking after me – and we do alright.' His face slowly turned the colour of rare beef. 'But if she *is* shaggin' this yoga bloke from the leisure centre, that's taking the mick, and I need to know.'

'Forgive me for asking, Mr Haddock,' I said, finding the name less amusing now I was face-to-face with 18 stone of solid muscle,' but you don't strike me as the sort of man who'd need any help to sort this out – by just asking the man in question, for example, not that I'm advocating it but …'

'Nah, you're alright.' He grinned. 'I got a caution, see? After last Saturday's match – some little Asif tried to wind me up, so I gave him some. Makes it ... er ... tricky. His mates claim I was saying stuff as I hit him.' He raised his palms in surrender. 'Me, officer, say something racist? No, sir, *As if* I would.' He laughed.

I didn't.

He shrugged. 'That's why I need you, darlin'. This yoga bloke might get scared, take a tumble down the stairs or something. And Jen might find out I'm asking and if there's nothing to it ...' He took in a breath and shook his head.

'You understand we can only establish the facts. We're not in the business of ... enforcing good behaviour.'

'No worries, doll.' He smirked and squeezed my knee with a sweaty hand. 'I got a mate for that if it comes to it – no damage, like, just a friendly warning – and I'll take care of Jen ...' For a moment he seemed to falter, and in the depths of his pinpoint pupils there glimmered something lost. 'Thing is, I never thought it ... not my Jen, but she's acting weird ...'

'Of course.'

'I need to be sure, one way or the other but if it ain't true ...' he tapped the side of his nose with one forefinger. 'Our little secret. My Jen, none the wiser.' He squeezed my knee again.

My instinct was to cut off his hand neatly at the wrist, but I controlled myself, merely removing his fingers from my jeans before rising to my feet. 'Confidentiality is in the contract,' I said, though it was always subject to small print.

'Then that's all hunky dory.' He beamed.

I PONDERED BEFORE I WENT TO SLEEP THAT NIGHT. THE leisure centre had a lot of footfall – fit sporty types, dancers, swimmers – but it also hosted activities for all ages and body types and hired rooms out to local organisations ... if I gave him a chance, Nate might not stand out from the crowd.

NEXT MORNING, I SLEPT LATE. I'D BEEN TORMENTED BY BAD dreams. Some were watery, but one had Nate playing netball against Sarah on the leisure centre court. Lizzie cheered from the side-lines while I was trying to referee a foul between Vincent Haddock and Brian Dunker. Alice, towering above the net like her *Looking Glass* namesake, scored goal after goal. Other nightmare fragments floated free and I woke up groggy; my bones ached like I'd sprinted the Grand National without a horse.

I downed two mugs of strongest Yorkshire to bring me back to life and headed down into the office to give Nate the good news about his assignment.

Nate wasn't there. It was Saturday.

Although we didn't keep strict office hours he only came in at weekends by special arrangement, but I had his file of Lizzie information.

I flipped through the reports of her death, and follow-up articles. I considered "best friend" Jodie Channing and the pictures of the girls together. Jodie probably knew more about Lizzie than anyone on earth. I might need to track her down, though I was still in the dark as to what I was looking for.

The inquest might give me a clue. Nate had made a note. The case was listed to resume on Monday. Good timing. The result might be imminent, but I couldn't take time out to attend. Besides, it would be tedious, hours of medical reports and legalese interspersed with heartbreak and tears. The verdict would be published, but not the full proceedings. I needed a proxy pair of eyes.

My phone reminder chirruped. Time to catch up with my blackmail suspect at the Assisi Pet Chapel.

THE QUAINT VILLAGE OF LITTLE CHARFORD WAS A MERE three miles inland of Haston, but it felt like another world. It was the kind of village that made it onto postcards and kept alive the ancient art of thatching.

I slowed for a group of youngsters in hi-vis yellow jackets trotting single file along the lane on an assortment of ponies. Dawdling the car behind them, I watched backsides rise and fall, and idly wondered why they had to do that. They peeled off into an even smaller lane and the backmarker turned briefly in the saddle and gave me a wave.

Two minutes further on I came to the Assisi gates. I pulled into the small parking area, and got out, breathing fresh country air. A faint smell of horse manure was not unpleasant. My first impression was restful – and very green. A manicured expanse of lawn swept down to the chapel building. From there the greensward gently undulated onwards to a line of conifers marking the boundary. Nearer, a few large, bare-branched trees reached into the overcast sky looking rather gloomy, but the grass was broken up by flower beds. As I walked down the long footpath towards the chapel, I realised the roses were beginning to shoot. The wind was kinder here than on the coast.

Stands placed near the chapel entrance held laminated cards, tributes laid below.

"Boo. You brought laughter into my life. Harry Bleasdale." I pictured an elderly man bending with difficulty to place the store-bought bunch of yellow chrysanths and felt quite sad – a suitable expression should anyone be watching.

"Mork Marsden. We miss you, loyal friend. Ben and Sid,

Bethany and Tom." A florist bouquet, two single roses tied with silk ribbon and a stuffed Winnie-the-Pooh adorned this one. I'd bet, a sibling named Mindy had gone on before.

I glanced around. No Basset ghost in evidence. Monty didn't seem to be here for his big send off. So why did he want me here?

Strolling through the stone arch into the vestibule, I found the listing of the day's services displayed on a board. I skimmed down the dozen or so names.

"Monty Mayford, 2pm. Songs, prayers and reading, followed by scattering of ashes. Family flowers only. Donations to SARC or PDSA."

A gap on the timetable explained the ease of parking, so I took a chance and turned the heavy iron ring. A quick scope inside confirmed the interior was empty. I sidled in.

Religious buildings are not my natural habitat. I'd been to occasional church weddings, including one of my own, and I'd attended Sunday school for a short time. I have a vague memory of hard seats, boredom and the innocent but whiskery embrace of the ancient woman who ran the bible study group.

'Hello, can I help?' A black-garbed cleric with rosy-cheeks stepped from the shadows behind the lectern. His face was as grave as it could look, but still had the slightly scary bonhomie of a garden gnome.

'I was ... err, just looking ...' I let my shoulders droop and sighed.

'Of course,' he murmured gently. 'Please look around all you like. Have you ...' the merest hesitation, 'lost a family member?'

I looked down at my feet and blinked a few times.

'Just take your time and if you need anything or have any questions, please don't hesitate. I'll be in the office – just through there.' He indicated a discreet door beyond a pillar and, with equal discretion, disappeared through it, leaving me to my grief.

I slipped into a pew, glancing at my naked wrist before fishing out my phone to check the time. Half an hour at least before anyone was likely to turn up for the Basset's send off. I'd give it a minute or two then have a chat with the gnome.

I wondered idly if the church sanctioned all this now. There'd been something about an animal Christmas service at the Haston non-denominational last year. A pair of beach donkeys had been a seasonal highlight, till they disgraced themselves in the aisle.

After a suitable time had passed, I tapped lightly on the office door and entered. It was a small space, richly hung with heavy curtains, cosy, and he'd made tea. I was warming to him.

'Joshua Clarke,' he said, standing to offer his hand. 'Take a pew ... not literally, of course.' I watched him beam expansively at his own wit and summoned a weak smile in return. The tea was about the same strength. My warming was rapidly cooling.

'I wonder if I might ask a few questions.' I kept my voice subdued, suitable for one soon to be bereaved.

He placed a booklet beside my teacup with the reverence accorded a holy text. 'That covers all the basics, but of course, I'm here to help.'

I spoke, quite movingly I thought, about my darling kitty and the thyroid problems that even Hill's wonderful food could no longer help; how it was time to think the unthinkable and plan the next step. We sipped our tea in companionable silence for a moment before I risked the next move.

'I wonder if I might sit in the chapel for a little while longer. Just to get a feel for it before I make a final decision?'

'I'm afraid we do have a service in a little while ...' He checked his watch. I reached for a tissue from the box he'd placed at my elbow with the now cold tea and dabbed my eyes. He bowed his head as if asking for divine permission before he gave his assent.

While waiting for the Mayford funeral party to arrive, I leafed through the brochure. The prices nearly made me cry for real.

The cleric headed to the vestibule and a few moments later I heard voices. The ghost of the Basset ran in, nose to the ground. He skidded to a halt when he got to my pew, looked up and waved his tail.

Okay, I'm here, I thought. What now?

Chapter Sixteen

❧❀❧

Alice fixed the plaited wreath around the urn which rested on a stand inside the chapel's porch.

'How clever to weave in his favourite toys,' Terence gushed as he kissed air on each side of her face. 'And rubber bones. He'd have absolutely loved it.'

'My thoughts exactly,' she said as brightly as she could, willing her lips not to tremble, her eyes not to fill.

'I'm so sorry, Alice, but you know that,' he said as he gave her a hug, releasing her to wipe his eyes with a white handkerchief as he made his way into the chapel.

Alice took a shaky breath. The string of sympathetic mourners that followed did not help her composure, and her eyelids ached with blinking but, somehow, she held on.

Colin arrived with his Basset, Brooke. The hound sat at his feet, looking up at him adoringly when he paused to murmur his condolences. It was so kind of him to come, and to bring Monty's sibling. He'd navigated her through all the "advice for small businesses" at the bank when she was starting *Dress to Impress*, then, as Basset "family", he'd become a friend.

Neither bad-boy macho nor metrosexual-handsome, his individual features were not remarkable, but added up to a pleasant openness. His cologne conjured the lifeboat crewman, rather than his office persona. She caught cedarwood and citrus, but somehow salt and saving the day always came to mind. Alice wondered why he hadn't been snapped up.

'Brooke's better behaved than her brother,' Alice said, patting the dog's head as Colin signed the guestbook. Then she felt disloyal. Monty hadn't been disobedient, not really. She'd just asked for the impossible, like leaving dug up items on the outside of the door, or ignoring potential chewing toys, like any shoe left temptingly in reach.

The only thing that counted was the love. He'd given that unstintingly every single day.

'Females can be more cooperative,' Colin said averting his gaze from her tears. The dog jumped up hoping for reward. 'But only when it suits them.'

Alice bent to rub the sweet spot behind Brooke's ears and the hound wriggled tail to toe, just like Monty used to do.

Colin spoke again. 'Do you remember when I lost my car key and Monty "found" it in the hole he'd dug?' He smiled. 'I'm telling that story.'

The lump swelled in Alice's throat. There wouldn't be a dry eye in the house when the time came for sharing at the open mic, but there'd be laughter too.

Colin moved away, making way for the small queue of people arriving in the porch and Alice was kept busy for a few minutes but then found herself alone. She checked her phone. No word from Pops; no news was good news, she hoped. Rehearsal over, he should be on his way. More mourners made their way inside.

Val, pink hair almost hidden by a navy scarf, shook hands awkwardly. She seemed uncomfortable, as if embarrassed to be representing the surgery where he died. 'So sorry,' she said, 'Dan's been called away on an emergency.' Perhaps she thought Alice would be offended the vet hadn't come in person, but she hadn't expected him. Monty was just one of his many patients, but Val had always said her Basset clients were on her personal favourites list.

Alice thanked her warmly for coming while Val scrawled her name in the book. When Monty had tried to eat a bee, it was Val who kept him calm and took out the stinger from his swollen lip when he wouldn't even let the vet close. He'd adored her ever since.

Carol's Westie, Betsy waddled her way into the porch, followed by her owner who was already swiping her eyes with her hankie. 'Oh, Alice,' Carol said, then passed inside, unable to talk further.

Alice glanced at her watch then scanned the footpath beyond the few late comers trickling in. No sign of Pops, though he had promised, hand on heart, to be here. As had her lodgers who had taken Monty to their hearts. Most would be off touring with their new show soon but in the meantime, Pops had wangled them a warm-up spot for the TV production. It was bad timing they'd all been called for rehearsal today. Theatre was a demanding mistress.

Joshua popped his head round the chapel door. 'All set?'

She checked the time again, then looked at the urn and raised her chin.

'I'll give it two more minutes.' She'd celebrate Monty's life and do him proud, but it would be much harder without Pops and the boys to lean on.

Her hopes were realised when she heard a toot of a horn and saw the theatre mini-bus swing into the car park. A moment later she heard voices as they hurried towards her.

Pops, sombre in a navy suit, wrapped Alice in his arms.

'Told you I'd make it, sweetie. I was finished in time, but there were no cabs for love nor money!'

'I'm so glad you're here,' said Alice, her voice catching.

'Lucky the boys could squeeze me in.'

'Squeeze you anytime!' called out one.

'Between you and me,' said Pops, looking into her face. 'I think they've already been at the Bristol Cream.' He wiped her tear away with his thumb.

'Prosecco, per-leeze. I'm allergic to anything brown — except me self-tan, natch,' called another voice from the back.

'Call that brown, Tango?' heckled another, and Alice wiped away another tear, laughing with the rest.

This cast had shared her house for months, regaling her with showbiz stories about her father — which he swore were lies — and extending Monty's repertoire of tricks along the way. Now they'd be leaving too, and her home would be so empty. She blinked the tears away as they lined up for inspection, their attire not quite as sombre as Pop's suit.

'Tango' did a twirl. 'Monty would've approved, doncha' think?'

'He'd have been thrilled.' Alice took the funeral urn off its stand and cradled it for a moment before passing it over to the chief pallbearer.

Pops smiled, tears brimming in his eyes. 'Ready, sweetie?'

'I am.'

'Shoulders back and best foot forward.' Pops took her arm, and they stepped together into the nave.

Chapter Seventeen

✣

I'm not judgemental. Okay, sometimes I am – but not over that kind of lifestyle choice. Still, I was hard pressed to keep from reacting when the funeral procession entered the chapel. I am aware, even today, some people do like to push the boat out and dress up for church. The good folk here had pushed so far it was halfway to Dunkirk.

Seldom had I seen a more glamorous pageant. RuPaul or Lily Savage might have been in there somewhere, but I was too dazzled by the shimmer of sequins to be sure.

· The overblown femininity made me wonder briefly about Alice. She was tall for a woman, elegant in a way that usually requires practice, and had a figure that might have owed something to good corsetry. She had large hands and feet and they were often the give-away, though her neck seemed positively swan-like. Whatever her background, dressed in simple black and on the arm of an older man to whom she bore a familial resemblance, she was not attempting the style of the rest of the funeral party.

These "girls" were truly fabulous. Coiffured and polished,

their eyelashes were long enough to start a hurricane. They paced a funeral beat in their stiletto heels, hips swaying to Cat Stevens' *I Love My Dog* which had started up from the speakers somewhere behind me.

A dazzling belle in a flame-red wig which reflected a faint orange tinge onto the face beneath, carried the dog's remains in a black and gold urn. The hound's ghost walked proudly before it, tail aloft, leading the company towards the lectern where the gnomish Joshua now waited. Alice walked in measured steps behind.

As the song finished there was a flurry of rustling fabrics. They were exotic birds settling to roost, though birds would not have left so much face-powder hanging in the air. Many tissues dabbed carefully around eyeliner, and I hoped all that mascara was waterproof.

We all looked dowdy compared to the main procession, but "Miss Pinkissimo" from the vet stood out amongst the sparrows filling up the pews nearby. A Westie raised its lip at me as the stout woman from the pier, settled into her pew, oblivious. Some ordinary folk helped me blend in, for which I was grateful.

No Brian Dunker though.

Then I saw a figure I had not thought to see. I hunkered down; my head bent over my hands as though in prayer as Colin Palmer went by. He was leading a familiar looking dog. Another Basset, this one smaller than the dead one, with longer ears. It was a wonder it didn't trip over them, but it ambled in a slow-motion sort of "run" with its nose close to the ground.

The cleric finished his welcome and launched into a moving elegy about the blue-blooded Pinnesari Hercules Montgomery aka Monty: his lineage, his good nature and his good works. He was a loving companion, a loyal friend, visited sick children in hospital and was even a doggy blood donor. He was everything a dog should be.

Pet funerals seemed no different to their human counter-parts. I bet he dribbled, put muddy pawprints on the furniture and bit the postman every chance he got, but the dark sides of the departed seldom get a mention at their send-off.

Then the urn-carrier started her reading. She'd just got to the part where "you cling together in joyous reunion" when the living Basset made a bid for freedom. The ghost dog ran up to it as it reached the central aisle and they touched noses. Then the living one sat back on its haunches and threw back its head. The howl was likely heard in hell.

It had our full attention. Evading Colin's hands with ease it loped along the aisle towards the back where I was sitting, quietly out of the way. There were several empty spaces between me and the aisle. It jumped onto the first and closed the distance fast.

Despite my flailing arms, it got its big paws onto my shoulders then wriggled its solid body onto my lap. Throwing it bodily off me would have been my first choice. But I didn't want to start a riot and it was a weight pinning me down. I could do little to fend off its cold, wet nose. Its breath was none too pleasant. I turned my head to find Colin, red-faced and apologetic.

Between us we hauled the beast off my lap and onto his, then I realised the red face was not solely embarrassment. A rising hysteria was sweeping the crowd, a hurricane of laughter passing from one person to the next as those who couldn't see quizzed for details. I suspected each retelling gained in entertainment what it lost in truth.

My own smile was as weak as the cleric's tea, and about as warm, but that made no difference. The dog sat, now docile at Colin's feet. He held it by the collar in one hand and used the other to hold back the tide of mirth – or made the token gesture.

One person who had not succumbed to the general amusement processed along the aisle towards us, one perfect eyebrow raised.

'Brooke, won't you introduce me to your friend,' said Alice, her hand resting briefly on the dog's head. Then she drew up to her impressive height and looked down at me.

'This is Penny,' said Colin, still spluttering. 'And I really am terribly sorry. She's usually *quite* well behaved.'

Did he mean me or his hellhound? Another tremor shook him, and he was off again.

Alice was not laughing. It was her pet's funeral. I thought she had the right to be aggrieved, but her anger was aimed at me rather than the dog.

'Penny who?' she demanded.

'Wiseman,' I said, standing to offer her my hand. She didn't take it.

'What are you doing here?'

The cleric bumbled to the rescue. 'Oh, it's her cat, my dear. She wanted to stay a while, decide if this was the right place to come …'

'Then I think you've seen enough.' Her voice was sharp enough to cut a throat.

I made an exit as dignified as one can when thrown out of a funeral.

The ghost dog wagged his tail as I went by.

Chapter Eighteen

The raunchy tones of Dolly Parton, giving her all about "the best friend" she ever had, mocked me as I hurried away. I tried to leave it behind by speed-walking across the greensward towards the distant carpark. Then suddenly I stopped.

Had I seen the dog before, the hound that pinned me to the pew, or was it just a similarity of markings. The photo with the Dunker's daughter, Jasmina, the one that had moved out of line. My ghost girl, Lizzie, had she nudged it somehow, and made sure I noticed?

I walked on slowly, lost in thought. If the dog in the chapel and the dog in the photo were one and the same, then Colin must have some connection to the Dunkers – and maybe Lizzie too. And he certainly knew Alice pretty well if he was at her doggie send-off.

But this was a small town. Could it be coincidence? Or was the ghost dog trying to send a message? If so, Monty was out of luck, because I didn't get what he was trying to say. What had he achieved except to get me thrown out?

My head hurt but at least my face was free from dog slobber and, almost at the Assisi's car park, I was out of reach of mad canines.

But fate loves one last snigger.

Yelling and excited yips signalled a commotion across the chapel grounds off to my right. A blur of movement resolved itself into a slip of a lad being almost towed across the grass. His posse of stubby-legged pooches were pulling their leashes taut and heading in my direction. I turned my head to look but kept on walking and somehow failed to notice the tan-and-white trailing a broken lead who brought me down.

I tried to avoid him, jumping with all the finesse of a carthorse over Becher's Brook. I ended in a puddle, bum-cheek deep. The escapee, enjoying the excitement, jumped on me in an instant. As I scrambled to get up, he licked my face.

I pushed him off, and the shouting resolved itself into words.

'Grab him!' The lad was yelling and the pup leaping around my feet was barking in appreciation of the game. I snatched his harness and held tight. The pup tried to yank my arm off, desperate to re-join the pack he'd been running away from just a second earlier.

The young man puffed to a halt. 'Thanks, thanks so much,' he wheezed, laying one hand on his chest while keeping a tight hold of the bunch of leads with the other.

He was older than he'd looked, his slight frame misleading me into thinking him a boy. Close-up he looked as if he might be old enough to vote – just. His baby face meant he'd probably look that way till he was fifty.

The other pups boiled around our feet, greeting the sibling with the urge for freedom as if he'd been gone a month. He'd not even been out of sight. Dogs!

'You're welcome, I think,' I said, bending at the knees to

keep hold of the troublemaker. His ears flopped across his face; his legs needed a steam press. The look was horribly familiar.

'Bassets,' agreed the lad as he struggled to regain his breath. I watched the freckles across his nose come into focus as the flush retreated. He grinned. 'They're a bit of a handful.'

'I can see that.'

'Cute though, don't you think?'

I murmured something indistinct as a pup found something fascinating at my feet. I labelled her a bitch and not just for the way she squatted. Now my shoe was fragranced – eau de puppy pee.

Cute was not what I was thinking.

'Oh, no! Sorry.' He clamped his lower lip between his teeth, but the snort shot through his nose. By then I was beginning to see the funny side. The pups were all waving tails and velvet coats and perhaps they had their good points. Not least because I seemed to have a growing interest in the breed.

'Bloody lead broke,' said their minder, glaring at the scrap trailing from the runaway. 'Look, I know it's a bit of a cheek, but would you mind walking back with me? Not sure I can manage on my own and there'll be hell to pay if one escapes.' He had brown eyes just like the pups. 'I can offer a clean-up and a coffee, if it helps?'

The thought of spreading puppy pee into the car was not a welcome one and, when he mentioned a flash coffee machine that could do a proper latte, I was tempted. More interesting still was the logo on his jacket. SARC. Sunshine Animal Rescue Centre – where Lizzie Nash had volunteered.

He was reed-thin and still puffed out from running. If he turned out to be a psycho, I could probably take him down. I took the broken lead and doubled it through the harness. It allowed me to walk almost upright as we cut across the lawns to a gate in the hedge.

The property next door was extensive. The farmhouse had been there when William did his conquering though it now sprouted carbuncles and turrets in unexpected places. Around this was an assortment of outbuildings including an impressive Tudor barn. It was probably original and in good shape, but one thing not original was the presence of CCTV. There were cameras everywhere.

'This is a bit posh for a rescue centre,' I said, nodding at his jacket.

'Ah, SARC is a tiny part of it – it's the Pinnesari Livery and Boarding Kennels. Mrs P supports the charity – lets them have space rent-free and pays their utilities. Covers any shortfall in their vet's bills too. She's a bit of a love – most of the time. These are her babies though.' He nodded at the tumbling pups. 'Basset breeding is where her heart lies.'

I followed my new companion, who had introduced himself as Van, to a more modest building where he put in a code as I made a show of looking away. Habit made me note which keys were worn and excellent peripheral vision made learning the code a breeze, but if I wanted to break in, the cameras would be a deterrent. Inside, the pups were restored to their mother dog who endured their boisterous greetings with good-natured patience.

'They'll all be leaving this week,' he said, as we walked back to his quarters. 'Other places would have let them go earlier but Mrs P won't till they've all been properly socialised. She has a thing about dogs being returned for bad behaviour.'

'People return their dog?'

Van nodded. 'Sure, they all come with a guarantee and if there's a problem it's better for the breeder to have them back.

They get trained and re-homed sometimes and sometimes …
er, not.' He was embarrassed.

So, put down if they didn't make the grade. Suddenly it
seemed a less than cuddly business.

'People who pay these prices expect perfection – and
there's our reputation to protect.'

'This is a puppy farm?'

He stopped dead. 'Jesus, don't let anyone hear you saying
that – they'll sue for defamation!' He'd gone paler still behind
the freckles. 'Mrs P's a reputable breeder, Kennel Club licence
and all. Pinnesari Calencia Rudebeck the Third was best in
breed at Cruft's last year.'

'Pinnesari Calendocia the Whatsit?' I said. Creatures with
bites at one end and kicks at the other turned huge eyes on us
as we passed the stable yard. I was distracted but I was sure
Pinnesari had been one of Monty's posh names.

'Rudebeck – Rudi to those that know and love him.' Van
grinned, then his face clouded. 'Her stud dog, a gutsy little
guy, but this could be his last litter. He might not even make it;
the vet's here again today. Mrs P's been out of her mind –
really crazy.' His fist curled at his side.

'Must be tough.'

'Yeah, I guess, but still not an excuse for a boss being so
…'

'I meant on you, looking after all the others,' I said mildly,
watching the colour rise in his cheek, and wondering what
she'd done to upset him.

He shrugged, regaining his composure. 'It's tougher on
her, I guess. I mean, if it was my kid …' For a moment he
seemed far away, then snapped back. 'Anyway, they're doing
everything they can.'

I couldn't help thinking of those bright-eyed pups.
'Nothing catching, I hope.'

'No, thanks be, but it's touch and go. He's had to have a major op so ... still, he's improved a bit so hope for the best. Here we go.' He unlocked the door, a standard Yale key this time, and ushered me in to his domain.

I used his bathroom, which I was glad to find neat and clean. I stripped off my jeans and gave the affected denim a good scrub. Pulling them on again I hoped the drenched area didn't suggest I'd been caught short. The shoe needed a wipe and I was good to go.

He looked me over, then rooted in a cupboard.

'Here, use this,' he said, gesturing at the damp patch.

I was amused to find his hairdryer had pink and purple hearts around the blower.

Over the latte I learned Van had a place at agricultural college in September but was spending his gap year helping with the horses, the Bassets and occasionally the rescue centre too.

'Didn't that teenager used to volunteer for the animal rescue bit, Lizzie Nash? She died a while back, but I'm sure SARC got a mention in the papers.'

'Yeah, poor kid. I heard about that. Some freaky accident. I didn't really know her. She was dead keen to learn, though. Even asked me a few questions about treatments and that and followed the vet round for a bit. Some people raised an eyebrow but there was nothing to it.'

'Nothing as in ...?'

'Young girls and older men ...' He shrugged. 'Got to be a bit careful and maybe she had a bit of a crush. I heard her dad came up one day in a bit of a state and after that, Mrs P said not to be alone with any of the girls — you know, sort of reinforced the standing instruction to everyone. But it was all something and nothing.'

A peremptory knocking made us jump.

His hand flew to his mouth. 'Shit! I didn't sign you in.' He shambled to the door and I could hear him murmuring as a deep female growl berated him for taking me into the Basset area. I decided I couldn't make it any worse but might offer reassurance. I was free of contagious diseases. That seemed to be her main concern.

Two women stood in the doorway. I assumed the eldest was the boss. Both she and her silent companion looked fierce. Mrs P was tall and rangy, with salt-and-pepper hair and a face my grandmother would have described as lived in. Her corduroys were worn and baggy. The other woman was her opposite.

Thin in an exaggerated way, lollipop head precarious on narrow shoulders, her bony wrists emerged from a cream sweater-dress fit for a premiere. The fingers of one hand stroked what looked like cashmere while the other swept a silky chestnut curtain from her face. Her heels were high enough to cause a nosebleed, but still she looked down a bare inch to dismiss me.

I ignored her and addressed the older woman. 'I'm so sorry for the intrusion. Van kindly came to my rescue after a close encounter with one of your pups.' I indicated the still damp denim.

'Ipsy's lead broke, Mrs P. We might've lost him.'

'I see. Then I thank you for your assistance. Losing one of my babies ...' Her weathered features softened, and she seemed almost on the point of tears.

The thin woman placed a hand on the boss's arm, and they turned away.

Mrs P called over her shoulder. Evan would escort me to the gate. Her tone left no doubt, right now would be best. A hint of steel despite the soft heart.

'Sorry,' he said as I shrugged on my coat.

'No problem. Who's the stick insect?'

Van grinned, then shrugged. 'Friend of hers. Mrs P seems to rely on her, though I can't see her helping muck out, can you?'

I laughed. 'Well, thanks for the coffee, Evan.'

He made a face.

'Van,' I corrected, and he smiled.

'Girlfriend – barmaid at the Dog and Duck, she prefers it.' His smile flickered for a moment, then he grinned. 'Says it sounds more … wicked.'

More a mode of transport, but they say love is blind so why not deaf as well? He seemed a nice guy, and I hoped the girl who caused that flicker wouldn't ruin that.

Chapter Nineteen

The Dog and Duck was bursting, decibels high. Alice had been doing her best to circulate but had finally given up.

She came to rest in a gap between the rough brick wall and a half-height barrier that separated her niche from the buffet table. It gave her breathing space and she could still look around her. Pops was swept in beside her.

'How are you holding up?' he asked.

'Fine, Pops. Really. Stunned so many people came. He had a lot of friends.' Splashes of exotic evening frocks flashed against more traditional funeral wear. A figure in a sparkling wig raised a glass in her direction and blew them a kiss.

'*You* have a lot of friends – and don't you forget it.'

She leaned against him for a moment, watching the scrum around the sandwiches and cake. 'Why do funerals make people hungry? Enjoy the worldly pleasures before it's all too late?'

'Never mind philosophy. What are you going to do about

this Wiseman woman? Should I dig out the water board and make her tell us what she's up to?'

'I don't think we'll need that,' she said, pointing to where Colin was in conversation with the barmaid. The landlord boomed, his words rising above the hubbub.

'Siobhan – get back to work. Now! Or you'll be losing this job an' all.'

The girl shrugged and said something more to Colin, her face pale and unhappy, then went back to serving as Colin threaded his way over.

'Alice,' he said as soon as he came within range. 'I'm sorry, I can't stay. I've had to put Brooke in the car. Siobhan offered to look after her out the back, but her dad's in a mood. Apparently, Siobhan's dog-sitting job has disappeared overnight, and I don't want the poor kid getting into trouble.'

The girl had trouble enough. The drama group's "Helena" was awfully young, Alice thought rather wistfully, to be having a baby.

But her own priorities were uppermost in her mind. 'The thing is Colin, you could help me, if you would.'

'Glad to,' he said.

'It's about Penny Wiseman.'

'Oh, look, I'm so sorry, I know there's no excuse for me …,' he said, turning down the offer of a drink and watching Pops head for the bar, 'but it was Brooke who misbehaved. I don't know what got into her. It really wasn't Penny's fault.'

'I know and …' Alice hesitated, biting her lip. 'Actually, I'm a bit embarrassed now. I rather think I owe Ms Wiseman an apology. I was rather harsh.'

'Oh, she won't cry about it. Tough as they come, always was, even as a kid.'

'You know her well?'

'We went to the same school – over twenty years ago,

would you believe? But I was the year above, and she only came back to live in Haston last year, so no, not really. Took over her dad's business so I know her a bit through the bank.'

'What does she do?'

'Ah, you'd never guess. Wiseman Associates – Penny's a private detective.'

'Good lord,' said Pops, handing her a drink and covering up her silence. 'How extraordinary.'

Colin nodded, grinning. 'Odd, isn't it? It's not all Philip Marlowe, but they do exist! I'd hire her if I wanted something dealt with discreetly.'

'Would you?' said Pops, while Alice tried to imagine why anyone would put a detective on her tail.

Colin looked away into the crowd, then back. 'Well, I sort of owe her. When we were kids, I got her into some trouble.' He paused, then gave a wry smile. 'She was supposed to be my ticket into the Smithson's gang.'

'The Haston Hood!' said Pops. 'Do tell!'

'More Milky Bar Kid by today's standards but you've no idea how much I wanted to join – they had secret passwords and everything.' He laughed. 'The initiation task was to shoplift something useful – booze or cigarettes. Only I didn't have the nerve.

'But I had some leverage over Penny because of my dad. You know he was on the lifeboats too?'

Pops shook his head; Alice was barely listening. A private detective!

'Penny nearly drowned – actually her babysitter did which must have been rough. Anyway, Dad helped in her rescue and …' He rubbed his hand across his face. 'I'm afraid I convinced her she owed me a favour. I'm not proud of it but I was only a kid.'

Alice narrowed her eyes. What kind of woman was she dealing with – and how could they find out who hired her?

'I know – it was a rotten thing to do. Course, she refused to get anything "illegal" and came back with two Cadbury's Flakes. No street cred in that!' Colin sighed. 'And she was caught. Had to pay out of her pocket money and never told them I was behind it. But I was so mad I hadn't got into the gang, I told everyone she'd lost her nerve – and she still didn't rat me out.'

'Well, well,' said Pops. 'A loyal friend. And, instead of going into petty crime you followed in your father's footsteps, I gather.'

'I do my bit – and the Smithson's are still up to no good. Penny did me a favour.' He smiled. 'One day I might get up the nerve to tell her that, but I don't think she's very keen on opening up old wounds – or on me.'

Alice had found her tongue at last, saying lightly, 'Is that the only reason you'd recommend her? Still paying off the debt?' She watched the heat rise above the collar of his shirt. 'Or do you want her to join your gang?' He blushed a bit deeper. 'It won't work,' she teased, while her mind still raced. 'She's a cat person – you have Brooke.'

'Didn't know about the cat. Still, you've a lot in common, you and Penny. Businesswomen, hardworking, loyal to your friends. You might even like her. And if you still want to find that driver, why not give her a chance?'

'I might just do that,' said Alice.

'Ms Penny Wiseman has an admirer,' Pops said as they watched Colin make his way towards the door. 'I suppose he's handsome enough if you like the tough outdoorsy type. So,' he turned to face her. 'Are you going to ask this Penny who she's working for?'

'I don't think she'd tell me. But she is a detective for hire –

I'm going to employ her to find Monty's murderer – then I'll
work out what she's up to at the same time.'

He clinked his glass to hers. 'That's my girl. Here's to
success on both counts.'

Alice's glow was short lived. She watched Terence make
his way across the room and hoped Pops would remember
what she'd said about steering clear.

'Are you ashamed of your dear old dad?' Pops had asked.

'It's for your own protection. If he finds out who you are,
he'll be all over you. He hangs round enough already because
he knows most of my lodgers come from the theatre.
Honestly, Pops, he's a stalker in the making for anyone with an
equity card. Best keep away.'

Terence waved a sausage roll in triumph as he
approached. Alice hoped Pops would remember and circulate
– and that Brian would not be mentioned.

'Went off alright in the end, wouldn't you say, and didn't
your friends look simply gorge?' The newcomer glanced at
Pops who hadn't moved. Terence's nose seemed to twitch. 'Do
I know you from somewhere?'

'Pops, this is Terence,' said Alice, trying not to grit her
teeth. 'From the drama group.'

'I don't think we've met.' Pops said held out his hand.
'Dominic Mayford – Alice's dad.'

'Terence Klein. Founder of the Haston Players and
former professional thespian.'

'How marvellous – anything I might have seen you in?'

Alice widened her eyes, but Pops pretended not to see,
intent on being charming, and on mischief.

Terence waved his hand, 'Lost in the mists of time, dear
chap, but some modest success – it set me up with my first
restaurant so I can't complain.' He smiled. 'But the theatre is
still my first love, albeit only as a lowly amateur now.'

'Ah, yes,' said Pops, smoothly. 'The Dream opens on Monday, I believe? I've heard such a lot about it. And about you, Terence.' Pops grinned at Alice. 'Director, I understand. Hardest job in the theatre. Like herding cats.'

'It is indeed.' Terence preened. 'So rare to find someone who understands. And the trouble I've had – even her ...' He nodded towards the barmaid who was now working under the landlord's close supervision. 'Starring role and got herself up the duff, would you believe! Catastrophe, dear chap – turning green more often than a traffic light.'

'Poor kid! She seems fine at the moment. Perhaps it'll be alright on the night.'

'I'm keeping all my toesies crossed!' Terence raised his wine glass. 'Still, a teensy bit difficult to suspend belief in a loveless Helena when she's practically giving birth.'

'The National would work the baby bump into an asset – as will a man of your talent, I'm sure. Besides,' Pops appraised the figure of the barmaid, 'it's not obvious. A well-cut costume can be made to hide a multitude of sins.'

'So true.' Terence sniffed and Alice prayed he wouldn't mention Brian. 'Suppose I do feel a teeny bit sorry for the little love – we could just put it about she's been at the choccie biccies.' He pursed his lips. 'Are you involved in theatre your-self perhaps?'

Alice held her breath.

'I've dabbled in amateur productions, but that was some years ago.'

'Oh, you should come back, dear heart. We're always short of leading men and you'd make a wonderful Prince Charming.'

'Ugly Sister is more my style,' Pops laughed.

'Ah, they're already taken, I'm afraid. Can't have our Brian's nose out of joint now, can we? It's his pièce de résistance.' His eyes flicked over the crowd. 'I thought he'd be here, Alice. Supporting you in your time of need – as you're *such* close friends these days.'

'The baby's a bit poorly,' she said, relieved to see one of the boys shoulder his way towards them. It was the work of a moment to divert Terence's attention. An introduction to the dressed-to-kill Toots McVay and her recent appearance on BBC Three was perfect timing.

Pops quizzed Alice as they sidled away. 'What was all that about?'

'What?'

'Professional thespian?'

Relieved, Alice was happy to enlighten him. 'He has fish and chip shops now, but he did voiceovers in the nineties. Remember the "Tower of Strength" ads, the household cleaning range?'

'Oh lord! The voice of the lovable loo brush! No wonder it was familiar.' Pops clapped his hand to his mouth.

His laughter was infectious, but whatever this Penny woman was up to, Alice resolved to find out. She'd be on Wiseman Associates' doorstep, first thing Monday morning.

Chapter Twenty

Before I left the Assisi carpark, I booked Nate a rail ticket to Chelmsford for first thing Monday morning, then broke the news.

'You'll have to get the eight fifteen to get there in time.' Considering Nate's allergy to sunrise was on a par with Dracula's, he took it rather well.

'An inquest? Great! Is it a murder?'

'It's Lizzie Nash – the kid in the bath. It's a courtroom so they might not let you take your phone in. Be prepared to take notes. I want to know who's there and what they say, particularly if they mention anything suspicious. She had some bruising on her arms – see if they explain that. It might be an hour or two, or all day, so it's an open ticket.'

'Wilco. Roger and Out,' he said, and I assumed the war games bug had bitten him again via Xbox or whatever.

I started the car and headed back to town to keep my appointment with Emily Dunker. Time to report my progress, or lack of it. I knew who her husband was giving the money to, but infidelity, or blackmail? I had no idea. I'd show the photos from the pier and ask if she wanted me to continue.

No need to mention I'd had a close encounter thanks to a loopy hound – but I was keen to get a closer look at the dog picture in Emily's living room. Could that have been Colin's?

I parked around the corner and approached the Dunker's semi on foot, squeezing past a small van with two wheels on the pavement. The logo said, *Your Comfort is Our Pleasure*, with a depiction of a sprightly blue-rinsed senior accepting a meal tray from a film-star gorgeous man.

In your dreams, I thought, and good luck using this bit of pavement if you're in a wheelchair.

In the bungalow opposite the Dunker house the curtains twitched. The ghostly tabby sat in a gateway licking its coat and paying no attention, but I felt eyes at my back as I walked up the Dunkers' path.

Wails of high decibel misery started as soon as I rang the bell. The front door was opened by the man I'd last seen handing over the envelope on the pier. He looked frazzled and his goatee needed trimming. There were dark bags beneath his eyes.

'I don't care what you're selling, we don't want it. Can't you bloody well read.' He pointed at the "no cold callers" sign stuck to the glass. 'And we've only just got him to sleep.' The last words were a defeated mumble as the door shut in my face.

At least I didn't have to lie, but I felt free to silently curse Emily Dunker. A simple text would have let me know her husband was home instead of wherever he was supposed to be.

The cursing had to be silent because, from somewhere nearby, floated the muted sound of a big musical number being murdered with girlish enthusiasm.

From the road I looked back. A driveway ran past the side door of the Dunker's house, leading to a garage beyond, though it seemed more playroom than a space to park a car. Inside the open doorway, a chubby figure in fluorescent neoprene was singing into a snorkel and boogying to the beat. I was surprised by the lack of volume and – given the talent – relieved.

Her dance spun her to face me and she froze, then gave a cheeky smile.

'It's my best favourite song!'

I wandered a little closer. 'It's a good one. You saw the film?'

'Zac Efron,' Jasmina Dunker said, melting a little. I'd go Hugh Jackman myself, but then I'm not eleven.

'You sing well,' I lied. Kids need encouragement and besides, she might tell me something useful about her dad. They see things, hear things, and adults don't always remember they're in the room.

'It should be loud but my brother's sick, so I'm not supposed to make a noise. He's throwing up and pooing at the same time – totes gross.'

'Nice.' I wrinkled my nose to mirror her expression. 'What's with the outfit?'

'It's to keep me warm in water.' She dug her toe into the concrete floor, and I could feel a wave of martyred grievance roll towards me. I decided against mentioning the tide would need to be at record high before she'd need it here.

'Right.'

'"Cos it's a dry suit!' she said as if I'd asked.

Ignoring a stroppy tone and letting a kid show off had worked to get me and my sister out of childhood snits. I invited her to tell me more and, after the technical wonders of the suit, the story tumbled out.

She should have been going to her first dive course this weekend which she'd been *promised* for *ages and ages*. Only now, and *all because* of her *horrid baby brother*, she *wasn't even allowed to go in* case everyone there got sick and she *didn't even have the bug*, so it was all *soooo unfair*.

I was sympathetic. I knew the trouble siblings could cause.

'You like the water then?' I hoped to distract her before her increasingly indignant moaning drew one Dunker parent or the other out of the house to see who she was talking to.

'Best free-style swimmer in my school last year.'

I remembered the certificate on that built-in shelving unit. Honesty compelled her to concede, now she'd gone up to the big school, there might be someone faster, but her confidence shone through. 'They're all much older. I'll still be best in year. And I'm going on the lifeboats when I'm old enough.'

'Open day?' They probably had an age limit or something.

'Duh! Search and rescue … saving lives! I might even get to go in a helicopter.'

'Been there, done that.'

'You saved someone?' Her wide-eyed disbelief was not flattering, and I was tempted to lie, but the child's innocence inhibited me.

'Nope, I went in a helicopter.' I sped on before her derision could find words. 'After I was rescued by the lifeboat.'

'Oh, wow!'

'Airlifted straight to hospital when they fished me out of the sea just off the pier. Those lifeboat guys are real heroes.'

I thought of Gail; imagined how her cold, limp body washed up on the shore the next morning with the plastic bottles and the seaweed. In my dreams her eyes were always open, looking into my dark space where the guilt tries to hide.

It didn't seem right to remind this child even heroes can't save everyone.

'I'm sure you'll be great,' I said. 'What do your parents think?'

'Dad says I can be anything I want – and I have to follow my dream! I'm going to be a pop star too!'

I thought she'd have more chance on the lifeboat, but stranger things have happened.

A window opened from above and Emily Dunker's head appeared. Her eyes widened, perhaps apologetically. In the kind of strangled whisper designed not to reach a sick child close by, she ordered her daughter in to do her homework. Then, ignoring me, she turned to speak to someone inside.

Jasmina lowered her voice. '*She* says I've got to *stop all this nonsense* and do my maths instead.' Her bottom lip came out and she kicked the doorframe with a thud. 'But Dad says she's gone a bit nuts 'cos of the new baby.' She went down to a whisper, 'Don't tell anyone but she even thinks the house is haunted – duh!'

Emily turned her attention back to us. We both thought it wise to move.

'Gotta go,' said the girl and scuttled into the house.

I strolled back to the road where the spirit of the tabby squeezed its eyes at me from Lizzie Nash's lap. The ghost girl sat on the Dunker's garden wall, weeping.

Chapter Twenty-One

I took one step closer to Lizzie's ghost and stopped, watching teardrops splash onto the pavement, fading rapidly to nothing.

The tabby jumped down and crossed the road. Lizzie wiped a tear away then stared at me, blank-eyed.

I muttered quietly and hoped anybody watching would think I was on the phone. 'You've got my attention, Lizzie, but I can't just hang about. Give me a clue.'

She turned towards the translucent tabby, now grooming itself on the opposite pavement. Then she faded, leaving me unsettled, with cold biting at my cheek. Was I just watching a recording of past actions or was she trying to tell me something?

I wandered towards the cat's ghost, puzzled by its presence. It wound around my ankles, and I felt a chill as it passed through. I tried not to react.

Tail erect, it walked sedately to the front door of the bungalow opposite the Dunker's house, where it waited, mewing silently for admittance.

Presumably it could just have walked through, but it gazed over its shoulder to where I was standing, then raised itself on hind legs as if to claw open the door.

I stepped onto the bungalow's path and at that moment, the door opened. The tabby slipped inside as a woman's broad back filled the opening. Her uniform was stretched in folds across her hips. She was a solid advert for their meals, but if I'd expected the good-looking chap on her van's advert, I might have asked for a refund.

She manoeuvred sideways through the doorway. Her hands were busy balancing plastic containers, and a thermal food bag dangled from one arm. I couldn't see how she could close the door without dropping something.

I stepped forward intending to help as she called out, 'Bye then, lovey. See you tomorrow,' to someone inside, then turned and caught sight of me.

She called again cheerily, 'Oh, your visitor is here, dear. Bye now.' Pushing the door further open with one elbow she headed past me. She muttered something rude as she went by.

I've been called worse, but this was a bit rich from someone who didn't know me. A hissed 'you should be ashamed' drifted in my direction as she climbed into her van.

I'm sure my mouth hung open, and I might have responded but was stopped by a command from inside the house.

'Come! Come in. The heat is going out.' A touch of asperity in the forty-a-day rasp. The ghost tabby was squeezing its eyes at me from the threshold.

I did as I was told. Stepped inside and shut the door.

She was stooped, leaning on a splay-footed stick, and wore a green dress which hung as if meant for a larger frame. The fabric shone in the dim light, like silk. A matching turban sat low on her forehead, just above pencilled arches where her eyebrows might once have been.

The air had the slightly thick feel that said no serious dusting had taken place for a year or two. The scent of ancient cat and recent smoke beneath the air freshener tickled my nostrils.

'*Gesundheit*,' she said as I fished for a tissue in my bag. She waved away my apology. 'Ach, English winter.' The word had a hint of "vinter" and, helped by the blessing, I cleverly surmised she was not a Haston native.

'Come, come.' She urged me into her lounge. 'You went to Emily's first. I saw you go. Well, you know he was often visiting that house, so maybe you saw him there. Sit, sit.'

She waved me to an armchair in which I sank to unexpected depths. She perched on an upright wing chair. A small table beside her held an overflowing ashtray and an open pack of Marlboro. For a moment I yearned for nicotine so badly I could taste it, but she was ready for our chat.

What were we chatting about, I wondered? I hoped we'd get to something useful before the real visitor turned up.

'I am Frieda, of course, and I am so happy you have come.' Happy turned into "hippy" in her accent and I imagined her young and carefree, with flowers in her hair.

She was waiting, head cocked slightly, eyes fixed on me.

'I'm …'

'Ach, I know who you are!' She waved away the introduction. 'Tell me,' she said, leaning so close I could see the lipstick bleeding into the lines around her mouth. 'Do you see him?' The tabby squeezed its eyes again from beside her sheepskin-slippered feet.

'The cat …' I ventured slowly, prepared to end my sentence according to her reaction. Her face broke into a thousand more wrinkles.

'Yosef,' she said. 'My little Yosef. You see him?'

'Tabby, smallish, three white paws?'

'That's him! How does he look? Is he …?' She swallowed, unable to finish the sentence so I told her what I could see.

'He's sitting at your feet. He looks fine.' Apart from being dead, of course, but I didn't feel the need to add that bit.

'Ah, my little darling. I still miss him, you know, even after so many months. I have a cat that comes sometimes but he is not the same as my little Yosef who was with me from a kitten. And so, I want to know …'

The doorbell interrupted us. Frieda went to see who was there. I went too, in case I needed to make a run for it. The tabby followed us into the hallway.

'Hi,' said a woman brightly, beyond the chain Frieda had sensibly put on before opening the door. Nice to know she was careful sometimes. 'I'm so sorry, I got caught in traffic.' She paused and then went on. 'Err … this is number thirty-four, isn't it?' I saw her shadow move as she stepped back from the doorway to check.

'I don't vant you now.'

'Ah, I know I'm a bit late, but you do still want me to contact him, don't you? Your husband, Yosef?'

'Tch!' Frieda expressed her opinion through her teeth and her accent was growing with her agitation. 'I haff someone better.' She pulled me forward with a nicotine-stained hand. 'See, she is here.'

I reluctantly stepped into the narrow gap and peered out. An oval face with a high colour regarded me with some hostility from under a red beret.

'And you are …?' she said.

'Not really relevant. Frieda doesn't want to talk to you, apparently.'

She took a deliberate breath, then squared her shoulders.

'Now look, I'm Amanda Bailey. I have an appointment to do a psychic reading here this afternoon.'

Ah, that explained the snarling by the meals-on-wheels lady.

She stepped forward and lowered her voice. 'I didn't realise she was a little ... vague. She was fine when she phoned for the appointment.'

'I'm afraid you've had a wasted journey, Ms Bailey. There really isn't anything I can do ... I can't let you in against the householder's wishes.'

She fidgeted with the gloves she'd removed and gave a theatrical little sigh.

'Yes, I see. It's tragic when they get so ... it's so sad.' Then we got to the real cause for sorrow. 'Of course, there is the matter of the fee ... late cancellation and travel expenses, I'm afraid. Not the full amount, naturally, but I do have a waiting list for appointments.'

'Okay. How much?'

She mentioned a figure. My mother brought me up better than to spit in her eye.

'No problem. Just let me have a copy of the signed contract, along with the cancellation policy and an invoice for tax purposes and I'll get a cheque out to you in the post.'

While she protested, I glanced over my shoulder to see the ghost of little Yosef sitting at Frieda's feet, gazing up adoringly. I watched as he gathered his haunches and leapt. He sailed right through her folded arms and landed behind her. Slightly affronted, he had a second go, and defied his memory of gravity for a split second as he landed on her shoulder. A moment later he was back on the floor washing his ears and pretending it never happened.

Mystic Mandy was beginning to repeat herself. I cut her off.

'No contract, no cancellation policy, no cheque, Ms Bailey. And unless you want harassment to be added to the charge of demanding money with menaces, I think it's time you left. Good day.' I shut the door.

Frieda was staring at me. 'That woman is a fraud. Contact my husband. Ha! We hardly spoke for thirty years, why would I want to hear him now? She has just googled me! But you, you have the sight. You see my little one.'

'He's upset he can't sit on your shoulder like he used to.'

'Yes, you see him.' She smiled and something was just a little off about it. Then she pulled a gun out of her pocket and pointed it at me. 'But who the devil are you?'

I raised my hands slowly, wondering how frying pan and fire had overtaken me so fast.

She motioned me back to the chair with the short barrel of the weapon, which was not a type I recognised. I'd not had much experience with firearms. Violence in Haston was generally more drunken brawls than shoot-outs.

I sank once more into the sagging armchair.

The gun was dark and threatening, an ancient relic from her glory days as a cold war spy, perhaps. The ticking clock seemed loud.

'I'm Penelope – Penny,' I said, as the gun jerked to hurry things along. 'I saw Yosef outside, and he wanted something, so I followed and was invited in … I'm sorry for any misunderstanding.'

'So, why did he want you to come?' She spoke to herself, her eyes focused inwards. I'd rather she focused on not pulling the trigger. 'Mm, I wonder.' She reached for a cigarette and turned the gun as if to shoot herself in the mouth.

She pressed the trigger.

A tiny flame popped into life. Saliva flooded my mouth and I swallowed hard.

Frieda drew the smoke deep into her lungs and chuckled. 'Your face, darling, it was a picture.' Hers was lit up with glee.

'Damn it all, Frieda. I could've had a heart attack.' And my nicotine craving flared into life.

'No, not you.' She blinked, regarding me as if I were something worth studying. 'You are young, strong. It is my heart that is coming to the end.' She shrugged as she answered my unspoken question. 'Soon … a week, a month or two, who knows? Not so long they tell me.'

I didn't know what to say.

'Don't be sad for me, darling. I have had a good life, lived in this house a long time and hope to die here. So, I am ready and now I know little Yosef is waiting, and big Yosef will be there too, somewhere.' She chuckled at my expression. 'We can spend eternity not speaking. We were happy enough in our way. I wanted … just to be sure there was something … beyond.'

We sat in the quiet for a moment.

Despite the clock on the wall, I fancied I could hear the ticks of her heart.

'So, now. What is it I can do for you?' she asked. 'There is a reason you were brought here, I think.'

'I see a spirit, Frieda. A teenager, Lizzie Nash. She was in the house opposite and then here, out in the street. I think she needs some help. Did you know her?'

Frieda's hand reached out and ground the cigarette butt into the ashtray, but her eyes never left mine.

'Oh yes. She had a face to make happy an old woman's heart – and innocence shining from her like the sun. But it was all a lie.'

'A lie?'

'She killed my little Yosef.'

Chapter Twenty-Two

❦

Alice hesitated at the narrow entrance between the minimarket and the betting shop. All weekend her resolve had held firm, but the reality of the dank doorway on a cold Monday morning brought doubts creeping in.

The typed card next to the top bell said 'Wiseman Associates', and a little fish-eye lens stared at her from above the door.

Layers of thick, brown paintwork were peeling, revealing more dull colours underneath; the bone-yellow button shone as if smeared with grease, it may once have been white; a rather unpleasant smell rose from the concrete doorstep.

Come on, Alice. You can do this.

The bell was dry. Not grease – just polished. A click came from the lock and the door began to buzz. She pushed it open and started up the claustrophobic stairway under a weak yellow light.

A female voice called from somewhere up above. 'Hello … just keep on coming. We're at the top.'

The stairs plunged into darkness.

'Oh, damn. Don't move! I'll find the switch. Then I'll put the kettle on.'

Light returned and Alice continued her ascent, somewhat cheered by leaving the smell behind and progressing towards a voice which sounded friendly.

Halfway up the second flight, a blonde head appeared over the rail above. 'Tea or coffee?'

'Tea, please.'

A second later. 'Chocolate digestives or ginger nuts?'

'Neither, thanks,' replied Alice, reaching the open door.

'Well, you don't have to watch your figure! But if you're sure. Go through, take a comfy seat and I'll be there in a mo'.'

Alice sank onto the sofa by the coffee table, a bit bemused.

'Here we are,' the woman said, handing her a mug and taking the chair opposite.

'You're not Penny …'

'Oh, no! I should have said. Sorry.' She held out a smooth, dry hand with short neatly polished nails. 'I'm Sarah. My sister and I are partners.'

'Alice Mayford.'

'Is it something Penny is dealing with already, Ms Mayford? Only there's nothing in the book about an appointment …'

'Just Alice, is fine, please. Yes. No. It's …' Distracted by frank appraisal from sea green eyes, which had a tiny fleck of gold that caught the light, Alice needed a moment to organise her thoughts.

'It's not the stairs, is it? I forget how steep they are. Just take your time.'

'Thanks,' Alice laughed. Sarah looked fit enough to run a marathon. 'The stairs are fine. It's just I was expecting Penny.'

'Oh,' Sarah's mouth turned down a fraction. 'Won't I do?'

'I'm sure you'd be just perfect … but I came to say sorry to your sister for my rudeness when we met – it's not quite the same if I make my apologies by proxy.'

'Pen won't worry – and I'll bet you had good reason.'

'It was at the memorial service for my Basset, Monty.'

Sarah's eyes widened. 'Oh, you must have been so upset already. I do hope my sister didn't cause offence.'

'There was a bit of commotion with another dog and – I'm afraid I didn't handle it very well.' Alice bit her lip. 'Actually, I asked her to leave.'

'I wouldn't worry about it. Pen's pretty thick-skinned and, I probably shouldn't say it,' her eyes sparkled. 'She has been known to put her foot in it quite spectacularly at times!'

Alice laughed. 'Can't we all! But this really wasn't her fault and afterwards I realised I'd been dreadfully unkind when she was already distressed herself.'

Sarah's brows drew together, causing the merest hint of shadow to appear. 'Then, afterwards, when one of the guests happened to mention your sister's profession, I wondered if I could enlist her services.'

'Like I said, we're partners – and we'd be happy to help.'

'Then I'd like to hire you to find out who killed my Monty, my darling Basset.'

'Right. We'd better start at the beginning.' Sarah opened a spiral pad and picked up a pen. 'Why don't you give me all the details?'

Alice explained, watching Sarah's neat writing emerge onto the page in an ink as vivid as her eyes.

'So, you want to find the driver who ran him down, as well as your Good Samaritan?'

'That's right, and I've asked some of the neighbours but there's a man who's quite … unpleasant.' Alice hesitated, folded her hands together in her lap. 'He doesn't like me much. He seemed to take exception to my friend when I moved in.' She outlined the *Get-a-move-on, Darling* uniform, and Jerry's fascinator.

A quick glance showed Sarah's snort was of amusement. 'Well, he's obviously got no sense of humour – or of style. But surely, he'd still say if he'd seen something important?'

'You'd hope.' Alice lifted her gaze to watch the other woman's face. 'But he may not. I'm trans – I don't make a secret of it – and my being gay might be enough just on its own.' She quoted his t-shirt slogan.

'Straight pride?' Sarah's eyebrows nearly disappeared beneath her fringe. 'Is that a thing or do you think he had it printed? He'd hate me too, then! Disgusting.'

Alice let out a breath she hadn't quite known she was holding, and warmth flowed through her limbs as Sarah went on.

'And this guy's let into Neighbourhood Watch?'

'He brought round a leaflet when I first moved in and wanted to discuss it but, well now I think of it, perhaps he was just ...'

'Trying his luck? We'll check with the local co-ordinator. See what they have to say,' said Sarah. 'We'll need a ruse to talk to everyone in the area really. We could pretend to run a survey – say it was to start a petition, pressure the council to work better for the community – that sort of thing. People love to have a moan. We could ask about rat-runs, drink driving, speeding – and work round to anything they saw that night.'

Alice had answered a dozen or more questions and was beginning to feel quite optimistic as they relaxed with their second cup of tea, then a head popped round the door.

Penny Wiseman froze when she saw them, then switched on a smile.

'I've come to apologise,' Alice said, getting to her feet. 'I'm afraid I was most dreadfully rude, and I have no excuse, but I do hope you can forgive me.'

'You're in mourning. I'm sure she understands, don't you, Pen!'

Penny nodded slowly, her eyes flicking from Alice's face to her sister's and back again. 'Of course, but you didn't need to come all this way in person.'

'She didn't just come for that,' said Sarah pointedly waving her notebook. 'She's a new client. I've taken all the details.'

Penny walked to the desk and placed her bag on it with care, then turned back to where the two women stood, side by side. 'And she's signed the contract?' she said softly, staring at her sister.

'She has!' Sarah smirked, holding up the document as proof.

'I really must be going,' said Alice, feeling the undercurrents. It was clear she'd learn nothing by staying. She'd look forward to seeing Sarah, working together to find the person who murdered Monty, and if Sarah knew what Penny was up to, that would be a bonus.

She slid her own copy of the contract into her bag. 'You'll be in touch?' she said to Sarah with a smile, then turned to speak to Penny who followed her to the door. 'And I'm so sorry about your cat.'

Chapter Twenty-Three

I sat speechless at my father's desk. Sarah filled my silence with how it hadn't taken her long to get her own client list underway, and wasn't it awful, running over someone's pet and not even bothering to stop, and how mean or just plain stupid people could be about their charming neighbours.

'Plain stupid. That about covers it.' I'd regained my voice. 'Sarah, how could you be so dumb?'

She gazed, wide-eyed and innocent as Lizzie Nash but I wasn't fooled. She'd always had a selfish streak when she saw something she wanted.

'You don't even like dogs,' I said.

'I think I can warm to this one,' she laughed. 'It's not likely to slobber on me – and by the way, why does Alice think you've got a cat?'

I refused to be diverted. 'I'm investigating *Alice*,' I said, 'I can't work for her at the same time!'

'I know *you* can't do it, Pen. But I can.'

'What?'

'Me! I can do it. It's only asking questions and maybe sneaking a look at a few cars – how hard can it be? Anyway …'

I was frozen on the track, rabbit-in-the-headlights; the train hurtled on at full speed.

'I'm a partner now,' she said, just as I started yelling.

I ranted about ethics and conflicts of interest, but she waved objections aside – just like she always did when she saw something she wanted.

'It's easy. We'll have a firewall.'

I stared.

'You know, like they did to stop insider trading – I won't tell you anything about my investigation and you don't tell me about yours. See? Problem solved.'

And with that she swanned out, nibbling on a biscuit. She left behind the dirty mugs and the throb of my tension headache. I took two aspirin with the dregs of the tea and, making a cushion of my arms, lowered my head gently to the desktop.

I hoped when I awoke it would all have been a dream.

Instead I was rudely awoken. More specifically, I was awoken while he was being rude – to our answering machine.

'What kind of effing place is it that can't even answer the effing phone!'

I picked up as he began another "eff".

'Mr Haddock,' I said. 'Penny Wiseman speaking. Sorry to have kept you. What can we do to help?'

I had not expected to hear from him. We weren't due to undertake surveillance on his wife until later in the week, but it seemed things had changed as he explained when he'd calmed down.

'My Jenny's going to her class tomorrow instead of Thursday, so you'll have to get a shufti on and sort it out, darlin',' he said. I could hear him breathing.

'That's fine, Mr Haddock. We'll send an operative to the leisure centre tomorrow. What time is the class?'

'Says she's going with a friend, but it's the first I've heard of this *Samantha*. Nah, betcha she's meeting a bloke called Sam. That's what I heard her call him on the phone. I should've been a detective! Money for old rope!'

With almost ungritted teeth I repeated my question. 'What time?'

He confirmed the details and hung up. Before I could get back to the serious business of finishing my nap, Nate's text arrived. The coroner's inquest on Lizzie Nash was due to start any minute and he was "going in undercover". I hoped he'd have the sense to take good notes and stay out of trouble. And not disguise himself as a policeman.

My mind was still half on the inquest, and on Sarah's executive decision to take on Alice Mayford – record time for putting her oar in, even for my sister – but time was moving on, and I remembered my appointment. I didn't want to be late. I locked the office and went down to retrieve my car.

Would Lizzie still be at the Dunker's house, I wondered as I drove towards it a few minutes later to update my paying client. A cat-killer Lizzie may be … but she was hardly going to hang around to boast about it. There must be something else – or would she not have moved on to … wherever it is they go?

According to Emily Dunker's apologetic text that had followed my last attempt to visit, the baby was much better, and Brian would be at work this morning. Emily had suggested ten thirty would be safe, but I'd told her to text me when he'd left. The second time I turned up on his doorstep he might be inclined to examine me a bit more closely.

I waited on Balham Road, around the corner from Emily's house as ten-thirty waved goodbye, and I wondered about getting the Seamaster back. When we made a profit, I'd told my sister. Definitely. But Sarah was keen to retrieve it as soon as possible.

'Suppose they sell it?' she said. 'As soon as the funds have been transferred you need to sort it out. Dad wanted you to have it!'

He'd wanted me to have the agency too, so he must have believed in me a bit, but how did he make it pay? It was a miracle according to the books he'd left behind, but the current keeper of the Seamaster might shed some light. I could ask – if I really wanted to know.

I sighed, then was distracted by the sight of Brian's car flashing across the junction ahead, going straight on Carton Drive. It was unmistakable, its gleaming bright blue paintwork marred by the orange splash of his company logo on the door.

I pulled out of my parking space, turning right towards the house. A moment later Emily's text beeped in my inbox.

No curtains were twitching this morning across the road. I hoped little Yosef was curled up as close to Frieda as he could get and was bringing comfort. No innocent-faced ghost girl was visible out here either.

Emily, still wan and watery-eyed, let me in and waved at the chair I'd occupied before. The radiators still clunked and gave out little heat. The baby clothes still lay folded in heaps. Pride of place was Jasmina's photo, her swimming certificate and the collage of baby pics. Nothing had changed. The RNLI calendar gave me a twinge. It was a while since I'd been up close and personal with a manly chest.

But then I realised there was one change. The photo of Jasmina with the floppy-eared hound was gone. 'What happened to the picture – the one with the dog?'

Emily went from pale to parchment in a heartbeat. She laced her fingers tight to stop the trembling.

Lizzie's ghost appeared in the corner, paying attention.

'Emily?' I said, gently. 'Are you alright?'

She swallowed. 'What do you mean?'

'You look like you might pass out,' I said. Or be sick, I thought. 'Have you caught the baby's bug?'

'I'm fine,' she whispered. Her eyes darted around the room as if she was trying to see something that wasn't there. Lizzie stood still. Impassive. 'It's just ... there's something wrong with it – the frame – it kept falling over so ... anyway, that doesn't matter.'

'Whose is the Basset?'

'It doesn't matter. It was nothing. Nothing! The frame was crooked or something – it just kept falling ...' Emily's eyes fastened on me. 'Anyway, you said you had some news.'

'Okay,' I brought up the photo of Alice on my screen, the best of those I'd taken with Dunker at the pier head. I had better ones I could've got from the office CCTV but didn't think Emily needed to know exactly how close my surveillance had become.

'Do you recognise her, Emily?' Pursed lips and the little furrow on her forehead told me she wasn't sure. 'She collected the envelope from your husband. Her name is Alice. Does that ring a bell?' The surname could come later, if it was relevant. She seemed under a lot of stress, and a revenge attack would not reflect well on the agency – especially if it made the papers.

'No, but he's paying her for something. She must be this "Honey".' Her conviction was rock solid, but assertion is not evidence.

'She could be a go-between.' This best-case scenario for my business may have made me too enthusiastic.

Emily's look was laced with both hurt and suspicion.

I hurried on. 'She could be up to her eyeballs in it, of course. I've no way of knowing until someone makes another move. Are you sure you want me to stay on it?'

'That envelope had a lot of money in it – I checked the on-line statement.'

'You know his password?'

'We did them both...' Suddenly she was wailing, 'But I never checked up on him, never! Not until he asked me what I was spending money on! We had such a row – he said I must have gone crazy.' She mopped at her eyes. 'And then Amanda said it could be his own guilt that made him look, and perhaps I should do the same to him ...' The rest was lost in another sniffle.

I thought this Amanda might have a lot to answer for. Emily might be better off in ignorance. She obviously didn't want to lose him. Only, no one likes being taken for a fool.

What did you spend it on? I wondered silently. There were a lot of women called Amanda. Maybe some men too in this day and age, but I'd heard that name recently.

I searched the filing system in my head until I found it. Yes! Amanda Bailey – the psychic who turned up too late to talk to Frieda across the road about "her husband", Yosef.

'I don't care about the money ...' Emily sniffed and hiccupped and mopped again. 'I do care about this "Honey"!' She paused for a moment. 'How are you going to find out?'

'I'm working on it,' I said vaguely, adding, 'If you want me to continue – but couldn't you just ask him?' The words were out of my mouth before I thought them through. I needed this client!

She wiped her sleeve across her eyes and took a jerky breath.

'I can't. He might leave me,' and, with that fear articulated, she began to sob in earnest. She waved away my apology but accepted the pack of tissues I offered.

I mumbled platitudes a little longer, and then made an excuse to give her a bit of privacy.

The bathroom, an extension off the kitchen, had been untouched for decades, or was fashionably retro. The door was heavy, tongue clunking into place as the key turned. White-tiles, white basin, fluffy pedestal set in pastel blue to match the towels. The claw-footed tub was long and deep. And empty. No drowning Lizzie Nash, fortunately.

But pressure pushed against my eardrums, a wave of misery. My cheek was ice. The radiator gurgled but was cold. 'I'll do what I can,' I muttered. A child was still a child, even if she killed a cat.

The key turned without protest to let me out. I was somewhat relieved.

If only Emily felt the same. Her eyes were swollen, lips chapped, fingernails bitten short. Her hair was lank across her forehead.

I pictured Alice in all her elegance; that kiss on Dunker's cheek, wiped clean with such a stylish gesture.

Questions itched like fleabites in my brain.

Chapter Twenty-Four

❧

'Hi,' said Sarah, holding up her clipboard as Alice opened the door. 'I'm ready to start, and I've had some thoughts on other things we could try.'

'Lovely.' Sarah's smile was cheering, and Tuesday morning felt a whole lot brighter for her presence. Alice had got up early to get to the bakery first thing, then found herself singing a showtune as she'd ground fresh Fairtrade beans. 'Coffee?'

'Yes, please. It smells divine.'

'Come on through.' Alice led the way into the kitchen, 'Croissant with jam, or pain au chocolat?'

Sarah groaned. 'I'm torn ... what a dilemma.'

'One of each?' suggested Alice.

'No! Too greedy. Um, pain au chocolat would be great.'

Alice poured the coffee, assembling plates and napkins, arranging pastries on her favourite serving dish. Sarah's wide green eyes were watching. Alice felt warmth tingle at her collar bone and was thankful she could turn towards the cold from the fridge. 'Milk or cream?'

'Cream please, since I'm already being wicked – and I'll

walk off all the calories door-to-door.' Sarah grinned and reached for the little jug Alice set before her at the table.

'Me too.' Alice picked up her croissant and added apricot preserve.

'You keep fit though? Yoga, Pilates?'

'Ah, you're a detective,' said Alice, glancing at her week's schedule pinned up on the fridge.

'And tap? You dance?'

'Reminder for the plumber.' She watched Sarah's lips part. Her own twitched. 'No, joking. I do a bit, for fun. Sometimes I do Bollywood or jazz – it all depends what mood I'm in. It helps offset my indulgences.' She raised a piece of croissant, though none had yet reached her mouth. 'You?'

'The gym,' said Sarah, swallowing her mouthful. 'Running track or cycle usually, and Zumba now and then. I like to power walk along the prom if the weather's good.'

'Me too. The pier and back most mornings.'

'We should go together sometime.'

'We should!' said Alice. She smoothed her napkin flat against the table. 'Monty used to keep me company,' then added quickly, 'Not that I'm comparing you to …'

'I'm a poor substitute for a dog,' said Sarah laughing, 'but I'd do my best.'

Alice had a sudden hope that, together, they might make sense of Monty's death.

'I have an idea,' said Sarah, as Alice stood to clear the table. 'We might pick up your Good Samaritan's trail. I'll bet the vet has security cameras. They probably caught you arriving, and might they look if you asked? Give us a print we could put out there?'

'I'll phone them now!'

Kathleen was sympathetic and went off to check, but the

answer dashed their hopes. Recordings were deleted after seven days.

'I should have thought of it yesterday when we were at the office – or Penny should!'

'I should have thought of it myself,' said Alice.

'You're grieving. Wisemans have no excuse. But,' the sparkle returned, 'not everyone's security is the same. She walked away, you said, the Pelham Street side of the surgery?'

'She must have – if she'd gone the other way, I'd have seen her from the carpark – or the window. It was only a minute or two before I looked, I'm sure. Unless she went into one of the houses along there.'

'I'll check that – she could answer the door!' Sarah shrugged. 'If not, there are shops, and some posh houses along Pelham. Some'll have CCTV and might be prepared to help – and when we find her – who knows, she might have seen the driver! I'll do that first, then knock on doors round here.'

Watching Sarah drive away, Alice suddenly remembered. She'd meant to pump for information – find out what Penny Wiseman was up to.

I'll do that later, she thought. Sarah would be back.

Taking a bolt of fabric to her cutting table she tapped out a step or two, the theme tune from *Happy Feet* looping in her head.

Chapter Twenty-Five

Monday evening had been unproductive, a scratchy little itch inside my brain stopped me from settling to anything much. Something about my visit to Emily's wasn't right, but I couldn't pin it down. I hoped a good night's sleep would solve the mystery. It didn't.

Sarah's diary confirmed she was out on enquiries about the Mayford dog. Her eagerness did not bode well. Her romances, whether with men or women, never seemed to last, and mixing business with pleasure had never bothered her. She'd never see this one could lead to trouble. Bull-headed. Perhaps that should be Basset-headed. I'd been reading up on the breed – they were stubborn too.

Then, at ten o'clock on Tuesday morning, distraction bounded into my office. Nate was full of the joys of spring a good month early.

'Hi Boss, I'm a bit late, but I had to make sure this worked before I brought it in.' He placed a small red object on my desk.

'A Lego brick,' I said, deadpan. Surprise only encouraged him.

'Coroner's report. On Elizabeth Anne Nash,' he said beaming, then his face folded a bit. 'Aged thirteen.'

I picked up the plastic toy and turned it over.

'Here.' He plucked it from my hand, twisted it in half, dropped the pieces back into my palm. 'You set it to go, then when you want it to play back, you just plug it in like a memory stick. Easy.' He waited for the praise.

'Nate, what have you done?'

'Recorded it,' he said. 'Not the whole thing – it'll only do an hour or two – but I got most of it and I made notes on the rest just like you said. Neat gadget, huh? Do you want me to upload ...?' He made a move.

'Stop!'

He stopped. He bit his lip.

I took a long, deep breath.

'Nate, do you know why I asked you to take notes?'

'Yeah,' but he looked genuinely puzzled. 'That's why I couldn't take any photos – some bloke in uniform told me to put my mobile in the locker. And I left the spycam at home – sorry.'

I was thankful for small mercies. I only had the audio to deal with – and it was going nowhere near the agency computers.

When I spoke, my teeth felt more gritty than the A12 in a blizzard. 'The penalty,' I said, 'for such a contempt of court, could put us both in jail for quite a while.'

Red spread from his neck like a bloodstain on a sheet. His freckles stood out like acne scabs.

'Holy shit!' he said.

I sighed. 'Where did you upload it?'

'Home.'

'Your personal laptop?' I said to clarify I meant device not just location.

He nodded towards reception. 'It's in my bag.'

'Go and delete the file and clear the ... memory thingy.' I called after him. Those were the kinds of things he knew about. I should have remembered that.

I looked at the Lego brick.

P.I. licensing was not yet here, but imminent – had been for years. One conviction might mean disbarment. There'd be a day when having a licence would be compulsory.

I picked up Dad's old ashtray, solid brass, heavy in my hand. A World War Two artillery shell, a sentimental relic of Grandad's wartime exploits.

He survived. The recorder didn't.

Nate crept round the door, averting his gaze from the shattered remains, and holding a ring-bound notebook like an offering. 'I wrote down some of it,' he said.

'Please, Nate, this is not TV. Recording is a no go.'

'You do it, though.' He whined, just a little.

'No!' I swept the plastic into the bin. 'Well, only when I have permission.'

A toddler struggling to understand why he'd been slapped could not have looked more miserable. I went on more gently, 'Or when there's no expectation of privacy – but then it's just to help me remember. We have to be careful, Nate. It's our careers.'

'Understood,' he said, staring at his shoelaces. 'I'll get on to the invoicing.'

He started towards the door, shoulders slumped.

'Listen,' I said. 'I want to read these notes – so I might have another job for you.'

Haddock wanted his wife followed, and now the timetable

had been unexpectedly brought forward. I preferred to look through his notes on Lizzie and see to my other business of the day. Nate wanted to do the "P.I. thing". What could possibly go wrong?

Nate phoned the leisure centre and made enquiries and was booked-in for the afternoon class. The tutor's name was Sam.

Samson James' photo on the leisure centre website showed lithe, dark limbs and a young, open face. His hair stood out in a mop of tiny plaits woven through with coloured threads.

I suggested Nate nip home to change into more suitable attire while I was still around, then he could go straight from minding the office to the class. In the meantime, I turned to deciphering his shambolic scrawl.

The notebook was stained with pale, weak tea – I hoped it was tea – and some of the ink had bled away in splotches. Despite the barriers, I could see the coroner had recorded a natural death: "Narrative verdict of drowning in the bath during a non-epileptic fit." It was written in Nate's very best capitals so that bit I could read clearly.

From what I could make out of the rest, there was nothing of great import, and the bruises on Lizzie's arms were dismissed as injuries unrelated to her death. Too old, apparently, possibly by a day or more. Further details were not recorded in Nate's notes – or were inaccessible without his personal Rosetta stone.

I gazed unseeing out of the window. A "narrative verdict'" meant no one could be one hundred per cent sure – a presumption of probability with no evidence to the contrary. No one seemed to know the cause. A history of fits was mentioned, low blood-sugar, even hormonal changes during puberty. But overall a verdict of a natural death.

I had a strong feeling Lizzie Nash might have a view on that.

A check of my notes so far got me wondering about her father. Nate had compiled a list of witnesses and interested parties in the courtroom. Lizzie's father, John Nash, wasn't on it. Odd.

Nate's early researches hadn't tracked down an address for Lizzie's stepmother, but her father was the sole adult resident listed in a one-bed flat whose address was in the file. Google maps confirmed the location and I was hatching an idea when I heard the door open in the outer office.

'Nate?'

'Yep.' His head appeared around the door, followed by the rest of him wrapped in his black greatcoat.

'John Nash wasn't at the inquest?'

'Nope, but his wife ... she was fit!' he said. 'Not tall, great hair, great ...'

I stopped him there. I got the picture. A better picture than the only one I'd seen – the one with her father at her graduation, but what she looked like didn't matter. I wanted to know how Lizzie had come to die.

Had anyone been sweating under questioning, I asked, noting Nate looked a bit sweaty himself, still wrapped up for the cold.

The gist was the stepmother had charmed the coroner's socks off, and the man had been all sympathy for the bereaved. He allowed a lot of questions to be put, but her legal team got nowhere with the negligence. The medic was off the hook. Nothing suspicious there.

Except there'd been no sign of Lizzie's father.

Taking my thoughtful silence for the end of the grilling, Nate finally took off his coat. 'What do you think?'

He posed before me in jersey bottoms with a hugely

sagging crotch and matching guru-orange vest. *Real Men Do Yoga* was blazoned across his chest.

'They're Matsyendra yoga pants,' he said. 'All the guys are wearing them. Cool, huh?' He raised his arms in a stretch and grinned.

The top almost matched his thatch of armpit hair. I suspected he'd stand out like an orangutan on an iceberg, but it was too late to change now. With a mental note to define 'suitable clothing' in more detail in future, I aimed for absolute clarity in my final instructions.

'Watch what she does and report back. Nothing else. Clear?'

I handed his notebook back and he bit his lip. 'Sorry about the stains – the train jerked a bit when I was adding in bits on the way back and someone's drink got spilled.'

'"Someone" might want to spend any spare office time making their notes legible.'

He grinned. 'Okay but can I upload the Haddock report via my phone? It'll be on audio, but I'll be pushed to get back and write it up before home time anyway and … I've got somewhere to be.' he said. 'I'll send it through as soon as I'm done.'

'You'll still have to type it tomorrow,' I warned, sighing at the media file obsession, but I made no impression on his mood. Maybe he had a hot date outside of cyber-space at last.

'Affirmative, Captain.' He raised a hand in a Vulcan salute as I left him to it.

I had somewhere to be too, something which put a smile on my face. First step, the bank.

For once that austere portico did not fill me with gloom. I'd phoned ahead to check and been assured my request would be no problem. I just needed the required ID and the funds in my account. I checked my passport and driving licence were both in my bag and set off with a light heart. Funds, thanks to Sarah, would not be a problem.

I presented myself at the desk and waited while procedures were followed. This included a tediously in-depth check of my documents with copies taken and logged and then another wait, while higher-ups were consulted to make sure all was in order. It was, and finally they were counting out my cash. I suppose a hefty pile in used twenties is a bit unusual in this almost cashless society, but it was the deal I'd made so it was necessary.

Colin Palmer, looking good in smart suit and high gloss shoes, ushered a customer through the hall. He nodded to me politely and I felt my pulse rise a fraction. Now I wasn't quite so beholden to him, I wondered if there would be any harm in a celebratory drink, or whether he still thought of me as a disaster.

I was glad he didn't stop just now. It felt wrong to be taking out such a large amount when I'd only just avoided the modern equivalent of debtor's prison, but I'd left plenty in the account. There was enough to pay all our bills and bankroll us for a bit – and Sarah had insisted.

I tucked the bundle of notes into my bag and hoped I wouldn't get mugged crossing the road to where the boss of Help4U Loans would be pleased to see the return of his cash.

'Penelope! Good to see you.' Jimmy Stark was leaning his tattooed arms on the counter, reading the *Daily Express* like any good working-class capitalist should.

To be fair I rather liked the man, despite his less than savoury reputation. He and Dad went way back, having triumphed in a fair few pub fights in their youth, so when I needed help, he gave me a decent amount against the value of the Seamaster.

'No deadline, no paperwork and I'll keep it locked away

where no one'll make me an offer I can't refuse. Private arrangement only. That do you?'

It did me nicely and I was grateful to Jimmy for it. I was even happier once I'd paid him back and was fastening Dad's Seamaster around my wrist.

Chapter Twenty-Six

I stepped out of Jimmy's doorway and headed across town. The pavement was bustling. My mind was bustling too. Something I'd missed at the Dunker house still niggled.

Irritated by the thought, I speeded up. Tired of dodging and diving, I tried to cross the road to where it was less crowded. I peered round a stopping bus, and nearly lost my nose to a passing vehicle. The van was blue, a bright stand-out blue – and suddenly I had it.

Brian Dunker's bright blue company car had sped past the turn for Balham Road where I'd been parked. If he'd been going to work, as Emily had said, he would have driven past me. He didn't. He continued along Carlton Road and must have turned only at the coast.

Drat! I should have followed the man.

I groaned up the stairs to the office, exasperated. I'd taken my eye off the ball, and the knowledge hovered like my personal thunder cloud. Nate was working hard deciphering his notes. Encouraged by my mood perhaps, he kept his attention on his task.

I rooted in my desk drawer for a tracker. I'd have to find a way to get it onto Brian Dunker's car, but no chance of that till he came back from "work". A least I'd have it with me when an opportunity arose.

Then I left to find my sister.

Sarah was still working her way along the road where Alice lived, with a clipboard and the optimistic efficiency of someone not yet bored with wasting her time – or with the ulterior motive of trying to impress. On seeing me, her face turned stormy.

'I don't need checking up on, Pen. I'm quite capable of doing simple tasks. I tie my own shoelaces and everything.'

'Sarcasm does not become you, sister dear. I'm not here for you, I'm here to check out something on another case.'

Sarah put down her bag, set both hands on her hips and snorted.

'It *is* a case … well, not an official case but it's connected to my blackmail one.' Her chin came up. 'Nothing to do with Alice Mayford,' I added.

The flash of antagonism retreated. So, it was our new client she was concerned about, not just me checking up on her. Worrying! In that case, I'd better keep the dog's ghost quiet, though Sarah was the one person who knew I saw such things.

While my parents had muttered about imaginary friends, she had accepted without question I saw Gail's ghost. Later, when Sarah asked if I still saw the dead, I told the truth. After all, who could she tell without sounding weird herself?

So now I told her about Lizzie haunting the Dunkers' house. I covered the basics, briefly. 'Her father, John Nash, used to live there. Now he lives in a flat just around the corner from your Miss Mayford. It's a bit odd because he didn't go to the inquest so I'm wondering ...'

'Maybe he was ill,' said Sarah, pursing her lips.

'He wasn't quoted in the news reports either. "Too distressed to comment" it was claimed.'

'Well, grief ...' she ventured.

'Or something to hide. I want to use your house-to-house enquiry as cover to get a look at Nash. I might even help you.'

'I've got it covered. Nate's volunteered.'

So much for his hot date.

'He might be late,' I said. 'I've sent him on a job, so in the meantime ...?'

SARAH HAD MADE A SURVEY FORM. IT SOUGHT OPINIONS ON everything from rubbish collection to medical services, via the need for speed bumps to enforce the residential twenty miles per hour.

'It gets them talking, then I steer the conversation without them realising.'

If a neighbour let the dog out and got him killed, they weren't going to admit it, no matter how well steered. But people love to gripe. Some, of course, love slamming doors in other's faces. Sarah had got nowhere, but she looked smug.

'Forms?' I said, holding out my hand.

She handed me a clipboard of them. 'Bring it back before Nate gets here, please.'

A dinky biro was tethered to the top. I held it up.

'I tell them I have to get the form signed or I don't get paid. It's hard documentary evidence for us.'

At least she was keeping focused.

'Only I kept losing pens, so Alice gave me the ribbon. Wasn't that sweet?'

Her smirk said her focus wasn't on the enquiry.

Leaving her to labour for love, I strolled around the corner. The houses backing onto the residence of Sarah's new best friend were in the same style as hers, but these hadn't been restored. Grubby cardboard labels signalled multiple occupation. I faked ringing the bell at the first few places, trying to ignore the smells: boiled cabbage, dope and drains not cleaned for decades.

Nothing too unpleasant from Nash's doorway though; dope still, but a hint of lemon polish from inside. He wore a tracksuit, but not the kind with saggy bottoms and pilled nylon between the thighs. His was smart, fitted, as if he might be set to coach the football team. His hair was almost military cut and his build was stocky, filling the narrow hallway. He listened politely as I explained my mission. then stepped back to let me in.

I tried not to think "lion's den". No obvious signs of suppressed rage or brooding violence. Then again, the lion's just a pussy cat till it's peckish.

He closed the front door but made no move to lock it.

'First floor,' he said.

I followed him up the communal stairs.

He left keys dangling in his own door. My phone was unlocked, ready in my pocket. If he turned nasty, I could phone for help, and I'm not too proud to bite and scream.

From the first-floor window I could see into the concrete yard of the flat below. Tall foliage was visible through the glass of a small greenhouse by the top fence. From this distance the plants could have been tomatoes – but given the fragrance around the doorway, I had my doubts. The fence bordered a narrow alley, a dumping site for unwanted furniture.

Beyond that was the shrubbery of Alice Mayford's garden where I could just make out the pale shade of a dog, his head tilted up towards this window. After a moment, the ghost hound, wagged his tail and disappeared underneath some kind of evergreen bush that obscured my view.

Left to my own devices in the lounge while John made tea in the kitchen, I noticed an etched bowl in opaque glass. I peeked inside and was disappointed. It seemed a waste not to put something prettier than supermarket tokens inside such a beautiful object even if they did come in different colours.

A row of well-thumbed paperbacks sat on another shelf, propped upright by a thick brown bible. Laid flat it made a good bookend. Was he religious, I wondered, or was it just a useful size?

The mantelpiece held the prize. A large photo of a school-girl in a burnished silver frame.

Lizzie Nash.

Draped across it, on a filigree chain, was a pendant, positioned as it would be if she were wearing it – a triangle contained within a circle, the whole surrounded by a heart of twinkling marcasite. The sort of thing a thirteen-year old might like. This looked like a shrine, but I thought I'd better judge his mood before I jumped straight in. I turned away as he returned carrying a tray.

'A survey for the council?' he said as he poured the tea.

'Not for them directly, but for local people, see if there's anything the council should be doing, or doing better,' I replied as we took our seats at the table.

He listened, sitting upright, his hands folded in his lap. 'Lots they should be doing. Potholes, dog mess.' He paused. 'That the sort of thing?'

'Exactly.' I jotted nonsense on my clipboard. 'Anything else?'

'Noise, drinking in the street late at night. I need my sleep. I work.'

'What sort of work do you do, Mr Nash?'

'Is that on your survey?' He sat forward, hands on knees and frown lines deepened between his brows.

'Oh, no, not at all, just curious … actually I find it hard to get up for work myself when I've had trouble sleeping so …' I babbled on, then my heartrate hit a high when he suddenly stood up.

'Here,' he said thrusting a hand towards me. I flinched, then batted an imaginary insect. I took the card he'd pulled from his pocket.

"John Nash, Plumber. Reasonable rates. Free estimates. No job too small." It was followed by a mobile number.

'Ah, thanks.'

'Anytime,' he said, then sat. He said no more but watched me closely. I went back to the form to give my pulse a chance to steady. I didn't glance at Lizzie's photo but tried to project a friendly interest in my task while wondering how to broach the topic of his dead child.

'Any problems with parking, Mr Nash?'

'I rent a garage.'

I put a cross in the box. 'Issues from a pedestrian point of view then? Cars using the road as a rat-run, speeding, hooters blaring … that kind of thing?'

He took a moment to think, blinking slowly as the wheels turned.

'Sometimes.' He shrugged, and I thought that was all I was going to get but he went on. 'Teen racers.'

'Oh, dear. And is this also at night, Mr Nash, keeping you awake?' My chance to empathise.

He nodded.

'Dreadful for you. A regular problem?' He shrugged again. I made a mark on the survey while wondering how to introduce the topic of Lizzie into our mundane exchange.

'Can you remember when this happened last, the approximate time would help ... it's so we can present the scale of the problem accurately.'

'Friday and Saturday nights are bad, early hours of the morning.'

I scribbled notes, nodding like a bulldog on a parcel shelf. Lizzie loved animals – should I mention the dead dog?

'Mm, one of your neighbours mentioned something ...' I flipped a couple of pages back. 'Ah, here it is. Monday of last week, soon after 10pm? She noticed because, as you say, mostly the noise is at weekends and much later.' I scanned the page as if checking. 'Yes, car engine, bit of a screech, like breaking hard, maybe even a bump, and then a roar as it powered away. Oh, it might have been the next street over ...' I gestured towards the window.

He sipped his tea. 'I always watch the headlines at ten. Switch it off about quarter past and get ready to turn in.'

The Basset had been run down about quarter past ten according to Alice, so here was my chance, but Nash went on without pause.

'If I heard a car, I thought nothing of it. Too busy watching that woman skulking about in the bushes down there.' He pointed at Alice's garden. 'Keeping out of sight of their windows.'

'Oh, my goodness.' I prepared to take notes in earnest as Nash gave me the best description of what he'd witnessed when the greenhouse light had been put on. My heart was doing a little skip of delight. Perhaps I could solve the Mayford case while I was here. Get one over on my sister and get Alice speedily off our client list.

The intruder was "solid, in dark clothing and wore a dark shapeless sort of hat with a drooping brim" – not much to go on after all, but it was an unexpected bonus.

Maybe she'd left footprints behind. A clever CSI could use them to estimate her height and weight. I'm not that smart, but even shoe size would be progress. It was over a week ago – still, we could get lucky.

'Right, sorry but I've got to be off,' Nash said as I finished writing. 'Job to do over at East Point.'

'What a lovely photo,' I said, in sudden desperation as he stood up to shepherd me out of the room. 'Your daughter?'

The shutters come down so fast I almost heard them hit the floor.

'I'll show you out.'

I was on the street in record time.

His card was in my hand though – and that had given me an idea.

Chapter Twenty-Seven

Tthe sparkle had faded from Sarah's sea-green eyes. 'I'm so sorry, Alice. I've nothing to report.'

'You're half-frozen. Come in quick.' Alice closed the door behind her. 'Let's get you in the warm.'

Alice helped untangle Sarah from her coat. 'I was so sure – but no one saw or heard anything. No one's at home who's willing to answer. Some are out – probably at work – I'll go back in a bit.'

'Get thawed out first. Hasn't your colleague come to help?' Alice urged her into the kitchen and put the kettle on.

'Nate hasn't turned up yet.' Sarah checked her phone. 'He should have let me know if – oh, that's odd, I've got no service.'

'Afraid we're in the Dark Ages here – it's a black-spot. The signal is so weak I have to tell my clients to use email.'

'You can get a booster – that should give you coverage. I'll sort out what you'll need sometime if you like?'

'You are full of surprises!'

'We aim to please.' Sarah grinned. 'But Penny's sent Nate

on another case and I suppose he can't get free.' Sarah took a sheaf of forms out of her bag and organised herself at the table.

'You did all those on your own?' said Alice. 'You must be exhausted.' Sarah did look weary. Not fruit tea then. 'Hot chocolate?' she suggested, 'Or latte, maybe?'

'Hot chocolate, lovely!'

'Good choice.' She reached for the mugs. 'I suppose you must have lots of clients – I hadn't thought of that. How does it work? I mean, is the whole team on each investigation or do you each do your own case?'

'Not sure really.'

Alice raised an eyebrow.

'I've only just joined,' said Sarah. 'You're my first client!'

'My good luck.' She brought the mugs and took the seat opposite. 'You must know, though what everyone else is doing. In case someone's ill, and you have to take over, or something.'

Sarah seemed faintly puzzled. 'We have a database, update things as we go along. I suppose I'd look there if I needed to – not that it would help with Penny.' She snorted. 'Penny's techno averse.'

'Me too, a bit. So how would you find out what she was working on – if you had to, I mean.'

'We do talk …' Sarah hesitated. 'Why do you ask?'

'Just curious. On TV P.I.'s seem to work one case at a time, but they'd never make a living. Wisemans must be doing well to be expanding – lots of business – and it must be so lovely to work with your sister.' Alice pleaded with her brain to stop the babbling, then raised her mug. 'Cheers,' she said, glancing at the pile of forms. 'So, what's our Plan B?'

Sarah tasted her own drink, eyes piercing Alice for what seemed far too long before she spoke again.

'Perhaps try for cameras along the main road. The driver might have gone that way so any vehicle speeding at the right time could be it ... then we'd have to track the owners and see if any damage was reported ...' She sipped her drink again, her eyes less focused as she mused. 'The best hope is this Good Samaritan and what she might have seen. I'll check for CCTV along the bus route too, because she's either fairly local or ... she wasn't driving so maybe someone dropped her off. I'll check the taxis for any fares about that time – they have cameras in their cabs – but it is a long shot, Alice.'

'I wonder where she was going?'

'That's a point. I'd check the pubs and clubs but it's the proverbial needle without a better description ... and you couldn't spend weeks scanning footage, even if we get it. Are you sure you can't remember anything about her?'

'I wish I could. Just female, slim and shorter than me.'

'There aren't many taller.' Sarah looked up, grinning as Alice stood to collect the empty mugs. 'That'll be the shock. It does strange things to the memory.'

Closing the dishwasher, it was Alice's turn to muse. 'Her coat was nice – good fabric and expensive buttons – not distinctive, sadly.' She straightened, leaned her back against the worktop. 'I'm sure I'd recognise her but it's so hard to describe someone's face. Individual features maybe – but they don't really help.'

'Can you draw?'

'Sketch a pattern, yes. Draw a likeness? Not a hope.'

'A professional could – but it might be expensive.' Sarah sounded glum.

'It'd be worth it to keep you on the case. Wisemans, I mean. Just to find out who was responsible.'

As she spoke, Alice began to wonder if that was true. She'd been so determined, but now ... perhaps she would have to accept it was impossible. Pointless even. Nothing would bring him back.

It had brought Sarah into her life, though.

'Do you want to talk about him? I'm a good listener if it would help,' Sarah asked, softly.

'Thanks, but …,' and suddenly the grief was overwhelming. Alice reached for a tissue to wipe her tears away. 'I'm fine, really.' She waved her hand, blinking. 'I don't want to be a bore …'

'You wouldn't be, and I'd love to hear about him.'

Tears rose again, but Alice fought them back, and wiped her eyes. 'If you mean that, one day I'll bore till you beg me to stop.' She offered the best smile she could. 'But not today. I have somewhere I've got to be this evening, and I don't want to explain my swollen eyes to all the fairies.'

Sarah blinked. 'Fairies?'

'In the Dream – Midsummer Night's one, a la Shakespeare. Or rather Haston Players version of it. It's been rather mutilated, but the fairies are from the local school and they're inclined to have hysterics. And Brian will be having a stage-fright meltdown. He always does. Of course, as soon as he gets into the spotlight, he's brilliant.'

'Brian?'

'Brian Dunker. He's our leading man. I'm only on the costumes, but he's sort of got used to me holding his hand, I think.' She laughed. 'Listen, why don't you come along? If you're not doing anything better, of course.'

'I'd love to.'

For a moment Alice felt her heart lift, then it dropped as Sarah spoke again.

'Could I invite Penny too? I think she'd be interested!'

Chapter Twenty-Eight

꧁꧂

As I left John Nash, I sent Sarah an instruction. It was succinct.

Intruder in dog's garden. Woman. Bulky. Floppy hat. Monday night. Search around bushes.

A unique footprint or hair caught would identify the villain in no time – but only on *CSI*. The dog was killed more than a week ago. There'd probably be nothing.

The Basset wanted something, but it was not my case. It hadn't hired my services, unlike Emily who was paying. Or Lizzie, who wasn't, but had hired me just the same.

I retrieved my car and drove to Carlton Drive, hoping Emily Dunker's heating would still be playing up. The shrine photo came to mind – Lizzie's glowing face. I might know just the man Emily needed.

I hoped Frieda would be up to talking, too. Lizzie had been animal mad. Everyone said so. Why was Frieda so certain Yosef's death had been Lizzie's fault? Perhaps there'd been a misunderstanding.

Frost bloomed inside my cheekbone. I had to find out more.

Brian's car was not parked in his drive, or in the street nearby. Their garage wouldn't hold Jasmina's hobbies and a car. Chances were high he was out. He might be at work by now – or up to no good elsewhere.

Emily might be in, though I could see no lights. Careful handling was called for. If Emily agreed, Nash would be face-to-face with Lizzie – and I had to see what happened. I'd need to be there – but what reason could I give Emily? I'd have to cross that bridge.

I risked knocking. No one answered.

Of course, Nash might refuse to come. His daughter died in this house.

I'd come up with no solutions by the time I'd crossed the road to where lights glowed in the bungalow opposite. I'd give it some thought.

I rang Frieda's bell and waited. I was on the point of leaving, when the security chain rattled, and the door opened a crack.

'Frieda? It's Penny Wiseman. Can I come in?'

She paused, but then removed the chain and shuffled into her lounge. The room was hot and stuffy and tasted of burnt tobacco.

She was wearing the same silk turban; the glowing green emphasised the sallow parchment of her face. The dress had been swapped for a robe the colour of Shiraz. It swamped her wasted frame.

I sank into the sagging armchair as she tucked the heavy fabric around her legs and turned bird-bright eyes to me. The ghost tabby curled up at her feet.

'So, you are still trying to help the child?'

'I am.' Silence stretched through three ticks of the clock,

and all was still, except the cat who curled his front paws under. He squinted his eyes.

'Good.' She pulled her collar closer. 'That surprises you?'

'A bit.' I had expected some resistance. I planned to mention helping a child in torment was the decent thing to do – beg if I had to. Point out the self-destructive side of anger. How talking to someone might help her too.

By someone, I meant me.

Her lips were pale, formed in a half-smile. I realised she'd left the lipstick off today, nor had she pencilled in her eyebrows, but her voice was firm.

'You did not think I would want to help?' She folded her hands in her lap and narrowed her eyes in much the same way as the cat. 'You told me sometimes my little Yosef is with her?'

'And once he was on her lap, yes.'

She closed her eyes for a moment. Air popped in her chest like a message sent in Morse.

'Then he has forgiven her.' She raised herself straighter in the chair. 'So, I must forgive also.'

She fumbled a cigarette from the pack and, as I held the lighter steady, I wondered if she heard the message from her lungs.

The flame flared in her eyes behind the veil of smoke, and illuminated the feathered lines criss-crossing her cheeks.

'Soon, she will tell me herself how this thing came to be.' She waved the cigarette. 'So, what is it you need to know?'

'Whatever you can tell me, Frieda. I'm working in the dark.' I gathered my thoughts. 'Maybe just tell me what happened because Yosef and Lizzie – they're still connected in some way – and tell me about her family. Her father, John ...'

More lines appeared around her mouth. 'Her father? Ach, not such a nice man. Too much beer, or whisky.'

She sucked in smoke. 'Not a good example for a child.' It

wreathed out from her nose and mouth. 'Such a temper, so much shouting ...'

'Yes?'

Her breath wheezed in and out.

'Sometimes I would ask, but what could I do? The mother would pretend – but I knew. I could see for myself the bruises. Lizzie, well, she would tell me stories for each one ... netball or riding horses or ... always some excuse. I might have believed – but Barbara, her bruises she always tried to hide. Pushing of a sleeve – or make-up that did not quite cover around her eye. I saw.

I am so clumsy; she would say or, *Such a silly accident.* Not so good at the deceiving as her daughter. Her eyes would be afraid.'

Frieda's cigarette glowed again, 'I should have said something to him – to someone.' Smoke dispersed lazily. 'Before ... yes, I should have said.' She paused, regret scoring deeper grooves around her mouth. 'But, of course, they loved him. Lizzie adored her father so what could she do. Then ... Yosef.' She stopped, took in more smoke. The clock ticked.

Killed was all she'd told me before, and Lizzie was to blame. I waited.

'Ach,' she breathed a lungful of smoke. I watched it curl around her thin lips as she exhaled. 'That afternoon, poor Yosef was so restless – he was not himself. He was ...' She balanced the cigarette in the ashtray, her jaw working as if she couldn't find the words. 'He walked so.' She sketched a circle with one hand, the other clutched the fabric of her robe. 'And noises, a wailing that he had never made. He fought me, scratched as if he did not know me. His eyes were,' she opened hers wide, 'like he was seeing things I could not see.

'Then he began to ... there had been rats and I thought *poison* – so this vomiting, it seemed a good thing.

'I phoned to the vet, and a taxi to bring Yosef there, but when he was sick again it was dark blood, from his nose too. I told the man, *drive like the wind*. Yosef — his head twisted from side and back and still that noise, that awful noise.'

She wiped her eyes and sniffed, coming back to the moment. Her cigarette had burned out.

'The vet, she did what she could do. Charcoal, she told to me. Oxygen. A drip for him. She asked, did I know what the poison was. I said perhaps for rats. She told me not to hope too much, but she would try.

'Then the test said no, not rats — some other thing.

She wiped away another tear, took a fresh cigarette from the pack, and lit it. 'Nothing could be done. I held him as he slept, told him I would see him soon. Then it was the end.'

She took a shaky breath then sat up straighter in her chair. 'I told them to do the tests — this post-mortem — to know what had happened. To stop this thing from happening to some other cat.'

She sighed. 'Even before the result was known, the girl had come. Her mother had explained her — told her she must say.'

'Lizzie?'

Frieda nodded. 'She came to the back door, like she always did. She stood in front of me, crying she was sorry. That it was her pill he had eaten. A strong one for her woman's troubles. She was so embarrassed, but her mother said she must confess. Poor child, I thought, she suffers so much she must take these special pills. I felt sorry.

'I told her. *Don't cry, it was not your fault.* Hugged her. Dried her tears.

'The vet said yes, it was that — good for us, this little painkiller, but so very bad for my little Yosef.'

'So, an accident?'

'I thought so.' Her smile was bitter. 'But then, when I have this post-mortem report. This painkilling level was very high. Some pills in his stomach too, not yet dissolved. The vet confirmed to me, the meaning. He was already poisoned – hours before.' Her thin lips curled almost into a snarl. 'She gave him pills before she went to school – and more when she came home!'

After a moment I spoke. 'Did you ask her about it? Or tell her mum?'

'No!' Her mouth clamped shut. She ground out her cigarette stub, jaw tight.

Lizzie's forgiveness was not quite total yet, but gradually Frieda's tension seemed to ease.

'Why could I not ask her?' she asked softly. 'Because it was too late. The child had died.'

She raised a bony hand to wipe moisture from her eyes.

We sat in silence for a while: her breath crackled in and out of tortured lungs. Her eyelids drooped; her body folded forward.

I gave her a moment to compose herself, and then it slowly dawned on me.

The crackling breaths had stopped.

Chapter Twenty-Nine

My rusty CPR bridged the gap until better help arrived. First responder and paramedic met on the doorstep. Defibrillation, competent and calm. Pulse confirmed. More crew arrived and hooked her up to more machines.

I stood out of the way, watching as they worked. A practised routine to each other: bp, pulsox, other things I couldn't decipher. They murmured to her: *Just relax, now darling; little scratch; we're going to roll you now*. Another said, cheerily, 'You're quite the frequent flier, Frieda. You'll be alright, my love.'

A short while later, the ambulance departed, lights flashing. As it turned the corner, I heard the first impatient whoop to clear the traffic.

She may be ready to take her final bow, but not here, not now – not on my watch. Adrenaline flooded out; relief swirled. I may have cried a bit.

. . .

I HAD ONE STROKE OF LUCK BEFORE I LEFT. BRIAN DUNKER had returned. The car was in his drive, tail end to the road. I took a casual step onto the path and leaned against the boot. An unnecessary adjustment to my shoe let me slip the tracker into place.

Lizzie Nash's ghost watched me from the garden.

Deliberate poisoning or something else? She'd wanted to be a vet but at thirteen how much did she know? Any search engine would have told her not to do it, but the road to hell is paved with good intentions.

Lizzie's thin shoulders slumped. She turned away.

She was bruised, I thought as I walked back to my car, and abused children sometimes do bad things. But whatever had happened to the cat, it should not have been a capital offence.

MY HEAD WAS FULL OF QUESTIONS. LIZZIE'S FRIEND MIGHT have the answers. But would she talk to me – and how would I recognise her?

They both went to Haston High. That much I knew. I checked the school sports gallery. There she was: Jodie Channing – tall, toothy, tawny-haired. Captain of the under-15's netball team.

School would have let out for the day – but social media is a blessing. Jodie's profile was secure – not so all her friends. She was tagged at Kelly's Café – ten minutes ago.

She was still there when I arrived, chatting with a bunch of girls, their school skirts turned over at the waist band, ties vanished into bags or pockets. She clocked me as I went in, then her glance slid away, uninterested.

I bought myself a latte and a chocolate fix and settled down to wait. One by one they drifted off till there were only three. I thought I might follow when she left, see if I could create an opportunity to speak. She beat me to it.

'You watching us?'

'Watching you, Jodie,' I said. 'I hoped we could talk.'

'Yeah? Like, what about?' I could almost see the dream, though I couldn't have picked which – model agency, casting director or maybe netball scout.

'Lizzie Nash,' I said. No point in pretence.

'Oh.' She brushed her hair back off her face, adjusted her hairband. 'You a reporter or something?'

'Sort of. I want to know a bit more about her, that's all.' I nodded at the chair opposite. 'Take a seat?'

She considered for a second, then waggled fingers at her friends as she sat down. They pretended to go back to their own conversation, sly glances betraying curiosity.

She shrugged when I asked if she wanted a drink, or anything to eat.

'Hot chocolate? Cream egg?' I urged. She had that skittish look. She might shy away at any second.

'Go on then, I'll have a Diet Coke,' she said. 'I'm not getting fat for anything.'

I paid for her drink at the counter and brought over the can and a glass. When I sat down, I noticed a Kit-Kat finger was missing. I was careful not to smile.

'What do you want to know?' she said, pushing the glass away and opening the can.

'What Lizzie was like, her home life, whatever you can tell me.'

'You doing a book or something?'

'Something. If I do, you'll get a credit.'

She tossed back the ends of her hair. 'Yeah, well.' Her voice softened. 'She was, like, my best friend.'

'You spent a lot of time together out of school?'

'Yeah, at my place or hers.'

'Which did you prefer?'

'Hers.' Her smile transformed her. Maybe modelling was on the cards. 'Her mum's so nice. Treated us like people, you know, not little kids.'

'I thought all step-mums were wicked?'

She snorted. 'Like you'd read in books when you were five! Barbara's alright.'

'Give me an example of "alright",' I suggested.

'Okay.' She thought for a minute then she grinned. 'She gave us wine with dinner.' Her face clouded a bit. 'Lizzie wasn't keen, but her mum said it made us "civilised" like the French.'

'Lizzie's dad drank a bit, I heard.'

'Yeah, well. I didn't see him much.' She gathered up her hair, examined the ends minutely. 'But ...'

'But?'

'Her mum said it was best to be ... careful when he was home. Like, he had a temper.'

'What did Lizzie say?'

'Nothing much. I mean, Barbara sort of told me when we were on our own so ...'

'Lizzie never said anything about her Dad to you, her best friend?'

She shifted in her seat, tossed back her hair again. 'She was ... like, in denial, I reckon. But I told her anytime she wanted to talk about it ...'

Her friends were signalling time to go.

'I'm sure you were there for her,' I said. 'Lizzie loved animals – wanted to work with them, that true?'

She glanced at her friends and back. 'Yeah, she was dead keen. But you need top grades to be a vet. Her mum thought it might be too hard, but Dan was, like, really nice about it –

leant us some books and stuff. He was going to help her – help both of us 'cos I thought I might go for animal technician or something – but then …'

But then she died.

'Dan?' I said, raising my latte and trying to sound casual.

'Yeah, he does all SARC's vaccinations and stuff. They only pay a bit, like if it's really expensive. He gives all his time for free …'

'He's their vet?'

'Duh, yeah. Daniel Kitson.'

And so good-looking too.

Jodie glanced at her friends. One pointed at the door.

'I've gotta …' she said, taking the Coke with her.

A second later she was gone.

Was Barbara cruel to be kind? Maybe. Perhaps Lizzie was too fragile. But, weren't parents meant to encourage their little darlings to reach up to the stars? And Daniel Kitson – did he bring out the girls' animal passions in more ways than one? Evan had dismissed the idea – but he'd also said John Nash had made some kind of fuss.

I had to get John Nash and his daughter's ghost in one place.

I checked the time. Six o'clock.

One more try at Emily's and then to home. Glass of wine, maybe. Pretend to be French.

BRIAN'S CAR WAS ABSENT, AND NO ONE ANSWERED THE FRONT door, but I could hear Jasmina mutilating a pop song in the garage. It was obviously a habit.

'Your mum about?' I said, sticking my head in at the door as my phone pinged.

I glanced at Nate's text.

Have updated Haddock file. Need to see you first thing ☹

I keyed a quick thumbs-up while listening to Jasmina.

'Dad's taking her to an eye appointment,' she said, pausing in her routine. The girl was wearing jeans and sweatshirt this time and looked much better for it. She was pink-cheeked from her exertions. 'Then on to Aunty June's to have a moan. I'm going next door for my tea then to my self-defence.' She grinned. 'Sausage, egg and chips and Bev won't make me do my homework. Result!'

I leaned against the doorframe. 'The moaning about you not doing your homework – or not wanting to eat your greens?'

'Not about me,' she said, with total confidence. 'It's my baby brother always crying and 'cos the heating's gone funny again, and the draughts and stuff. It's her nerves, Dad says, but not to worry 'cos she'll be okay. Shall I say you wanted her?'

'No problem, I'll pop back tomorrow.' Which I would, I thought, as I walked away. I didn't want someone to fix that heating before I got my chance to suggest Nash.

Chapter Thirty

s I reached home my phone pinged once again. This time it was Sarah.

Am at the Jolly Roger. be here 7pm. ticket at box office. it'll be fun! S xx

An improvement on my own plans – microwave meal for one, and large Shiraz to hide the taste. An evening out might do me good, though I wished the pier theatre was not the chosen venue. All that swirling water below and Gail's dead eyes watching.

Still, my brain was whirling like a kaleidoscope and until the colours fell into a pattern, nothing would make sense. Distraction would be useful. My conscious self could watch, or doze, through whatever treat I had in store while my subconscious did its thing. Snoring might provide amusement for my sister.

THROUGH THE PIER ENTRANCE, PAST GLASSED-IN AREAS EDGING the central walkway, endless coins dropped into slots. Occasionally the chug-a-chug preceded a cascade of falling metal. Cheers were transitory. The machines were always hungry.

My stomach rumbled so I stopped briefly for dinner. I finished my Big Mac and took the fries to go, then stayed on the central walkway leading to the theatre entrance, ignoring the dark mass of fairground rides each side.

The Jolly Roger, mid-way along the pier and two thirds its width, looked welcoming. The expected welcome too from Howling Gail, whose pale shadow I could make out beyond the theatre's bulk. Gail had made that joke herself just before I nagged her into going in the water.

Her shade raised a hand; I did the same. Acknowledging her presence was the least I could do. She faded to nothing as I stared into the darkness.

I'd overheard my mother talking a while after I was rescued. If not my imagination, then "survivor guilt" was the cause of my symptoms. Fair enough, I'd thought. I survived, and I was guilty – but I learned to stop talking about what I saw. Threats of counselling had dwindled but the ghosts remained.

The first time I'd been to the Jolly Roger, Gail had brought me. Memories of Peter Pan and Wendy flying in an obvious safety harness were disappointing to a child expecting magic. I had no high expectations of this "midsummer night", not in February put on by amateurs.

Leading man for the Haston Player's *Dream* was Brian Dunker – that much I knew. Why Sarah thought the show "interesting" was still a mystery.

The clerk handed me my ticket. 'You'll have to hurry. You'll miss the start.'

Walking slightly faster to the auditorium door, I was ushered to my seat as the house lights dimmed. I barely made it before the gold curtain lifted and the first act swung into full flow. What I had not expected was a semi-musical. Puck hit the first high note.

Bludgeoned might have described it better.

'Why am I here?' I whispered, but Sarah got no further than 'Alice' before loud shushing drowned her out. A torch flashed along our row. We were cowed into silence.

The show was not too bad, I suppose, if you like that kind of thing. People running through fake trees spouting rhyming couplets: one chap – ass's head and a fake Suffolk accent – fawned over by a matronly fairy queen; Helena was young and pale and sweaty, fearful in the spotlight. She was prompted loudly, swallowed and soldiered on.

Chilly draughts distracted me from banks of thyme and eglantine, but not enough to stop me recognising Brian. His Demetrius was arrogant and selfish, ranting about his wife-to-be who'd run off with a lover. Ironic given his own wife's worries.

His singing was truly impressive though; his voice took clear possession of the high notes and growled the low ones tunefully, and the slap-stick moments following his enchantment had the audience in stitches.

His acting skills surprised me – his role as the "good husband" hadn't fooled his wife of late. But even he couldn't carry the entire cast alone.

Other laughs were strained, and the first half crawled on for a year – or fifty minutes in real time. Then came the interval. The audience went in search of alcohol. Sarah and I let a few spectators pass, but we stayed put.

Unless my sister was both masochist and sadist, there must be a reason she wanted me here.

'Alice?' I prompted.

Sarah grinned. 'She does the costumes. Aren't they great?'

They were rather snazzy and, had there been a mute button, the show might have been worth watching.

'That's hardly front-page news,' I said. Or worth the bruising on my eardrums.

'You should be pleased I've found you a connection! I read your case notes. It's more than you've managed.'

'He works in textile sales. She's a dressmaker, Sarah. It's hardly rocket science – and I can't note every detail.'

'You should! But Alice can't be a blackmailer –'

'How can you be so sure?'

'– she's not that devious. Smart too – she knows you're up to something.'

I glared, thinking about cats being let out of bags.

Sarah shrugged. 'Not me. You wrecked poor Monty's funeral, and she probably saw you earlier and added two and two – it's hardly rocket science!'

'Okay, Smart Alec. What did she say?'

The corners of her mouth turned down. 'She was fishing. Wanted to know about your other cases – and no, before you ask, I played dumb and changed the subject.' Her frown grew pensive. 'Do you think that's why she came? I rather hoped she hired us because she fancied me.'

'Excuse me, could I get through?' We stood, backed up against the row behind to let a returning couple pass.

'Don't get involved,' I warned. A waste of breath. She'd do exactly what she wanted. Always had. I thought I might try to remind her Alice was a client. 'What about your investigation. Any luck?'

'I updated *my* casefile. You could have read it!'

I rolled my eyes. 'We don't have a team of twenty to keep informed! Just tell me.'

She sniffed then admitted she'd discovered nothing.

'Really disappointing, but I'm going back tomorrow. I'm not giving up – besides, I do think Alice likes me!'

Yes, wasting my time.

'Okay,' I said, leaving that aside, 'but what about the garden, did you find anything useful in the search?'

'It was too dark. I'll do it tomorrow.'

'It was full daylight!' As full as winter gets anyway.

'Alice is in a blackspot. I only got your text on the way here. After a week, what am I searching for, anyway? A footstep, a hair caught in the bushes. Ridiculous!'

'The description of the woman was pretty useless, but I saw the dratted dog's ghost under the bushes.'

'Well, why didn't you say?' She grabbed her phone.

'I wasn't going to put that in a text!'

She completed the log-in as she spoke, 'I'll flag it up as urgent and check it out first thing tomorrow.'

'You don't need to flag it ...' Her fingers flew over her keypad. 'You're just doing it to wind me up – it's only you on the case!'

'What if I get run over by a bus?' She grinned.

'I'd know to do it anyway,' I muttered as the lights went down. 'Stop being such an ass.'

An enchanted Bottom gambolled on. We both giggled and were shushed.

AFTER THE PERFORMANCE WE MADE OUR WAY INTO THE FOYER. I thought it might be worth hanging around a bit. Brian and Alice were out of reach until they left the backstage area, but I might see them interact and my sister was clearly biased.

Sarah was happy – too happy – waiting for her client to emerge. I was wasting breath again, explaining why professional and personal should stay poles apart. My sister was more stubborn than the ass. She was waiting for me to finish when she suddenly grew tense.

A woman with the shoulders of a rugby player homed in like a guided missile, leaning close to 'mwah mwah' Sarah's cheeks.

'Hello, Clare. What a surprise.'

Ah, mystery solved. An ex-girlfriend. The relationship had been brief, the woman hard to detach. Sarah usually exited with grace, but this ex was proving tough.

Clare's eyes raked over me. 'Who's your friend?'

'My sister, Penny.'

The family nose could have given her a clue. I smiled. She didn't. She just locked in on her target. 'I found some of your CDs. I'll bring them round. How about tomorrow?'

'Just keep them, Clare,' said Sarah, taking a step away. 'Really. Don't worry.'

Clare paused, and then the green-eyed monster blinked behind her eyes. 'I know there's someone else. Why won't you tell me who it is?'

Big girls don't cry. The refrain went through my mind, but it looked like this one might.

'There was no one, Clare, honestly. It was just ...'

'So why don't we meet up for a drink or something. I mean, if you're on your own again and I'm on my own – just talk, that's all.'

I was about as useful as a goldfish at a car rally. I debated whether to butt in or make my excuses and leave them to it. Then a voice I recognised spoke from behind me.

'Sarah. So glad you could make it.'

Alice was radiant in a little black dress and legs all the way to the ground. Sarah glowed a little brighter. I held my breath, wondering if there would be fireworks to end the evening.

Alice acknowledged me, then turned to Sarah's ex and held out an immaculately manicured hand.

'Hello, I'm Alice. I don't think we've met.'

Clare turned and walked out into the night.

The crowd, not large to begin with, had dwindled to a trickle and I had a clear view as Sarah raced down the theatre steps and out into the night. I saw Clare stop. My sister, the peacemaker. She'd do her best, though Clare's body language said she was holding tight to her conclusion.

Alice watched the interaction. 'I hope it wasn't something I said.'

Confronted by Alice's perfect grooming and her slender six-foot frame, I wished I could, occasionally, look that polished. The green-eyed god was working overtime. It made my reply a little sharper than I intended.

'Nope, just something you are.'

She arched one eyebrow, and I realised how my words might sound. I might have put my size six boot right inside my mouth.

'No, hell, I didn't ... gorgeous, that's all I meant ... they've broken up quite recently and I ...'

Her lips had begun to twitch, and I wondered if she had been teasing me, but all she said was, 'They've broken up? What a shame,' and then switched on her megawatt smile as Clare stomped off and Sarah started back towards the foyer doors.

I slunk away.

Chapter Thirty-One

Watching Penny stop to talk to Sarah outside the theatre, Alice was grateful her days as Alan were a long way behind her – and amused she'd taken the wind out of Penny's sails. Clearly, Sarah had told her sister Alice was trans and, though it was hardly Penny's business, Alice smiled, pleased she'd been on Sarah's mind at least.

'Can I get you a drink?' Alice waved at the bar as Sarah returned. 'It's open for a few minutes yet. And we could sit over there?' She pointed to a sofa that had just come free.

'Lovely, but I'm buying.'

'Cheers,' said Alice a short while later, raising her bitter lemon. 'Are you okay now? You seemed a bit … fraught – not with Penny, with …'

'Ancient history,' said Sarah, dismissing the ex with a wave. 'Your show costumes were fabulous!'

'Thanks – and I'm sorry I was so busy earlier – Titania's zip broke and half the fairies got into a scuffle. Broken wings everywhere – but it's all over now – well, until tomorrow anyway. Just the matinee then, and it'll be done with!'

'They were so cute.'

'They are really.' Alice lowered her voice as a group of mothers crossed the foyer with their grease-painted children. 'Most of them, anyway. They come from the local school – and parents buy lots of tickets – but it doesn't make life easy.'

'Never work with children and animals?'

'At least I don't have to be on stage with them.' Alice paused. 'Monty used to love it all. He did some commercials when he was a pup, and a turn on stage sometimes ...'

Sarah briefly touched her arm and they were silent for a moment. Then Sarah cleared her throat. 'Penny thinks I should have a look around your garden as soon as possible.'

Alice bit her lip. 'I only checked the fence really – it's a bit of wilderness out there so ... should I have been more thorough?'

'It's just elimination – there'll be nothing there to find.' Sarah was reassuring.

'No handily dropped credit card?'

'Wouldn't that be nice! I'll take a look, then go door-knocking again tomorrow – and there's still a chance of CCTV.'

'I don't think my Good Samaritan is the woman in my garden. Even with her coat she was slim ... quite skinny even ... and she helped so much. She even phoned the vet.'

Sarah frowned. 'I thought you were in a black spot? Or is that only one network?'

'It's all of them ... at least, it used to be. Perhaps that's changed ...'

Sarah pursed her lips. 'Did she ask which vet – or for the number?'

Alice shook her head slowly. 'Kitson's is nearest,' she said, 'but she didn't stop to look it up. She must know it – but they don't know her, not from my pathetic description.'

'Hmm. What made you think she was skinny, not just slim. Her face?'

'When I was kneeling, she was standing right beside me. Her legs were thin.' She closed her eyes to picture it. 'Her shoes were very high heeled, and incredibly shiny – not just with rain – but patent leather.' Her eyes flew open. 'No mud!'

'Not the woman in the garden!'

A sparkle of excitement lit Sarah's face. Alice suddenly had faith that together they might work out what happened to her beloved hound.

Her thoughts were interrupted by a jangle of keys. The foyer had emptied, and the caretaker was waiting to lock the front doors.

'Look,' Alice said on impulse. 'Why don't you come back to the house? We can carry on with this over coffee – or something stronger.'

Chapter Thirty-Two

I'd put Nate's text out of my mind earlier, but now I was home it began to niggle. I wouldn't get to sleep till I knew what he'd done. I should have gone with him. He'd have been disappointed, but I could have lurked nearby and still given him free reign.

Dad had been of the 'sink or swim' school of teaching so I was often out of my depth, and he could be cutting. One of the reasons I'd gone to London to complete my training.

I'd hate Nate to think he'd failed, even if he had.

Especially if he had.

The video report had been uploaded as promised. I opened it with some trepidation. His nose loomed way too large before he adjusted the focus. 'Hi, it's me,' he said, then mumbled something that could have been the date and time, both of which were clearly displayed in one corner of the screen.

'Haddock, case number 0246 ...' he started more confidently but then another voice broke in.

'Oi, whotcha saying about me? And who to? Give that here, you.' There were rustlings and random syllables. Evidently a scuffle for the phone. A minute or two later, a woman's face flashed by in close-up. Then the screen went blank. I recognised her from the photographs her husband had provided.

The follow up action showed an appointment had been made for Jennifer Haddock to see me. Ten o'clock tomorrow morning.

I decided my beauty sleep might be more restful if I had the full story. It was just past eleven now, a bit late to call him but getting it off his chest might save Nate a sleepless night brooding about it.

The phone rang before I had a chance to make my call.

'P-Penny, I'm so sorry. It's Alice, Alice Mayford. You've got to come. They're taking her to ...'

A voice mumbled in the background and I heard a vehicle door slam.

'The General,' she said. 'It's Sarah. She's been hurt.'

Time stood still for a heartbeat.

Then I grabbed my car keys and ran.

No news is good news. The words circled like a mantra. I paced the hospital waiting room, trying not to think the worst.

I found myself staring at Alice, legs splayed like a broken-legged giraffe on a low plastic chair. She rested her forehead against her palms and stared at the floor. She began to mutter.

'Why did I give her the keys?' She spoke into her lap. 'I should have told her to wait. I was only going to be a few minutes, but we'd been talking, and she was suddenly so keen

...' Her eyes flicked up to my face. 'There was the patio light and she had the torch on her phone. She said she'd have a quick look round but it's such a mess out there – I'm so sorry.'

I silently cursed Sarah for an idiot. I cursed the dog's ghost too. If he hadn't made an appearance she wouldn't have been out there. She might have had the sense to wait till daylight!

Alice's voice rose. 'If I'd been there, I'd have called the ambulance sooner or maybe it wouldn't have happened at all with someone else to hold another light, but I stopped off to get us some Chablis ...'

Ah, a drink with Alice. That explained my sister's eagerness. And then what did you do, Sarah? Walk into a branch, trip over your feet? Not just getting a bump or scratch but ending up barely conscious ... concussed ... or worse.

Idiot!

'What's taking them so long!' Alice asked, and I wanted to scream out the same question to the weary woman on reception.

We raised our heads at the squeak of rubber soles, but it was a policeman crossing the waiting room. He had a quick word at the counter and the woman pointed into a corridor. Somewhere down there, in the labyrinth of this old building, Sarah was being examined. We watched him turn a corner out of sight.

A moment later, our vigil was rewarded. A small man with a stethoscope walked purposefully around the corner that had swallowed the policeman.

I jumped in the moment he'd confirmed my identity. 'So, how is she? Can we see her?'

His face was kind. 'Not yet, I'm afraid, though she is conscious. The blow to the head was substantial, but the skull is a pretty good design for protecting the brain. However,' he held up both hands as if to fend us off, 'head injuries can be very serious, and we'll be doing another scan and keeping her under observation for a day or two at least.'

'So, when can we see her?' I asked again, wincing at the plaintive note.

'Someone will take you through as soon as she's up to it. Keep it short please.' He scrutinised Alice. 'Family only for now.'

An impulse made me jump in.

'My sister's fiancée.'

She mouthed a silent thank you at me behind his back as he stopped to exchange a few quiet words with the returning police officer.

'Miss Mayford?' The policeman's expression was politely bland. 'I understand it was at your property where the incident occurred. May I have a word?' He indicated the plastic seats to one side and Alice obediently sat down. 'I'll just be a moment.' He stepped to one side to take me further in the opposite direction.

'Penelope Wiseman? Sarah Wiseman's next of kin?'

'Yes, her sister.'

'And you were notified of your sister's admission by the hospital?' he asked.

'No, by Alice.'

He nodded and wrote something in his notebook. 'And can you confirm what time you received that call, and your whereabouts when you received it?'

I gave him the answers and he wrote those down too, and by then my brain had clicked into gear. The police do not ask these kinds of questions to keep themselves busy or impress the public.

Sarah's injury was no accident.

'What happened?' I said, but he flipped the notebook closed.

'That's what we're trying to establish. Your sister's not been able to give us a coherent account as yet ...' He may have said more, but a nurse approached, and he stepped away.

'Ms Wiseman? Would you like to follow me?' she said.

Seeing my sister trumped everything.

I tried to hang on to the consultant's positive words as we passed through double doors and turned down endless corridors. We walked for what felt like forever then suddenly we were outside her ward. I smothered my hands with antiseptic gel under the nurse's watchful eye and would have done the same with bleach if it meant I could find Sarah safe and well.

We finally arrived at a wide open-plan area; neon bright. There were eight trolley-beds, four on each side with rails like giant cots. The nurse's station ran along the middle. Some beds were occupied; assorted white-faced visitors grouped around them. The over-heated air was heavy with the smells of disinfectant and desperation and assorted bodily fluids.

A tremor travelled along my spine and I swallowed uneasily. My vibrant baby sister did not belong here. The nurse drew me to the far end.

Sarah lay motionless, the machine nearby pulsing a quiet rhythm. Her nose was lost in gauze and steri-strips, and around each eye-socket a stain was spreading. Her lips were leached of natural colour. A tuft of matted hair stuck up from dressings that wound around her head.

'It's the impact to her skull we're keeping an eye on. All the signs are good, though. Try not to worry.'

Sarah's arms lay on the sheet, her wrists blue-veined and vulnerable; a plastic thingy was clipped onto her index finger. Not worrying was like not breathing.

The nurse collected a chair from a stack nearby and set it by the bed. She patted my shoulder. 'Talk to her. It was a nasty crack, so her brain needs time to unscramble. She might not make much sense. If she seems agitated, be reassuring and keep her calm. No sedation until we see how she's doing, but I'm here if you need me.' Then she drifted away on silent shoes.

'Sarah?' I whispered. 'Can you hear me?'

For a while she didn't respond, then she stirred and groaned.

'Sarah? It's Pen.' I squeezed her hand gently. 'You're in the hospital. You're going to be fine.' I hoped my voice sounded more confident than I felt looking at her battered face. I wiped my eyes with the back of my free hand and sucked in one uneven breath.

'P-Pen?'

'It's alright, Sarah-bear. I'm here.'

I watched for the twitch of a smile that might accompany the baby-name. It would usually provoke a storm of protest.

'P-Penny-lope.' The childhood mispronunciation might be retaliation or maybe she was just lost in her own dream. I couldn't tell.

'You had an accident,' I said, not wanting to upset her.

Her fingers scrabbled on the sheet and I heard the beeps increase. 'Attacked!' she said clearly, then subsided into mutterings from which I picked out random words. 'Dark' and 'shadow' seemed reasonable, as did 'tall', but 'bug-eyed' was too far. The rest was jumbled syllables and moans. Her agitation grew.

Some horror-film nightmare was stirring in her brain. 'You're safe now, Sarah-bear. No aliens here, just you and me and lots of lovely people who're going to make you better.'

'Alice,' she mumbled. Question, accusation or just articulating random thoughts – it was anybody's guess. Alice's frantic voice and worried face rose in my mind.

'Don't worry, Sarah-bear. Everything's going to be okay,' I soothed as she slipped further into her dream and I considered Alice.

Did she know more than she was saying?

Chapter Thirty-Three

✥

Alice rose to her feet as the nurse approached Penny in the waiting room, but the policeman made it clear Alice was going nowhere.

'Miss Mayford, if we could ...' His open palm suggested she resume her seat and he sat in the same row, leaving an empty chair between them. He opened his notebook and turned to face her. 'I won't keep you long, but I'm sure you're as anxious as we are to get to the bottom of what happened.'

'Of course.' Alice watched Penny disappear into the depths of the hospital. Refolding her legs under the chair as best she could, she clasped her hands in her lap to stop them fidgeting.

'So, I understand you are Ms Wiseman's – that is, Ms Sarah Wiseman's – fiancée?'

'Um, no, not really.' The heat rose in her face. 'That's just what we told the doctor so I could get in to see her. Sarah's just ... I mean we're ...' She tried not to flinch at the trite expression. 'Just good friends.'

'Good friends?'

'Yes, well, we only met a few days ago but she's ... I'm ...'
How to explain! 'She's helping me find out what happened to
my Basset.'

His eyebrows rose.

'I reported it to you – the police I mean – but ... I understand it's hardly your top priority, of course, so I hired Sarah
privately.'

Alice took a steadying breath, and gradually, under his
gentle probing, told the story of Monty and how Sarah had
been helping her, not only professionally but listening when
she needed someone to talk to.

He listened gravely, nodded encouragement now and then
when she faltered, and took notes.

She was proud that, for once, she avoided the tears that
were never far away when she thought of Monty. And now
Sarah had been hurt. She swallowed, blinking away the rising
tide, and tried to keep her voice steady.

'As a sort of a thank you, I'd invited her to see the play –
I'm Haston Player's wardrobe person – only afterwards she
had a bit of a run-in with her ex so I thought I could return
the favour a bit if she wanted to talk about that.'

Alice decided it was not his business how much she'd
wanted to know if Sarah was still attached.

'And the ex's name is ...?'

'Clare. But I don't know her other name, I'm afraid.' She
glanced along the empty corridor. 'Penny might know.'

He jotted a few words, then looked up again. 'Just one or
two more questions, Ms Mayford. Can you run me through
exactly what happened when you came back to your house?'

'Yes, of course.' Alice turned her attention back to him.
'The lights were on in the front hall and in the kitchen, so I
called out to let her know I was back. But she didn't answer,
and the kitchen was empty so ...'

He held up his left index finger as he made a note, then said, 'Back from where, Miss Mayford?'

'From the Jolly Roger – on the pier. Where the play was.'

'Sorry, can we just backtrack a minute?' He flicked back a page, scanned briefly, then looked at her. 'You didn't come back from the play together?'

'No, I stayed behind to finish up in the dressing room, so I just gave her my keys. She wanted to search the back garden – we'd just realised it could be important about Monty – didn't she tell you?'

'So, you're saying you weren't actually at home when the incident took place, but she was searching your back garden at night because of something you'd discovered about a dog?'

'She had a torch …' His expression made her realise how unlikely it all sounded – but it had made perfect sense at the time. A sudden surge of enthusiasm that they might find something useful.

The policeman's pen flew over the page. He finished and closed the book before he spoke. 'I think it would be best if we continued this down at the station, Ms Mayford. If you would consent to helping with inquiries in a more formal setting and to us taking some forensic samples – just to establish a clear sequence of events – it would be much appreciated.'

Alice frowned. 'I want to see Sarah first.'

He stood up and planted his feet firmly, his face impassive. 'Restricted visiting at this time, Ms Mayford. By your own admission, you are not family or even a long-standing friend, so I'm afraid that won't be possible. Let's get these other matters cleared up and perhaps come back later, shall we?'

Chapter Thirty-Four

❦

At four o'clock in the morning, Sarah was taken for another scan, and I wandered out to get a coffee – or the brown stuff that masqueraded as it. I was waiting for my drink to be dribbled luke-warm from the machine when the ghost of a tabby cat wandered to my feet. It sat, washing.

'You look familiar,' I muttered, causing a fellow caffeine addict to give me a wide berth.

Yosef stretched and yawned, and then began to walk away. He stopped and looked back at me.

'Right,' I said, collecting my paper cup of sludge and set off in his wake.

I had to ring the bell to gain entry to the ward. I said I'd come from Carlton Drive, to visit my neighbour, Frieda.

'I know it's late,' I said. 'But I'm off abroad for work tomorrow and this could be my last chance to see her …' The last bit might be true. As I'd stood outside the Dunker's house and heard the ambulance siren wail, I'd wondered if Frieda would make it to the hospital. Now the tabby wanted me to visit.

The care assistant let me in and pointed out the side room door.

Frieda was asleep or seemed to be. She opened her eyes as I lowered myself into the creaky chair beside the bed. A tube split into two under her chin, snaked behind her ears then emerged to rest beneath her nose. A pump somewhere hissed quietly.

'Do you haff a cigarette?' she said, then coughed and chuckled. There was something wonky in her smile.

Her dentures were missing.

The little cat leapt onto the bed. He levitated just above her stomach, looking smug. I passed on the news.

'He is here. I feel him. Almost I can see him.' Her eyelids fluttered as if she were drifting away again and I prepared to go, but she spoke, her eyes still closed. 'So, what next will you do to solve this mystery?'

I thought she shouldn't be worrying about that, but she seemed to read my mind.

'I may be old, but I am not dead yet. I have nothing to do but lie here and wait. For the nurse; the doctor; the undertaker.' Another chuckle. 'Come, tell me. What more do you know?'

'Not a lot,' I admitted. 'I spoke to one of Lizzie's school-friends. I think you were right – her father caused the bruises on her arms. They were a day old at least. The coroner was satisfied. A tragedy, but not a crime.' I tried not to sound disheartened.

'You must look harder!' Her voice was strong and for one horrible moment I thought she'd try to get up, but she slumped back. Her face was whiter than the pillowcase but her grip on my wrist was strong. 'She has come to you for a reason, you know this. She must not suffer longer. You must bring her peace!

'This coroner,' she said, subsiding. 'Did he say why this thing had happened?'

I thought back to Nate's scribbled notes. 'Not really. All sorts of things – hunger, previous fits – her periods of course, poor kid. Any kind of stress seems like it could have had some bearing, but it's all just guesswork.'

I didn't like to add that I'd quizzed Nate, but no one had mentioned the cat's death. Whatever reason Lizzie had for giving him the pills, the result must have been stressful for the kid in itself – especially if she had been trying to "help" him.

'I do have one idea,' I said, 'but I need Emily's cooperation at the house. I'll try to see her again tomorrow. Later today, I mean. I want to get Lizzie and her father face-to-face. See what happens.'

'You must take care. He is a dangerous when he is angry, Penny.'

'Not to a woman who'll kick him in the family jewels if he tries anything.' Jasmina Dunker wasn't the only one with some ideas on self-defence, and I had steel toe caps in my boots.

Her face was grave, and I had a sudden thought.

'He didn't ever hurt you, Frieda? Did he?'

A bead of moisture trickled from the corner of her eye and was soaked up by the pillow. 'He did not hit me.'

'But something happened?'

She paused. The rattle in her chest was more pronounced.

'I need to tell you something ... a confession.' she said. 'I did not lie to you – I did not speak to Barbara or to Elizabeth about the post-mortem report, this is true but ... I did speak to her father. This stress the coroner said, that made this terrible thing more possible – it was my fault.'

'I'm sure that's not right, Frieda.'

'Well, I will tell you, and you will then agree, I think. So, it was the day I got the report from the vet, the day Elizabeth was to die.

'Her father was coming home – beer on his breath already and not even three o'clock. I called out and he came. He saw that I had put the chain on the door. He stared, was offended, I think. He said he was sorry about Yosef.'

She swallowed and I held the straw and cup to her lips so she could drink.

'And he seemed … even then I thought perhaps I would not tell him everything – it would do no good, but I told him I had the report – that Yosef was poisoned'.

A post-mortem? It was only a cat!

He was laughing.

'I shouted at him then – said how she had fed my Yosef one pill and then another, and then more again. I said how Elizabeth must have enjoyed watching him suffer, must have been happy because – even then – she gave him more!

'So, what did that make him? I asked. What sort of father raises such a child to do that to *only a cat?*

'A man who drinks too much, I told him, a man who beats his wife, a man whose child is too scared to tell the truth about her own bruises. This man I hold responsible – he is to blame, not the poor child who needs a doctor to help her!'

Her tears soaked the pillow; she made no move to wipe them away.

'Ach, I was so angry.'

I cleared my throat and swallowed. 'What happened, Frieda?'

She took a rasping breath. 'He told me I was a fool, a wicked, stupid woman – yes, but stronger of course – called me names I will not repeat. Shouted in my face that I was evil, telling lies! That it could not be too soon till I was in my grave just like my cat.'

She put her hand up to her mouth as if to stem the flow of words, but her eyes opened wide. 'Now there is her ghost and I am afraid. Did he hurt her, scare her so much …? Was it my fault? You must find out!'

Her voice was fading. I put my hand on top of hers. 'I'll do my best, Frieda.' I said softly. 'I promise.'

I had to get John Nash back into his house and, for Frieda's sake, I had to do it soon.

My thoughts were spinning as I went back to check on Sarah because, if I found out what happened, would it set Frieda's mind at rest – or would I be confirming her worst fear?

Chapter Thirty-Five

⁂

'Thank you for your cooperation, Miss Mayford. We'll keep you informed as to when we've cleared everything at the scene. In the meantime, do you have somewhere you can stay ... a friend or family?'

'My father's waiting to collect me.'

'I'll walk you out.' The detective strode beside her to the front desk where Pops was waiting.

'If you could just let us have the address so we know where to contact you ...?'

'The Grand Hotel,' said Pops, and then, 'I've booked a suite, my darling, so we'll be fine for as long as all this takes.'

'It's so they know where to come to arrest me,' fumed Alice as they climbed into the taxi.

A quick shower and a change of clothing in her room made her feel slightly better. Pops had obtained jeans and a t-shirt in her size from some all-night store. Her own had been taken away and, police resources for anyone of her height and build, were limited.

Having vented her annoyance on the short ride to the

hotel, Alice found her anger at the detectives had been holding her together. 'They should be out there finding out who did this!' She accepted the brandy glass Pops handed her.

'Medicinal, for the shock,' he said as she began to prowl the lounge between their bedrooms.

'They admitted she was in no fit state to give a statement, but they still suspect me.' Alice's voice suddenly failed. She stopped, hand over her mouth, unable to go on.

'Sweetie, they're just covering the bases – and they let you go! No one who knows you would imagine you could do anything so vile. Once they put their brains in gear, I'm sure they'll work that out. Besides, have they seen your nails? My girl wouldn't spoil her manicure getting into a fight!'

He led her to the sofa, put their glasses down and folded her into a hug. 'Come on, now. You've had a horrible time and no sleep, your friend has been hurt, and it's absolutely fine to have a darn good cry.'

'But after you've done that,' he said, as her sobs subsided, and he held her at arm's length studying her face. 'Then the Mayfords follow the spirit of our Viking ancestors. We pull ourselves together and go back to conquering the world.'

Alice sniffed and mopped at her eyes with his hankie.

'Do we, Pops?'

'Well, you do, sweetie, I just have a fit of the vapours.' He nudged her. 'See, I knew there was still a smile in there somewhere.'

He leaned back on the sofa and stretched out his long legs, keeping his arm looped around her shoulders. 'So, your friend Sarah, what *was* she doing in your back garden while you were at the theatre?'

'Searching for clues about Monty. She went on ahead and I stopped for some wine on the way.'

'Lovely girls like you don't have to get their fancies drunk, sweetie.'

She ignored the comment and the twinkle in his eye.

Her tears started up again. 'She was so broken, Pops. Lying there, so helpless, blood everywhere. I should have come home with her. She'd have been safe then. And now they think it was my fault and they're right! I should have been there!'

Her father handed her a fresh hankie and gathered her back into his arms until the worst had passed.

'Now, here's the thing, Alice,' he said eventually turning her loose. 'This was *not* your fault. There is no possible reason for you wanting to hurt this girl. There's no evidence you did – because you didn't – so let the detectives get on with their job and find the who, why and whatever, and you just wait and see.' He frowned. 'She's an investigator, you said. There could be any number of people upset with her for finding out their secrets. I'm sure the police will look into all that. And then there's the baggage with this ex.'

He smoothed a strand of Alice's hair and tucked it behind her ear. 'I don't want you involved in anything that might get you hurt.'

Alice blinked at him and handed back the hankie.

'Seriously, Pops? That's your advice? My *friend* has just been hurt in *my* garden and you think I should just – what? Stay out of it? Keep away? Leave her on her own thinking I don't care?' Her words had driven her to her feet.

He opened his mouth, but she cut him off. 'And what about Monty? She's investigating what happened to my baby boy, Pops. Suppose that's the reason she got hurt?'

'Okay, okay, I get it.' Her father held up his hands. 'And I love you for it, my feisty darling, but please – for your old

Dad's sake – take care. I don't want it to be you lying out there bleeding next time.'

'Lying out there bleeding,' Alice echoed, frown lines appearing between her eyes. 'Oh, that's odd.'

Pops raised an eyebrow.

'He wasn't. Monty. Bleeding, I mean. Not a scratch on him – isn't that strange?'

Chapter Thirty-Six

By eight thirty in the morning Sarah had responded to the medics about pain levels, but not made much sense otherwise. Questions about what happened caused agitation and the doctor's advice had been to leave all that till later. Their tests proved she remembered her name, the year and who was allegedly running the country. The queasy rollercoaster of concussion was apparently receding. Regular observations showed improvement in her prognosis, if not her temper.

Dozing on the chair beside her bed had cricked my neck and cramped my legs; bad dreams plagued my catnaps; my mouth was drier than the sand sheet in a budgie's cage.

'You're snoring again,' Sarah mumbled as I surfaced for the umpteenth time. 'Go home!' She sounded annoyed. This was encouraging.

I wiped the dribble from my chin with as much dignity as I could muster and had a word with the new doctor on duty. Satisfactory, she said. No guarantees but the signs were good.

Home I went.

. . .

A QUICK SHOWER AND INTO THE OFFICE, HOPING THE IRATE Jennifer Haddock wouldn't take too long. Emily Dunker had not yet answered my text, but I had to get John Nash into that house.

Nate sat at reception picking at his thumbnail. His hair stuck up as if he'd started combing it then forgotten what he was doing; the bags under his eyes rivalled mine.

'My bad. Sorry, boss,' he mumbled to the floor. 'I so screwed up.'

'All part of the learning curve,' I said with only an inward sigh. 'Come through and tell me what happened.'

His eyes flicked to my face as he got to his feet. 'Shit-a-brick, you look worse than me. You okay?'

'*I* am.' I wilted into my chair, rubbing the heels of my hands across my eyes.

'So, who isn't?' he said, taking a seat.

'Sarah.'

'Sarah!'

'She was attacked. Back of her head took a battering and they smashed her face as well.'

'Jeez ...' He'd got to his feet, pushing the rest of his hair into vertical.

'She's going to be fine.'

'Shit! I mean ...what happened?'

'She was in Alice Mayford's garden ...' He was still standing, fists clenched, face suddenly chalk white, '... but it's the concussion they're keeping her in for, and she's improved a lot overnight. They don't think there'll be permanent damage.'

'Thank Christ,' he said, slumping into the chair.

'She doesn't know what happened – well, not much – something about bug-eyed aliens so watch the news for

UFOs.' Laughter tried to bubble out. 'She's fine!' I dug my nails into my hands, tried to focus. 'If the police find whoever hit her before I do, they can count themselves lucky!'

He turned a whiter shade of pale beneath his ginger freckles.

A mixture of emotions played across his face. Shock and horror, and a flicker of fear. Violence was not my usual response to … anything. But the sight of my baby sister, bloodied and hurt … I took a breath. 'That's why I didn't phone last night, Nate. Sorry. I didn't mean to leave you hanging.'

'But she's going to be okay?'

'That's what they say, but you'd better tell me what happened to you. The client's wife will be here any minute.'

'Yes, but …' He looked like he might be sick, but I hurried him on. I could do nothing for Sarah right now, but I could protect her investment. I hoped.

'I need to know the worst. Let's have it, Nate.'

He was suddenly interested in the hangnail again. 'She said I was taking photos of her … her …' The tips of his ears turned red and he shifted in his seat. 'Up her skirt. And everyone was staring so I scarpered into the nearest gents. I was doing my report when she burst in – into the *gents* – and grabbed my phone. Said it was evidence, and she'd get me arrested.'

If his head had hung any lower, it would have been on the desk.

'Nightmare,' I said. 'We will sort it out.' I let that sink in, and when he risked a look, I nodded. 'Now, you went to the leisure centre …'

He sat up a little straighter. 'I went early, like you said, but she didn't show. I was going to pack it in, go and help Sarah …'

I watched him swallow nausea as he mentioned her name. I wondered again if he was a bit smitten with my sister.

'Then the target turned up and I followed her to the studio. She waved to someone inside but didn't go in, so I walked past, but that corridor's a dead end. I pretended I was lost. She asked if she could help.'

'Oh.' My pained expression mirrored his own.

'Then she went to the coffee shop upstairs, so I went too. She stared a bit, so I sat a couple of tables back and pretended to do sudoku.'

'Out of her eye-line at least. Good thinking,' I said, trying not to shake him till his teeth rattled and he got to the point.

'The yoga guy turned up and they were holding hands, heads together and,' he bit his lip. 'I know you *said* just to watch, but I couldn't hear, so I moved to the next table. And I know you said it was okay to record if it was in a public place so …'

I could feel my forehead crease. What had I said?

'I put my phone on to record and skidded it underneath her chair only,' he worried at the hangnail again, 'she moved her foot and kicked it out a bit, then turned to look. I made a grab for it and ran.'

'Right,' I responded calm as cucumber and any other cliché I could find to halt the urge to scream. 'That's when she accused you of up-skirting and threatened to call police?'

'Yeah, and yoga guy said he'd take a rusty knife to my …' He moved his hands into his lap and swallowed. 'So, I said I was working for you, and she said she wanted to see the organ grinder not the monkey, and I made her the appointment.'

Nate looked marginally better; one layer of despondency lifted from his shoulders. It landed back, with extra weight when I said. 'What's on the recording, Nate?'

He mumbled. 'It was only for a minute.'

He laid the phone on the desk as the door buzzer sounded. Three jabs followed by a continuous drone.

I sent him to answer as I listened.

JENNIFER HADDOCK SPORTED AN IMPRESSIVE CLEAVAGE AND A lot of bling. Her features were sharp which matched her tone as she swept past Nate and into my office. 'You his boss?'

Nate trailed in behind.

She strode to the desk and tried to tower over it. Her blonde updo added a couple of inches which helped.

'You will tell me what your *associate* was up to! And I should warn you, my husband has considerable influence with the police!'

'Take a seat,' I suggested and nodded at Nate. He subsided into a chair near the door.

She sniffed, then sat, and glared across the desk. 'What's going on!'

I kept my voice pleasant. 'I understand from my colleague you attempted to steal his phone.'

Her mouth opened.

'And coerced him into revealing personal details by threatening to have him arrested.'

'He was stalking me and then he crawled under my bloody table and tried to take a photo up my dress.'

'He dropped his phone and was attempting to retrieve it,' I corrected.

She crossed her arms. 'Sam will say what happened.'

'Ah, and will your husband's police contacts be taking a full statement from your son?'

She blinked and stuttered, and half rose from the chair.

I watched her, saying nothing.

She deflated faster than a souffle in a chef's worst nightmare, letting out a long, deep breath. Resignation dulled her voice. 'I suppose it's Vinnie you're working for.'

Her husband's words drifted across my mind superimposed across the boyish face of Samson James. *Me, officer, say something racist?*

'Under the terms of our contract,' I said gently, 'I am obliged not to answer.'

She twisted her wedding band and shook her head. 'He's always been a daft bugger. Thinks every bloke's after me.'

'I am obliged to report our findings to my client – but only concerning the question asked, and it may take a day or two for the full report to be available,' I offered.

She thought for a moment. 'And he just asked if I was doing the dirty on him?'

I sipped my tea, watching her over the rim of the mug as she squared her shoulders.

She shook my hand as she left. I wished her luck.

When Nate came back from seeing her out, the greenish tinge had reappeared on his face. He fidgeted in the doorway, moving a small rucksack from one hand to the other.

'It'll be fine, Nate. We'll reassure him she's not playing away, and we'll still get paid. Don't worry.'

'It's not that. It's …' He came towards me struggled to pull something out of the bag. He laid an object on my desk and backed away a step. His hands were shaking.

'I'm so sorry,' he said.

Oversized goggles mounted on a military-looking helmet. Two black protruding lenses.

Bug-eyes.

His arms were wrapped around his body as if to hold himself together, but it was no use. He cried like a child: sobbing, snotty-nosed, like his world was ending.

'I'm sorry,' he wailed. 'I didn't mean to …'

He shook, chest-heaving, misery gurgling in his throat as he folded from the waist, fists pulling at his hair. 'It ... it was an accident.'

All I could do was stare.

An accident? The contusion on the back of Sarah's head. The damage to her face.

'Sit!' I said.

He collapsed into the chair, hands covering his mouth.

I let the sobs run their course before I spoke. 'Tell me.'

'I – I saw her note – on the Mayford file – it said ...' his voice caught as his chest jerked to supress another bout of crying. 'It said it was urgent – important. I thought ... I thought ...' He scrubbed at fresh tears and, when he could continue, he went on.

He'd felt bad for not helping with the survey when he'd promised. The "night observation kit" he'd bought on-line had just arrived. It had seemed like fate.

'It shows where the ground has been disturbed – I thought, if someone had hidden something ...'

I waited.

He swallowed. 'I ... I went to the front door, but no one answered, so I thought I'd just ... there's an alley at the back, things to climb on. Only, when the lights came on – what if she called the police or something ... I was already in so much trouble.' His gaze flicked to my face, got nothing, focused on the floor again.

I felt like I'd been plunged into a blast-chiller. One change of expression and my whole face might crack.

He wiped his sleeve across his nose. 'I was in the shadows, in the bushes. I hunkered down. Kept quiet. I thought whoever it was, they'd go back inside.' His tongue moistened his lips.

I could imagine him crouching in the dark, pale face

turned away. I could imagine Sarah, too. Coming through the garden to the bushes, out of the range of brightness. A little torch beam at her feet to stop the stumble over the rough surface, flicking light from side to side.

'The client – I thought it was her – she'd got so close. Another step or two and she'd be almost tripping over me – so I got up to run.'

A shadow rises, looms out of nowhere, seeming scarcely human even as the light flashes over.

'She screamed. I ran, scrambled back over the fence and … I didn't recognise her – these things are no good for that – and I didn't know she was hurt. I promise you.'

She flails back. Her head cracks on the uneven paving slab. After that, another fall or two, a scramble to get back towards the house, to safety – a minute or two passes and Alice finds her, bloodied and confused.

'You've got to believe me! I didn't know!'

'Stupid,' I said, not quite knowing if I meant him or her or just the whole sorry tale.

His hand dug into his bag and came up holding something.

'I did find this,' he said, putting a clear bag on the desk and stepping away – a disgraced puppy offering a long-buried bone might have looked that hopeful.

This bone was a syringe.

Chapter Thirty-Seven

I left Nate in the office under strict instructions to help no one. I told him to polish the abject apology he'd be making to my sister – and warned him it had better be good. Whatever his future held was entirely up to her.

I sent the hypodermic off to be tested before I left the office. An old friend worked at the university science lab and owed me a favour. It might have been thrown over from the alleyway, but it would be good to know what had been in it. Dotting the 'i's and all that – and the dog had wanted it found.

'There might be fingerprints,' Nate offered, still hopeful.

'Then they'd be messed up by yours – even if we had the means to find out.'

'Couldn't we get a lab to check? I was wearing gloves so it might be okay.'

I gave him a look to indicate he'd wandered into fantasy land again, but it was wasted.

'They were the touchscreen ones my mum bought me for

Christmas.' A touch of his usual cheeriness tried to surface. 'It was cold as a dead man's feet out there.'

'Even colder lying on the concrete, bloodied and bruised,' I replied.

His cheeriness departed.

On the way to the hospital I considered the police investigation. I didn't want detectives wasting time on the "attacker". Nate was idiot, not villain, but as the injured party, it was Sarah's decision how to handle it, and it was her client's property Nate had trespassed on. When Sarah was awake, we'd need to discuss it.

Sarah slept on.

She'd been moved into an ordinary ward and was sedated so she could get some proper rest. The nurse assured me she was doing fine.

I needed to move on with getting John Nash into the Dunker house. I'd sent a text to Emily and the reply arrived to say the coast was clear as Brian was at work.

I left toiletry basics and a bottle of squash in the locker by Sarah's bed and crept away. I left a soft toy on the top. It was cute and the first thing she'd see when she woke. Watching the bruises spread around her eyes wasn't going to help anyone.

The panda watched me leave.

The net curtain fell back into place as I walked up the Dunker's front path. Emily hurried me inside. I thought the rush was to keep cold air from flooding in, but the hallway was just as frigid. She was wearing a long shaggy cardigan over a jumper, and woolly tights under a thick calf length skirt. I took off my coat reluctantly in the hall. The living room was no warmer.

Under the window, in front of the radiator, Lizzie's spirit hovered, her gaze fixed on us as we entered.

Emily's eyes were still red-rimmed, not disguised by the glasses on her nose. I remembered Jasmina mentioning her mother's eye appointment and, as she checked the electric fire was up to maximum, I said, 'New specs?'

Her hand went to the frame. 'They don't help much. I still can't ...' she faltered, adjusting their position slightly. 'I keep feeling a bit woozy, and something keeps sort of flickering ...'

'Varifocals take a bit of getting used to, so I've heard,' I said, as I huddled in an armchair drawn close to the fire; its heat was negligible despite the glow.

'That's what Brian says – and before that it was stress, or tiredness or whatever else he could think of to imply I'm imagining things! He thinks I'm going mad.' Her laugh was as hollow as the clunking of the radiator. 'I do too, sometimes, but never mind all that.'

She perched on the other chair, twisting her hands in her lap. 'What have you found out?'

'Alice Mayford,' I said 'Wardrobe mistress for the Haston Player's current production of the *Dream*. Ring any bells?'

'Oh, the tall woman. What about her?'

Mildly I said, 'I showed you her picture.'

She was vague, glancing over to the window where the radiator hissed, and Lizzie waited. 'Let's have another look?'

I pulled up the same photo as before and handed her the phone.

'She does look familiar,' she said. 'All that theatrical nonsense! I suppose it's where they met.' The radiator gave a metallic clank. Emily's hand jerked.

I caught the mobile as it fell, waved her apology away and

went on. 'She has a dress-making business. It's possible Brian knows her through his work. Only, there's nothing to suggest they're having an affair – in fact, it's my understanding he's not her type.'

Her chin came up. 'He's very good-looking.'

'She's gay, Emily, so whatever's going on, I don't think sex is the motive – at least not directly.'

'Blackmail then.' Her lips twisted. 'If she's not this "Honey" then she must know who is!'

Lizzie drew closer. My cheek ached with cold and the rest of me was chilly. The radiator clunked again.

'The heating's pretty noisy,' I said, seizing my chance. 'And it's none too warm in here.'

'It never works properly – just stops and starts. Except the baby's room – that stays snug which is very odd, because all the radiators can't be faulty except that one, or so the agent's maintenance company says.' She pulled her cardigan closer around her body.

'I might know someone who could take a look.'

'It's not our responsibility …'

'He might do you a report you could use as leverage to have it fixed. He's a one-man band. Reasonable rates.'

Lizzie's ghost rotated slowly, and the draught seemed to increase. The radiator hissed and from somewhere at the back I heard a door slam.

Emily leapt up. 'Damn it!'

I followed her into the hall and through the kitchen.

'I shut it tight, I know I did.' She opened the bathroom door and closed it again, pushing against it, making doubly sure.

We'd just got back to the living room when we heard it slam again.

Emily jerked to a stop. 'I don't care what Brian says …' she muttered.

Lizzie floated close and stared at her. Emily backed against the wall, eyes closed, her hands shielding her face from Lizzie's gaze.

'… I'm getting Amanda back,' Emily said, 'and I don't care what it costs.'

The girl's ghost turned to me; her eyes so dark they seemed to suck out all the light.

'Stop it, Lizzie,' I said. 'There's no need for all this. You've got our attention.'

Very slowly, Emily opened her eyes and stared at me.

Lizzie backed away, watchful.

'Oh my god,' whispered Emily, peering around the room. 'Lizzie Nash. You can see her!'

'Let's sit down, shall we? I don't think she'll disturb us for a while.' I hoped. 'How do you know who she is?'

'Amanda told me. She's this amazing psychic.'

I remembered the persistent woman coming to Frieda's door, and ignoring the cat. I hoped Frieda was resting comfortably. Emily was still enthusing.

'Amanda told me all sort of things. Not the name at first, but she got the gender right away.'

Well, fifty/fifty.

'She just felt the presence, and then said the spirit was confused and needed help. She offered to perform a ritual, to help her to pass over.'

'An exorcism? You must be kidding!'

Emily's mouth drew into a line. 'It was a "blessing ceremony". Amanda said it helped uneasy souls to move towards the light.'

'I'll bet that "blessing" wasn't cheap.'

Emily swallowed. 'You sound just like Brian! I bet you don't work for free!'

'The detective work I charge for, Emily, but this thing – whatever it may be – I keep it very quiet. I don't take payment for it and,' I suddenly realised why Frieda chose that particular "psychic", 'don't go telling anyone about me!'

'It was Frieda across the road who said it might be Lizzie. When I said about the atmosphere, she said the girl had been ... troubled. I was furious the agent didn't tell us she died here. I'd never have moved in if we'd known, but they never said a word.'

Buyer beware, I thought. Or tenant, in this case.

'I phoned Amanda straight away and she had to do a reading to be sure. After that, she said it was Lizzie, and she passed on all sort of things, and how Lizzie wanted to move on, but needed Amanda's help.'

I'll bet she did, I thought, deciding the value of anything this Mystic Mandy said was not worth pursuing. 'Where on earth did you get her from?'

'Facebook,' she said. 'What was I meant to do? Brian thought I needed stronger pills, my sister said it was lack of sleep – no one would take me seriously! I thought I was losing my mind – then I saw the advert and thought, what have I got to lose?'

I thought the fraudster had done her research, then dipped her bucket till the well ran dry.

'Brian checked what I was paying, and we had such a row, but that doesn't matter now. You can just ask Lizzie what she wants and then it'll all be over.'

If only it was that simple!

'She can't speak to me, Emily,' I said.

'She could to Amanda!'

'It doesn't work that way for me.' Arguing would be

useless, no matter how much I wanted to. 'I have to work out why Lizzie's here and what she needs.' Where to start, I thought. 'Lizzie was a student at Haston High, Emily. When you were working there, did your paths cross?'

'I saw her occasionally, but I didn't know her, not really, poor kid! I help those who have special needs, mostly. I do remember her step-mum at the parent's evening, though.'

'Barbara?'

'She was lovely, so interested in the students' work, quite charmed everyone, especially the head. She said, as a step-mum, there's still a bit of prejudice – I could relate to that. One or two of the staff were a bit catty about her, but Barbara was like me with Jasmina. Just concerned as any mum would be.'

'In what way?'

'She worried Lizzie was working harder than anyone realised, having to put in a lot of extra hours, especially with biology and maths. Barbara's a senior researcher at Biotech Analytica. It was pretty clear who was helping Lizzie get her grades!'

Barbara's medical background had been put to some use then – not a doctor like her father, but I knew of the medical testing place at Gerrard's Cross. They ran clinical trials for everything from flu vaccines to cancer treatments.

Biology and maths must be key for anyone wanting to be a vet. Lizzie would have needed top marks. More stress on her, but it sounded like Barbara was protective.

Lizzie stirred and drifted closer.

'And her father, was he there?'

'I don't think so. He might have been working or ... no, I don't remember.'

'Emily,' I said, feeling the prickle on the back of my neck as Lizzie came closer still. 'I want to get Lizzie's father in this house and see how she reacts. He's the plumber I mentioned. Will you call him?'

She hesitated. 'Will he want to come here though, after everything?'

'I don't know, but I think we have to try.'

While Emily was phoning. I checked the app for Brian's tracker. I felt a little guilty that his wife was helping my enquiry while I'd done so little to help hers.

The signal now put him parked to the east of the town and in a familiar location. A sour taste rose in my mouth. What was he doing near Alice's house when he should be at work?

Chapter Thirty-Eight

Alice approached the curtains, wrinkling her nose at the hospital disinfectant permeating everything. She peered through the gap, then tiptoed to the end of the bed. Sarah stirred.

'Alice. How lovely,' she murmured, and began wriggling herself upright.

'I don't want to disturb you,' said Alice lending a hand to adjust the pillows at Sarah's back. 'The desk said it was okay, and I wanted to bring you something.' Alice had laid the fruit basket and magazines on the locker next to a soft toy someone had left there.

'That's so nice of you. Pull up a chair. I'm only dozing because I'm bored.'

Maybe, thought Alice, but Sarah was very pale. 'Only, if you're sure.'

'Seriously, there's not even a good reason for keeping me in. They said they'd look at discharging me this evening, but only if there's someone at home to keep an eye on me overnight. Otherwise I've got to stay here until tomorrow. How ridiculous is that!'

'Is it so unreasonable? I mean, suppose you passed out or something with no one there.'

Sarah snorted. 'I'm fine – it's just a headache and a few bruises and a lot of embarrassment – and Penny's got to be out and about earning a living so I'm not landing on her.' She made a face. 'Besides, she's in a grotty little bedsit over the office, and there's no way I'm staying there.'

Her eyes were too bright, her lips trembled very slightly. 'I want to go home, to my own apartment, with peace and quiet.' She blinked, then gave a rueful grin. 'Trust me, hospital is not the place for that. Every five minutes there's something – if not on the medical side, it's offers of tea, toast, painkillers … never-ending. Next thing, they'll wake me up to ask if I want a sleeping pill!'

'I think they're just trying to make sure you're okay.' Alice kept her voice gentle.

Sarah sighed. 'I do know that, really I do – but I just want to be left alone for a bit. Oh, not you,' she added as Alice started to rise. 'I just mean from all the other patients coughing and snoring – and the incessant coming and going. They're ill, I know but … oh, lor' you'll think I'm such a bitch!'

Then a tear traversed the bruising and Alice reached out to cover Sarah's hand with her own.

'Sorry,' Sarah sniffed. 'I'm being pathetic.'

'You'd hardly be human if you weren't a bit emotional – and I'm sure I'd be just the same. The last thing I'd want is to be surrounded by total strangers.' Alice watched another tear follow the first.

'This is so stupid. The police came and I couldn't tell them anything!' Tears flowed faster. 'I'm such an idiot.'

Alice passed tissues and held her hand as Sarah began to cry in earnest. She'd like to give the police a piece of her mind. 'You've been hit on the head and had a horrible shock – of course you're having trouble remembering. Anyone would!'

When the tears had reduced to a trickle, Alice passed a new pack of tissues from her bag.

'Sorry.' Sarah mopped her face. 'The police officer was really nice about it, only – now they've had the medical report and a look around, they think I might not have been hit. I might just have fallen – how embarrassing is that? Or been pushed over – because I'm sure someone was there. I have this memory I can't quite bring into focus – it's just a dark shape. Someone tall and thin, I think.' She groaned. 'I just want to find out what happened, then get on with my life, but most of all I want to get out of here!'

'Look, do say no if you want to. I mean, you don't really know me or anything, and it is where you were attacked but the police have finished at the house now and ...' Alice stopped herself rambling and started again. 'What I'm trying to say is, you could come back to mine – be discharged into my care or whatever they call it. I know,' she held up a hand although Sarah hadn't said a word, 'it's not ideal, but I could just look in on you now and then, in case you needed anything, and I have lots of space now the cabaret boys have gone. No one else is booked in until next week so it'll be quiet ...'

Sarah was staring at her.

'Of course,' Alice added, 'I'd quite understand if you'd rather not.'

'I'd do anything to get out of here!' Sarah said, then her hand flew to her mouth. 'I mean ... yes. Oh, yes please!'

Alice smiled. 'I'm on my way home now, so I'll get every-thing ready, and then collect you after the *Dream* finishes if that would work. It's a schools' matinee and when that's done, I can be home all evening.

'It's a date,' said Sarah, not looking quite as pale as she had. 'And we can sort out the next steps for Monty. I've still got some CCTV to check. There has to be something.'

'I've been thinking about that, Sarah. It is odd she knew the vet's number right away, even if she did have a phone signal. Then there's the car. She seems to have been the only one who saw it. What if … what if there was no car?'

Sarah frowned. 'What about Monty's wounds, though? There must have been something that caused those injuries.'

'That's even stranger. I've been thinking about that and I don't think he had even a scratch.' Alice thought back. 'He was muddy and wet, and I sort of assumed he was bleeding, but I had no blood on my clothes when I got home and none in the car – I've checked.'

'Internal injuries, wouldn't show, I suppose,' said Sarah, 'But given the amount of blood a paving stone can cause, then a speeding car …' She touched her hand to her bandaged head. 'What if she did something to him – or the woman in the garden did and then this woman with the shiny shoes just found him?'

'But then why would she lie about the car?'

'Or perhaps,' said Sarah, thoughtfully, 'they were both involved.' Sarah struggled up against the pillows. 'We need to find out what Monty's injuries were.'

'Well, you're not going anywhere,' said Alice, laying her hand on Sarah's shoulder. 'You need to rest, but I'll call in and ask Dan on my way home, and we'll put our heads together later.'

Sarah leaned back on the pillows and the smile in her green eyes glowed against her pallor, but her eyelids were beginning to close. As Alice left, her head buzzed with the thought that, at last, they were getting somewhere.

Chapter Thirty-Nine

I left Emily looking nervous, despite my assertion Lizzie's ghost would behave herself. I had no idea if that were true, but Emily seemed happier for it. The ice shard in my face had melted a little so I hoped Lizzie was content for now.

In the car, a check of Dad's watch confirmed I'd missed hospital visiting hours, so I did the next best thing.

When Sarah answered her phone I said, 'You sound sleepy – did I wake you?'

'I was only dozing. Alice just left.'

'Right.' A moment's silence. 'So, have the police been in?'

'They seem convinced I'm making the whole thing up and just fell over my feet.'

I heard a rustling as though Sarah was fighting the bedsheet and her voice was weary. I wondered if she'd be better off not knowing her "monster" was our employee – and if the police weren't investigating there was no reason to rush in. I could postpone telling her anything till she was brighter.

'Okay, don't worry. We'll get to the bottom of it. More

importantly, what's the doc's latest verdict – are you going to live?'

'Not only that, but I can get out of here as long as some-one's with me for twenty-four hours.'

I processed that and thought about logistics. I knew my sister – she'd die before she moved into a grotty bedsit. In her apartment I only drank clear liquids in case I spilled some-thing and brought down fire and brimstone on my head. No way I was moving in there. Besides Lizzie was scratching at my consciousness, and I had to find out what Alice and Brian were up to, and the Monty enquiry fell to me until Sarah was back on her feet.

'We'll work something out,' I said more to myself than to her, but she snorted.

'Don't worry, sister mine. I'm not going to kick you out of your bed so I can fester under the eaves in squalor. I'm going to stay with Alice.'

'She's my suspect, Sarah!'

'Don't be ridiculous. You know perfectly well she's not having an affair with that man.' There was a tiny pause, then she continued, sounding smug. 'Or why would she ask me to stay?'

'Oh, I don't know, Sarah – off the top of my head – I'd say guilt cause you got bashed in her garden, needing to keep you under her nose in case it's related to whatever she's up to, a way of making sure you don't give up on the "murder" of her dog – something I haven't even thought of yet … whatever!'

'I'm very tired,' she said frostily, and I realised a full-scale argument was probably not what the doctor ordered, or she could just be playing the "poorly me" card because she knew I was right.

Except she was poorly. Drat. Still, some good might come of the situation.

'You could do a bit of snooping around, sort of bring Brian up in conversation and see what she says.'

'Spy on her, you mean.'

'Exactly.'

'A fine way for a guest to behave and,' she cut me off before I could protest, 'she is kind, and lovely, and she likes me – and if you can't see that, Penelope Wiseman, then Dad was right. You're a useless private detective.'

The line went dead.

WELL, NORMAL SERVICE HAD BEEN RESUMED, BUT I TRIED NOT to let her parting shot sting. She was hardly at her best – or worst.

It may have been her final comment that made me conscientious. I spent some time in the car with my laptop, diligently checking her field reports from yesterday before I headed off, but everything was negative. No one saw anything, no one heard anything, no one was saying anything – except John Nash and his mysterious woman in the garden which hadn't got us anywhere so far.

I called up the CCTV Sarah had found via the off-licence around the corner from Alice Mayford's house. It hadn't snowed in Haston this winter, but the images looked as if they'd been filmed in a blizzard. I fast-forwarded to just before ten o'clock.

The camera captured close-up images of faces as customers entered the premises, but in the street beyond they were shadows in grainy black and white walking past the line of parked cars. One such shadow walked slowly, stopping at each vehicle for a moment, then patting the windscreen before ambling on. It took me a moment to work it out. Gathering road-mending money with the parking fines or "Tirelessly working for residents" as the council slogan puts it.

I ran the tape forward slowly. Customers came and went. People passed by. A classic hunched VW silhouette was captured as it pulled into the kerb. A passing vehicle briefly flashed up the outline of two figures in it. Headlights blinked off. The driver got out and walked towards the camera.

The streetlight was behind; it gleamed on slick patches of pavement but left the driver's face in shadow. The short, squarish figure, bundled in a bulky coat, splashed through the standing water. The walk said female. As she came past, I glimpsed a few details: buttons glinted on her sleeve, dark gloves, but nothing was visible of her face. The hat hid it all. A large floppy hat. She crossed the road and disappeared towards the alley that ran behind Alice Mayford's garden. The entrance was out of camera range.

"Solid, dark clothing and wore a dark shapeless sort of hat with a drooping brim." John Nash's vague description fitted.

I fast-forwarded a few minutes until the car's passenger emerged. She was smallish and slender, her face a pale blob, hair sleek and dark. She adjusted her belt and raised her hood, as she gained the pavement. She walked away in the direction of Alice Mayford's road, stepping around the puddles in spike-heeled shoes.

Tearing open the Cadbury's Curly Wurly I'd excavated from the glove compartment, I chewed and pondered. Two women arriving in the area together, and there was the syringe. It might take two to move a dog that size if it was unconscious. Walk it to the road though, before you sent it off to sleep but would the dog go off with someone it didn't know? Weren't they supposed to guard their homes against intruders?

No car engine, no thump, no scream of brakes or revving as the vehicle roared away from the dog's hit and run. The missing Good Samaritan had mentioned a car and a thump, and the vet hadn't contradicted that idea or Alice would have said, but had he confirmed it?

I chewed, sticky caramel clinging to my teeth, chocolate covering my tongue. A sweet sensation to counteract the one I had inside. Dad was right – I was a bad detective.

I'd need to talk to Alice, and then Daniel Kitson was the place to go. I could find out what he had to say about Lizzie Nash while I was there.

I checked the tracker. Brian Dunker's car hadn't moved.

Time to visit Alice.

BRIAN WAS NOT JUST DROPPING SOMETHING OFF IN PASSING. The signal had been stationary for nearly an hour by the time I drove past Alice's house. His car was a short distance away, sandwiched in a long row of parked vehicles.

I swung onto Alice's driveway and rang the bell. Inside I heard a masculine voice call out, 'I'll get it' and he was still looking over his shoulder as the door opened. Alice shouted out, 'Hold on', but it was too late.

His being there did not surprise me, but the outfit he was wearing did. A snazzy full-length number stretched tight across curves. Not the potbelly which might have been expected but a voluptuous feminine figure topped with a blonde wig. The scarlet bow around his mouth was made more disturbing by his dark goatee beard.

'Er, hello,' he said. 'Can I help you?'

I have no idea what I said in return, but I was distracted by Alice's arrival. She hurried me inside and closed the door after a swift look up and down the street.

'Penny, what a surprise,' she said. She was not the only one surprised. 'What brings you here?' Her face suddenly lost colour. 'Not Sarah, she's not …'

'She's fine.' I said. 'I just thought I'd check up on how the police were doing and …' I let my eyes drift to Brian and my voice tail away.

'They've gone! Collected up everything they could find – sweet papers, crisp packets – all the debris. It's a lot cleaner now, but I don't know if they found anything useful.' She babbled as the overdressed elephant in the hallway hovered, shifting his weight from one gold high-heel to the other.

'Oh,' Alice was no actress. 'Sorry, Penny. This is Brian. I'm just fitting his costume for the next production. You remember him from the *Dream*, don't you?'

'I do,' I said turning to the man in the dress. 'It's a big change from Shakespeare. What's the production?'

The answer was a nanosecond slow.

'Lots of cross-dressing in Will's plays, you know.' He brushed a blond strand out of his eyes. 'But this is for *Some Like it Hot.*'

'Sure,' I said. My knowledge of the Bard might be shaky, but I'd seen the classic starring Marilyn Monroe. Unless he was playing her part, this costume was over the top. I glanced at Alice. A skilled dressmaker would be needed to get a fit that good on a figure like his, and perhaps supply the padding too.

'Brian, didn't you say you have to get to work?' Alice said, subtle as a slap in the face with a wet fish.

'What? Oh! Yes. I'll just,' he slipped off the heels, picked them up in one hand and, lifting the dress hem with the other, scurried up the stairs.

I watched him go, then turned to Alice.

'As Sarah's out of commission, I've been reviewing her

case notes,' I said as she gestured for me to precede her into the lounge.

'Then Sarah updating everything as she went along made perfect sense! Sarah said it was in case she was "run over by a bus", but that you didn't agree,' said Alice breezily, then paled. 'Thank heavens it wasn't a bus that hit her!'

Nate was more runaway bicycle, and without her update he wouldn't have been there – but I was not about to drop that into the conversation. Sarah had obviously had no qualms complaining about my working practice to her client. Putting information where it might be hacked had seemed an unnecessary risk when it was just me, but I supposed I might now have to agree she had a point.

Silently, I groaned. She'd never let me forget that she was right.

Maybe I could solve her case though – that might even the score. 'So, Alice, I thought it might be worth speaking to the vet about exactly what …'

'Monty's injuries were,' Alice finished. 'We had the same idea earlier! I tried to speak to Dan, but he was out on a case and Val was tied up with a patient. I was going to go back later, or phone him at least,' she glanced at the wall clock, 'only time's running out on me today. The matinee starts at two.'

'Don't worry. I can go and have a chat.'

She agreed without hesitation, and she might have been slightly relieved not to hear the grizzly details of her dog's demise, or at getting me out of the house. As far as I knew Brian Dunker was still lurking upstairs in a glittering evening frock.

I wondered how Emily would take the news her husband might be happier if she let him wear her clothes.

Chapter Forty

The surgery reeked. A huge St Bernard swung his greying muzzle in my direction and air freshener fought a losing battle with shaggy dog and methane. The moth-eaten pet and his equally ancient owner took up a large part of the waiting room. The methane may not have been entirely from the dog.

I waited at the reception desk as Kathleen, armoured in blue nylon against the furry hordes, turned her smile on the schoolgirl who held a rodent in a cage. Wet sawdust and ammonia added to the pungent aroma. The receptionist logged the details while I waited my turn, breathing through my mouth.

I had believed Monty's death was just a random driver's bad behaviour. Now it seemed that something else was going on. His ghost sat at my feet and I read reproach in his eyes.

The vet nurse I'd seen on my first visit emerged from the consulting room along the corridor and called the cage owner. 'Would you like to take Hubert straight through?' The badge pinned to her uniform reminded me her name was Val. Her hair was unforgettable, still in-your-face Pinkissimo. I wondered if her timekeeping had improved.

She smiled vaguely at me before following her patient.

'Hello, again,' Kathleen said. 'How's your cat?' A flicker crossed her face – perhaps remembering I'd never returned to collect the thyroid-helping crunchies.

'She didn't make it,' I said, feeling a little guilty as the woman mirrored my expression. She may have been faking too, part of the job. Monty joined in the general sadness without effort. His face was perfect for it. 'I'm actually here about something else, something for Alice Mayford.'

'Alice, that's right, you're a friend of hers, I remember. Did you get to Monty's funeral alright?'

'I did, thanks.' The Basset stalked a tight circle, then sat peering up at me. 'She asked me to check a few things for her. She's a bit distressed as you can imagine.'

'Bound to be, poor thing, but … oh dear, is it the invoice? I'm afraid it can add up a bit. We offer time to pay if it's a problem. Just tell her to phone, or email if it's easier, and we'd be happy to set up a payment plan.'

It was clearly going to be a shock.

'She hasn't got it yet.' She'd not mentioned it anyway. A look might be useful. 'Perhaps I could take her a copy? I suppose it lists the tests, drugs, that kind of thing.'

'Of course, it does.' She appeared scandalised anyone would think otherwise. 'We have a very clear charging policy but,' her fingers clicked over the keyboard and then she frowned, 'it doesn't seem to have been made up yet.' She looked up from the screen. 'Even if it had, I'm afraid we'd have to post it to her – it has to go directly to the client.'

'Of course, only she's got a few questions about exactly what happened, and she asked me to have a chat to the vet on her behalf.'

'It's so hard to understand when it's sudden, isn't it? But Mr Kitson's out at an emergency just now and I don't know how long he'll be. Perhaps Val could help, only I don't know what we can tell you. Confidentiality ...'

'For pets?'

'For clients,' she said reprovingly. 'We'd have to have their permission to share the clinical records.'

'What if Alice wanted a copy of the file to look at? What would she need to do?'

'She'd have to request it in writing, but that's usually where there's some dispute or ...' She drew back, her face suddenly suspicious. 'Alice has always seemed very happy with our care.'

The Basset had rolled over and put all four paws in the air as she spoke. The surgery had failed to save him, but I didn't want to push Kathleen too hard. Questioning her hero's competence would snap her mouth shut faster than the *Open All Hours* till.

'Alice is very happy. She told me how lovely everyone is. She highly recommended it, but this is more about the nature of Monty's injuries. You see,' I glanced around, leaned over the desk and lowered my voice, 'we may have identified the driver. The car's being traced, but it would help if − and this is really why I'm here instead of Alice − too upsetting but if we knew what exactly had to be done when he came in, it might help establish impact speed, or bumper height or ... well, with the weight of the dog and so on so we can sort of reconstruct it − like they do on *CSI*.'

Her eyes had opened wide. 'Fascinating!'

'She'll send the request officially, no problem, but if there's anything you could tell me while we're waiting for the paper-work, Alice would be so grateful.'

'I shouldn't really but ...' She bit her lip. 'Let's see what I can do.' Her fingers began to crawl across the keys, her speed seemed that of a sedated tortoise.

Val reappeared at the end of the corridor and headed towards us, glancing at Kathleen's screen as she passed, then stopped.

'What are you looking at that for?'

Kathleen turned defensive in an instant. 'I was just telling this lady, we need Ms Mayford's written request to disclose these records.' She turned to me. 'The British Veterinary Association insist and there's data protection ...'

Val frowned. 'Didn't I see you at Monty's funeral? I thought you were there because of your cat?'

'Yes, but Alice and I got talking and ...'

She cut me off. 'You're an investigator. Someone said so, at the wake.' Her glance flicked to the older woman. 'I hope you haven't said anything you shouldn't, Kathleen. If there's some kind of problem and we get sued ...'

Kathleen sniffed. 'She asked if the bill had been sent out – but it hasn't yet. I told her I couldn't give her any details, anyway.'

'I *am* an investigator,' I said, interested in how she'd jumped straight to legal action. 'I'm working for Alice.' I hoped Kathleen wouldn't mention I'd claimed Alice as a friend before I went to the funeral.

'By sneaking a look at his medical records? I don't think so.' Val's hands went to her hips.

Kathleen twittered my nonsense about crime reconstruction; Val was not impressed, but I was distracted by a semi-transparent figure flickering into view along the corridor. Monty's ghost still sat at my feet, but he was also trotting towards me, ears swinging.

No. This was a different Basset.

He greeted Monty, nuzzling his face before they began to

chase each other around the waiting room in a ghostly game of tag. I looked a little closer and could see small differences. The white splotch on the back of the newcomer was larger and a different shape; his feet were freckled where Monty's were all plain; the streak of lighter coloured fur between his eyes was an exclamation mark, where Monty's branched above his brows.

Their circuits were making me dizzy, and I was in their path. Each time they passed through, ice crystals vibrated along my thighs and up along my spine. I tried to bluff it out, but the world was starting to spin.

'You've gone quite pale.' Val said. She glanced at the St Bernard owner. 'I'll be with you in just a moment, Mr Carroch.'

She guided me to a seat, though I resisted to take a small detour round the ghost dogs now tussling on the floor. The second dog tumbled over, legs in the air, then gambolled away, swishing his hindquarters. While Monty was a neutered male, the newcomer seemed to have all his bits intact and no shame about showing them off. They set off again romping around the waiting room.

I heard the glug of the water cooler.

Val handed me a paper cup. 'Here,' she said. 'Sip this and feel free to stay until you feel better, but you'll get no information without proper authority, so if this is all a ploy ...' She shook her head. 'It won't get you anywhere. I'm afraid.'

She turned away. 'Come through, Mr Carroch. I'm sorry to have kept you waiting.' She gave me one last glance as they walked past, the St Bernard as stiff-legged as his owner. The Bassets, whose tussle had ended in a no-score draw, watched them leave. Monty curled his lip in their direction. Then both dogs looked up at me.

I sipped the water. My brain tunnelled through detritus

until it found a gleam. Was the light-coloured VW Beetle on the CCTV tape precious metal or fool's gold?

The last time I was here I'd watched Monty as he relieved himself in their staff car park. He'd chosen as his target a custard-yellow Beetle.

I still wanted to see the vet about Lizzie. He'd "lent her books and stuff" according to her friend. A generous gesture. The sceptic in me wanted to know why, but for now there was little point in staying. Dropping my empty cup into the bin, and avoiding the ghosts, I left.

Once outside, I walked round the building to the back where the barrier pole into their car park was not designed to stop pedestrians, but I didn't need to walk around it to see the VW. I snapped a clear shot of the registration plate.

A door unlocking made me glance towards the surgery's back door. Val stepped out, cigarettes in hand and talking on her phone. 'I don't know, but if Alice sent her to ask questions ...' Our eyes met and she stopped talking, then turned and disappeared back inside.

'Nice car,' I said to empty air.

Chapter Forty-One

❦

'Thanks for breaking me out of jail,' said Sarah as Alice held the door to the bedsitting room.

'My pleasure.' Alice had chosen the most spacious room for her guest. 'I hope you'll have everything you need.'

She checked the bedroom one more time, pleased the towels she had laid out gave off a faint air of honeysuckle, while the yellow and white colour scheme made this room feel bathed in sunshine even on such a grey day. She'd hoped to get flowers. Hothouse freesias or an early daffodil or two would have made a nice welcome, but she'd been more concerned with getting to the ward on time.

'It's lovely, and really, thank you.' said Sarah. 'You can't imagine how relieved I am to be out of there, being poked and prodded every half an hour – and the smell of antiseptic and the rest – and never a minute to yourself.' Sarah's lip trembled, and Alice glanced round quickly, checking the tissues were in place. Sometimes a good cry was the best therapy.

She patted Sarah's arm.

'Make yourself at home. Feel free to use the lounge – it's just you and me – or come and find me in my workroom at the top of the stairs whenever you like. But don't worry if you want to rest. I'll knock from time to time.' The instructions from the discharge staff were clear. Sarah must be checked on regularly. 'I'll pop my head round the door if you don't answer, but if you're okay just call out and I won't intrude – unless you invite me in,' Alice couldn't help but add.

Before Sarah could respond the doorbell rang.

'I'll see off whoever that might be, don't worry. It'll all be peace and quiet, I promise.' Alice backed out, closing the door behind her and ran down the stairs.

'Pops! What are you doing here?' she said as she let him in.

'Being offered coffee by my loving daughter. Hopefully.'

'Yes, but – we'll have to be quiet. Sarah's resting and I don't want anything to disturb her.'

She shepherded him into the kitchen ignoring his smirk and waved him to a chair while she tried not to clatter too loudly with the coffee maker.

'Finished rehearsals so early?'

'If only, my sweet. We've technical run through in a bit, then the show's big numbers tonight – but then that's it until tomorrow afternoon when the magic happens. You are still coming to support me, sweetie? Despite having your lady-love to stay?'

'Don't call her that!' she said, swiping at his arm. 'And yes, of course I'll be there. I wouldn't miss it for the world.' She poured the coffee and placed his cup at his elbow.

'I've brought you two tickets – perhaps you might like to invite *Sarah* to come too – I think, as your father, I should get a look at this woman you're so taken with.'

'Very funny! But she might not feel up to it, Pops. '

A voice spoke from the hallway.

'And she's got two panda eyes which don't need showing off in public.' Sarah stepped into the kitchen. 'I hope I'm not interrupting.'

'Not at all.' Pops beamed, leaping to his feet as Alice felt the heat rise in her face. 'I'm sure Alice can do you a cover-up. My girl's a whizz with make-up, you know, amongst other things.'

'Stop it, Pops, you're embarrassing me.'

'But I'm proud of you, sweetie.' He turned to Sarah. 'She's re-designed my stage look a few times. Made me half my age and twice as glam – but that's probably not quite what you'd be aiming for. I'm Dominic Mayford.' He held out his hand.

'Sarah Wiseman. I'm not sure I'll be up to it, but thank you for the thought, and it's lovely to meet you, Mr Mayford.'

'Dominic, please,' he said, bowing over Sarah's hand, with a twinkle at Alice. 'I trust you're feeling better.'

'You should be resting,' chided Alice, ignoring her father and settling Sarah in the chair with the plumpest cushions.

'What kind of show are you in, Dominic?'

'A talent show, and I'm the host – it's going to be on prime-time telly. I do hope you'll be up to coming along – it'll be loud and OTT, maybe not quite suitable for invalids, but you'd love it I'm sure.'

'Pops is the most talented of the lot,' added Alice.

'Thank you, sweetie.' He blew Alice a kiss then turned his attention back to Sarah. 'So nice when your nearest and dearest appreciate you, but it would be such a shame to waste the second ticket, so do come if you can.'

'I'm sure Alice has lots of friends she could invite.'

'Ah, but she'd rather go with …'

'Pops!'

'… her new house-mate, I'm sure.' He twinkled at Sarah. 'But you must take it easy if those are doctor's orders. Alice tells me you have a sister, perhaps she'd like to come? I could get to meet more of the family.'

'Aren't you going to be late for rehearsal?' said Alice, hands on her hips.

He held up his palms, laughing. 'Yes, indeed. See you again soon, Sarah, I hope.'

Alice marched him into the hall then crossed her arms. 'Just popped round! Honestly! I should never have told you she was here.'

'I don't know what you mean,' he said, eyes open wide, then nudged her gently as he stepped out into the porch. 'Good taste, sweetie. She's gorgeous, even with the panda styling.'

Alice shut the door a little more firmly than she should have, reminded herself Sarah needed calm, and took a breath.

Sarah giggled as Alice returned. 'He's quite the charmer.'

'He's a nightmare!' Alice said, then giggled back. 'I do love him though, and honestly, there have been times when I don't know what I'd have done without him.' She smiled. 'It would be lovely to have your company at the show tomorrow, if you feel well enough.'

'Well, I didn't like to say in case you had someone else in mind – but if you're sure, I'd love to!'

Chapter Forty-Two

O n the short drive back to Alice Mayford's house, I
phoned the office. I wondered if I still had staff or
if Nate had run away with his tail between his legs,
but I needn't have worried. He answered the call with the
proper Wiseman client greeting.

'Nate? It's me.'

'Hi,' I could hear the click of his jaw as he went back to
chewing gum, but his usual exuberance was missing.

An image rose of a black beret flattening his ginger quiff.
Frank Spencer, alive and well and living in Haston – but
casting the first stone seemed unwise. I was still smarting a bit
from Colin Palmer's dog slobbering over me while the Assisi
congregation looked on. Especially with Colin laughing
himself silly.

Undercover is tricky and Nate was trying – very trying –
but perhaps it was time to show him a glimpse of light at the
far end of the tunnel.

'I haven't spoken to Sarah, Nate, but I'm on my way to see
her now. I'm sure she will forgive you – eventually.' I thought I

heard a sniff. 'Now, I need you to do something for me. You'll need to write it down.'

'Sure – lemme just grab a …' Sounds indicated a kerfuffle and I imagined the pen under the desk and Nate scrabbling for it. There was a thump. 'Ouch! Hang on a mo'… yep, fire away.'

I recited the VW's registration. I made him repeat it, correcting till he got it right. 'Licenced keeper and address, please – Val something, with luck. Text me when you have it, then check to see if it got a parking ticket last Monday evening. You'll need to give a reason. Say the driver might have witnessed an incident outside Moppets Off Licence and we've been hired to look into it. Got that?'

'I'm on it.'

'And, Nate?'

'Yep.'

'Don't do anything else.'

'Right, boss! Over and …'

'Out,' I finished with a grin as I parked the car.

Alice led me into her kitchen and offered coffee, explaining Sarah was due a check in a few minutes. Clearly no one was going to disturb the wounded on Alice's watch – not even a sister.

With a minimum of noise, Alice fussed with the machine until it began to hiss and spit. In this house Sarah was probably too far away to hear. I hoped she'd left a trail of breadcrumbs to find her way back to the kitchen.

Alice took the mugs down from a shelf I'd be hard pushed to reach. The cute cartoons on the china were in different poses but were both on the same theme. These long-eared hounds were beginning to haunt me in more ways than one.

'The vet needs your permission before they'll give me Monty's records,' I said.

'Data protection or are they trying to hide something?'

'Maybe both. The Royal College of Vets have rules apparently, but I saw something.' I explained the VW Beetle on the CCTV. 'I know you couldn't recognise anyone, but there's the possibility the car belonged to that nurse, the one with the pink hair – and a warden was issuing tickets so we might get lucky. We'll know more when Nate's checked with DVLA.'

Alice's shapely eyebrows drew together. 'But she was there. She helped Dan in the operating room.'

'Oh.' Sarah hadn't made a note of who the surgical team was, and I hadn't thought to ask. It would be tricky telling Alice about the syringe without explaining how I got it. I had to talk to Sarah before I could mention Nate's involvement. 'Perhaps she was on call or something and it was just coincidence – or maybe it wasn't her car at all.'

'Monty did make a sound that night,' Alice said thoughtfully, putting my latte on the table. 'One of his little huffs as he went off up the garden, but nothing like he would have if he saw a stranger. I thought he was scenting a mouse or something.' She shook her head as she poured her coffee and sat down. 'But why would she want to hurt him? She's always been lovely.'

'Why would anyone – that's the question, and I have no clue, except ...' I stopped. Except, the other Basset ghost had to mean something.

'Except?'

'Nothing.' I couldn't explain that to her either. Not without sounding mad. A text pinged and I relayed the information Nate had sent. 'Valerie Church is definitely the keeper of the Beetle at the surgery. We'll have to wait until tomorrow to see if a parking ticket was issued. Let's get your dog's treatment records and hope they tell us something in the meantime.'

'I'll have to do a letter, or an email, I suppose.'

'Maybe both,' I suggested. 'Just in case?'

'Actually,' she said, standing up and reaching for her own phone from the counter, 'I'll ask exactly what they need.' A minute later she hung up. 'Answer machine. I'll try again in a bit.'

She went to check on Sarah, while I sipped the very decent coffee and let ideas swirl in my head while the caffeine did its thing. I could almost feel my brain cells lighting up like a pinball machine. My phone pinged with a text. Nate had news on the syringe. It had held a mix of drugs with complicated names, an opioid mix. Despite Nate's dyslexic typing, some names sounded familiar, including one whose recreational use was growing according to the news – but it was meant for animals as an anaesthetic. Ketamine.

The question asked with any crime is "who benefits" – but what if the beneficiary was not a person? I finished the latte and let the wheels turn.

Fact one – Dog One was taken to the vet. Fact two – Dog One went into the operating room. Fact three – Dog Two recently died and was haunting the vet surgery. Fact four – Dog Two was male enough to have pups.

I knew of one daddy dog who was very ill – and a blood relation of Dog One.

What did one Basset have that another might need if they had to have – what was it the Pinnesari lad had said – "a major op"?

'Monty gave blood, that's right?' I said as Alice came back into the kitchen. She nodded. 'Maybe someone needed an emergency transfusion.'

'They'd call the blood bank. That's the point of the donation service. If they needed more, they'd have asked donors to go in.'

Barking up the wrong tree. My brain cell lights went out.

'Sarah's awake,' Alice said, 'and says you can go up. Second floor, first door on the right.'

I was dismissed.

'YOU'RE A BETTER COLOUR,' I SAID, PEERING ROUND THE door. 'Less green. Except around the eyes.'

'I feel better,' she agreed, sitting up against her pillows. 'So, thanks, I think – and thanks for the cuddly panda too!' She stuck out her tongue. I replied in kind.

The room was white and pastel yellow with a big window overlooking the garden and smelled of something flowery. 'Nice digs.'

Sarah smirked. 'They are, and Alice is looking after me which is lovely.'

'Lovely.' I echoed, as I propped myself casually against the doorframe.

A small silence blossomed in the fragranced space between us. Her eyes narrowed and she tilted her head.

I stuffed my hands into my pockets and fought the urge to whistle.

'What have you been up to?' she said.

'Nothing,' I replied. 'Er, have you remembered anything about …' I pointed to the garden beyond the window.

'Nothing useful – why?' She had that "tell me or you're grounded for a month" look she'd inherited from our mother.

'Um, that bug-eyed monster …'

Her mouth twisted. 'Alright, no need to mock. I was semi-conscious. I think I can be forgiven for one flight of fancy … what?' I'd held up my index finger.

'Not entirely without foundation.' Laughter was inappropriate and rising as fast as her indignation. 'You're not going to believe this ...'

'If you're about to make a joke about little green men from Mars, Penelope Wiseman, I promise you will live to regret it!'

'How about one lanky ginger lad,' I said, trying to keep my face straight, 'from Wiseman Associates and on the trail of buried clues.' My snort suppression was failing. I was running out of air as the cartoon unreeled before my eyes.

'Nate? But ...'

'Wearing night-vision goggles.' I gave in, sliding down the doorframe, clutching the pillow Sarah had thrown against my stomach.

'Stop that!' she said, and after quite a while, I did.

'You're saying Nate attacked me?'

'You terrified the life out of him,' I said, having regained some control, helped by having to catch a heavy shower of pillows. 'There he is, being a bush in the shadows, all Mission Impossible and everything, when this green figure lurches out of the grey mist and blinds him with a torch. He leaps up; you fall over backwards, and he legs it over the fence as fast as his spider limbs will carry him.' I'd stopped laughing. 'He'd no idea who he'd disturbed, or that you were hurt. He nearly wet himself when I said you were in hospital.'

She closed her eyes for a moment, then opened them. 'Green figure out of a grey mist?'

'The goggles are cheap rubbish off the internet. He'd have seen more without them. And you know the saddest thing?' I said, getting to my feet.

'What's that?'

'He did it all for you. Saw your "urgent" flag on the file

about the garden search and thought he'd help out – sort of a "sorry" for not giving you a hand earlier.'

'I'm not sure whether that makes it better or worse.'

'Mm, but despite all the odds he found something.' I perched on the end of the bed and explained the syringe. 'The right dose and the dog could have been walked groggily out into the street before he keeled over. If it was this nurse, he'd have let her get close, but it doesn't explain the other woman. Or why they'd take him.'

I left a pause, then went on. 'What do you want to do about Nate and the police – and who gets to tell Alice that her intruder was on our staff?'

'You'd better leave it to me,' she said. 'You've got to get hold of Monty's records!'

Chapter Forty-Three

A lice hurried into the hall as Penny's boots clumped
down the stairs.

'Kitson's aren't picking up the phone, but I've left
a message. Here.' She handed Penny the letter. 'This should
do. I've emailed them a copy too. I'd come with you, but
someone's got to stay with Sarah.'

And, thought Alice, closing the door, I still don't know
who to trust. A sick feeling lodged in her stomach. Her Good
Samaritan was suspect. The vet nurse who'd always seemed so
kind might be involved, and Alice was no nearer discovering
what Penny's interest in her own life could be.

A soft footfall from above helped Alice make up her mind.
One part of the mystery at least might be solved, if she was
prepared to risk it. 'Come and sit with me in the lounge,' she
said as Sarah descended. 'I need to ask you something.'

'I hope it's a favour – because I need one from you, too.'

Alice sat on the opposite end of the sofa and wondered if
she really wanted to ask. 'You go first,' she stalled. She found
herself hardly listening to the story of Sarah's "attacker".

What was she going to do if she asked the question and Sarah just refused to answer?

'He's a trainee, you see, and he was doing it for the best of reasons only, I'm afraid he's over-enthusiastic and then he panicked thinking you might have him arrested. It was your garden he was trespassing in so if you want to report him ...'

'You're not taking it any further?'

Sarah shrugged. 'It was an accident and he didn't know anyone was hurt, and he did find the syringe.'

'Penny didn't tell me about that.'

'It was a bit difficult until she could say how she got it.'

'So, she had to talk to you first.' Alice paused, smoothing the cushion in between them, marshalling her thoughts. 'She's very loyal – to you, to this employee, to her clients. Colin said it was one of her strengths.'

Sarah nodded. 'That's true.'

'So, if I were to ask her why she was really at Monty's funeral, I don't suppose she'd say.' She watched Sarah lose a little of her recently returned colour, but the woman's emerald eyes were steadily fixed on her own.

'I don't suppose she would.'

'Would you tell me, Sarah? If I asked?'

Sarah spoke mildly. 'Are you asking?' Her eyes widened slightly but never wavered.

Alice took a breath. It seemed loud. She felt her toes were edging towards a precipice. Would the question destroy something that already felt important to her? Would the answer? She hesitated.

'Asking,' Sarah said, breaking the silence, 'would put me in a difficult position, and I would much rather that you didn't.'

Alice's heart was racing, pulsing at her throat. She swallowed. 'Can you tell me anything?'

'Investigations happen for all kinds of reasons. What's

found is not always what was expected, and sometimes it's just nothing, nothing at all. I'm sure that's all it is.'

Alice lifted her hand to Sarah's cheek then, with great care for her bruises, tilted her chin upwards. She met no resistance. 'Thank you,' she said and leaned in for a kiss.

'Of course,' said Sarah cheerily a few minutes later. 'You should tell me *all* your secrets just in case.'

'I'm not sure I have any – not the deep and dark kind anyway.'

'Can't you make a few up – I do love a woman of mystery!'

'Maybe you should tell me all yours first,' said Alice as the doorbell rang. 'But it'll have to wait, I'm afraid. Duty calls – I've a fitting to do.'

Alice followed Brian to her workroom with a lightness in her step. It may still be February, she thought, but spring was on the way.

Chapter Forty-Four

I'd left the Mayford household with Alice's full authority to proceed, but it got me nowhere. The surgery was dark though it should have been open till eight. A notice apologised and gave emergency cover details.

Not much use to me.

I wandered round the back. If there were lights inside none were spilling into the night. I could hear something like a dental drill, faintly whining and making my teeth ache in sympathy, but the only illumination was the security lamp. It had been tripped by a black cat which froze, then ran for cover. It blended into the shadow of the wheelie bins near the storeroom door.

The spirit of the elderly St Bernard I'd seen inside earlier sniffed around the VW Beetle. He ignored the other option, the Toyota Yaris, and once satisfied, he cocked his leg in the same spot Monty had. His arthritic joints seemed less bothersome now he was dead. He trotted round the bins. The cat arched his back, then spooked and took off at speed. The dog's ghost chased after, barking silently in glee.

A moment later he returned, seeming philosophical about his failure. He faded into the storeroom brickwork rather like the Cheshire Cat. Briefly I wondered why he'd disappear in there but then realised it made sense. They'd hardly pop him in the kitchen fridge to keep fresh until disposed of. There had to be facilities for that somewhere.

I was fading too, and nothing could be gained by hanging around watching the deceased enjoy themselves. Hard work deserved more than a microwave meal for one.

Lamb Tikka Masala and poppadums somehow followed me home.

THE NEXT MORNING, AS I WAS WONDERING WHAT THE STAR OF India used that could linger through repeated toothpaste brushing, Nate bounded into the office. All bright-eyed and bushy-tailed was one way to describe it. Sickeningly cheerful for an employee in disgrace was another.

It transpired a call from Sarah had unlocked his doghouse door. Good intentions might pave his road to somewhere less pleasant one day, but this morning he looked ecstatic to have the office as his destination.

On his best behaviour, he pledged to chase up the potential parking ticket. If that proved the Beetle was near the Mayford house the night Monty died, I told him to tell me straight away.

I could do nothing about Lizzie till her father's visit to the Dunker house this afternoon, and I'd speak to Emily face-to-face about her husband's dress-sense after that. Sarah might get confirmation of my cross-dressing theory in the meantime, if she chose to help.

She'd called me first thing, enthusing about some TV show which I really mustn't miss, and got huffy when I said I'd had quite enough amateur theatricals for this year, thank you very much. Her attempt to sweeten it did not make me all a-tremble.

'But no, listen Dominic Mayford's famous!' she said. 'He's …'

'So are lots of people I've no interest in,' I cut in, suddenly empathising with Emily Dunker's view of all thing's thespian. 'Besides, my partner fell over her own feet and left me to pick up the slack so I'm a bit busy. Seeing John Nash for one thing so unless it's of vital importance, Sarah, I'll give it a miss!'

'Oh, well. It's not *vital* so please yourself,' she said. 'But you'll wish you had!'

That gloating note crept in. She knew something that I didn't, something that gave her the upper hand.

I'd crawl through broken glass before I'd ask.

I turned to my first task: getting the dog's medical records.

GLANCING AT THE EMPTY STAFF CAR PARK AT THE VET, I FELT the gods might be against me, but was cheered by a text from Nate. Parking ticket was "green light".

Kathleen's greeting smile was at low wattage this morning. I suspected she'd been told to guard her tongue.

'Mr Kitson's out till after ten on house calls and it's more than my job's worth to hand out information.'

'What about the pink-haired nurse? She assisted with the surgery. Maybe she could help.'

'Last minute holiday.' She sniffed. 'Alright for some, swanning off to Spain.' Perhaps it was envy making her prickly.

I was about to slink away and had reached the door, turning to say *I'll be back* then hesitated. A bit too Arnie? As I was reconsidering my parting shot, Val Church came into view along the corridor. I opened my mouth, then stopped. She looked different.

Her hair was no longer the vibrant magenta that had first caught my eye. Her face was paler too. She stopped between the reception desk and the door where I was standing. She spoke silently to someone who wasn't there then walked back towards the consulting rooms.

I could see right through her.

'Oh, I'll be back,' I said, no longer caring who I sounded like, because if Val was in Torremolinos, I was in Timbuctoo.

Chapter Forty-Five

I left the waiting room and wandered around the building, restless, waiting for Kitson to show up.

That custard-yellow car crumpled in a ditch came to mind. Was Val distracted because she knew I'd come back to talk to her sooner or later? Did she panic and do something stupid to herself, or did someone do it for her and if so, why?

The dripping ghost of Gail Monterey surfaced from the dark depths of my mind. One death on my conscience was more than enough, but whatever happened to the vet nurse, I'd take an even bet her death was no coincidence.

By the back door, the St Bernard's ghost wandered around the car park, looking lost. Val's spirit stopped to rub his head then entered the code on the storeroom door and went inside. Habit stored the numbers in my head. She must have done that a thousand times. I wondered again about echoes of life.

Lizzie Nash was more than an echo. The heating failure, the slamming door, and her touch on my face that had begun the root-canal ache once more. Kitson had questions to answer about her too, but more flies with honey than with vinegar as they say. I'd try to play nice.

Eventually, his car swung around the corner. I stomped back to the waiting room with the Monty authorisation in my hand. The magic key.

The two ghost Bassets were still playing tag around the waiting room, but stopped, ghostly tongues lolling, eyes on Kitson as he paused at the counter long enough for Kathleen to explain my interest.

'You'd better come through.' He stood aside so I could precede him along the corridor. His door had an impressive array of letters etched under his name on a brass plate. I caught the scent of sweet cologne as I passed him. Too sweet, like funeral lilies hiding something grim.

He waved me to the chair beside the desk. Black leather upholstery sighed as he sank into his own. He looked a little deflated this morning. A heavier weight than gravity seemed dragging at his eyes and mouth.

His desk was uncluttered: a sleek computer, a wire tray with incoming post, a recent copy of *Vet Times*. The only personal item was a model of a bell. The sort of bell that hangs in church towers while a voice lisps *Esmerelda* and a town goes up in flames. He saw me looking as he started to log in. 'Liberty Bell. Memento of my salad days.'

'Philadelphia?' I said, placing the faint accent at last, and flicking to a fresh page in my notebook. 'You're American?'

'No, just lived there for a while.' He glanced at my poised pen, perhaps deciding now was not the time to reminisce. He clicked the mouse and nodded at the screen. 'Kathleen will print you a copy of the records to take away, but I'll need to look at the file. My memory isn't what it was.'

The wry twist of his mouth invited disbelief. I was inclined to disbelieve a lot more than his bad memory. The window behind him framed Val's ghost who stopped once again to rub the St Bernard's head.

'Perhaps your vet nurse might remember?'

His smile dimmed a little. He cleared his throat. 'Ah, Val's on annual leave but ... here we go.' He pointed at the screen. 'The medical jargon might be a little hard to decipher so why don't you just ask, and I'll explain.'

'I'm sure I can get someone to translate if necessary,' I said. 'Did you realise straight away the dog had been run over?'

He tilted his head. 'I'm not sure what you mean. Alice herself explained what happened.'

'Did she? I thought it was another woman who called ahead.'

'We logged a phone call ...' He glanced at the screen, 'but it was Alice, I'm almost sure, who told us he'd been hit by a speeding vehicle.'

'Who took the initial call?'

'That would be me.'

'Don't you use an out-of-hours emergency service?'

'We do, but I live here,' he pointed at the ceiling. 'If I'm here working late, sometimes I pick up on autopilot, and if I've already answered I can hardly tell a client to go elsewhere.' He shrugged.

'Did you recognise the caller's voice?'

'No. Is there any reason I should?'

My pen moved steadily across the page. 'What did she say, exactly?'

'Just that Alice's dog had been in an accident and could they bring him in.' He shrugged again.

'She knew it was Alice's dog?'

'Ah, oh. I'm not really sure ...' He blinked at the screen but found no answer.

The poor memory. Convenient. I went back a step. 'You said Alice told you it was a speeding vehicle?'

He sighed softly. 'I may have been mistaken. My focus was on getting everything ready for surgery as quickly as possible. A few minutes can make all the difference. Perhaps the caller gave me the details …'

'You were certain before he arrived, he'd need surgery?'

He nodded. 'Ah, yes, so the caller must have told me something because I was preparing the theatre. A collision with a moving vehicle might mean broken bones – pelvis is the common one – or liver or kidney damage and so forth. The faster we can get the patient triaged the better.' He touched a key. The visuals changed shape and colour, too dense for me to read. He was confident now, on solid ground. 'We did all the usual things on arrival – electrolytes, blood chemistry, haematology and so forth. The test results are all here.' He angled the screen further towards me.

I ignored it, watched his face.

'Alice said he was out cold.'

He raised a hand to smooth the furrow between his brows. 'He never regained consciousness, I'm afraid.'

'Did he have head injuries?'

'No, but blood loss would cause a shut-down …'

'Alice said he wasn't bleeding.' I cut in. 'Not from anywhere at all. No blood loss.'

'That's not …' He stopped, took a breath and spoke again more quietly. 'He *was* bleeding. Internally, I'm afraid. Much more serious, and rather more than we'd expected as it happens. We concentrated on that rather than any minor abrasions which, I am certain, must have been there.'

Except they weren't. No blood on Alice's clothes, or her car. Any proof was gone, ashes round the chapel's roses. And he was "afraid" a lot. Verbal tic or subconscious tell?

I looked at my notes. 'Did you give him drugs?' Usage must be monitored to make sure no one was making a little extra on the side.

'Hartmann's – there were no contra indications so that's standard. Nothing else.' His gaze was steady but the mix in that syringe must have meant a bit of fudging somewhere. 'Not until we'd finished the assessment and the surgery was underway – then yes, of course, sedation and pain relief.' His palms opened towards the screen. 'It's all recorded.'

'If he didn't wake up, why would he need pain killers?'

He held up a forefinger like my maths teacher when I defined pi as perfect with chips. 'It reduces post-operative pain if we give it during surgery. Any vet would do the same.'

That sounded like he'd expected the dog to wake up, but that thought took me nowhere.

Back to basics.

'What was cause of death?'

'In layman's terms, his heart stopped. He was probably thrown a distance, so his internal organs were ...' He shifted in his chair and shook his head very slightly. 'I thought he was going to make it, but the bleeding was ... well, we simply couldn't get it under control. But I don't see how this helps you.'

Neither did I. Nothing made sense, but I needed something to prove the dog had not been injured. 'Broken bones though – you took x-rays?' I caught the slight hesitation before he confirmed they had. 'So, they could establish the height of the car bumper from where the breaks were.'

He shook his head. 'He could have been thrown over the bonnet, or clipped by a wheel or well, landing causes fractures too. Forgive me, but I don't think you'd find them useful.'

'Still,' I said. 'I'd like to see them.'

His jaw tightened and a small tic jumped in his cheek. 'It's the interpretation that's in the file – that's what the client pays for. The original images seem to have been mislaid. Of course, if they'd help, I'd try to find them but ...' he shrugged. 'They'll tell you nothing.'

They'd already told me he didn't do x-rays. They'd told me he knew why Monty had gone under his knife – and that meant Val knew too. Now she was dead.

Val's ghost crossed the yard at the back, stopped to rub the St Bernard's head. Film on a loop.

Kitson steepled his hands and rested his chin on his fingertips.

'I'd like to speak to Val.' I said. 'Do you know where she's gone?'

'Off to sunny Spain on some last-minute impulse, so she said. Leaves me at the mercy of the agency but what can you do?' While he was speaking his blink rate increased. A good liar; not a great one.

'When's she due back?'

'Couple of weeks.' He glanced at his watch. 'Look, I'm sorry but I have another appointment so ...' He got to his feet and held out his hand. I took it. It was clammy. His cologne was working overtime.

'Just one more thing, before I go.' I paused, so I could be sure I had his full attention. 'How well did you know Lizzie Nash?'

Chapter Forty-Six

A lice found their seats, so happy Pops had swung the third ticket. Sarah sat back, watching cameras gliding around, steered by industrious people wearing over-sized earphones, while Alice checked Emily had the best view.

'I can't believe I thought my Brian was having an affair!' Emily peered with interest at the technicians running about the stage adjusting this and that, or just muttering into mouthpieces while lights changed intensity and colour.

Alice kept her thoughts to herself. Brian was an idiot – all that stupid secrecy – but she was keeping her fingers crossed that he would do well – and Pops would be none the wiser about her involvement in Brian's transformation.

It was a big night for Pops, too. Now her phone buzzed and displayed his number. She fought against the tide of spectators flowing in, till she found a space where she could hear what he was saying.

'It's madness, sweetie. Total chaos back here. I need to hear the voice of sanity for a moment. Did you persuade your lady love to come? Shall I blow you both a kiss?'

He's nervous, she realised with surprise. 'Sarah's here, Pops, and we'll be cheering loudest at the best act of them all. Just be your fab self. You'll knock their socks off!'

'Of course, my darling – though my fans prefer stockings or so they claim.'

A voice in the background said, 'Five minutes, Mr Mayford,' and Alice heard her father's murmured thanks, then the rustle of movement.

'Time to get this show on the road, sweetie. See you on the other side.'

'Break a leg!' she said, and then the line went dead.

Back in the auditorium, the noise level had risen, with an air of expectancy as two o'clock approached. The crew had found their starting places. A few empty seats remained here and there, but last-minute arrivals were scurrying in to claim them.

Alice slipped into her aisle seat and exhaled. She felt she'd been running hard.

'Everything okay?' Sarah asked.

'It's all madness back there, Pops says. I think he has a touch of stage-fright.' She shifted her weight and crossed her legs, bumping Sarah's in the process. 'Sorry, I'm almost as nervous as he is.'

'Not as nervous as me,' said Emily Dunker from the seat the other side of Sarah. 'I don't know whether to hope Brian wins or hope he doesn't – but if I'd realised it meant so much …'

Emily certainly looked the most worried; her eyes were practically popping, and her hands moved constantly. She looked amazing though. Alice had enjoyed doing her make-over. Sarah's too – the black eyes were still there, but you had to get close to see them.

Getting closer was what Alice was hoping for, and why

she'd let her in on Brian's secret, but right now Sarah's thoughts seemed elsewhere.

'I don't know what Penny's going to say when she finds out I told you about an ongoing case,' Sarah said. 'She'll probably murder me.'

'I don't see why. You've solved the mystery – and the client is happy. Aren't you, Emily?'

'If it's anyone's fault,' said Emily, not quite answering the question, 'it's Brian's. All this cloak and dagger stuff.'

'He didn't want to worry you, and he thought you'd disapprove,' Alice said.

'I do! But that would have been better than keeping it secret and driving me half-crazy.'

Not for me, thought Alice, but she said mildly. 'You were crazy enough to have him investigated. You could have just asked.'

'Yes, well,' Emily shifted under Alice's gaze, 'that wasn't really my idea.'

Sudden hush descended as the house lights faded, and the cue was given for applause. The whooping reached a crescendo as a figure tripped lightly into the spotlight. A small, wiry-haired man wearing an oversized shirt, his face cut with deep-cut lines, seemed weary as he took the mike off its stand and waited for the noise to die. The "applause" sign changed to "silence". The audience obeyed.

'Warm up,' Alice muttered to Sarah behind her hand, drawing a stern look from the official patrolling the aisle.

Some blue-ish jokes in a Billy Connelly accent issued from the stage, then came the big build up. 'Your host for the evening, gi' a humungous Haston welcome to the amazin', the fabulous … Miss. Dee. D'Vine.'

Cue cards were held up and the whoopers and callers went into overdrive as Pops sashayed onto the stage to the opening bars of Jolene, resplendent in Alice's latest creation. The sea-green gown was sculpted to the hyper-feminised figure and showed off a décolletage few could wear so well. Alice felt a thrill of pride.

Dee stood well over seven feet tall, but she didn't need height to dominate – she was magnetic. She launched into a throatily tuneful version of the Dolly Parton number, breaking off now and then to relate what she'd do to any woman who might try to steal her man. The audience lapped it up.

Sarah leaned close to whisper, 'Amazing! I'd never have recognised him!'

'Hello, Haston,' Dee purred in a dusky voice as the applause faded. 'How are you all tonight?' She paused. 'Such a pleasure to be here at the fabulous Pavilion Theatre.' Her nails were talons as she opened her arms to encompass the rococo-style surroundings. 'We were offered the Jolly Roger – and all the nice girls love a sailor, don't we, ladies?' She arched an eyebrow and peeped at the audience sideways through jewelled lashes, 'I bet you wouldn't turn down a bit of jolly rogering, would you, darling?' She pointed at a man in the first row and hoots went up around him. 'Lovely boy! See me later,' she said and blew him a kiss. 'But the Pavilion has the best address – the top of Queen's Parade – and queens just adore a parade. Isn't that right?'

The audience, more than half in full drag, went wild. Stomping their stilettos and cheering madly while the cameras panned around.

'Tonight though, it's all about who's going to come out on top in our wonderful contest – tonight, on this very stage, we are immensely excited to introduce the superstars of the future. But only the very best will go through to the National finals. The prizes there will be staggering: not only a stunning wardrobe by Valentina Harper Couture; not only a fabulous wig selection from Diva Hair Inc; not only a year's supply of cosmetics by Bea Hind, but also,' her voice dropped from the rising crescendo to a low purr, 'fifty thousand pounds.'

She waited for calm, 'And the best prize of all – drumroll please – a year's contract with the number one international theatrical agency, Eleganzah Elite Management.

'So, there is everything to play for and back-stage our contestants are warming up and getting their nerves under control. Let's just have a little peek.'

Attention switched to the huge screen showing competitors nervously primping backstage. Alice scanned the faces but couldn't spot Brian. A chirpy girl with a Claudia Winkleman haircut collected one-liners from would-be superstars, while the crew did incomprehensible things with bits of tech.

Dee dusted her face with a huge brush. She waggled her fingers at them before the action returned to the live stage.

Dee introduced the panel: Rikki Karn, soap star and tabloid darling; Demi Golden, body activist and plus-size model; Jett Lux, record producer; and Paul Westlake, one half of comedy duo Westlake and Breeze, whose acrimonious split left him free to join the celebrity circuit on his first solo gig.

The first hopeful stepped out. The competition was underway.

In the first round, each contestant had two minutes to sing or lip-synch followed by feedback from the judges and the scores. A board displayed a running total. Dee D'Vine updated the overall positions to camera with much milking of the drama.

Brian came on last. Alice waited for his entrance, torn with the same hope and fear she saw on Emily's face. Pops gave the build up from the autocue mentioning Marilyn curves and trade-mark pout, a talented beauty with a voice to die for.

'So please give your warmest welcome to – Miss. Honey. Trapp.'

Emily sat forward, hands clasped between her knees until the cue, then she clapped with so much enthusiasm Alice wondered if she might do her hands some damage.

Several of the audience leapt to their feet as, on stage, Honey paused for a heartbeat, basking in the moment. Noise thundered around the auditorium, and the cause of it all held out her arms to embrace her public. She shimmied on strappy heels to the microphone centre stage. The hours of practice that made her sway effortless paid off. In the spotlight, resplendent in the perfectly fitted gown, her make-up flawless, Honey Trapp looked every inch a star.

And the final touch – the neat goatee, powdered to pure white and twinkling with diamond lights. It dazzled around the scarlet lips and this crowd loved it. She swung into *Don't Rain on my Parade* – her voice swooping effortlessly through the notes. The audience went wild, stomping and cheering.

The reaction might have been helped by pre-theatre alcohol filtering in bloodstreams but, even so, Miss Honey Trapp was a class act.

The judges were fulsome, Dee D'Vine air-kissed her cheeks and, as Honey left the stage, the crew sprang forward to do the reset. Honey was second on the leader board. The second round – the comedy slot – would decide the winner.

Emily was pale under her make-up. 'He's …'

'Amazing!' completed Sarah, squeezing the woman's arm. 'Miles above the others – and I don't just mean the heels.'

'You've no idea how hard he's worked!' Alice chipped in. 'And the dieting, and the exercise plan – you can pad the extra, but if you still want to breathe, even corsetry has its limits.' She laughed. 'All those pier walks paid off!'

Emily shook her head. 'I thought he was wanting to look good for, you know ...'

'A new love? Not a chance, Emily. He adores you!'

Emily's breath huffed. 'Not enough to tell me the truth, though.'

'He was ...'Alice stopped, unsure of how to explain. 'He was a bit afraid, I think.'

'Of me? That's absurd!'

'For you,' Alice said, gently. 'You'd been under a lot of stress with the house move and the baby and everything and he was worried ...'

'About my state of mind,' Emily finished.

Sarah squeezed Emily's hand. 'Penny will sort it out,' she said.

'What's left to sort out?' said Alice.

'The heating,' said Sarah quickly. 'Penny knows a very good plumber.'

The audience was called to order, cameras rolled again, but even as the second half got underway, Alice wondered why the temperature of her house affected Emily's state of mind.

The contestant order reversed in the second half, so Honey Trapp went first. The audience laughed and heckled good-naturedly around them, and Honey's adlib talent was tested and approved. She 'read' the judges perfectly, a blend of insult and humour that had them laughing at themselves and when scores were done, only one act could rob Honey Trapp of the prize. Shantay Awayday had timing, excellent material and a large following in the crowd. The judges gave their feedback, the numbers were crunched.

Alice's nightmare became reality. The scores were tied. Pops would make the final choice.

'What are you going to do?' asked Sarah.

'About what?' said Emily, her face alight with excitement.

Alice couldn't answer. She was listening to the announcement. There would be a lip-synch challenge to help Ms Vine make her decision. Both contestants were preparing backstage.

'Meanwhile, for your delectation and delight, we are going to show the audition tapes for both of our finalists to you, our live audience and to our tie-break judge, so you can see the amazing journey these two contestants have already made.'

'Oh no,' said Alice.

Sarah and Emily stared at her. 'Monty's on that tape,' she whispered, 'and it's too late to tell Pops now.' All these months of telling Brian to come clean – why hadn't she taken her own advice? Pops would recognise her darling boy, and the workroom where Brian had made his tape and the revelation would be in public view.

The audition tape came on the screen. Monty stared into the camera, and moments later Dee D'Vine's dramatic faint went viral.

A runner summoned Alice to the dressing room.

Chapter Forty-Seven

P ops was half lying on the sofa under a coverlet, a water glass on the table beside him, his wig and dress on their stands as Alice hurried into his dressing room.

'Pops, are you okay?'

She perched beside him and he asked everyone to give them some space.

'Honestly, darlings, I'll be fine.' He was all calm reassurance and Alice felt like sinking into the floor as he spoke to those hovering. 'I don't know what came over me but I'm already much better. Just give me a few minutes to recover, lovely people.'

As the door closed behind the last of them, he turned his serious face to her.

'I'm so sorry, Pops.'

'I can see that, sweetie. You're paler than your girlfriend.' He sighed. 'I don't want my swansong to be a fit of the vapours and I've a horrid feeling I may have overacted – but I cannot announce a winner, my darling, until I know what's going on.'

Damn, now she was going to cry. He was being kind – as if she didn't feel guilty enough. The truth came tumbling out.

'Brian – Honey – had put so much into it – the preparation and the practise sessions and everything. He was so good – a real chance – and I couldn't tell him to withdraw – but then, but then – you got the job and your career and … and you weren't *supposed* to be judging.'

He sighed again. 'Honestly Alice, did you never think to just tell me? I might have been able to clear it with the producers – it's not as if *I* have a relationship with him and there's no rule about who designs his costumes.' Her father pursed his lips. 'Now it is a tiny bit tricky. If it comes out later that you're his dress designer …'

'Bit more than just his costumes, I'm afraid.'

'You'd better come clean.'

'It was because of you – actually. I mean, I've known him for ages – I buy most of my fabrics from his company, and one day he mentioned he'd seen you in a show. I boasted a bit – okay, a lot – and said how we'd worked on your make-over for Vegas.

'So, when he wanted to go in for this, he asked for my help, so I agreed to coach him. Design the make-up and make him some outfits and be his personal trainer too – sort of Jill of all trades. He swore me to secrecy so if it was a disaster Emily – his wife – would never have to know.'

'His wife doesn't know?'

'Didn't – until today.'

'I thought you wanted the extra ticket for Sarah's sister!' He sighed.

'Sorry – but the thing is, Brian's been trying out at open nights around the clubs, but this break would make all the difference – and he has a child. Dressing up in amateur panto is one thing, but he's not sure how his daughter will react to drag – especially if her mother thinks it's weird – but now Emily's seen for herself how good he is.'

'Weird is only what critics say until you make it, sweetie, after that it's "werking it". As for daughters whose fathers wear dresses for a living,' he squeezed her hand. 'They can surprise you. Still, this is a conundrum. How are we to get out of it, and still get your friend what he deserves?'

He threw off the cover and got to his feet. 'Let's see what I can do.'

ALICE SLID BACK INTO THE SEAT NEXT TO SARAH AS DEE D'Vine returned to the stage.

The welcoming rapture faded, and Dee purred in the spotlight. 'Thank you all so much for being patient while I had my needs attended to – don't be naughty, you in the front row, or I'll invite you backstage with me next time – and what would your wife say?'

'Now, darlings. I really don't feel up to making the big decision – whichever I choose, someone is going to hate me.' Dee held the back of one hand up to her forehead in the classic tragic pose. 'I simply can't bear it. But seriously,' she took her hand away, 'In our midst tonight is a much better judge of talent than little ol' me, and he has kindly agreed to help me out. Please give your warmest Haston welcome to CEO of our generous sponsor, Eleganzah Elite Management. Mr Johnny Richards.'

Alice could hardly bear to watch as the two contestants sang their numbers then, after a horribly tense moment, the man with all the power made the decision.

Honey Trapp stood dazed and glowing in the spotlight, the winner's crown perched on her curls as Emily applauded wildly.

The cameras panned round again, then came an announcement. They needed to rerun a couple of the links, and the audience were instructed to wait until they were released.

'What did you mean before?' Sarah asked Emily as they all subsided back into their seats and the immediate excitement had been subdued by watching the stage reset again.

'When?'

'When you said hiring Penny wasn't really your idea.'

Chapter Forty-Eight

I was consoling myself with a hazelnut latte and a large éclair in my favourite café after reading Emily Dunker's text. My two-clock appointment was no more.

Plumber postponed. Something's come up.

I'd have to wait another day to see Lizzie with her father – and after Kitson's reaction I was even more intrigued.

I was inclined to believe Daniel Kitson about Lizzie. If his acting was that good, he'd deserve an Oscar and I'd have swallowed the rest of his lies. The phone call, the dog's death – smoke and mirrors and the nurse, too. Something there had him needing clean underpants. But about Lizzie his indignation rang as true as the Liberty Bell.

'You're working for her father?' he said after he snatched his hand away as if I'd set fire to it.

I said nothing.

'She was just a kid, and I felt sorry for her,' he said, his chin rising. 'She was bright and had an empathy for the animals so why not encourage her ambitions?' His index finger stabbed towards me, 'And that was all I was doing. I was never alone with her. I made damned sure there were always other people around and yes, she had a bit of a crush – but I never did anything to encourage that. In fact, as soon as I realised how it was going, I made it very clear she had to keep her distance.'

'How did she take that?'

'None of your goddamned business.'

'When did you have this conversation?'

'Still none of your business.'

'What if I told you her death was down to stress?'

'Not true. No one knows what makes a kid have a fit. The coroner was absolutely clear. No. One's. Fault.' He glared. 'Now I think it's time you left, but you can tell John Nash he'll not be getting a penny out of me!'

IF JOHN NASH HAD TRIED TO BLACKMAIL KITSON OVER HIS relationship with Lizzie, he hadn't got much out of it. Kitson might have lied but that grotty one bed flat in the mean streets behind Alice's house did not speak of wealth. Which was odd, because I'd always thought plumbers could pretty much write their own ticket. Divorce could be expensive though. Funerals too.

I ate the last crumb of my éclair and sipped my latte. Nash and his wife had split up after Lizzie's death – perhaps Barbara took all the money. She had a good job. According to Lizzie's friend she was a doctor of some sort, but Barbara's name had not shown up on the medical register. A researcher at the Biotech Analytica lab according to Emily Dunker. Not a medical doctor, but it must pay pretty well.

I remembered from years ago, some controversy about

that lab – animal experiments came to mind. Barbara's father did something with "mouse models" that sounded nasty. Perhaps that was where his daughter's talents lay.

Googling Biotech, I checked the websites for vegan vitriol, but came up empty. No animals at risk; they tested drugs on humans. They covered cardio-vascular, renal, and metabolic trials right through to annual flu camps. Their website assured me risks were minimal and, if I cared to join a trial, my time would be generously compensated, with a full medical thrown in, and I'd be doing the world a service.

I was glad I had other priorities right now.

Was Val's death an accident, I wondered? Kitson had seemed tired and edgy and the "lost" x-rays sent alarm bells ringing. I'd take a bet he knew her holiday was a lie – but it was a long way from a dog's death to murder – especially of his own assistant.

How did she die? No accident reported, no unidentified bodies found according to the news. Of course, some don't surface quickly, especially the drowned.

The sea was always one of my first thoughts. Had she gone down to the pier in a fit of remorse about Monty's death? The railings were waist high, but no trouble to the determined. But why would she – and why now. Much more likely she was silenced.

If Kitson had done away with her, drugs seemed a likely choice. Even on controlled ones there must be some sort of 'wastage' allowance. Bottles break, needles snap, pills are dropped and crushed underfoot.

Only, theft of a dog was no worse in law than that of a laptop, the usual penalty community service or a small fine. Intentionally caused its death? A couple of years in jail. Not worth murder, surely. And then he'd have Val's body to get rid of.

Why would he take that risk?

I stared at the crumbs on my plate, getting nowhere, searching for distraction.

Sarah's phone went to voice mail. Then I remembered she was at some show this afternoon – she'd have turned off her phone. She was supposed to rest but she'd never done what she was told so that was no surprise.

That made me think of hospitals, so I phoned the General to see how Frieda was doing, hoping she wasn't tormenting herself over Lizzie's death and that the ghost of her cat was bringing comfort. Not a relative so I could get limited information, but they did confirm she was resting comfortably, whatever that meant. Hanging on, I guess. ·

Thoughts hopped from one topic to the next. From tabby cats to mournful looking hounds.

Bassets – a sudden thought. Sick Bassets. Helen Pinnesari and her stud dog!

I tracked down the number I wanted. Fresh-faced Evan answered on the second ring.

'Yeah, Rudi died yesterday,' he confirmed. 'Mrs P's in bits. She's locked herself away.'

Nothing to gain by going there, but most ghosts show up for a reason.

I was stuck. Lizzie Nash and Val Church, Bassets and Brian Dunker. Stymied on the lot of them. At times like this I wish I had more hobbies.

Later, in the early evening, I stared at the cracked ceiling to escape the prizewinning literary novel I'd mistaken for entertainment. My thoughts meandered back to Kitson and his vet nurse. He had the means and the opportunity.

He was well thought of. His charity work, a busy practice … and a successful lifestyle to protect. He was hiding something, and now there were two dead hounds. If Val had threatened his reputation, or if it meant he'd lose his licence, would he kill to keep them?

Her ghost seemed on a loop, but still, it didn't mean I should ignore it. And why the St Bernard? Put peacefully to sleep, he'd likely end up cremated, scattered somewhere, mourned by his loving owner: why would he hang around?

Only ... a human body was hard to dispose of ... but who worried about a dog disposed of in a shallow grave? No one, unless it's yours!

What were the chances the St Bernard was not the waste waiting for disposal in that outhouse?

My brain sparked like a fuse before the bomb goes boom.

If Kitson was a murderer, there might still be time to keep the victim from going up in smoke.

Chapter Forty-Nine

J eff Smithson was a disappointment to his mother. While
most of his family kept defence barristers' wigs from
getting dusty, Jeff went to the dark side. He joined the
police.

Over the years he'd risen slightly higher than unleavened
bread. He made it from police constable to detective constable. He'd got there through determination and a working
knowledge of the best bacon butties in town.

We'd helped each other out a time or two.

'Evening, all,' I said when he picked up the call.

'If it isn't that bad Penny turning up again.' His voice was
not exactly warm, but it was a bit fuzzy. 'Wa's happening on
your mean streets?'

'Something big and nasty. You free?'

'Cheapish,' he chuckled. 'Blacksmith's Arms, half an
hour?'

'More beer than blood in your veins already from the
sound of it. I'll swing by and pick you up.'

'You can stand me a decent malt for that remark. As I won't be driving.'

I blew a raspberry down the phone.

'Fair enough,' he said. 'A pint'll do to start.' He inhaled audibly, then started to cough. Marlboro – I could almost smell it. I tried not to imagine thumping his back. Hard. It was easier when I remembered we weren't actually going to the pub. He'd be heading for AA one day soon.

AA! I suddenly remembered Lizzie's father and the "supermarket tokens" in that beautiful glass bowl. Not tokens but sobriety chips – different colours for different time periods. A quick tap into the internet showed me the symbol for AA – it matched the pendant he'd draped over his daughter's photo. He'd taken the pledge.

DC Jeff Smithson might one day do the same. He didn't quite lurch to the car, but it wasn't far off. What with the beer and the smoke and the dead badger he must've had for supper, his breath fell through the door before him. I was glad we weren't on mwah, mwah terms – cheek to cheek would need a gas mask.

'This about Sarah?' he said as he tried to fit his bulk into the passenger seat.

'Why, what's she done?'

'Har, bloody har! Even if she was pushed in that backyard, there's not much hope of catching the scrote. Some doper from over the back alley, probably.'

I wondered if he was out of the loop, or whether Sarah hadn't got around to mentioning her non-attack. Better remind her next time we spoke. They might have better things to do, like catching murderers, maybe.

'Something else happening,' I said. 'Much bigger.' The more I'd thought, the more I was convinced Val's ghost was heading into that storeroom for a reason. I needed someone with a legitimate purpose to make the discovery.

We pulled up a turn away from Kitson's surgery and Jeff listened as I explained.

'You'll still owe me a pint,' he said.

'Get the credit for solving a murder before it's even been reported, and I reckon you'll owe me one.'

He grinned. 'Fair dos and all I have to do is wander by this vet's parking area and take a decko?'

'If I'm not back in ten minutes, stroll past and keep your eyes peeled.' I said as I collected a shapeless dark coat and a baseball cap off the back seat.

He crossed his arms over his stomach and closed his eyes. I wondered if it might be better to take him with me but it's tricky asking a copper to watch you trespass.

'Go'orn,' he said, tapping his temple, eyes still closed. 'I've set me alarm.'

Tugging the cap low, I went.

Surgery hours said they'd shut at five today. There were no lights on the ground floor, or the flat above. No cars in the car park. Just the loop of Val and the St Bernard. I hoped that meant whoever collected the pet corpses hadn't been and gone.

Once past the parking barrier, the security light blazed, and the camera's on-light blinked from above the back door. All it would capture was an average person in a baseball cap. I nipped into the shadow of the wheelie bins and hoped any watcher would assume a cat or rat had tripped the sensor.

Val came and went. Nothing else went by. I nudged the bin nearer the doorway until, as long as I kept low, it screened me from casual passers-by. The main building remained dark. I hoped it was as empty as it looked.

The numbers on the keypad surfaced in my memory on

command, but I froze when the door unlocked with a clunk. Nerves pricked the back of my neck. I waited.

Nothing moved. No lights came on at windows. No one raised an alarm. After an age I breathed again and slipped inside.

Three red eyes, each one paired with a green, stared like devil cats. Three different locations. Two at ankle height, one stared me in the face. My palms were slippery inside my gloves and the torch was small, but I held it steady. No one blinked as I lit a bright circle on the concrete floor.

My devil cats were a tall fridge, a chest freezer and one huge walk-in that might be either. Power was red, thermostat was green.

I opened the fridge first. Bottles, cardboard boxes, bags of clear liquid. Not what I was looking for. I moved on.

Lifting the creaky chest freezer lid revealed a multitude of packages in different colours. I moved a few, but nothing here was big enough. I closed it again.

Reaching for the handle of the walk-in, I took a breath, and pulled. The door opened silently. What no Hammer horror screech?

Air stirred behind me and as I turned something bumped my shoulder. The smell of leather, it's taste against my teeth. I bit.

'Jesus wept!' hissed Jeff, pulling his injured hand away.

'Idiot!' I hissed back.

He grimaced, evil incarnate, my torch beam under his chin. 'Would've been funny if you hadn't of chewed me fingers off.' He nodded to the huge plastic bag, bone white in the freezer's own cold light. 'That it?'

I read the label. Carroch. St Bernard. 55.3 kilos and a reference number. 'Only one way to find out.'

I put the torch between my teeth and punched a small

hole with my penknife whose blade was legal – just. Slitting the plastic wrapping slowly, I concentrated on keeping a straight line. I was not that keen to see her in the flesh.

Jeff crowded me away and the bag rustled in his hands. His horrified expression made me wish I'd chosen some other course. I steeled my nerves and risked a look.

Bleached to grey in the torchlight part of the corpse had been revealed, and it was a dreadful sight. My stomach flipped and tried to rise through my throat. I had exposed a vision that would haunt my nightmares for a long, long time.

One giant frosted paw.

Chapter Fifty

Brian and Emily had been whisked away for interviews by the TV crew and the party was breaking up. Alice put down her glass. Even make-up couldn't disguise Sarah's pallor now, and an evening of celebration was not what the doctor ordered.

'Let's go,' said Alice, steering Sarah towards the cloakroom. 'You look done in.'

'I am a bit. Wasn't it wonderful though – and now the national finals!' Sarah accepted her coat from the attendant. 'Amazing for Brian – and his outfits were gorgeous. You must feel a little bit 'enery 'iggins.'

'As long as I don't look like him!' Alice laughed, shrugging into her mac and lifting her hair from under the collar.

Sarah giggled. 'I mean it, Alice, take a bow. Brian said he couldn't have done it without you.'

'Maybe, but his voice won it really – and that's not down to me.' They walked out into the crisp air of early evening. 'The woman in the pink top, she's responsible for the husky drawl. She's a voice coach now. They used to do a double act at uni, with Brian in drag and Karina as the frumpy friend in Huddersfield's equivalent of Footlights. I wish I'd seen that.'

Sarah took her arm and chatted on as they walked across the car park. 'Perhaps they'll recreate it when he's famous – as long as his wife agrees. Brian looked almost as thrilled with Emily being there as he was with the win.' Sarah paused. 'How did you change her mind?'

'Oh, I didn't change it,' said Alice lightly, unlocking the car. 'She accepted Brian's not having an affair with me – I explained why – but said this was all a waste of time and money and he should stick to sales.' Alice folded herself into the driving seat.

'Did you persuade her how good he is?' Sarah clicked her seatbelt into place.

'Hardly.' Alice put the car in gear. 'I pointed out that when Brian failed miserably, he'd be pretty devastated but a loving wife cheering him on could help him see life's not all "A Star is Born". But if she wasn't supportive – well, no one likes "I told you so" from their nearest and dearest, and by the way, did she know his voice coach had taken "Honey" to an open-mic last month – and Karina's such a lovely woman.'

'Manipulation, Miss Mayford!' Sarah laughed. 'And Karina was more interested in catching your eye than his.'

'Emily didn't know that.' Alice grinned as she turned onto the main road. 'Of course, now he's won, Emily's worried everyone will think he's the gay one – but she'll get over it. Once she starts to meet the trans queens and female queens and every other sort of queen, she'll realise how amazingly all-encompassing drag is.'

By the time they reached home, Sarah's liveliness had faded into silence.

'Why don't you go straight up?' Alice suggested as they took off their coats. 'I'll bring you a hot drink if you like.'

'It's a long time since I was sent to bed at eight o'clock, Alice!'

She sounded like a grumpy child, but perhaps now was not the time to joke about it, nor to mention how tired she looked.

'The doctor said you weren't to overdo it, though. Just a thought.' Alice trailed Sarah into the lounge.

She was wondering whether to go up to her workroom in the hope Sarah might doze on the sofa if she were left alone or stay to keep an eye on her, when the doorbell rang.

Penny stood on the doorstep, looking almost as weary as her sister.

'Come on in. Sarah's through there,' said Alice, adding quietly. 'Perhaps you can persuade her to follow doctor's orders and get some rest.'

'Sarah follow orders?' Penny snorted, but when she saw her sister, she seemed to take the idea more seriously.

'You should call it a day before you keel over, sis – you're pale as a ghost.'

'You should know!'

The sharp response caused a sudden pause but as Alice perched on the sofa arm beside her, Sarah went on more softly.

'And you're a fine one to talk, Pen – have you looked in the mirror lately?'

Penny dropped into the armchair opposite and sighed. 'It's been a long day, and,' she shot a swift glance at Sarah, 'thinking of things ghostly, that vet nurse with the pink hair has done a disappearing act. A last minute holiday apparently – but I have my suspicions, and yes,' she cut in as Sarah opened her mouth, 'it's because I can't trace anyone who knows where she's gone – and I think she may have used that syringe in the garden to drug your dog, Alice, then scarpered before you could recognise her. Then there's another dead Basset in the mix.' She pushed on without explaining how she knew. 'The posh Pinnesari male, I think.'

'Rudi died?' said Alice. 'What a shame c'

'Do you know his owner?'

'I've met her a time or two.'

'Damn,' Penny brushed her hair out of her eyes again. 'I was hoping you could ask what was wrong with him.'

Alice thought for a moment. 'Pops knows her a bit. He got Monty from her, but they aren't close friends or anything ... still he might be able to find out something.'

'If anyone can charm it out of her, I expect he can.' Sarah grinned.

'Great, can you ask him now, Alice?'

'I'll text, but I doubt he'll answer. He's celebrating.'

'Oh, right,' said Penny. 'Your dad's show went okay then?'

'Brilliant – and Brian won! It was so exciting, and Emily was thrilled to bits.'

Penny blinked and stared at her sister.

Sarah shrugged. 'You should have been there, Pen. You were invited!' Then she giggled, her eyes over-bright. 'Brian's just won the regional heat of the UK's new reality contest – to find Britain's next amateur drag superstar. Alice is his coach and costume designer.'

'Well, that explains the dress and the lipstick!' Then her forehead creased. 'But who took the incriminating photo?'

'The friend who got him a gig – and shared a cheap family room at the Premier Inn. She sent the print photo so Emily wouldn't see it on his phone!'

'And she bats for our side, so it was just a joke.' Alice thought she'd better make that clear.

Penny rolled her eyes. 'Brian's a drag queen?' She shook

her head, speechless for a moment, then sighed. 'Well, now I know why Emily bailed on me this afternoon.'

'Alice got her to support him and,' Sarah smirked. 'I can clear up another mystery. Want to know why Emily hired you?'

'Other than the obvious?'

'You came highly recommended! Your admirer wanted to remain anonymous. Apparently, it's bad form to tout for business for your clients.'

'He sang your praises to me as well after Monty's funeral,' chipped in Alice. 'Said all sorts of complimentary things. He's definitely a fan – but I think he's shy.'

Exasperation gave way to understanding on Penny's face.

'Colin Palmer!' squeaked Sarah with glee. 'You used to have such a crush!'

'He's protecting the bank's investment,' Penny blustered.

Alice watched her colour rise.

Chapter Fifty-One

❦

Friday dragged itself into being. Heavy cloud shrouded the sky. Gusts kicked against fences and dustbins and tugged at the car as I drove to Emily's.

I was still coming to terms with my failings. DC Jeff Smithson had not been nearly as impressed by my detecting skills as – allegedly – Colin Palmer was.

'Penelope Wiseman, super sleuth,' Jeff had chortled as we stood looking into the vet's freezer last night. 'Just wait till the boys at the station hear about this! It'll be on a par with "body found in graveyard" – hold the front page!'

'You could keep it quiet,' I'd suggested without much hope as I tucked the St Bernard's frozen paw back inside the wrapping. 'Telling tales might backfire – you were in on it after all.'

'Nah. I was doing my duty investigating a possible crime in progress when I found you, and learned you've finally flipped!'

Reputation is all in this business and I saw mine go swirling round the pan as I trailed him to the door.

He stepped out into the flash of headlights as a car turned

into the carpark. The security light blazed again. 'Shit,' he muttered.

In his shadow, I ducked out, pulled the door closed and hunkered down behind the wheelie bins as the car door slammed.

'Evening, sir,' I heard Jeff say. 'DC Jeff Smithson. Just checking everything's secure. We've had reports of prowlers in the area.'

Either Jeff rattled the door to demonstrate its security or Kitson had approached to check.

'May I see your warrant card?' A rustle of fabric then, 'Appreciate your vigilance, officer.'

'Have a nice evening, sir.' Jeff's footsteps moved away at a measured pace.

I held my breath. Silence seemed an eternity, then the keypad beeped, and the storeroom door unlocked. White light spilled into the yard. I didn't dare move until I heard the creaking of the freezer door, then I scuttled from my hiding place and ran.

I WAS STILL WINCING AT THE MEMORY AND MY LOW MOOD seemed appropriate for seeing Lizzie's ghost face-to-face with her father at the Dunker house. Whatever happened I'd take a bet it would not be fun.

Emily was a contrast. Vibrant in a way I hadn't seen before. She whisked about getting coffee, putting biscuits on a plate, chatting cheerfully.

'Have you heard?' she said, and it seemed kinder to let her tell it all over again. How funny Brian had been; how amazing he'd looked; how talented she'd always known he was. More detail, much more – I let her babble on as we took what felt like our usual chairs in the living room and I watched black-eyed Lizzie drift closer. The buzz in the air was not all Emily's.

'And Jasmina is so excited. Not the least worried about her dad wearing women's clothes and make-up.' She raised her eyes heavenward and shook her head. 'Says diversity is all the rage and went off to school this morning with a huge smile on her face.'

'Great.' I glanced at the Seamaster. If Nash was punctual, he'd be here any minute. I was listening to Emily with half an ear and pondering whether plumber and punctual were contradictory when the doorbell sounded.

'Right,' Emily said, her smile fraying slightly at the edges. 'I'll be happy when this bit is over, too.' She went to let him in while I nodded at Lizzie. The dead girl had waited a long time. I was keen to see why.

Emily led the way, and Nash held his almost military bearing as he paused in the doorway. I half expected him to salute. His face was immobile, more deeply seamed than it had appeared before, his expression solemn, and growing puzzled when he saw me.

Lizzie occupied the corner of my vision. She had raised one hand, her fingertips resting on her lips, and seemed focused on her father. She drifted to the centre of the room, reaching the other hand towards him, but his attention was on me.

'Don't I know you?' he said. 'You came to my house.'

'Oh yes,' I chirruped, hoping Emily would not make another startled sound. I should probably have warned her. 'On the local services survey, wasn't it? A few days ago.'

'Asking the same questions here then?' Emily opened her mouth, but I jumped in before she said anything I might regret.

'Not at all, just a social visit – and I don't want to get in your way. Would you rather I …' I waved a hand at the door and his shoulders relaxed a fraction. Dismissing me, he switched attention to his client.

'I'll start with the boiler. Alright with you?'

'Of course. It's in the kitchen.' Emily followed him out. Lizzie watched them go.

I'd placed my bag carefully on the table to give the wide-angled lens the best view of the room and nudged the volume up a little on the baby monitor. Emily had set it for one-way sound. I could listen in from the kitchen if necessary. At my suggestion, the baby was with its aunt. Restless spirits can be … unpredictable.

I didn't expect much from the camera. Ghosts don't appear on film or whisper into microphones, but it would be foolish not to cover all the bases. I could still gauge Nash's reactions. Live images would go to my phone, but the sound quality could be iffy so as back-up I'd use the baby monitor. Of course, I wasn't budging from the living room unless I had to, but he might not show any reaction unless alone, even if he felt her presence. If I was ejected, I could listen from the kitchen. *Belt and braces*, as Dad used to say.

Lizzie stayed where she was, staring at the wall dividing us from the kitchen as if willing her father to come back. She turned to me from time to time as if to check I was still there.

'Which rad' upstairs is working properly?' Nash said as he and Emily crossed the hall.

'The nursery. It's always warm.'

Perhaps I needn't have worried about the baby.

I took a step or two towards the door to see if I could hear more, but pressure on my eardrums muffled sound. The floor felt unreliable, as if my feet might start to sink into a pool of quicksand. Lizzie looked at me and I stopped moving, swallowing down the sudden queasiness.

'Ok,' I muttered. 'I'll stay put.'

I sat again and sipped my lukewarm coffee. After a while the footsteps came down the stairs and went into the kitchen. The discussion was turning out more heat than the boiler and I could hear Emily's loud complaints and Nash's quiet rumble of assurance.

'There's nothing I don't know about this system,' he said as they came through the door. He laid a hand on the radiator. 'This one the worst?'

'It's stone cold most of the time and noisy too.'

'Let's have a look then.'

Emily picked up her coffee cup and raised an eyebrow at me.

'It's probably cold,' I said. Nodding at her cup, then tilting my head at the door.

'Oh, I'll make some fresh. Tea or coffee, John?'

'I'm good, thanks,' he said, taking a cloth and brass key from his bag, not interested in us. Emily left and I stayed put, leafing through a magazine, and if Nash thought my staying odd, he didn't say. He twisted the key until the radiator spluttered into the cloth. Then tightened the screw again.

He was half turned away from me, kneeling with his tool bag open beside him but it became apparent he was doing nothing. The fire made an amber halo of his short grey hair and the fake flames glowed through Lizzie crouched beside him. Her hand seemed to rest on her father's sleeve, her mouth close to his ear as if whispering. I could hear nothing, but there was a stillness about John as if he was attuned to her presence.

I had made no sound, hoping he might forget me, but a sudden noise from the hallway caused him to raise his head. The front door had crashed open and then closed, and I heard the clump of sturdy footwear crossing the hall.

Nash stood, the fabric of his jacket stretching across his shoulder blades. His arm swiped across his eyes and I realised why it had taken him a moment to rise and turn.

'Sorry,' I said automatically, turning my face away, then stopped. His face was grey and bleak, red eyes turned to me without seeing. 'Are you okay?' I said.

He didn't seem to hear. Lizzie was by his side staring at me, her hand still on his arm. I could feel her presence, an emotional wave, unsettling, like static in the air before a storm. The hairs on my arms started to rise. A sudden ringing sounded in my head. I blinked, my eyes scratchy, as if the air was full of dust.

Nash seemed cemented into place, lost in another world, and had he slumped unconscious to the floor I would not have been surprised, but something held him. Lizzie's touch, or just the force of longing that shimmered in the air like something tangible.

'John,' I said. 'Are you okay?' My voice sounded muffled to my own ears, as though from far away or long ago.

Nash touched the spot on his arm where Lizzie's hand rested, and his eyes held a despair so deep I was afraid it might swallow him completely.

'What is it?' I said.

His mouth worked. It took my brain a moment to register his words.

'My girl,' he said. 'My little girl.'

Lizzie watched, the grief on her face no less than his. I felt the tears spilling from my own as he sank once more to his knees, arms dangling boneless at his sides.

'Lizzie's here,' I said. 'Right here beside you. She's trying to talk to you, John.'

He lifted his hands, scrubbed their heels into his forehead as if to drive the pain further inside his skull. His breath caught on the words. 'She's always with me. I hear her voice. I hear her all the time – I should just go to her – but I'm a coward, such a coward.'

Lizzie's hands covered her mouth, her eyes infinite black holes drawing me into her mind.

'That's not what she wants.'

He suddenly blazed. 'Who are you to tell me what my Lizzie wants?'

'I see her, John. She's here, right here beside you. She wants you to live.'

'You can't know that.' Fear glazed his eyes. For a moment I wavered, suddenly afraid I'd got it wrong and I was seeing violence not despair.

'I can't put it right.' He bowed his head. 'I wish I could.'

'She's kneeling in front of you, putting her arms around you. She's hugging you, John. She doesn't want you to be in this pain.'

'You see her?' His voice was raw with longing.

'I do – she's right here. She's reaching out to touch your face. I think she wants you to know how much she loves you.'

He seemed to come back to himself. 'No,' he said, the denial harsh and bitter as he got to his feet. 'You're lying.'

'She's here and trying to tell you something but you must listen – I think you need to listen.'

He was breathing hard, a man driving himself beyond his limits, his teeth clamped, jaw rigid. His hands were fists and I wondered if he'd lashed out at Lizzie, fuelled by alcohol, goaded by Frieda – a bewildered bull tormented by the lances of his daughter's cruelty and sickness. I took a step out of range.

His nostrils flared and his eyes flicked around the room, but underneath the pain, a need to believe. I searched for details to convince him.

'She's wearing jodhpur jeans, riding boots. Her hair is longer than in the photo in your flat, but now she has a fringe. She's not wearing her glasses.'

He shook his head, but I could see suspicion now. 'So what, you saw her at the stables, with her contacts in and after she'd changed her hair,' he said, but underneath was desperation. Hope or fear?

'She has ...' I stepped back another pace, trying to think of something to help him believe, but I'd find no proof in the physical. 'She's standing right beside you – and she wants you to know she forgives you.'

The last was interpretation, but I was sure I had it right. John's eyes grew wide, and I hated to think how hard the blood was thumping in his ears. My own was throbbing, though the intense storm pressure had eased a bit now I was doing Lizzie's bidding.

John swallowed once, and then again. His chin came up in a challenge. 'Forgives me?' he said. 'For what?'

'I – I don't know, but there's something ... something that hurt her. Something you did or didn't do, that made her unhappy.'

His jaw was tight, the words barely allowed space to leave. Thick veins in his neck pulsed and his fists were clenched. He almost hissed into my face. 'I know your sort. After her funeral, psychics, mystics, crawling out of the woodwork to take advantage, mumbling vague messages then demanding money. Filthy bloodsuckers, the lot of you.'

I'd stepped back under the onslaught, cursing Mystic Mandy and all her breed under my breath.

'No money – I'm not after money, I swear. I just want to pass on whatever Lizzie wants ...' I'd been watching as she steepled the fingers of both her hands together, wondering if she was showing me a heart and how this was meant to convince him, but she changed the shape until she'd made a triangle, and then a circle once more, and suddenly I understood. The pendant John kept on her photograph – the AA symbol.

'The drinking. That's what she wants. For you to take the next step on your journey. She wants you to know she's proud of what you're doing, and you have her forgiveness.'

He stared at me, and slowly his hands unfurled. 'I'm supposed to make amends,' he whispered. 'How can I? It's too late.'

'She's still here, John, watching over you, wanting you to forgive yourself, wanting you to live.'

I fancied some of the despair loosened its grip a little. He rubbed thumb and index finger across his eyelids, then down across his mouth and took a shaky breath.

'Can she hear me?'

'I think so. She's right here, ready to listen.'

I stepped towards the door, and this time Lizzie let me go.

As I walked into the hall, I was distracted by Jasmina, bright and bubbly as ever, she was beckoning me from the kitchen door.

'Wow,' she said her face aglow, 'You see dead people!'

Chapter Fifty-Two

❦

'Thanks for doing this, Pops.' Alice walked beside him to Helen Pinnesari's door.

'It's for our boy – how could I not? And besides,' he patted her arm. 'Helen might appreciate some company.'

Alice still hesitated, wondering if being here was quite the right thing for her or the Basset breeder. She could hear pups yapping and squeaking and each sound tugged at her heart. Monty's soppy mournful face rose in her mind. Nothing could ever replace you, she thought.

'Come on, sweetie. It's nearly twelve now, and she's expecting us. We can't dither on the doorstep all day.' He lifted his chin at the security camera. 'We have a mission.'

Alice pressed the bell in two short, sharp rings before she changed her mind.

The door swung open, the volume of yaps increased, and Alice braced herself for the sight of rolling pot-bellied turmoil around her feet, but they were caged behind a pet gate further along the narrow hallway. The lump swelled in her throat. A temporary reprieve.

Alice switched her attention to the older woman who had opened the door, shocked at how Helen had so swiftly aged. The laughter lines around her mouth had deepened; crow's feet had become talons clawing grooves around her puffy bloodshot eyes.

Pops stepped forward to peck Helen's cheeks and somehow it turned into a hug. Alice could do with a hug herself, but Helen clung on to Pops like a rock in a stormy sea.

'Dominic,' she said. 'Dear man. Still handsome.'

'Helen, how lovely to see you again – though, if I may say so, you seem a bit under the weather. Would you rather we came back at a better time?'

The woman blinked and swayed a little. 'Course not. Glad to have the company.' She touched cheeks with Alice, then stood back to let them enter. 'So sorry, my dear. Poor Monty. Car accident! Horrible!'

She clinked the ice in the tumbler of clear liquid she'd picked up in passing. The lemon slice nearly sloshed over the side as she waved it towards a door to their right.

Scratched leather seating was heaped with well-chewed cushions, and dog-fragranced throws in rich burgundies and greens. It was warm and chaotic and though Alice itched to tidy up, it did feel welcoming.

Helen waved them to the sofas around a low scarred table and opened the door to the adjoining room. The pups piled in, chubby bodies with short thick fur tumbling in black and tan patterns across the rugs.

'They keep me going, them and blessed Saint Gordon's.' She gestured with the green bottle she'd lifted from a tray. 'Don't know what I'd do without them.' A tear slid off her nose as she poured. She ignored it, merely closing her eyes for a moment before giving a small sniff. 'Ice, lemon?' Their refusals didn't register.

Several pups were playing tug-of-war with knotted ropes but two had bounded over to Alice's feet and were trying to climb her jeans. She gave in and lifted one in each hand onto her lap. They wriggled for a moment chewing on her fingers, then jumped off again to romp with their siblings. Pops bent to fuss ears and pat rumps from the sofa opposite her.

'To absent hounds!' Helen, standing at the head of the table, raised her glass and they did the same. Helen gulped half of her drink then blinked blearily at the pups over the rim. 'He's gone, you know. These are the last of my Rudi's babies. Sorry,' she mumbled, slurring slightly, drawing her sleeve across her face and subsiding into a seat.

'No need to be.' Alice could feel her own tears welling.

'Stupid of me. Miss that dog.'

'I'm so sorry for your loss, dear heart.' Pops moved to beside Helen and put his arm around her. 'Whatever happened? I thought he was doing well.'

'Tried everything to save him. Prognosis good after the s'gery! S'what they said, but he never really ... just went down ...'

'How very sad to lose him in his prime.'

'We love 'em too much, tha's the trouble, Dominic. Love 'em like our babies. Should've had lots more – more little Rudis, little Montys too.' She sniffed, held on to Pop's arm for a moment then moved away. 'Would have if not for that girl. Attention span of a gnat. Never,' she said, holding up one finger, 'trust anyone to look after your babies!'

'Good lord, darling. Whatever did she do?' said Pops

'Can't. Promised not to say.' She hiccupped. 'Not her fault – not really, I s'ppose. Young girl – monthly horror. Same thing at her age – Ha! Five days a month when you can't bloody think straight, then five more with your innards scraped out with a rusty blade. Who'd be a woman, eh? Still … bloody menopause put a stop to it!' She looked at Alice. 'Least you don't have these problems … or do you? Often wondered about the hormones …' Her hand clamped over her mouth. 'Bugger! – sorry, too much gin … too much …' She started to sob, hands over her face, rocking back and forward on her seat.

Alice perched beside her, one hand on Helen's back looking past her at Pops for a clue but he just widened his eyes and got to his feet.

He poured straight tonic into a fresh glass and put it at Helen's elbow, 'Here, darling, better than more G&T for now. I'll just pop to the little boys' room if that's okay.'

Alice stroked the woman's shoulders, murmuring reassurances now and then until the sobs lessened and Helen gulped a few jerky breaths. Handing her the tonic glass, Alice tried to balance the queasy feeling of intrusion with the idea Helen might be better for getting it off her chest. Alice's own railing against fate had helped her cope with Monty's loss – a bit.

Not to virtual strangers though. Alice was still going to have a stern word with Pops for abandoning her.

'I really am so sorry.' Helen sniffed, drawing away. 'I didn't mean to be rude about …' She waved her hand vaguely in Alice's direction.

'It's fine.' Alice smiled. 'I wish more people would just ask – open curiosity is so much easier than ill-informed judgement.'

'Judgement. Well, I can't judge anyone.' Helen looked at her hands holding the glass, took a sip, then sighed. 'Whatever I might say, thing is, kid made a mistake. I shouldn't have been so harsh, but her mind was hardly on the job. Kept going off sick, then when she was here, she distracted my lad.' Her smile was weak. 'And I could hardly have her working here – not after …' She scooped up the pup at her feet. 'So, let's see how you get on with these littl'uns, shall we? Maybe someone will cancel their order.'

'Actually,' said Alice, 'I'm so sorry, but I don't think I'm quite ready yet'. The lump in her throat was growing large again.

Besides, she had an idea where they might find a girl who'd lost a job recently and might have had a reason for going off "sick".

THE DOG AND DUCK WAS NOT BUSY, AND SIOBHAN WAS WIPING the tables with a hygiene spray with no great enthusiasm. She perked up when she saw Alice and hurried behind the bar to take their drinks order.

'I wanted to say thanks again for opening night,' she said as she filled the glasses. 'I thought I'd be giving the front row an eyeful when that zip went, and I was in such a state already – you were an absolute lifesaver.'

'No trouble, it's what I was there for and your "Helena" went down really well. You were good.'

'Thanks.' Dimples appeared briefly making her look even younger. 'I just wish I hadn't felt so ill.'

'First night nerves?' Pops asked. 'The actor's curse!'

Siobhan placed their drinks in front of them and waggled her hand. 'Sort of.' She leaned her elbows on the bar and lowered her voice. 'Actually, it was more morning sickness. Can you imagine getting it at six o'clock every evening? Who knew that could happen?'

'Congratulations,' said Alice. 'I did wonder, but I didn't like to say. I hope you're feeling better now.'

'I am thanks.' Siobhan rolled her eyes. 'No one told me it

was going to be that bad, but I've been fine the last few days.' She smiled at them both. 'Sorry, not what you want to think about just before you eat! Anyway, thanks again.' She handed them the menus and the engagement ring caught the light. 'Pick a table. The kitchen'll be open in about ten minutes.'

'Love the sparkler,' said Alice, pointing. 'A new development, I think?'

Siobhan coloured, pink washing across her cheeks prettily as she held out her hand for inspection. 'Van asked me yesterday. Still a bit unreal to be honest.'

'When's the big day?' asked Pops.

'We haven't set it yet. He's going back to Writtle in September – degree in animal welfare – and I'm going to college nearby. We'll probably do it before that.' Her smile faltered for a moment then she sighed. 'It'll be good to get out of here, but he's got to finish his work experience across the road first.'

'Oh,' said Alice. 'He's not working at the Pinnesari's place, is he? We've just come from there.'

The barmaid took a step back, retrieved her spray and cloth as she muttered. 'Well, I'd better get on before Dad has another go at me.'

Alice glanced at Pops who stepped into the breach.

'She's an odd old duck,' he said, 'the woman who runs it. Three sheets to the wind when we got there, then started crying about one of her dogs who just died. Said it was some kind of accident.'

Siobhan twisted the nozzle of the spray round and round, her expression grim as it turned.

'Thought you'd be friends. Bassets and all that,' she said, glancing up at Alice.

'Pops knows her a bit – it's where he got Monty – but I've only met her a time or two. That's why it was so strange, her being practically drunk at this time of the morning. I mean, we were potential customers and she knew we were coming.' Alice leaned forward, her elbows on the bar. 'Is she always like that?'

Alice watched the girl's expression soften. 'Nah,' she said, 'To be fair, that 'd be because of Rudi. Poor love only died a couple of days ago and he was her baby boy, you know?'

Alice knew.

'He was gorgeous.' Siobhan went on. 'Full of himself mind – but lovely with it. A real snuggle-bunny when he wanted to be.'

She put down the spray, came a bit closer. 'Helen was alright, till he had the "accident"'. Her fingers emphasised the quote marks. 'Then she went completely barmy.'

'All stages of grieving I suppose,' offered Pops. 'Wailing and gnashing of teeth, then diving into a bottle.'

'Yeah, that I could understand,' Siobhan's lips tightened, and she resumed her cleaning, 'but she said I'd left some pills where he could get them. I'd never even seen the bloody pills. Not that she listened. Just went full psycho and ordered me off the premises. I was only temping, so I've got no rights, apparently.' She rubbed a little harder than was necessary at an invisible mark on the bar. 'Van would've walked too – but he needs this for his course. Good job she didn't know we were together, or she might've fired him too.'

'Ghastly for you. Nothing worse than unfair accusation – and she shouldn't be upsetting you like that, not good for the little one,' said Pops.

'To be fair, she didn't know about that – I hadn't told anyone – I wasn't sure what I was going to do.' Siobhan stroked her thumb over the ring.

'Sensible,' said Pops, 'Wonderful how things sometimes

turn out for the best.' He sipped his drink. 'But what made her think you'd been so careless?'

'My own stupid lies,' she sighed. 'I worked there in the mornings so the sickness wasn't too bad mostly but some of the time I was so tired I could barely stand up, and it was just too much. I didn't want anyone knowing so I told her I was having,' she looked at Alice, 'you know, women's problems.'

'Of course,' said Alice. 'Good cover story for dashing off to the loo a lot too.'

Siobhan smiled. 'Yeah, I thought I was being so clever.' She lowered her eyes and stroked the wood grain with her fingertips. 'Only the pills he ate were extra strong *Feminax* so ...' she shrugged. 'That was it.'

Alice broke the silence. 'You didn't want to tell her?'

'I might have − but she was so sure it was me and she was yelling and stuff and that stuck-up friend of hers was always lurking about listening − anyway I thought I'd go back later, or write to her or something, but then ... well, what was the point. It's not as if I wanted to go back anyway.' She crossed her hands across her stomach. 'I had more important things to think about.'

'Much more important,' agreed Pops, while Alice's thoughts raced ahead.

'Who do you think these pills did belong to − they can't have been Helen's.'

Siobhan shrugged. 'Her friend I guess.'

'Do you know her name, this friend?' Alice heard her voice − too sharp, too eager.

Siobhan drew back a little but then shrugged again.

'Sure. It was Barbara. Barbara Nash.'

Chapter Fifty-Three

❧

I'd sworn Jasmina to silence about the ghost, adding for good measure no one would believe her as people were quite rightly sceptical of this sort of thing. Her mother pitched in.

'Even your father thinks it's nonsense, so don't mention it to anyone except Penny and me, okay?'

John was upset, I told them. 'Let's just give him some space.'

'He's not going to do anything to himself, is he?' Emily bit her lip. 'I mean, should we call someone?'

'I think he just needs to grieve,'

'I could ask the doctor if there's counselling or something – sorry, I forgot Jasmina's check-up was today.'

Jasmina rolled her eyes.

'Losing a child,' Emily wrapped her arms around the girl, 'how can you get over that?'

Jasmina squirmed in her embrace. 'We'll be late,' she grumbled, then suddenly caved in and hugged Emily in return.

'Would it be alright with you, Emily, if I stayed for bit, to make sure he's okay? Sometimes a stranger is easier to talk to – less embarrassing.'

'Why not.' Emily shrugged. 'If you think it might help. We should be back in an hour or two, but you know what these appointments are like – they're always running late.'

She left, Jasmina chattering beside her. I could only hope she'd make sure the girl kept Lizzie's presence to herself or her daughter might be referred to mental health.

I paused outside the living room door, fresh tea gave me a reason to intrude, but I thought he might be ready to ask questions, or answer some. I couldn't hear anything, so I tapped lightly and pushed the door enough to see inside.

John was in the armchair by the fireplace, Lizzie sat on the floor beside him, her head on her father's knee. He straightened when he heard me and wiped his face with his hands before he turned.

'It's only me,' I said. 'Everyone's gone out for a bit so there's no rush, but I thought you could do with this.' I held up the mug.

Lizzie raised her head as I put the tea on the table at John's elbow. The dark pools of her eyes still spooked me, but my ears were not roaring with her distress.

'She's still here?' John said. Then he touched his heart. 'She'll always be here.'

'Sitting at your feet.' My chair sighed as I settled.

'I'd give anything to see her, to hold her one more time.'

'I wish I could make it happen.'

'She was so ... alive. So full of the future.' He smiled, a lifetime of heartbreak in it. 'All the things she wanted ...'

I waited a moment before I spoke again. 'She does still want something.'

The embers of John's suspicion flared for a moment then died. 'I'd give my life.'

'I don't know what she wants exactly, but she's still here.'

A door slammed and he jumped. 'Someone else is here!'

'It's the bathroom door, John,' I said. 'It keeps doing that.'

John's eyes widened. 'Ask her.' He swallowed before he could go on, 'Ask Lizzie, was I right about the key?'

Lizzie had risen, arms stiff by her side, fingers curled into fists as she stared at John. I copied her stance. 'She's doing this. She's angry, seems upset.' I sat again. 'What happened with the key?'

'Barbara said Lizzie turned it – but Lizzie never locked the door. If something happened when she was in the water … that was the nightmare. Ever since the first seizure, we had a rule. Lizzie just put something on the handle – a hairband, bracelet – it didn't matter what, it told us she was in there and no one would go in unless she didn't answer when we knocked.'

'She had been cleared,' I pointed out. 'Medically, I mean – a week or two before …'

'That's what Barbara said but I wanted to keep the system going, just in case, and Lizzie had promised – but later I wondered. Maybe Lizzie resented me for asking, wanted to say no, but I pushed her into giving me her word – and then she broke it. I was furious she'd put herself at risk. The nightmare had come true and I blamed her.' His face was wet.

Lizzie still clenched her fists. Was this what she wanted, to make him admit his anger as a kind of catharsis? But then why was she slamming that door over and over?

Lizzie clasped her hands together, staring at John with such intensity I thought he must be able to feel it, but he was gripping the arms of the chair, eyes closed, reliving the worst day of his life.

'I tapped on the door, called her name. She didn't answer. I turned the knob, but the door wouldn't open. I called again, nothing. I bent down, tried to look through the keyhole but I could only see the gleam of the tiles. I shouted but she didn't answer. I started to panic.' His eyes flew open.

'I had to get in! The door was solid – hardwood. I barged it with my shoulder, but it didn't budge, I just rebounded. I started kicking at the lock, hard as I could – I was wearing work boots, but the lock held. I kicked and kicked but it wouldn't give. There was a gap under the door – and I thought if I pushed the key through it would fall, and I could bring it under on newspaper or something.

'But Barbara was screaming it would take too long. "Just kick it in, kick it harder". She kept yelling. "Kick it in!"

'So, I kept on and it began to break. I could feel the catch starting to bounce in the frame, the metal bending and then I was through.

'Her head was underwater, hair floating. I was desperate to get her out. I grabbed her under the arms and hauled her over the edge.' His chest heaved. 'She wasn't breathing.' He fought for control as he lived it again. 'I did what I'd been trained to do – I took the course each year – but nothing worked. I kept waiting for her to cough up water, start to gasp in air.' He shook his head.

'Barbara was just standing there. I shouted at her and she went to phone the ambulance. I kept it going, CPR, but even before they came, I knew. I knew I'd lost her.

'The paramedics ordered me away. I stood there, watching, praying, but she didn't breathe. I couldn't bear to watch what they were doing – I looked away.'

I could imagine. How could any parent bear it?

Lizzie's tears mirrored her father's.

'The key was lying on the mat just inside the door. I

thought it must have jumped out – but I remembered seeing through the keyhole before I barged the door – I thought I had – but Barbara said no, that was after – that I'd run at it first and I ... I wasn't sure – I couldn't be sure.'

'But?'

'I knew something was wrong – I saw the bruises on Lizzie's arms. They'd argued the day before about the old woman's cat, and I thought Barbara might have shaken Lizzie – her temper could be ... terrible.'

'Why did you stay?'

'Barbara said if I ever tried to leave, she'd take my girl. She'd made sure everyone thought I abused them. She got me so worked up, told me someone at the stables was turning Lizzie's head and maybe more, but when I went up there and made a fuss, somehow it all got turned around and I ended up the villain – the bloke said I was the one with the problem. I was a drunk, I'll admit to that, but I was never violent, not to her, and not to Lizzie. Barbara made sure if I made any move against her, my girl would be the one to suffer.

'But after Lizzie ... well, Barbara had no hold on me. I couldn't even bear to look at her. I moved out, went to a bar – then to a hotel with a bar – then the minibar in the room. I stayed drunk for as long as I could.'

Perhaps the speed might have raised some eyebrows, but a grieving family breaking up is hardly news. So, the house is rented out again. The neighbourhood moves on.

Only, where did Barbara move to? Friends? She didn't seem to have them. Family? Her parents were a fair distance away. An unofficial sublet ... perhaps. Or did she have somewhere to go already?

'Is that what Lizzie wanted me to know?' said John. 'That she didn't lock the door? But if she didn't then ...'

'Did you think Barbara could have caused her death?'

'I asked the coroner's office, but nothing said Lizzie was held down or struggled or was drugged or … I could prove nothing! But I know I failed her. I failed my girl. I wasn't there in time to save her and I was out drinking when I should have been at home protecting my girl.'

'You couldn't have saved her, John.'

'I might,' he said, misery creasing his face in deep folds. 'Barbara said she'd checked on her just a little while before, so if I'd been home a few minutes earlier …'

'Perhaps she did – and that's when she locked the door – when she saw Lizzie was …' I looked at the ghost girl who shook her head. 'Or if she was still alive, then maybe she was in trouble then … and Barbara did nothing about it?' Lizzie wiped away a ghostly tear. 'Could Barbara have watched Lizzie drown and done nothing to save her?'

'She … she was always jealous, said I loved Lizzie more than I loved her – that she'd take her away from me if I ever crossed her … oh, god. Once the old lady told me about the cat, I'd have done anything to get my girl away, because then I knew … but I was too late.'

'What about the cat?'

His laugh was bitter. 'My girl wouldn't harm any creature – she loved them! She thought it was an accident. Took the responsibility though I had my doubts even then, but a deliberate overdose – she'd never have done that!'

Live cats give those that hurt them a wide berth. Would dead ones be different? Yosef's ghost seemed happy enough to hang out with the girl.

'Only one person liked to watch things suffer and it wasn't my little Lizzie. It was the monster I let into our lives. My fault.' He sobbed. 'All my fault. How could my baby ever forgive me for that?'

'I don't know, John, but it seems she needs you to forgive

yourself. She's at peace now.' Lizzie lifted her hand, as if she might stroke his cheek then her image flickered, a film frame expanding into pixels until the shape was lost and nothing was left but white space which slowly changed to blend in with the background.

She was gone.

A need to see Barbara Nash face justice flowed like lava through my veins, but it seemed that even Lizzie recognised the impossibility of that. The ice in my cheek where she had touched me was thawing, the memory of cold would fade. The memory of a sad ghost and her grieving father would take much longer.

When I left the house later, I'd begun to think ghosts had done with me in this neighbourhood – but then a little tabby tried to wind around my legs and passed straight through.

Yosef wasn't quite finished yet.

.

Chapter Fifty-Four

❧

Back in the office, the morning brightened further when Alice passed on what she'd learned from the Basset breeder. A poisoning with painkillers – and those for "women's troubles" too. My brain went super-nova – flashes everywhere.

Frieda's cat and Lizzie took the blame – now the Pinnesari Basset and the kennel maid. Only the dog hadn't died straight away. First there was an operation, done by Kitson – who had enough contact with Lizzie Nash and her cold-blooded step-mother to believe John Nash violently abusive.

Nate came bouncing in. 'Naproxen,' he said in much the same tone as Archimedes said "Eureka". 'The active ingre-dient in over-the-counter medicines for, um … you know.'

'Period pain, Nate. Don't be coy.'

'Yes, well, it's bad stuff if you're small and furry. It does horrible things.'

'Such as?'

'Intestinal bleeding, confusion, nausea and wrecking your kidneys,' He looked up from his notes, 'That's if you're lucky.

Otherwise it just kills – messily. Vomiting blood is one of the many highlights.'

'Great,'

He gave me a concerned look.

'Great you found out – not great it does horrid thing to pets, Nate. I'm not a monster.'

'If you say so, boss.' It might be time to remind him of things alien and goggle-eyed, but then again it was more fun to have him back to his usual self, as long as he was in the office where he could do no harm.

"Okay,' I said, 'so we have a dog that ate this stuff and needed an op, and a closely related healthy dog that was dognapped, doped with animal anaesthetic and later died in surgery. What does it suggest to you, Nate?'

'Wrecked kidneys. Transplant?'

'Smart thinking, Robin!' He took a bow.

What had Kitson's receptionist said? I checked my notes. Something about the vet's training in America at the best hospitals.

A few keystrokes confirmed pet transplants were not allowed here. No "informed consent". Other countries had other rules.

The United States was okay with it in cats, as long as the donor animal was adopted by the recipient's family, regardless of the outcome. I gathered this was not generally a common-or-garden mog in need of rehoming, but one certified disease-free, surplus to research requirements. Their usual fate would be euthanasia.

A kidney for your life? A recent documentary on human organ trafficking had turned me similarly queasy.

'See if you can find any US vet hospitals doing trans-plants.' I flipped through my notes again. 'Kitson's got a connection with Philadelphia.' Nate went off to trawl while I checked out how the gory deed was done.

The procedure was successful in cats for three main reasons – "improved microsurgery techniques, the ability to use an allograft from an unrelated donor and the development of better post-op immunosuppressive drugs" – but dogs were trickier. The animals needed to be related, and it hadn't been done often, even in the States. The chances of rejection were much higher, and it was sickeningly expensive.

More sickening was the idea of carving up a family pet for spare parts.

Nate stuck his head around the door. 'Philly has a big teaching hospital with a feline kidney transplant programme running since the early 90s. Cats, dogs, chimpanzees … it's all the same plumbing, isn't it?' offered Nate.

Who knew? Not me – I couldn't change a washer on the tap.

But I intended to ask Daniel Kitson.

I'd also been wondering about his actions regarding Val. Him checking his storeroom after PC Plod had gone had seemed reasonable – after all, someone had been seen lurking, but now I got to thinking. Why not do it while the professional was on site? Jeff was not a shining example of police expertise – but Kitson didn't know that. It made more sense to check with reinforcements handy – unless he had something to hide.

He'd opened a freezer – the one that creaked. The one with the small packages.

I should have another look.

I WAS IN LUCK. NO ONE WAS ABOUT AT THE BACK OF THE surgery except the ghost of Val still going through her loop. The St Bernard was still there. She fussed him each time she passed.

The staff car park was empty of the living and their cars. I hoped that meant no one was watching the security too closely and kept my face averted. A hooded parka was my disguise this time.

I let myself into the store and pulled the door closed, thankful no one had changed the code. My phone's torch lit the way. As I lifted it, the lid made its familiar creak and the internal light came on. I held the lid with one hand, balancing my phone on the freezer's edge so I could turn over the contents. The packages varied in size, their labels giving ID numbers and weight of the pet inside. Guinea pig, cat, chihuahua, another cat. I picked that one up, bracing the freezer lid against my shoulder so I could use both hands to trace the shape within. The frozen feline was still recognizable. Head, front legs, back legs. Against the belly, I could feel a knobbly fist-sized lump. A lump rose in my throat which I had to concentrate on swallowing before I could continue.

I slit the plastic and drew the edges apart. The moggy's expression was blank in death, eyes closed, nose and whiskers white with frost. Bound to the torso with sticky tape was another package. The knife cut again. I peeled back the wrapping, fighting my desire to look away.

Half a foot's six inches, but this one was shorter. It had been severed side-to-side across the arch.

Five little piggies went to market. These had painted nails in vibrant pink.

The same pink as her hair.

I'D BEEN EXPECTING IT, BUT STILL IT WAS A SHOCK. I DROPPED the package and took a step away. The lid fell with an emphatic thump and a sharp noise that took me a moment to process. My phone had shattered.

I'd need another to call the police, and fast. For all I knew the collection for the crematorium was imminent. The evidence would go up in smoke.

As Kitson lived in the flat above and his car wasn't in the carpark, it was a fair bet he was out somewhere. I could explain Val's whereabouts to the receptionist, get her to call the police and stand guard against the disposal of the evidence until someone showed up to collect it.

It was a plan.

As I approached the desk, the two ghost Bassets followed a trail across the waiting room, noses to the floor, intent on whatever phantom smell had caught their attention, but Kathleen's focus was on me. Whatever instructions she'd been given had starched her face.

'I'm not allowed to talk to you,' she said as I drew near.

'I only want…' That was as far as I got.

'I just said – I can't help you!'

'I need to …' The words clogged in my mouth. How could I explain her colleague was in pieces out the back and I needed to use her phone urgently? Acid rose in my throat.

'Mr Kitson's not available and I can't tell you anything.' Her manner was brittle. Her hand rested on the phone.

Perhaps if I caused a nuisance, she'd call the police herself – but she might just call her boss and he'd hardly want the law involved.

I dithered. Should I leave to find another phone, try to explain to Kathleen why I needed hers, or just wrench it out from under her hand and dial 999?

'I can't wait,' I muttered to myself, but as I reached forward the phone began to ring.

'Suit yourself,' she said, then, 'D. Kitson Veterinary Practice. Kathleen speaking. How can I help?'

She busied herself at the computer summoning the caller's

details as questions circled through my mind. Would Jeff Smithson's story of our St Bernard discovery have done the rounds of the police canteen? Would anyone take me seriously? And if they did, how long would it take to organise an official search? Could they even get a warrant based on my snooping?

I watched Val's ghost cross the waiting room.

Could I persuade Kathleen to look?

'What about Val?' I said, when she'd replaced the receiver. She huffed but didn't flinch. Ignorance is bliss. 'She's not on holiday. She's ...'

'Away for two weeks in Spain!' Kathleen sat back and crossed her arms.

'She won't be back,' I said. My breakfast threatened to make a reappearance. I swallowed.

'Don't be absurd!'

I gave it up. She wouldn't believe me and Kitson would hardly risk her having keys to the back. If I phoned the police from here, she might even tip him off – and how long would it take him to organise disposal?

'When's Kitson back?'

She glared. 'Mr Kitson's taking some personal time.'

'Convenient.' I said. 'All the pets in the area unexpectedly in the pink?' Pink, Pinkissimo. I swallowed again.

'One day off! He's entitled!'

Perhaps it was best not to bring a dismembered corpse into the conversation – as long as the corpse in question wasn't about to be collected.

'The thing is,' I said, 'Alice is worried – well, fixated a bit, actually. She's wondering if the ashes she got back were really Monty's and she keeps imagining he's in your storehouse out the back, all cold and alone for days ... she's in a bit of a state.'

She softened only slightly. 'There's no question of a mix-up. Our collection's Tuesday afternoon, so it was only a few hours. We'd have made a special arrangement otherwise, so he'd be ready for her on Saturday, and the procedure is very tightly controlled.'

Today was Friday. But there were a lot of dead pets out there. A special arrangement would risk questions being asked. My guess was Kitson would try to keep to the normal schedule.

'No extra collections on busy weeks?'

'No, we have plenty of storage ... what's that got to do with anything?'

I held up my hands. 'Just curious.'

'Look, if you're trying to get Alice to claim for damages or something, it won't work. No one did anything wrong!'

'Then there's nothing to worry about – but don't you find it odd Val's disappeared just as we're asking questions?'

'She's on holiday!'

Val passed me, floating gently from reception along the corridor, through one of the doors off to the side.

'What's through there?' I pointed.

'Surgery suite,' she said. 'State of the art. He had the very best of treatment!' She drew her mouth tight.

'Perhaps,' I nodded. When I'd been loitering in the car park the night they'd shut early, I'd heard machinery. Something that sounded like a dental drill.

Not a drill. A saw. I shivered. What kind of man does that?

'Kathleen, please, put yourself in Alice's shoes.' I watched Monty and his ghostly playmate start a tug-of-war. Ears rose and fell in soft folds as they adjusted their grip. 'You know how much she loved that hound. I just need to put her mind at rest, and for that I need to ask some questions.'

Kathleen huffed and blustered but eventually she said. 'You'll have to speak to Mr Kitson, and you can't. He's gone fishing for the day.'

I glanced at the photo of the cruiser and wondered if he had his passport with him. Would he run if he thought he was about to be exposed? Could my earlier incursion into the storeroom have spooked him?

Perhaps I'd need to call the coastguard as well as the police.

'Sure it's only a daytrip?' I said.

Kathleen sighed. 'Look, he's hardly going anywhere for long – not without the love of his life.' Her finger pointed to the flat above. 'And believe me, Barbara wasn't dressed for fishing, not in those high-heels.'

My jaw dropped like the dunderheaded dimwit in a kid's cartoon. No wonder Barbara Nash had dropped off the radar. As I pulled my face back into shape, Kathleen must have realised there was a way to make me leave. She turned a shade more helpful.

'If it's that important you might catch him if you hurry. He was stopping at the bank before boarding The Liberty. She's at the mooring off the pier.'

Calling the police could wait. Val wasn't going anywhere, and this could be my only chance to confront him – and find out where Lizzie's stepmother fitted in.

Chapter Fifty-Five

❧❦❧

Catching a glimpse of Kitson's blond head spurred me on to jog along the top promenade. I sped down the steps and onto the pier trying to catch up.

Addicts fed coins into slot-machines inside the arcade, but the outside was deserted. I was steaming inside my coat, but the chill wind numbed my cheeks and turned my nose to ice. It didn't matter. Nothing was going to stop me, though covered kiddie rides and shuttered booths made me zig and zag. Ahead, the wooden bulk of the Jolly Roger Theatre blocked my view as Kitson disappeared beyond it.

An obstacle suddenly blocked my way. I swerved to treat it like a roundabout but Jasmina Dunker, bundled in a cherry-red duffle coat was not easy to shake off. She scurried at my side. 'Want to watch me rehearse?' She pointed to the theatre and skipped a little. 'I've got a solo in the school show. It's gonna be ace.'

'Love to,' I lied. 'But I'm busy right now.'

'Dad's the same.' She kept pace as I jogged on and unlike me, she had enough breath left to chat. 'Alice is making him a brill new dress with feathers and beads and everything, and mum's going back to work part-time next month – the sprat is going to day-care.'

'Great.' I gulped in air. 'Won't you be late?'

'Nah, I'm early!' She skidded to a halt as I stopped abruptly at the theatre entrance. 'I could help you for a bit?' she said.

"Fraid not.' I gave her a nudge towards the door. 'Go into the warm.' I didn't wait but strode on past the building to the open pier beyond. Kitson had reached the gate to the narrow fishing jetty. Once through, he could be away down the iron ladder onto the pontoon, then a dinghy hop to a cruise to somewhere with no extradition treaty. Maybe the girlfriend was being dumped. I'd have no chance to stop him.

He was struggling to turn his key. Cold lock, cold hands – neither made for speed. Gail Monterey passing through him on her way to say hello didn't make it any easier. My own flesh goose bumped. Not just the usual spirit chill, but the taint of something dank and slimy from the seabed hung in the air.

I slowed, walking silently towards him. 'Having trouble?'

Kitson swung to face me. The key jerked and dropped, then rattled between the boards. It was swallowed by the darkness below.

'Butter-fingers,' I said. 'But I'm glad I caught you.'

'Caught me?' He spluttered. 'Caught me doing what? I'm just going fishing!'

'Of course.'

A wash of micro expressions marred his handsome features. Blinks and twitches and darting eyes suggested panic wasn't far away, but his lips parted in an almost convincing smile. I guess surgeons learn to act cool under pressure.

'You're Alice Mayford's detective.'

Nice to be remembered.

Hands in his pockets, he leaned back against the gate. 'You still on the trail of whoever ran down her dog?'

'Amongst other things,' I said. 'But we can start there if you like. How much did you charge for the transplant?'

His jaw tightened. One ratchet more and he might break some teeth. He said nothing.

'You did a great job. First Alice's dog died, then the other one. I wonder what Helen Pinnesari will say when she understands what you did to get that kidney.'

'She'd lose her breeder's licence. Be barred from keeping animals.' He straightened, pulled his lapels closer against the cold. 'There goes everything she loves in life. Good luck persuading her to talk.'

And the physical evidence was up in smoke. Damn. Still, small scale in the scheme of things, but he was hung up on the dog.

'I am sorry about Monty. He should have resumed normal life with no one the wiser – I set it up that way.' He shrugged. 'But if it does come out, the penalty's a joke. The Brits may say they love their pets, but the law sure doesn't.' He shook his head. 'The things I've seen some people do and get a slap on the wrist – and I tried my best to save those dogs.'

'What made you try it anyway?' I was suddenly curious. *Transplants for Dummies* special offer on Amazon?'

He shrugged. 'I'd seen it done in the States ...'

'I've seen Olympians smash world records – I still can't run fast.'

'... and Barbara said she'd worked on organ rejection research – she knew how everything needed to be connected. She said she had done trials with her father's transplant programmes.'

'Allograft rejection,' I suddenly remembered. 'But that was mice, not dogs.'

'He researched on other species though. It's the same basic anatomy so between us it was worth a try.' He shrugged. 'Barbara couldn't bear to see Helen so upset, and Rudi was going to die without it.'

'Monty wasn't! And it was only needed at all because Barbara poisoned the breeder's dog.'

Sea spray flew up into the wind. He wiped a hand across his eyes. 'It was the kennel maid ...'

'Nope. Barbara got the poor kid fired – and it was your girlfriend that did the deed.'

His top lip curled as if a fishhook caught and held, but his confidence was draining like water from a landed cod as I went on.

'Her transplant expertise was another fiction, I imagine. She's not even on the medical register. I doubt she had much practical experience, but you didn't look too closely, did you? What was it, white knight blindness? Alcoholic husband, domestic abuse – child abuse even – she's sown the seeds so well. Your armour's a bit rusty though. You didn't spot how good she is at killing things like dogs and daughters.'

He paled but I'd pushed too far. He came out fighting. 'Rubbish! She showed me her daughter's inquest report – no one killed the girl.'

'Barbara didn't hold her down,' I agreed. 'But she poisoned a cat Lizzie loved and convinced the girl it was her own fault. In that state of mind, Lizzie had another fit. Just one of those things? I doubt it. Barbara was ready to move on. She had you. Lizzie was unwanted baggage. Barbara wouldn't risk playing second fiddle to the girl a second time – but how could she leave her with an "abusive" father and still play the heroine? Much better to be bereaved – and serve her husband right.'

'That's ridiculous. She couldn't have known what would happen!'

'True, but I think Lizzie's days were numbered. Teenage suicide, perhaps? Guilt over the cat and an overdose of those handy pills?'

'Speculation!'

'Perhaps – but she is a killer ... or did she make you murder Val?'

White round the gills. Dead white, like the face of Howling Gail who'd drifted back to take an interest. She stared at him for a moment before pursing her lips. A sudden gust of chill blew into his face. He flinched against the waist high rails, now boxed into a jutting corner, sea on two sides with five-foot six of solid me in front.

I tensed.

He swallowed, looking to his right where Gail was leaning in. I could almost feel the hairs rise on the back of his neck. His eyes flicked between the space Gail inhabited and me, barring his way.

'Val's on holiday.' His voice barely carried against the wind.

'She was murdered, then bagged up in bits in your freezer.'

His smile was meant to persuade me of his innocence, but it had been beaten out of shape and nailed back on askew. 'It wasn't me,' he said. 'Barbara said it was an accident! I just agreed to clear up ...'

I don't know what might have happened next, but I can only assume boredom and curiosity brought the girl skipping from behind me. A flash of red escaped my grasp as she flashed by.

'Hi, Mr Kitson,' said Jasmina brightly.

In a split second, he had grabbed her, drawn his arm around her throat and pinned her to his body like a shield.

'I think I'll be going now,' he said staring at me. Glancing at the top of Jasmina's head, then at the sea slapping and gurgling down below, he added, 'I don't think it's swimming weather, do you?'

I held up both my hands as if he'd pointed a gun. Jasmina gave up struggling and looked to me for the next move.

'Let's not do anything rash,' I ventured, aiming for calm and confident and fooling no one. Tension constricted my voice into a squeak. 'Listen, if you haven't hurt anyone, now's not a good time to start.'

'I never touched Val,' he said, 'I was going to pay her off, but that doesn't matter. Barbara will convince everyone it was me. That's what she does …'

I saw Jasmina begin to tense, and hoped she'd have the sense to keep still and quiet while I talked our way out.

I should have known better.

'Get off me, creep,' she yelled, dropping dead weight in his hands, forcing him to bend forward to keep his grip. I reached for her, but she'd braced her feet and jumped straight up, hard and fast. Her arm caught my face and I missed her coat by a fraction. I heard his nose break as her skull made contact. The metal rail caught his lower spine, but without purchase on the wet boards, momentum won. He fell backwards.

He might have had a chance if he'd have grabbed the bar, but his hands held fast to her duffle coat – good durable material that wouldn't tear. He disappeared over the rail.

Buttoned inside her coat, despite my desperate lunge for her legs, Jasmina followed over the rail into the cold North Sea churning below.

Snatching the life belt from the rack, I scanned the choppy

waves, and caught sight of her coat, sinking. I unreeled the line and threw, just as I realised the girl had shrugged it off and was treading water with limited success off to one side. Her clothes were seaweed dark. The belt landed nowhere near, and the currents, treacherous as I well knew, swirled it in a useless circle.

I tugged the line, but it remained out of her reach. Her head went under and she came up spluttering. A wave slapped her in the face and her arms began to flail. Panic killed faster than cold.

I grabbed a second belt and scrambled over the fisherman's gate, targeting the ladder. As I half climbed, half fell down the rungs, I saw the dinghy, a sturdy rubber inflatable, moored at the far end of the pontoon. If I could get its engine started, there would a be chance. I flung myself down the last few metres, but even as I reached the platform, a figure clambered aboard and hauled the rope to slip the mooring.

Kitson bared his teeth at me, blonde hair dripping as he pulled the cord to start the engine. It spluttered into life and the boat began to move. For a second I hesitated, hopeful he would turn. I could see Jasmina moving, her chin above water level but her actions were sluggish. This water was cold, too cold to keep the brain functioning for long.

The dinghy pulled away. No rescue there.

I heard a voice cry from above and a figure leaned over the rail, a mobile in his hand. I prayed the teenager was calling out the lifeboat, not uploading video to his blog.

As I stripped off my coat and shoes, Kitson pulled away. He didn't look back, not even when Gail flew through him to the bow end of the rubber boat. It was riding high above the peaks as he increased the throttle. The engine growled, labouring to full power. Gail seemed to hover just in front as it picked up speed. The front of the dinghy rose, the stern weighted by its occupant. The wind caught the underside and turning it in a graceless somersault. Kitson tipped into the waves out of my sight.

A gull screeched overhead. The second it took for Kitson to capsize was wasted. Gail Monterey now floated just above the water nearby, hair plastered to her pale features reminding me what drowning was. I took a breath.

Jasmina, head tipped back, barely broke the surface of the water. Lifebelts floated near, but she had no chance. Cold had stolen movement from her limbs.

I jumped. The shock was huge. Water closed above my head. My entire body seemed to freeze in an instant, turkey-skin lumps erupting from my flesh. I exhaled further than I thought possible and then gasped in air and water. Fortunately, not much of the latter, though the drops were needles stabbing at my lungs.

I flailed, inching in the girl's direction. I couldn't see her. I could only pray she was still above the water. The waves were brown hills I climbed one after another, but even from the top I couldn't spot Jasmina.

Metallic sand-logged water slapped my face, hair channelled rivers into my eyes and the dark shadows of the pier's legs blurred. Already my feet were numb, and my teeth chattering.

Swimming had never been my forte, but I did my best to move in the right direction, a hampered one-armed stroke towards where I hoped Jasmina was, lifebelt clamped under the other arm. Without it I'd have been sinking already, but I was inching forward. Gail hovered, always a wave or two away.

She had saved me once. I hoped she was not just following that path but leading me to Jasmina. How lonely Gail might be in her afterlife, how much she might enjoy Jasmina's company – and why would she help me? All my years of "sorry" had made no difference to her. I brushed the thoughts aside, kept myself moving.

A flash of pale shape in the brown, blurred in my salt-soaked vision. I tried to kick towards it. Something bumped me. Frozen lumps of flesh that used to be my hands reached out. Jasmina's ashen face swung into range as I hauled her towards me. Her eyes were wild. She fought, pushing me away and down. The lifebelt bobbed up like a cork. I followed, grimly holding on.

I reached for the girl again, and again she flailed, but this time I was prepared. I locked my arm across her chest, tethering her shoulder blades against my breastbone.

'It's okay. It's me, Jasmina. It's okay.' I held tight with one arm, the other looped through the lifebelt, repeating my litany until she understood and calmed, or grew too tired to care. I swung her around, hauled her as far as I could over the lifebelt's surface, her cheek against the far side of the ring. I braced her body with my own and tried to fold her fingers around the mesh winding round the lifebelt. Each time I failed, my tears added to the brine.

Waves slapped my face. My hands began to lose their grip. The current spun us round.

The tide threw me against something hard and unforgiving. It jarred me loose, a fly swatted by the gods. I floated free. I had no strength to close even that small gap. Some instinct deep within Jasmina finally closed her fingers on the rope. I knew that instinct – it had kicked in when Gail had saved me all those years ago. I hoped it would save Jasmina now.

I drifted into deeper darkness, the pier looming above as I was pummelled by swirling water into a forest of dank pillars. Flung this way and that, the currents eager hands pulling me one way, pushing another.

Gail floated near, crooning a lullaby that sounded only vaguely like the cries of gulls. Lost souls of the drowned, calling to the living, she'd told me once. It was fitting to hear her voice – but now I couldn't quite remember why.

No energy left to kick; my efforts made no difference anyway. I let myself hang, suspended in water that seemed blood warm. I was floating, not in water, but on a warm feathered cloud. Brown foam-flecked hills passed to each side and that was fine. One covered my face. Its caress was gentle as Gail's fingertips on my cheek as she soothed me to sleep.

The world loosened its ties. I felt Gail's arms slide around my waist, folding me into her warm body. She whispered, 'I've got you,' into my hair, just as she had when thunder rolled, or the bogeyman came in the night. Her voice was deep, her arms strong.

Beneath the salt, rotting metal, and the seaweed's ripeness I caught a hint of citrus, a drift of woodsmoke in the wind. The familiar scent of *Eau Sauvage*.

I let everything go.

Chapter Fifty-Six

A voice called my name from far away. A voice that woke a memory of citrus aftershave. I was snug and the surface beneath me was moving. Rocking. Not like a baby's cradle swings; more cruise ship with broken stabilizers. I was curiously unbothered.

With no desire for change, the growing bluebottle buzz was an irritation. When I tried to wave it away, I found my hand restrained by another.

'Relax,' said a familiar voice. 'I've got you. You're going to be fine and so's Jasmina, thanks to you'

Eau Sauvage and brine. A heady mixture, but the fly turned into the drone of an outboard motor. Awareness of Colin Palmer's breath mingling with mine snapped reality back faster than a broken bra strap.

'Get off me,' I said firmly, sitting up – or that's what happened in my head. Sadly, a froglike croak and feeble twitch seemed to be the true result. Diesel and wet wool blended with Colin's aftershave. I struggled like a landed fish against layers of restraint.

'Keep the covers on and hold still, Penny. The ambulance is waiting on the shore. A couple of minutes and we'll be there.'

The rocking became bumpier as we hit the breaking waves. 'No time,' I croaked, my eyes unsticking enough to let me see him looming above me. 'Got to get the foot out of the freezer before it burns.'

'It's fine,' he soothed. 'They'll warm you up. No one's going to freeze your feet.'

'Idiot! What about Dan Kitson?' My voice was getting stronger. I coughed and spat and pushed the oxygen mask away, then glared through salt-stiffened lashes. He remained unmoved, having the temerity to grin as he jumped over the side.

Shingle crunched and I was lifted and laid out on a stretcher.

'No!' I said, pushing helping hands away. 'I'm not going anywhere. I need a phone.'

'Stop causing havoc, Penny. They're trying to help.' Colin glanced over his shoulder. 'We've got to get back out to find your friend. I'll see you at the hospital.'

'I'm not going to hos ...' I might have saved my breath. He nodded to the medics and disappeared from view. They finished strapping me in and loaded me on board the ambulance. 'I need a phone,' I growled. The warmth crept into my limbs making them heavy; exhaustion claimed me; sleep was irresistible.

Sometime later, I woke from a dream of being hugged by giant teddy bears. A cool draught touched my skin as the covers were disturbed. A stern-faced doctor, watched by two acolytes, prodded and poked without exposing my privates to all and sundry and I tried to be grateful. "All" pronounced the grim reaper had better things to do than visit me today and

"Sundry" laughed. The man in charge didn't twitch but gave his verdict: no lasting damage evident, but core temperature a little low. 'I might suggest you swim in warmer waters in the future.'

Sundry mumbled something and the doctor grunted.

'Lucky for the girl you were there. Without the lifebelt ... well.' He patted the cover. 'She'll live to tell the tale and you're famous on YouTube. You might want to thank the lad – he called the coastguard before he switched to film directing.'

Certainties of modern life – death, taxes and social media.

'What about the man in the boat?'

'A friend of yours?'

'Not exactly.' No friend of mine or of Jasmina's.

His face turned solemn anyway. 'Well, they're still out looking – but I'm sorry, there's very little chance anyone could have survived this long.'

I had expected it – Gail Monterey had given her life to save a child; now she'd taken Kitson's life to save another and I had a feeling she'd finish the job – but with Kitson dead, it seemed likely Barbara Nash would get away with murder. He'd dealt with Val's body so his DNA would probably be on it – but would Barbara's? If she'd been clever, and without him to tell his side, there'd be no proof she'd been involved. She might get away with it.

Not on my watch!

I subsided like a model patient until the entourage had left, then asked a passing healthcare assistant for a phone.

'There's a queue,' she said. 'We've only got the one – budget cuts.'

'It's to call my mum,' I lied. 'She is in her eighties and she worries.'

'I'll call for you from the desk.' I wanted to slap that bright smile right off her face, but my rage was not at her.

'She'd got dementia – she'll panic if it's an unfamiliar voice.'

'Poor thing.'

Whether she meant me, or my mythical mother was unclear, but she brought me the phone. I'd give her ten out of ten when the inevitable survey made the rounds, especially as she didn't listen in.

'It's me,' I jumped in as soon as I heard Sarah's voice. 'We've got a situation and I need ...'

'I'm sorry, I can't ...'

'What?'

'... come to the phone right now, but leave a message after the beep ...'

Beep was what I thought – or something like it. I hung up, then stabbed the buttons again.

'Nate. I'm in the hospital. Minor accident. I'm fine. I need you to set up an observation asap.' I gave him the details.

'The vet's storeroom door,' he repeated. 'Watch and record who goes in and out. Don't get caught. Got it, Boss.'

'Go now.' I added. 'And don't *do* anything,' but I was speaking to dead air. If my toes weren't numb, I'd have crossed them, too.

I redialled and this time my sister answered.

'Penny! Are you okay? The hospital called! We're on our way.'

'Good. We have a situation. I'll explain when you get here. Hurry – but swing by somewhere and get me some clothes. Mine are soaked through.' And nowhere to be seen.

I had a vague memory of my underwear being cut off – but perhaps I had been dreaming.

'But ...'

I ignored the interruption. 'Just get the warmest stuff they have. Asda will do, it's on your way. Jeans, sixteen, not skinny!

T-shirt and jumper, size 18, loose fit.' No time to fret about the lies I tell myself. 'Knickers,' I almost heard her thinking same to you, but levity would have to wait.' Size fourteens 'll do – they always come up big. Bra forty, D cup. Thick socks – two pairs; trainers size six – number sevens.' Room for socks and feet. 'And a coat – anorak or parka – something padded.' The harried assistant had been stopped by a patient three beds down, but her eyes were on the prize. 'Don't waste time, Sarah. Get here fast.'

'But …'

'I'll be in the pick-up zone in fifteen minutes.' I hung up just as the assistant managed to free herself. She hurried up with her hand held out.

With thanks, I confirmed 'mum' was hunky dory, and she scurried off to assist the next person whose day had taken an unexpected turn.

If Barbara Nash had any influence with Kathleen, any minute now those much-loved pets could be sent off to the Assisi crematorium as a special collection. The grieving owners would not suspect a kilo or two of pink-haired human had been added to the mix.

No time for an official discharge, I had to get to Barbara Nash and get some proof of her involvement before all the evidence turned to ashes – and I had a quarter of an hour to come up with a plan.

Chapter Fifty-Seven

❧❀❧

Alice turned the Hyundai sharply into Asda's carpark. 'What are we doing here?' She killed the engine, bemused by Sarah's sudden desire to shop.

'Buying Penny something dry to wear.'

Alice felt her eyebrow's rise.

'And she's an eighteen.' Sarah's eyes gleamed as she almost skipped towards the entrance. 'I knew she'd put on weight!'

Staying out of the sibling rivalry seemed wise. The hospital's call to Sarah had not suggested threat to life, but neither had it implied Penny would be discharged within the hour. Curious.

'I'm glad Penny's okay,' she said, watching Sarah toss a pack of briefs into the basket she'd scooped up, 'but why can't we just detour to her flat and pick up her own clothes?'

Sarah checked the rack for sizes and pulled out a pair of mid-rise jeans. 'No time! We need to pick her up in,' Sarah glanced at her watch, 'Argh! Ten minutes. Come on.'

Alice followed, taking a mustard sweatshirt from Sarah's grasp and swapping it for the same size in royal blue. 'Better

339

with Penny's colouring,' she said, then followed in her wake. Sarah bundled a bulky quilted jacket into Alice's arms, then gathered an assortment of items in a supermarket dash around the section. Deodorant, moisturizer, and hairbrush landed in the basket in quick succession as Sarah flew onwards. Alice grinned and tossed in lip salve and a pack of elastic hair bands on the way to the tills. Speed shopping was rather fun.

Some beeps, a swipe of the card, and two minutes later, Alice pulled out into the stream of traffic. 'So, now tell me properly. What are we doing?'

'She's planning a jail break.'

'The police are involved?'

Sarah laughed. 'I don't think so!' Then stopped. 'Actually, they could be. No! She'd have said. I think.' She shook her head as if a thousand thoughts were stirring up like hornets. 'The hospital said she was fished out of the water at the pier. Perhaps they think it's a mental health issue. Lord knows she can be fruit-loop nuts at times but she's not suicidal.'

'I suppose we'll find out soon enough,' said Alice taking the lane signed to the General's pick-up zone.

They'd barely stopped when a figure in a raincoat and little else dove onto their pile of purchases on the back seat. She flattened herself below window level. A split second later the coat flew out the window and the naked Penny hissed, 'Drive on! I nicked the coat and I don't want to get stopped for it! Head for Kitson's.'

Alice pulled away, pausing briefly to wave her credit card at the ticket barrier, while Sarah craned her neck towards the back seat. Sarah fired questions. They remained unanswered.

A quick glance in the mirror showed Penny's elbows, knees, and various parts in between, as she wriggled into the clothing. Swearing was fast and fluent as she tore off labels and bashed herself against the seats in the limited space.

'I hope we're not aiding and abetting anything serious,' said Alice, changing lanes to head towards the town centre.

'You went to see Kitson,' Sarah prompted. 'How on earth did you end up in the sea?'

Penny's flushed face appeared, band held between her teeth as she pulled her hair back in a ponytail and secured it tightly. 'It's a long story and we don't have time! Kitson's dead and I'm not sure I care, except without him here to defend himself Barbara Nash will wriggle free – she seems to be good at that – and I'm not letting that happen. And heaven knows what trouble Nate's got in by now!'

'Take a breath, sis!'

Alice was pleased to note Sarah seemed as puzzled as she felt. 'We've got until we reach the vet. Twenty minutes at least.' Alice said, reasonably she thought, 'So you can explain a bit. What's Barbara Nash got to do with anything?'

'She's Kitson's girlfriend! And your Good Samaritan. It was probably all her idea to ...' she stopped. Their eyes met in the mirror. 'To hurt your dog,' she finished.

Alice pulled into a layby and twisted in her seat. 'You know what happened to my boy,' she said, 'and I'm not driving anywhere until you tell me.'

Chapter Fifty-Eight

Desperation sharpened my voice, but I took a breath. I dressed it up as best I could, but it was not a pretty tale. Carved up for a kidney. Killed to save the poisoned dog. Hubris by the vet, who'd believed Barbara's fantasy of competence.

Then there was Val's involvement. Some of the blame was hers. Barbara might have taken Monty on her own, but with her husband's window overlooking the garden, would she have risked it? Would Monty have gone so willingly to greet a stranger? Besides, why put yourself in the firing line. This way, if it went wrong, she could walk on by. Her modus operandi to a tee.

'Helen said Rudi was her baby,' Alice said. 'She'd pay a lot to save him.'

'Transplants in the States are around thirty grand. Illegal ones – who knows. Fifty, maybe? More? And then the drugs to keep him going. I expect they'd cost a fair bit.'

'They did it for the money!' Alice wiped away a tear.

'I don't think so – not Val anyway – and maybe not entirely your vet either. I know it doesn't make it any better, but I think they saw it as a chance to save the poisoned dog – not knowing Barbara was the one who poisoned it to make the whole thing seem necessary. Then Monty died – and Barbara's fake expertise came to light. When the Pinnesari dog was dying too, Val had second thoughts. My turning up probably brought things to a head – and then ...' I shrugged. 'My guess is Val wanted to come clean, but Barbara killed her to prevent it.'

'She's ...' Alice fell silent. Sarah raised her hand to her mouth.

'Dead, I'm afraid,' I checked the Seamaster, 'and the evidence could go up in smoke any minute. I've left Nate on guard so sorry as I am for all the losses, can we get back on the road so we can nail the bitch?'

Alice started the car without a word and her foot went to the floor.

'Careful,' Sarah leaned into the turn.

'Don't worry. I was taught stunt driving by an expert.'

It wasn't reassuring.

'So, what's the plan?' Sarah hung on to the door.

'Val's not officially missing yet, but they know it was Kitson in the dingy. Jasmina's in no shape to be interrogated and I ducked the police.' I hadn't stopped to see Jasmina for that reason, but she was on my mind.

Kitson had swum like a brick. I wasn't sorry. Except if Val's body disappeared. She'd be just a statistic on the missing persons list and Barbara would walk away.

If we could get bits of Val discovered in the storeroom, DNA might prove Barbara complicit, but she could play the innocent woman under duress. She'd had experience. Her acting skills must be as good as Brian Dunker's.

I couldn't let that happen. Val and Lizzie's deaths were down to her. I was working for them now.

'Barbara has to be caught red-handed, trying to save her own skin. Her moving the body is the only thing she can't explain away, but if that gets incinerated ... we've got to make her think it's about to be discovered – and the body parts are in the cold store Nate's keeping watch on,' I said.

At least, that's what I hoped – but when we did a drive past, he was nowhere to be seen. Sarah dialled his mobile and I hoped he had it on vibrate if he was hidden within Barbara's hearing.

'He says he's in the pub around the corner,' she said, and my core temperature rose towards volcanic as Alice got us there. Without waiting for the others, I jumped out of the car and marched straight in.

Nate had taken a corner table, his iPad propped against his pint. I hoped whatever he was watching with such intensity was worth him being fired – from a cannon if I could find one at short notice.

'Penny!' he said. 'No one's gone in or out yet.' He beamed.

'That you know of,' I clarified.

'I'd have seen,' he said, turning the iPad towards me. A wide-angled view from above the vets' car park was displayed. Anyone approaching the storeroom door would have to pass within the frame.

I let out a breath. 'You hacked their security camera?' I said, impressed for once. The moment passed.

'I never thought of that,' he said. 'It would have been so cool! I just flew a drone over and parked on top of it.'

'Well done.' Sarah filled the silence while I was wondering where Nate had got a drone from ... but maybe this was not the time to ask because I'd had an idea.

Chapter Fifty-Nine

※❦※

A round of drinks later, we'd agreed a rough way forward. Nate drank his beer looking smug while the rest of us sipped our no-alcohol of choice. His moped licence didn't qualify him to drive so that was down to the rest of us, though Alice had the hazardous bit of trying to engineer a crash.

'You're sure you can do it, without getting hurt?' I asked her.

'Think of another way, Penny!' Sarah butted in. 'It's too dangerous.'

'I'll be fine,' said Alice. 'Jerry taught me – he's an expert.'

'You're sure?' I said.

'She killed Monty. Trust me, I'll stop her.'

'Right.' Sarah's glass met the table with emphasis. 'I'm coming with you.'

Alice beat me to the protest 'You've already had one concussion this week. I'm not risking you getting another!'

While Sarah ignored the reference to her injuries, Nate found a sudden interest in his shoes.

'Well, you're not doing this alone.' Sarah said, staring at Alice. 'This woman's a killer!'

Alice had a lot to learn about my sister's stubborn streak, but the lesson would have to wait. I butted in. 'I need you to drive Nate around, Sarah. Apparently, that thing,' I said, pointing my chin at the drone picture. 'has a limited range, and Nate can't fly it and follow on his moped at the same time – and you'll feed Alice directions.'

'You can do that!' she snapped.

'I'll be too busy. If Barbara has time, she might find another way to keep herself in the clear. She's got to think Val's body is the only thing that could trip her up, but she's psycho, not stupid – We need to push her into action while she believes no one knows Val's dead.'

'Poke a sleeping bear with a sharp stick. Brilliant! It's not like it's dangerous or anything!'

I shrugged. 'She'll want to know what Kitson said to me – and if there's anything I can prove.' I turned to Nate before Sarah could dig deeper. 'You're sure she didn't spot you? It'll fall apart if she's seen you skulking.'

'No chance.' Nate got to his feet, lanky, carrot-topped and way too memorable for my liking. A mouse-brown L'Oréal make-over and taking six inches off his height might help – but one would take longer than we'd got and the other … well, nothing to be done about that. A stoop and he'd stand out like Quasimodo.

I glanced at the drone's output again as Nate went on. 'Invisible man, that's me. I only walked past once to check out drone landing sites.'

Barbara would recognise my face, and Alice's. Nate was the only option to meet her head-on. At least if things turned nasty, he could probably sprint faster than all of us – though I'd back Sarah if she were fully fit. I'd have to hope Barbara hadn't been looking out of her window when Nate had sauntered by.

The screen still showed no activity. In fact, it was suspiciously motionless and with Nate's record with gadgets an uncomfortable thought grew in my mind.

I peered at it. 'You are totally sure it's working?' This would all be for nothing if our quarry had flown before we flushed her out.

'Should be,' he said. My eyebrows lowered to match his own. 'It's on a motion-sensor to conserve battery power, but there's always a risk. When the power's gone, the visual will go dark.'

'How long?'

'Dunno, the spec said five hours but that's only the camera. The drone battery is a lot less. Flight time's about twenty minutes, then it's crash and burn.' The cloud lifted. 'I've got a spare battery for that though so I can switch it before we start.' He patted his pocket, then bit his lip. 'It's in the office.'

'We'd better get a move on then.' I looked at Alice. 'You're sure you can do your part, Alice, and stay in one piece?'

'Easy as falling off a log. One of the first things Jerry taught me was how to crash safely.'

Sarah moved to protest again as "oxymoron" floated through my head. Alice patted her arm. If I'd tried that, Sarah would have ripped my hand off.

'It'll be fine,' Alice assured her, 'but darling, don't take your eyes off that screen, because we're depending on you.'

'Right then!' I said. 'We have a plan!'

NATE AND I CABBED IT TO THE OFFICE TO GET HIM KITTED out. I called in a favour on the way. A friendly car dealer gave me an unofficial 'rental' now and then. We'd have our unmarked white van within the hour.

While Nate went to borrow a white coat from the pharmacist a couple of doors away, I cobbled together a reasonable facsimile of the Veterinary Medicines Directorate logo which Nate got busy laminating on his return. Stuck loosely onto the vehicle it wouldn't pass close inspection, but our target wasn't likely to stroll out to check. I turned my attention to a headed letter of authority and a matching ID badge bearing Nate's staff photo.

I slipped this into a plastic holder on a lanyard while Nate shrugged into his borrowed lab coat. It was short in the sleeves – but then so was Nate's shirt. It didn't scream mad scientist any more than his hair sticking up or the manic gleam in his eye, but the combination was worrying. I hoped Barbara Nash would not expect a fake to look so … fake.

'What do I do if she phones up to check I'm legit?' he said, looping the ID round his neck. Unlike its wearer, it looked convincing.

'The number's genuine.' I tapped the plastic, 'but she'll get a recorded message. The VDM closes at four today. There's an "out of hours" number on the letter head.' I handed him the clipboard with the paperwork I'd prepared. 'If she tries that she'll get through to Sarah, so you're covered.'

'Roger that,' he said, 'And if there's no one in?'

'Then we'll keep trying, or go to Plan B.'

I hurried him down the stairs before he could ask about Plan B. I was still wrestling with version A because a lot depended on Nate playing his part, then on his prowess with the drone.

Heading to meet with Sarah in the pub, Nate had time to think. 'What do I say if she asks me something about the VMD?'

'Ignore it. Stick to your guns. You've orders to clear all the fridges and the freezers of all containers relating to drugs and waste disposal. Routine procedure when the premises are no longer under direct supervision of the licensee. You're just a removal man – you know nothing.'

He bit his lip. 'What if she lets me in, though?'

'Trust me, Nate. She won't let you through the door.' I blinked away the vision of pink-varnished toes pale with frost. 'She'll say she doesn't have the entry code, or authority to give you access – whatever it takes to keep you out. You'll concede you've no remit to break in, then slink away with your tail between your legs. Just make it crystal so she knows …'

He grinned. 'I'll be back!'

His impression of the Terminator was no better than mine.

BARBARA NASH STOOD, ELEGANT IN HER STILETTO HEELS, facing me with a small smile on her lips. Signs of mourning were conspicuous by their absence. She was crisply attired in a sheath dress and accessorised for a night at the opera. Half a carat on each ear alone.

'Penelope Wiseman. This is a surprise,' she said, then opened the door wide and invited me in. The spider's invitation to the fly must have sounded much the same, but I hoped for a bit of role reversal in the offing.

'Barbara.' I said preceding her into the sitting room of Kitson's apartment.

'Can I offer you something? Coffee, tea, a glass of water perhaps – still or sparkling or,' – a twist to her mouth, 'do you prefer it with a dash of salt?'

'I'll pass thanks.' I kept my voice untroubled, as we took seats either side of the triple-glazed French doors. Outside a huddle of fluffed up feathers sheltered ineffectually from the cold. The wind might have been whining as it sliced through the balcony rails but inside all was silent.

'I'm sorry for your loss.'

She hesitated, a barely noticeable pause in the act of crossing her legs, then smoothed the hem of her skirt and regarded me coolly.

'I've had the *Gazette*'s reporter giving me the gist of your involvement. Did you have a cosy chat before poor Dan went for his swim?'

'Does it worry you that he might have told me everything?'

'Good heavens, that does sound sinister.' She raised an eyebrow. Her smile stretched tighter than a whip about to crack. 'Please, do go on.'

'Organ transplants. Very lucrative when owners will pay almost anything to save their beloved pets.'

Her shoulders loosened a tiny fraction. 'I'm sure you're right – but what has it to do with me?'

'It was your idea – and you were there when Monty died.'

'Was I?' Her eyes opened wide; her head tilted as her smile grew wider. 'Well, I found him. Poor thing,' she said, her voice saccharine and ice, 'lying there, hardly breathing, and I got him help. The creature was still alive when we reached the surgery as I'm sure Alice Mayford can testify.' Her smile relaxed, spreading like a stain. 'Well, he must have been, mustn't he, if poor deluded Dan tried to perform a transplant? But as for me – I walked away into the night. I'm sure your client will tell you that.'

'You walked round the building, in through the side door, and straight into the operating suite You tried to put his kidney into the other dog. You'd told Kitson you could do it – only you didn't have the competence to match your boasting and it all went wrong.' My hands were curling into fists.

'Oh, dear,' she placed one elegantly sculpted nail on her chin and sat forward theatrically, 'Is that what he said before your little helper tipped him into the sea? I'm afraid it isn't true. Would the girl be able to persuade anyone, do you think? Children are so very prone to making up tall tales.'

Lizzie would've told the truth about you, I thought, if she'd had the chance. I took a deep breath.

'Cat got your tongue?' she said, and all my rage went cold.

'The transplant was needed because you fed painkillers to Helen's dog – the same ones you gave to Frieda's cat.'

She smiled and re-crossed her legs. 'I told Lizzie so many times she shouldn't let that mangy cat inside the house, but – didn't she admit to leaving those pills lying around? I'm sure I remember her confessing to the old woman. It was an accident waiting to happen, some might say.'

'Just like Helen Pinnesari's Basset. Another convenient accident – only this time you couldn't gaslight anyone into a confession.'

'But I don't need to, Penny. There's simply no proof against *me* – and unless the little girl on the pier thinks she heard something to the contrary, this is all just speculation.'

Only the hope of justice for Lizzie and for Val, and all the pets she'd killed made me grit my teeth and tell Barbara what I needed her to know.

'Jasmina heard nothing,' I said, 'so at least you don't get to rip another child apart.'

'Well, then,' she said, standing. 'I think we're done here, don't you?'

From the window, she watched me leave. I hoped she was convinced I knew nothing of Val's death, and that she enjoyed her triumph.

If all went to plan it wouldn't be for long.

THE VAN WAS PARKED AROUND THE CORNER. NATE STOOD ON the pavement; the drone cradled in one arm as he fiddled with its innards.

'Done,' he said, as I reached him. 'New flight battery installed. We'll be good to go if and when she makes a move.'

'Well then, let's rattle her cage and give her a reason to get going. Nate, this means you're up,' I said. I hunkered down in the back of the van, keeping out of sight and he got in the front. Sarah drove us around the corner and drew up outside the vet.

Nate took hold of his clipboard and headed to the door.

Less than ten minutes later he was back, flea firmly in his ear.

Chapter Sixty

T he drone had watched and relayed Barbara's actions
after Nate left. She'd taken a heap of empty bags
into the storeroom They'd been heavy as she packed
them into the boot with the excess on the back seat when
she'd run out of space.

Now, as we set off in pursuit, I craned my neck from the
back of the van to peer though the upper windscreen into the
dark. I was almost convinced of Nate's competence as I
watched the drone's LED lights die at his command. Then its
shadowy shape dipped out of sight.

My heart sank with it.

Nate muttered a few words of Anglo-Saxon origin, then
fiddled with the controls. Suddenly, the flying box was there
again, just visible above the streetlights, its buzz lost in the
engine's moan as we went up the hill.

Whenever Nate leaned out of the way to let me, I watched
the camera output on the dash. For someone so skinny, he
seemed to take up a lot of space, but the image of Barbara's
Yaris up ahead was clearly captured.

Her car moved sedately through the maze of streets. While we could follow on the screen, all would be well. Lose it and picking out one individual vehicle would be tough. Haston's rush hour couldn't be compared to a city jam, but cars look very similar from above. A blip and we could lose her – and the chance of any kind of justice. Maybe I should have just called the police. But Barbara would deny all knowledge – and where would be the proof of her involvement? I was sure even her basic medical expertise would be enough to have destroyed her DNA on Val's body.

'Keep steady,' I said as Sarah started to speed up. 'We can't get too close or she'll see us.'

Alice came through on the phone. 'Where is she now?'

'London Road,' Nate said. 'Just over the top of Bolton Hill.'

'There's no turn off for a mile or so after that,' said Alice. 'I might be able to arrange it along there.'

Sarah's hands tightened on the wheel.

'She'll be fine,' I said.

A face-to-face collision at a controlled speed, then 999 to say there were body parts on board and Barbara would be caught red-handed. That was the plan and Alice was confident she could make Barbara stop. This friend of hers had taught her a few tricks and no one would get hurt.

I hoped.

Nate spoke, excited. 'Alice! She's speeding up.'

'Don't do anything dangerous!' I chipped in.

A snort from Sarah suggested I might have considered that a bit more before we started. She spoke into the phone. 'Alice, it's national speed limit along there. Wait for a slower bit.'

'Eleven minutes of fly time left,' Nate offered, trying to be helpful.

'There's a thirty-mile limit just past the next turning,' I said. 'Alice, can you meet her on that stretch?'

'I'll try but ... oh, no!'

Sarah's voice rose an octave. 'What is it? What's happened?'

'Nothing it's fine. Just an idiot pulling out to pass me, and now there's more traffic catching up.'

The aerial view showed Barbara's car sweeping past an oncoming vehicle. Alice's Hyundai was being boxed in by the car ahead and tailgated by a vehicle which had caught her up. Now Alice was in a convoy that swept past our position as our quarry put her foot down on the open road ahead. The drone kept her in sight.

'I'll never catch up. My little bus just isn't fast enough on the straight. What about your van?'

'Speed limited to fifty max, and slower up the hills,' I said, wishing something faster had been available.

'We can't let her get away!'

I echoed Alice's sentiment. Val was disappearing for a second time.

'Go through Maize Lane,' called Nate into the phone. 'Next left. Then through Brisson Cut. It's half the distance.' His eyes were on the screen, but his driving lessons had taken him on the back roads around this area. 'She's being held back by slower stuff now. Nowhere to pass. I think you'll get to the crossroads before her.'

Six tense minutes later and Alice was back on the main road.

'I see you,' I said, 'but there's too much traffic. We can't risk someone getting hurt.' In the mirror Sarah's look was laser.

'Someone unprepared, I mean.' That didn't come out

quite how I meant it. 'I don't want you getting hurt, Alice.' I clarified.

Saved by Nate. He broke in. 'She's turned onto the lane to Jessop Flats.'

'I'm there.'

We saw Alice make the turn, and pick up speed, and Barbara pulling away. One glance in her mirror and she'd know Alice was behind her. Her car leapt forward, then the screen went black.

'Battery's out,' said Nate, sounding not unhappy. 'A minute over their estimate so that's not bad.'

'Nate!'

'That road goes nowhere – it just twists down towards the tidal marshes. There's nothing but an empty cottage on the lane and a lot of mud beyond. And the drone won't crash – just kidding – it's got a reserve to bring it down safely ...' He'd raised his voice above the sudden screech of tires and screaming metal.

'Alice!' yelled Sarah, swinging the van onto the road Alice had taken.

'Alice,' I yelled in my turn. 'Can you hear me? Alice?'

No reply.

Sarah gunned the engine to its limits and threw us round the twists and turns.

'Slow down! We'll smash into them, Sarah!' I shouted, bouncing off the unforgiving metal while dialling 999. 'Ambulance,' I said, 'and police – traffic accident, Jessop Flats. Two vehicles ... might be three.' I yelled, the phone flying from my hands as we took a sharp bend and Sarah hit the brakes.

We skidded, careered across the road and ended with our wheels spinning in the ditch.

It was choked with too much debris to be much of a drop.

Whiplash and seat belt bruising notwithstanding, we were miraculously intact.

I hoped the same was true of Alice.

There was no screaming. Was that good or bad?

Ignoring all the bits that hurt, I scrambled over the seat and almost fell into the road beside Nate and Sarah.

'Hi.' Alice walked past her Hyundai, which was slightly crumpled but neatly parked about ten yards ahead. 'Good job I kept out of the way, Sarah. You drive like a maniac.' Her laugh turned to a hiccup, then a shaky indrawn breath.

Between us and Alice's car was Barbara's. It lay at a skewed angle in a deeper section of the ditch. I bent to peer in, half afraid of what I might see but I need not have worried. The driver's seat was empty.

A smear of something wet and dark glistened on the steering wheel in the light of Alice's headlamps and that was it. Except for thawing plastic packages spilled from split bags.

'She'd already crashed when I came around the corner,' said Alice. 'I swerved and just glanced off the wreck as I came past.'

Above the ticking of our cooling engines the tide was beginning to slurp its way across the deep marsh cuts bringing debris and dead things inland.

'I don't think she'll get far,' I said. 'Not in those shoes.'

A dark part of my soul yearned for Kitson's body to float in to see his girl.

No such luck.

Aftermath

At the time, watching torch bearers track Barbara's route across the marsh, a waft of stale cigarette smoke, and a whisper at the threshold of my hearing, made me wonder about Frieda in the hospital. When I learned she had breathed her last while we watched the emergency services search, I became certain.

Frieda had been present in spirit, little Yosef probably smirking on her shoulder, as Barbara stumbled thigh-deep in freezing mud and the tide rose all around in silent threat.

May Frieda's sleep be peaceful and her mind at rest. I hoped her little cat would forgive me for not sharing Lizzie's innocence and Barbara's evil deeds in person. I'd told the story to Frieda's scattered ashes in the Garden of Rest. She wasn't there. Her voice was my imagination.

There are better things to do in my afterlife, than wait around here in case you drop by for a chat.

It would be so nice if that turned out to be true.

Barbara was rescued in the end. Maybe it was a pity I'd involved the police – she wouldn't be the first to drown alone out on the flats – but she'll stand trial. The lawyers are still arguing the charges but a car full of body parts is hard to explain away. At least Val's family won't have to spend years wondering if she's out there somewhere, lost. That's a tick on the plus side of the ledger.

Some good for John Nash, too. He asked me to visit Lizzie's grave, but she didn't appear. 'She's at peace,' I told him as we laid the flowers. 'She's gone on to … wherever it is they go.'

'I thought she might be here, to say goodbye.'

'She's said goodbye,' I told him, gently. 'Now you have to do the same.'

I left him kneeling there. Perhaps she'll come back one day and lay a hand against his cheek. Perhaps she won't, but maybe he'll think she did. Truth is thin gruel for the soul; it's what we believe that makes us happy.

My sister believes herself in love and is nauseatingly chipper – her romance with Alice is new and shiny, and they seem ridiculously pleased with life. In the way of new lovers everywhere, they're desperate for the world to follow in their footsteps. Starting with me, apparently.

Colin Palmer had waved away my thanks – saving lives was too commonplace to make a fuss about, he'd said, grinning – but when I asked him out to dinner, he said yes.

'A thank you, or the start of something?' Sarah's curiosity breaks out like a rash each time we talk.

'When I know, you'll know,' I tell her honestly, and she smirks. She'll probably work it out before I do, but I'm in no rush. Some dishes are more flavoursome slow-cooked.

Some scorch. Some dry up.

My stomach rumbled. Well, we'll see.

As for the Wiseman Agency, Sarah says it's my decision whether we go on. I hear McDonald's is hiring and I love their fries but it's not quite the same as being your own boss. Though I might need to moonlight now. Drones are cheap but the camera Nate bought with it cost a bomb. All on the company credit card.

'It was fourteen days approval,' Nate said, staring at his feet. 'I just wanted to see how it worked. I was going to send it back and get a refund.'

The drone's battery reserve may not have functioned quite as advertised, but the chances of money back seem low — unlike the drone when it cut out and smashed into the tarmac somewhere along the A133. The few bits we recovered were not helpful, but I live in hope.

Once I'd paid that bill, Wiseman was almost broke again, but all was not lost. The overdraft was history and enough petty cash remained for a meatball sub and Cadbury's Creme Egg.

Things were looking up.

THE END

About the author

Wendy Turbin lives near the sea, walks a dog or two for the Cinnamon Trust, and is owned by Little Ernie, a cat who spooks at invisible things. An avid reader of crime fiction, she has long been a fan of the private detective from Chandler to McDermid, from Grafton to Galbraith.

This combination of facts may explain why her novel contains a PI, a pier and a pet – and a ghost girl in need of help.

Over the years, Wendy has worked in international logistics, customer service banking, and education – but she has always been a writer. Like many others who doubt themselves, few of her tales have seen the light of day, despite the Creative Writing core of her OU Bachelor's degree.

But recovery from a severe bout of depression a few years ago led Wendy to re-evaluate her priorities and then she came across the University of East Anglia's amazing MA Creative Writing Crime Fiction. Ever the 'learnaholic'', the idea appealed. Write a whole novel while studying crime fiction? Yes! In a "seize the day moment" she applied. She was thrilled and terrified when offered a place.

Fuelled by huge mugs of tea and a lake of Prosecco, she wrote the book and achieved the MA.

Now her world is all murder and mayhem – and she's very happy with that!

Acknowledgments

I owe a huge debt to a lot of people without whom this novel would never have emerged blinking into the light. Here are some of them:

Henry Sutton, Course Director of the MA in Creative Writing (Crime Fiction) at the University of East Anglia, you and your team helped me fulfil a dream.

The generous and patient tutors included Laura Joyce, William Ryan, Tom Benn, Julia Crouch and Nathan Ashman. I learned so much from you all. Thank you for everything.

My fellow students, you were, and you remain, amazing, the best writing buddies anyone could wish for. So, thank you Laura Ashton, Judi Daykin, Antony Dunford, Jayne Farnworth, Natasha Hutcheson, Louise Mangos, Elizabeth Saccente, Matthew Smith, Karen Taylor and Bridget Walsh. Time murdering our "little darlings" was well spent. Long may it continue. I raise a glass to you all.

Blu Tirohl, a massive thank you for your veterinary expertise, and correction of my misunderstandings. Any errors that remain are all my own.

Ruth Dawson, your perception, and your eagle eyes have been invaluable.

Jenny Parrott, *Sleeping Dogs* is a better novel for your editorial insight. Thank you for your advice.

Finally, my grateful thanks to Rebecca Collins and Adrian Hobart for taking on my debut novel. I hope it will be the first of many we will send out into the world together.

Hobeck Books – the home of great stories

This book is the first in the Penny Wiseman murder mystery series, Wendy is currently working on the second book. There will be many more to follow after that.

If you've enjoyed this Penny Wiseman murder mystery, please sign up to **www.wendyturbin.com** to read about Wendy's inspirations, writing life and for news about her forthcoming writing projects.

Also please visit the Hobeck Books website **www. hobeck.net** for free downloads of short stories and novellas by a number of our authors including Wendy. If you would like to get in touch, we would love to hear from you.

Finally, if you enjoyed this book, please also leave a review on the site you bought it from and spread the word. Reviews are hugely important to writers and they help other readers also.

Printed in Great Britain
by Amazon

55246350R00214